Fortress of the
Shadow Reich

Kate Haley

Special thanks to Viktor Thompson,
Hannah Bond, Juliet Aabryn, and
James Robinson.

CONTENTS

Visit **www.katehaleyauthor.com** for
deals and current news from the author.

1

Gunshots sounded. They echoed across space and time. Wherever they were, they weren't happening here. Vincent couldn't tell if they were from his past or future. He kept waiting for the bullets to hit him, to tear through his body and end his life. Instead, he was drowning. Blood and oil filled his mouth and nose. He couldn't draw breath. A voice older than all his memories called to him. It whispered his name in his ear, tempting him, drawing him further down.

He sank deeper into the warm embrace of the ooze. It pulled hungrily at him. The fingers of death caressed his skin. He had avoided them for so long, longer than he had any right to, and now they were finally claiming him. The voice washed away all concerns. Vincent could remember this voice calling to him his whole life. Someone who yearned for him. A grace that had spared him.

He jerked.

Darkness sparked like an electric shock. It was in his veins. Pain. Nausea poisoned his stomach. There was nothing he could do. The Prince had him in his clutches. Vincent had always known it would end like this. He had been marked. Claimed. The Prince had made

Vincent his toy. He had intended for the old Hunter to die from the tonic, mad as a raving dog, thrashing and drowning. That's why the memories were stolen. That was his fate.

But he had cheated death.

He had cheated the Prince and the Darkness. He had cheated cruel fate and the evil of insanity. They were not masters to be cheated lightly. They would take what was owed, one way or another. They were patient. Determined. Dangerous. Now they were collecting.

"Vincent!" the Prince hissed in his ear.

The monster's limbs tightened, oozing around Vincent, crushing the air from his lungs. The goo that comprised the Prince's current form crept over Vincent's face. It seeped into his nose. Forced its way into his mouth. Vincent could feel himself choking on it, as though the Prince's dribbling fingers were sliding down his throat. It slithered into his lungs, his stomach, pushing and groping. Vincent couldn't even scream. He could feel the Prince's hands inside him, trying to rip through his lungs to clutch his heart. The only reason he wasn't already dead was the Prince's desire to torture him. He had reneged on their deal. That was unforgivable. The Prince would make him know.

But he cheated death again.

Vincent woke, throwing himself forward. He tangled in the blankets of his bed, covering his mouth with a hand as he coughed, choking and gasping from the dream. A dry cough. He looked at his hand. Clean. Vincent closed his eyes and took a deep breath. His lungs expanded painlessly. He was fine. There was the ever-present itch at the back of his throat – that tickle for an old drug that made him cough – but that was as bad as it got these days. He hadn't coughed up blood in years. Not since Egypt.

He sighed and rolled back onto his pillows. The nightmares were getting worse. Still, after all the things he'd seen in his life, that must just be a sign that his brain was working properly. It was still strange to be able to see clearly again. To be able to observe the Darkness without being a part of it. He thought of his current case and grimaced. That was Darkness. He'd known it as soon as he'd seen the body of the first child.

However, for today at least, the case was in the hands of the authorities. Today was the big day. They had been putting it off for so long. There was always another monster or cult or demon. There always would be. So, today, that was someone else's problem.

Vincent could see his suit hanging from the corner of his dresser. Fred had laid it out for him. She had been rather firm about the state of his presentation today. He had no interest in tempting her wrath. With a weary sigh, he climbed from the bed and began to prepare.

* * *

The church was a beautiful old wooden building, with timber beams and arches supporting the vaulted ceiling and gothic spires. The pews were cushioned with velvet, a luxury that had survived the crippled economy. Not that Tony could complain. His family were doing well. Years of Prohibition and depression had been good for their business. It wasn't a business he was overly involved in, but he was finally at an age where he was starting to see it. His uncle Elia Ferro ran the family, and Ferro made a point of keeping his nephew close for his power, and blind for his delicate sensibilities. Tony didn't begrudge him that. Family was family, after all.

He was standing in the main aisle, nervously straightening his cuffs, when Ferro's hand slapped him on the shoulder. Tony smiled over at his uncle. Ferro was beaming at him, his wide smile lighting up his scarred face.

"*Congratulazioni!*" he bid, hugging his nephew.

"*Grazie zio,*" Tony hugged him back.

"Are you sure I cannot change your mind, boy?" Ferro muttered, holding him by the shoulders. "Your mother is losing it."

Tony held back a sigh. He was all too aware and had been present for too much crying and rending of garments. Fortunately, an excuse to get out of the conversation was coming through the door. Two men stepped into the church, both in their best suits and long woolen coats.

"Gio!" Tony exclaimed, tearing himself from his uncle's hands.

"Tony!" his cousin called back. The broader and heavier of the newcomers caught Tony in a fierce bear-hug. Tony gave as good as he got, the two men laughing as they embraced. Gio stepped back first and looked the younger man up and down. "*Mamma mia,* kid! Look at you!"

4

"Giovanni!" Ferro greeted him warmly, striding over.

Gio quickly turned to his uncle. They clasped each other's shoulders and kissed cheeks. When he stepped back, Gio held an arm out to indicate his companion. The man was half a head taller than Giovanni, with neatly combed black curls and square glasses. He wore leather gloves and a thick scarf under his heavy overcoat.

"You remember my mentor, Professor Owens?" Gio introduced.

"*Si!* Of course!" Ferro shook the Professor's offered hand. "*Benvenuto!*"

"*Grazie, Signore Ferro,*" Owens returned flawlessly. The Professor had a cool disposition that under no cultural circumstance was going to cater to a familial embrace, but his crisp handshake was affable. A wry smile touched the corner of his lips as he moved onto Tony and shook the boy's hand. "*Bravo, Tony. Alla buon'ora.*"

Tony grinned at him sheepishly as his uncle and cousin laughed.

"*Grazie,* Professor," Tony dipped his head bashfully as he shook the man's hand. "I assure you, I wasn't the hold up."

"Never believed you were," Owens grinned.

"Miss Winifred wanted to see you when you arrived," Tony passed on. "They're through that door and down the hall to the left."

"You're relegating him to the bride's family?" Giovanni joked.

"Elevating!" Ferro backhanded his nephew lightly in the chest.

"I'm more the part on their side anyway," Owens smiled, patting his apprentice's shoulder. "*Scusami*, I really shouldn't keep the lady waiting."

"*Certo!*" Ferro agreed. "What lady Winifred wants, she gets."

"She certainly does," Owens agreed, excusing himself and heading for the door.

Giovanni grinned and slapped Tony on the back.

"You know what you're in for today, or you been a good man and keeping out of the ladies' way?" he teased. "Between her family and ours, Satan himself might be easier to contend with."

"*Mamma mia!*" Ferro shook his head. "You don't know the half of it!"

Tony rolled his eyes. A giant murderous fiend probably would be easier to deal with than his family. He'd been getting an earful all month. No one was going to let this go. Everyone had an opinion. He could see the bombshell hovering on his uncle's lips. In the next thirty seconds Gio would know. He'd have an opinion too. Maybe it would have been easier if the Professor had stuck around. Tony didn't blame him for running off to Lucy's family. He was, after all, lining up to do the same.

* * *

Traditionally the bride was readied elsewhere and brought to the church in her full glory. Lucy didn't have time for that. At least, up until this moment she had been adamant she didn't. Now she was standing in a small storage room off the side of the church, looking at herself in a long mirror. Her sleek silk dress was cut with such a wide neckline it was nearly off the shoulder, and the back plunged. Her soft curls had been tamed with ribbon and flowers. She tugged the delicate cuffs of her sleeves nervously as Helen finished fussing over her hair. Lucy didn't believe she had ever looked this pretty. Maybe it was worth making time for. Especially since she was actually getting married today. It really was happening.

She'd been putting it off for some time. That was how she phrased it when people asked. It was just 'oh, some time now' since she'd gotten engaged. It was more than two years since Tony's proposal and their adventure in Egypt. It wasn't that she hadn't wanted to marry him – of course she did! It was just that there was always something else to do. Something more pressing. She thought of her current mission and grimaced. That was urgent. Children were dying. After what she'd seen last night… well, she'd nearly called the whole thing off today to go monster hunting. But she couldn't do that. Not to him. Not again.

Now that she was finally here, standing in her dress, ready for the day… she was prepared to admit she was genuinely excited. Fred and Helen were both fussing over her and the Cooks were looking after their son Toby, who was at an age where he didn't like to sit still. It was nice to have them there, and she was so grateful, but there was a small part of her heart breaking at the memory of her own family. At the thought of her mother, who should have been there. Her side of the church was going to be significantly smaller than her groom's. Although, if her parents had still been alive, there was no way they would have let her marry Tony, and her family would still have been smaller than his.

Then there was his mother to contend with. Things had been going fine, mostly, until a month ago. No, that was a lie. Things had been going steadily downhill with Missus Carlotta Marzia Segreti since she had found out her youngest son was getting married. At first it had been wonderful, *'Bravo!' 'Salute!' 'Che bello!' 'Evviva!'* and too many people had been heaping praise on her in Italian. Next thing, Missus Segreti decides her son is marrying above his station and the bride is too snooty. Then she finds out what Lucy does and suddenly she's too wild and reckless. Then Lucy won't commit to a date because people are *dying* and she's trying to help, but Missus Segreti says she's just not committed to her boy and is fishing for something better.

Lucy took a deep breath and stopped grinding her teeth. Missus Segreti was Tony's problem, and why he had decided to make the problem worse a month ago was beyond his bride, but that was not her circus and those were not her monkeys – no matter what the paperwork said at the end of today. She was marrying Tony in less than an hour, and no cultists, monsters, ritual sacrifices, or future mothers-in-law were going to stop her.

The door opened and a man walked into the room. Fred and Helen turned to him, but Lucy could see him just fine reflected in the mirror. She took in the expensive suit and steel grey hair. He was clean cut and neatly combed. It took her a second and then her jaw dropped and her eyes popped.

"Oh my God!" she exclaimed.

"Well, aren't you just the cat's pajamas in that getup, kid," he grinned at her, the humor testing his scarred face.

"She looks like a little angel," Fred grinned. "When she shuts her mouth…"

Lucy ignored the instruction and kept staring, completely agape.

"You shaved!" she continued. He'd also had his hair cut, but she couldn't manage to articulate that.

"Fred was very strict about the state of my presentation," Vincent admitted severely.

"You have to walk her down the aisle," Fred reminded. "All things considered, you haven't done too badly, Sir."

"You look very handsome," Helen smiled, popping a spare flower from Lucy's hair through his buttonhole.

Vincent sighed as a means of accepting the compliment. He looked over the room. Helen always looked like the first kiss of dawn, and today she had accentuated it with a pale pink frock. Fred had gone all out, abandoning black and grey for midnight blue and even consenting to a dress.

"You ladies all look radiant," he nodded to them.

"All doled up and polite." Fred raised an eyebrow at him. "What have you done with my boss?"

Vincent was spared having to answer by a knock at

the door. They bid the visitor enter and a tentative expression poked its way in.

"I don't mean to interrupt," Owens apologized. "Tony said Winifred wanted to see me?"

"Stuart!" Fred crossed to him and caught him in a hug he was unable to escape.

"Hello Fred," he smiled as she squeezed his ribs and kissed his cheek.

"Glad you could make it, Owens," Vincent rescued him and shook his hand. "When Tony told me what train you and his cousin were taking I thought you were cutting it a bit fine."

"Apologies, Chancellor," Owens deferred. "Things have been rough down south, as you well know."

"Things have been rough everywhere," Vincent muttered. "If this wedding wasn't being run by Winifred and the Mafia, we might have decided to find a very different way to spend the day after what we found last night."

"Tsk, tsk!" Fred hissed, shooing them. "You two ain't talking shop today. Not here. Stuart, we've got you front row. You're going to be accompanying Helen today. If anyone asks, you two can come up with whatever story you like for how your engagement is coming."

Owens laughed at her. Everyone else grinned at him. Lucy liked Owens, even though she barely knew him. They had only met briefly before, but he was scholarly, polite, and handsome. He was also someone Fred was particularly fond of, and anyone who could get Fred to like them that much had to have a lot going for them.

Lucy was giving him her best cheeky grin.

"She's not joking," she told him.

The situation dawned in his eyes, and for a brief moment he didn't know where to look. The surprise gave way to composure. Patience settled behind his glasses like class was in session.

"Then it would be my pleasure to escort the next most beautiful lady of the event, besides our dazzling bride," he flattered courteously.

"Fred's standing right next to me," Helen pointed out.

"And your opinion of her can be as biased as you like," Owens conceded. "But let's not pretend that with those severe eyes and dark clothes she doesn't look like the Morrígan."

"How far is flattery getting you these days, Stuart?" Fred grinned.

"Your husband hasn't had me hanged yet," he replied glibly.

Fred laughed at his response, but she had things to sort. Once she was satisfied that Vincent and Lucy knew what they were doing, she ushered Owens and Helen from the room. They had to take their seats, and Fred had to reclaim the young ring bearer from the Cooks. Lucy was fairly certain Fred was hanging onto the rings and would pass them to Toby only for him to carry the few short steps required during the ceremony.

Now the hardest thing Lucy and Vincent had to do was wait. They were not good at waiting without weapons in hand. The patience of the hunt was one thing. The patience of dawdling while everyone else fluffed around with frivolities was another. Lucy was the one who sighed first.

"Are you alright?" Vincent asked.

"I still can't believe you shaved," she replied.

"You take exception to the strangest things, kid," he grinned. "But that wasn't what I was asking, and you know it."

"I'm excited," she admitted. "Now that it's finally happening."

"But...?" Vincent led, clearly hearing something in her voice.

"But I can't stop thinking about those kids," Lucy shook her head. "All those missing children... knowing that they all probably ended up like the one we found last night... and the cultists got away! They could be out there murdering right now! We should be stopping them!"

"And we will," Vincent assured. "As soon as we've gotten you safely married, I promise, I'm going to find the mage responsible, and I'm going to hang her and her followers from the Brooklyn Bridge – show them how we deal with witches the old-fashioned way."

"I don't imagine Fred would approve..."

"Anyone who uses their magic for rituals like that deserves more than a hanging, and Fred would be the first to agree," Vincent insisted. "She might even come and help me do it."

"We could ask Owens and Gio to join us too," Lucy suggested. "If they're feeling restless after their trip."

"Won't you be off honeymooning?" Vincent raised an eyebrow.

"Well…" Lucy pulled a face.

"You've done the same thing with your honeymoon that you did with your wedding," he accused.

"What's that supposed to mean?!"

"I wasn't being subtle, Lucy. You've been putting this off, and it wasn't just because there was work to do. If you're marrying him for the wrong reasons–"

"I'm marrying him because I love him and I want to marry him," Lucy retorted. "Are those the wrong reasons?"

Vincent stayed carefully quiet. It didn't do to irk the bride on her wedding day. Lucy huffed softly at his side as she calmed down.

"When we came back from Egypt engaged," she began softly, "everyone expected it to be a shotgun wedding. I could tell. Everyone who knew us thought I was in trouble and that was why we were engaged."

"Well… they had a point…" Vincent commented.

Lucy glared daggers at him. He didn't flinch. Her anger was unyielding, but his composure was unflappable. They spent several of the seconds they needed to waste locked in that stalemate.

"I wanted to prove them wrong," she glowered.

"By using Fred's magic to keep yourself safe instead of taking any kind of responsibility for your behavior in the last two years?" Vincent queried. "You held out on the wedding to prove everyone else wrong, when you were, in fact, getting yourself in frequent trouble. Don't think I don't know about your trysts in the stables."

Lucy stayed very quiet. Vincent had an infuriating habit of phrasing things in a way that made her sound like an irresponsible child. She also hadn't realized he knew, although, in hindsight, she should have known better.

"The real question," Vincent continued, "is does Tony know? Because I do not believe he would approve of your methods."

"I told him I've taken precautions," Lucy grated. "And he trusts me."

"He really is rather dim, isn't he?" Vincent sighed.

"No, he isn't," Lucy bit back. "He's brilliant, and we've been working on something genius. You'd be surprised."

"He's more powerful than a dozen steam engines, I'll grant you," Vincent conceded. "But talent and power does not a genius make. I know you don't see it, but you're both still children. His brain isn't even fully developed yet, and let's not pretend that the blood is well spent fueling it in matters that concern you."

"You're just saying those things because you're so old," she grumbled.

"Rude," he smiled. "What I'm trying to say is you're going into your wedding inflicted with an old witch's curse and your future husband doesn't know."

"You think it's bad luck to get married while cursed?" she asked.

He stared at her for a moment, waiting for any sign that it was a trick question, and then slowly and patiently replied.

"Yes, Lucy. Everyone does."

"Fred hasn't said anything," she protested. "She said it wasn't dangerous."

"Fred has a liberal concept of the dangers of magic, especially her own," he sighed. "I'm not trying to scare you, kid. I'm just trying to get you to be responsible. Fred and I won't be around to protect you two forever. On this day of all days, I want to believe that you can be an adult. I want to believe you know what you're doing. This is a marriage, Lucy, starting with a wedding you've been pushing out and a honeymoon you never planned. I can see why some members of his family are concerned."

"We agreed to go wherever we wanted for our honeymoon and pick a spur of the moment destination," Lucy retorted. "It's not unplanned, it's spontaneous. As for why his family are all getting sore – that's not my fault. That's the name thing and that was his idea. You were as involved with that as I was. In fact, you started it."

"How did I start it?!" Vincent exclaimed.

"One night at dinner. You said that you and Fred were the last Temples, and you were concerned about the future of the Temple estate. That's where Tony got the idea from."

"I thought it was your idea..."

"Nope," Lucy shook her head. "He said I was basically a Temple in all but name and that instead of taking his name I should take yours and be your heir. He said he'd take the name too, so that we had the same. Said we could take over from you and Fred one day and keep the house and the people safe."

Vincent was quiet a moment. Lucy elbowed him gently.

"See? He is clever," she insisted.

Vincent chuckled concededly. He probably thought the entire affair was a superstitious disaster, but Lucy was happy and she thought they were doing the right thing. That was what was most important.

There was another knock at the door, and the priest let them know everyone was ready for them. It was showtime.

Vincent set Lucy's veil and tucked her hand in his elbow. She held her bouquet carefully. It was possibly heavier than it ought to be, but that was her decision, and she was easily strong enough to carry it. Vincent led her out the door and into the main church as the music started.

All eyes were on her as she came down the aisle, but she didn't register any of it. The thin film of white across her face made the world seem to glow. It blocked out all distractions and crowds. Her attention was completely focused on Tony. Even from here he looked so nervous. So awed. Seeing him there brought all of Vincent's previous scolding to the forefront of her mind. She blushed a rosy pink as butterflies hatched through her stomach. He looked perfect. He was perfect, and there was so much room for her to mess everything up.

Her fears proved unfounded. She didn't trip or stumble, with either her feet or her words. It was a simple ceremony. They hadn't wanted anything more. All concern vanished like smoke in the wind as the priest told Tony he could kiss the bride. It took all of Lucy's self-restraint not to launch herself into his arms and make the first move. She settled for a half step forward. His fingers brushed her face as he kissed her, pretending it was the first time. She was vaguely aware of cheering, but was perfectly content to keep ignoring her crowd.

Everything felt like a dream, like she was moving through life half asleep. She felt like she was floating. Tony led her back down the aisle as people stood and cheered. The next stop was the reception, but all she wanted was to run off with him alone. Vincent was right, they should have planned a honeymoon. Tony was hers now and she didn't want to share him. His hand was warm at her waist as he held her close, but both gave their attentions to the congratulations of onlookers.

He led her out to the steps of the church. The air was cold and the sharpness of it was like a welcome slap in the face. It woke her up. A photographer was already set up on the stairs. Immediate family gathered around and the flash went off. She wasn't sure if she had smiled especially for the photo, or if the smile on her face was incapable of faltering.

Until everything went bang.

She moved without thinking. They all did. She had her pistol out of her bouquet and in her hand before she knew what she was doing. Tony had pulled her in with one arm and drawn his gun with the other. He stood alert, half shielding her with his body. All around them everyone was suddenly armed. She looked for the source of the sound.

Across the street, a car was burning. An explosion then. Not just any explosion. Not just any car.

Fragments of white ribbon blew down the street, the flames smoldering as they were rubbed out by the icy road. The wedding car. Their car.

Whispers started up instantly. Who could have done this? Who would have dared?

Lucy felt Vincent's hand on her shoulder, but it was Tony she looked to. There was a hardness around his dark eyes. Shadows. They were deeper than she'd seen in years. The corner of his mouth twitched as he looked back at her. He straightened, letting the immediate fear of the attack slip from his shoulders.

"Your family or mine?" he asked.

2

Tony's flippancy had been short lived. The car had exploded when a member of his family had started the engine to drive to meet them at the stairs. His cousin's kid, Manni. Whether or not he or Lucy had been the intended targets, and that was the most popular theory currently, someone had died and his question still stood. Unfortunately, the Mafia and the Hunters were not short on enemies. A bomb like that was perhaps more in keeping with gangsters, but an old-fashioned shoot out was more likely. The Hunters' current mission had been making some powerful enemies. Possibly the type to commercially outsource their vengeance.

Either way, the patriarchs were taking it personally. They were standing on the balcony outside the reception, which had become a tragically somber affair. Ferro was smoking. Every now and again he would tap his cane. Both of them were drinking. While they had been prone to troubles in the past, their common desire for blood and answers in equal measure was bringing them together.

The door to the balcony opened and Owens wandered out to join them. His scarf was tucked tightly around his neck, the collar of his thick jacket turned up around it, and his gloved hands thrust deep in his pockets.

"Gentlemen," he gave them a brief nod. "How goes the throat wringing?"

"Too soon to tell..." Ferro answered bleakly, tapping ash over the railing.

"How are the children?" Vincent asked.

Owens shrugged. "I don't know them well enough to comment. They seem alright. Fred has it in hand, I daresay. Antony's sense of humor hasn't been permanently damaged. He saw you two out here and commented that it was nice to see the family getting along."

"That boy has a smart mouth..." Ferro commented.

"His wife thinks it's more than just his mouth that's smart," Vincent grimaced, sipping his drink.

"Are you being rude about your son-in-law, Temple Senior?" Ferro grinned, twisting his scars.

Vincent's grimace deepened. Owens joined Ferro's grin.

"*Oui*, this is the first wedding I've been to where both parties changed names and no one's fleeing the state," he remarked.

"*Sicuro che*," Ferro agreed. "I cannot believe you let them talk you into it!" He pointed his cigar firmly at Vincent.

"Lucy was telling me you've already written them into your will," Owens commented. "She said as soon as they signed their names over today they became leading beneficiaries, along with Fred."

"*Per l'amor di Dio!*" Ferro exclaimed.

"What's it to any of you?" Vincent growled.

"You're a brave man, Doctor Temple," Ferro declared. "If I did that with my family, I would be sleeping in a bulletproof locked room."

"The kids won't stab me in the back for an inheritance no one wants," Vincent replied.

"There's no such thing as an inheritance no one wants, Doctor," Ferro disagreed. "Especially not with your money."

"That money comes with Fred and a mansion full of cursed items." Vincent drained his glass. "You don't get one without the other."

Their conversation was interrupted by one of the waitstaff ducking out the door and handing a note to Vincent. He took it politely and scanned it over. His usually severe face went bleak. Ferro's expression darkened in kind. They'd been waiting for that. Vincent's people had come back with an answer first. He didn't show the note to anyone else. Instead, he folded it and pocketed it.

"I think I'm going to go for a walk," he announced. "Mister Ferro, would you like to join me?"

"*Si*, I think I will."

"Is this the kind of walk that involves taking the biggest guns you can carry?" Owens asked drily.

"Oh, I see you are familiar with this pastime too," Ferro smiled at him. "Care to join us, Professor? My nephew says great things about you. He says you're even better than our good Doctor Temple."

"Well, I have the benefit of being half his age..."

Owens smiled.

"Half?!" Vincent exclaimed.

"Closer to it than not, Sir," Owens said.

"Three fifths…" Vincent grumbled.

"Comme je l'ai dit…" Owens commented.

Vincent didn't speak French, but he glared daggers at him anyway. He knew the man well enough even if he didn't know the words.

"Saddle up, spring chicken," he ordered. "We're going for a walk."

* * *

The address Vincent led them to was a rundown brownstone with a wrought iron fence. The gate was shut and icy slush gathered in small clumps around the cement bricks at the base. The three men wore heavy winter coats over their wedding attire. It had occurred to Owens that they possibly should have changed first, but he regularly dressed this way and he wasn't going to be the one to start suggesting anything sensible to these two. He'd seen that murderous look in the eyes of people before. He was just lucky no one was directing it at him this time.

Vincent went first. He popped the lock at the gate with practiced ease. On the street the day had been fine. On the other side of the gate the sky was darker. It wasn't dramatic, but it was noticeable. An eerie silence settled in the air. Ferro shivered like someone walked over his grave. The other two knew the feeling. They had the right place.

"Gentlemen," Owens addressed them softly. "How do we want to play this?"

"Scope first," Vincent muttered. "I want all exits covered. No one is getting out of this place until I know who bombed that car and why."

"*Bene*, we play it smart, Professor," Ferro agreed. "If the good Doctor's informant is right, someone here wishes us and our families ill."

"We check the property, block all the doors, save the one we use," Vincent directed.

"This way," Ferro led on, drawing a handgun from his coat and stalking down the side of the house. He walked carefully, with his cane firmly grasped and raised to avoid unnecessary noise. Vincent followed close behind. Owens brought up the rear.

They stepped carefully in single file down the tight squeeze of the passage beside the house. The yard out the back was small, but home to a rough plank swing that hung limp, covered in slush. They were nearly at the back door when they heard the noise. A low growling, deeper than the hum of an engine.

"That can't be good..." Ferro muttered.

They turned. Something the size of a bear squeezed around the other side of the house. It was hairless with dark mottled skin. The limbs were like those of a greyhound, but strangely elongated and dangerously and massively mutated. Huge claws scratched the earth where it walked. Fangs dripped grey saliva from its mouth. A dozen eyes blinked from strange places on its long face.

"Hound!" Owens snapped.

The warning was unnecessary. They had all seen it. It was impossible to miss. It growled like a rumbling train. They scattered. Ferro fired at it as he dove up the stairs to the back door. The creature moved so quickly it seemed to shimmer, dodging Ferro's bullets as it lunged. Vincent leapt. His coat was undone. He drew his sword from beneath it. Man and beast collided. Its claws pierced his arm. His blade slashed across its side. They rolled apart. Blood blossomed across his sleeve.

The creature's hide was tough. Vincent's sword had left a deep scratch down its body, but nothing more. It pawed the ground, watching all three men with its numerous mismatched eyes. The scratch down its side began to tear. Vincent perked up, readying his blade again. The laceration ripped open to expose rows of sharp fangs. A fresh growl shuddered from the new mouth, snarling out of the beast's ribs.

Everyone paled. Turning this thing into a four-legged truck of fangs and claws looked all too easy, and probably fatal. There wasn't time for planning though. It lurched for Vincent. Ferro shot it from behind. His bullets struck. Two, just behind the shoulder. They glanced off the hide, leaving ugly welts. The injuries split in half, cracking open to expose new blinking eyes. It didn't slow it down.

Owens ran for the swing. He jumped one side of the frame, using a dagger in his sleeve to slice the top of the rope. Vincent followed him. He rushed back from the monster, blade raised defensively. He didn't want to cut that thing again if he didn't have to. It was gaining. The yard wasn't big enough to escape it. Vincent raced under the swing frame, the dog chasing after him. Owens leapt. He lashed out with the rope, catching it around the neck. He bound it tightly. The monster thrashed as he choked it. Owens looped the rope around the swing, tying it down. It snapped at him. He leapt back. His foot caught in the uneven ground and he staggered.

Vincent snatched Owens by the back of the coat and hauled him out of the way. The younger man straightened, regaining his footing. He gave Vincent a grateful nod. They stood a moment and watched the beast thrash against its bindings. Vincent opened his mouth to speak, but his comment became a curse and they bolted. The monster snarled and pulled. The swing frame crashed behind it as it began to drag the wooden structure. It twisted and flailed. Claws and fangs caught the rope from different angles and slashed it. It was free.

Owens ran back towards the house, cursing in French. Vincent went towards the fence. He was the one it followed. He ran as fast as he could, ducking and weaving. The thing snarled and snapped at him, clearly not appreciating being tied up. It snatched at his ankles. He risked slashing at it with his blade. Still better to cause damage than take it. His sword caught its paw. He didn't stop to find out what new horror that had caused.

Ferro fired at it again. He emptied his gun, opening new eyes down its spine. Those eyes saw him. He paused to reload. It saw him stationary and vulnerable. It swerved towards the back door.

"*Merda*! How the fuck do you kill this thing?!" he

roared.

It was racing for the stairs. He didn't have time to get away. Holy bullets were supposed to kill monsters. What did you do when they didn't work? He drew the sword from his cane and slashed out, trying to drive it back. The blade caught its cheek and opened a small mouth beneath one eye. Now it could bite him twice in one go.

Then Owens was there. He leapt the railing, kicking the beast in the side of the neck with both feet. It staggered. He snatched the discarded cane, shoving it straight into the creature's main mouth. It choked roughly as the cane stabbed it in the back of the throat. With one hand he yanked the cane, forcing the monster's head to the side. With the other he drew his pistol, pressed it to an eyeball, and fired. Three shots echoed in quick succession. The body flailed and twitched at each bullet. Then it fell limp.

Owens tucked his gun away and carefully pulled the cane from the creature's sticky mouth. He kicked the monster's body to the ground. With one gloved hand he scooped up some sleet from a pile by the stairs and wiped the cane free of dog slime. Then he handed it back to Ferro. The gangster was standing at the doorway, wide-eyed, staring at him. Owens smoothed his clothes and straightened his glasses. Ferro finally broke his stare as Vincent approached them.

"Him?!" Ferro demanded. "He's the man your lot fired?!"

"Excommunicated," Owens corrected. "Or tried to. Luckily for me, Doctor Temple here isn't very good at doing what he's told."

"Well, I have a job going, Professor, if you're ever–"

"*Merci Monsieur* Ferro, but my current employment is fine, and Louisiana has much better weather." As though to emphasize his point Owens pulled his coat tighter. "I suppose there's no point attempting surprise after that racket, so let's see what kind of man keeps such a guard dog *monstrueux* ..." He moved to the door and jerked the handle, snapping it open and starting inside.

* * *

Lucy was hiding in the bathroom. The light was glinting off the mirror and she could see it perfectly from where she hid in her stall. She was alone in the room and hadn't bothered to shut the stall door. Carefully, she dabbed at her tears with toilet paper. It was not the most glamorous condition to find herself in. These certainly weren't the tears she had thought she might cry on her wedding day.

The bathroom door opened and she quickly pushed the stall shut, dimming the light. She held back her tears and waited. Footsteps crossed the tiled floor. She watched shoes appear in the gap beneath the stall. They were not women's shoes. They were very familiar polished Italian leather shoes. She stepped back and took her fingers from the door, letting it swing back slightly. Tony pushed it the rest of the way open.

Lucy pressed her trembling lips together as soon as she saw him. Somehow it made her want to cry harder.

She was undone by his presence. Her walls were crumbling and they were all battlements he had long cleared. He took one look at her, stepped into the stall, and pulled her into his arms. She did not have enough tissue paper for the overflow of tears. Tony held her tightly and kissed her hair. Lucy shivered and sniffled in his arms. It took a few long seconds before she could speak.

"He was your cousin," she whispered. "Why am I crying?"

"Because you care," Tony replied. "Because you're a beautiful loving person and you just watched someone get blown up in front of you on your wedding day – with a blast that more likely than not was meant for us. That's enough to mess anybody up, Luce."

"I just..." her voice trembled and the tears took her again. She couldn't make them stop. When the weeping wouldn't subside, she forced her words out through it. "W-when I was getting r-ready... I kept th-thinking about m-my mom. I k-kept th-thinking she sh-should be here. I was thinking about my mom and dad... and a-all those p-people across t-the y-y-years... and the kids we found... and Manni was just another person I f-f-failed..."

"You never failed anyone," Tony assured, squeezing her. "You've never failed at anything as long as I've known you, *mi amore*. The devil himself shot you in the chest because he wanted you out of the way – and you survived!"

"Out of pure spite," Lucy sniffed.

"Out of pure something." Tony kissed her. "You're

right, your mom should have been here. She could have teamed up with my mother and then the two of them could have leapt up all indignant, handkerchiefs waving, when Father Marcello asked if anyone objected."

Lucy's laughter spluttered through her tears.

"But none of that is on you," Tony continued. "You didn't fail, Luce. Other people did. Your mom shouldn't have needed anyone to save her. The failure there was on your dad. He shouldn't have killed her. Just like whoever killed those kids, or whoever blew up Manni, or the people responsible for all the other horrors we've dealt with shouldn't have done what they did. The fault lies with them, completely and utterly with them. You step up and do your best because of their failures. You're incredible, Lucy."

She sighed and rested her head on his shoulder. "I'm sorry I'm hiding in the bathroom crying."

"I'm sorry you didn't get the wedding day you deserved," he replied.

She slid her arms around his neck and tiptoed up to kiss him. She hadn't realized she was cold until she noticed the warmth of his lips on hers, the heat of his body against her, and his hands on her back. This was a better kiss than the one in the church, even if it was happening in a bathroom stall. Perhaps because it was. She didn't need an audience for her love. She preferred to have him alone. A sigh escaped her lips as she let him go.

"Maybe we did..." she whispered. She dried her eyes and took a deep breath, composing herself as she looked up to him. "Where did Vincent and Ferro go? I know they left."

"They didn't say," Tony answered. "Uncle Elia asked me to let them have this one. They looked like they wanted to do this themselves, and I don't think they want us killing anything today."

"Too bad," she replied. "I don't trust them to deal with it alone. They've been drinking and they're angry."

"Sounds like someone else I know," Tony smiled at her. "Don't worry, Professor Owens went with them."

"They took Stuart?"

"They certainly did," he confirmed. "I didn't know you were on a first-name basis with him."

"I think I'm pushing the boat a little on that," she admitted. "I call him Stuart because Fred does. Do you think he knows magic? Is that why he went and Fred didn't?"

"I don't know," Tony replied. "I've never sensed anything about him, but that doesn't mean anything one way or the other. He's a Hunter though. I thought most Hunters don't practice magic, not properly anyway."

"He's an ex-Hunter," Lucy shrugged. "Maybe he picked it up after Whitehall had him excommunicated. Maybe it was why they threw him out."

"But Vincent's been Chancellor for two years, how come–?"

"Don't know," she said. "They're still friends, I think, but Vincent never reinstated him."

"Weird..." Tony frowned.

"Very weird," Lucy agreed. "But that one isn't my fight. For all I know, Stuart doesn't want his pin back. That's their business. Ours is making sure they don't get set on fire."

"I'm not letting you follow them, Lucy," Tony smiled. "Not this time. Today, it's their fight. You don't have to stay here. I'll take you home. I'll take you ice-skating at the park. I'll sail with you to Italy. I'll take you anywhere you want, but not to a battlefield."

She bit her lip in thought. Tony didn't take a stand with her often, but it was getting near impossible to make him budge when he did. Also, he might have a point. She wasn't thinking clearly. She was upset. Perhaps it wasn't the best time to draw a weapon and seek vengeance. She was the one who was supposed to better than that. Demurely, she turned her eyes up to him.

"Home sounds good..." she suggested.

He smiled and kissed her. Home was safe. Home was easy. Home was a very reasonable request after the day they'd had so far. It was also not lost on either of them that he was finally allowed in her room now.

* * *

The house was dark and cold. No one had been heating this place for at least a day, maybe longer. Most of the curtains were shut. Daylight filtered through the occasional window, but only in thin weak beams. Still, the building seemed more like it was going through a state of inoccupation rather than becoming run down.

The Darkness was present, but it wasn't a curse. Not yet.

Vincent stepped carefully through the hallway, after Ferro and Owens. Everyone had their weapons fully loaded and at the ready. Vincent made sure the barrel of his pistol entered every room before he did. The guard dog outside had been a less than welcome surprise. They could do without another.

He poked the nose of his gun through the next open doorway, following slowly. Nothing. That was fine. They might have swept the bottom floor, but there was a lot of house to go. Something above him creaked. He paused. Waited. A knock. Single, sharp. His eyes narrowed. He ducked back to the hallway and pointed towards the stairs. Owens appeared from another room, his eyes questioning. Vincent gave him a nod. They'd both heard it.

Vincent went for the stairs. Owens went to grab Ferro. Vincent took each step slowly, as silently as he could. The creak of the house was inevitable. But it was louder upstairs. It came again. Vincent quickened his pace. His tiptoed to the second floor. He could see the door to the room above the one he had been in. It was shut tight. He crept up to it. The other two followed. He signaled them hold. They took the hint, staying on the other side of the doorway and keeping their backs to the wall. Owens quietly grabbed a statuette doorstop from a nearby room. Carefully, Vincent removed his scarf and looped it around the door handle. They all stood wide. He pulled.

Bang! The shotgun blast ripped through the wood

door. It was followed immediately by another. Owens tossed the doorstop at the stair railing. It smashed through and crashed loudly down the stairs. Someone kicked the remains of the door open. Vincent bashed them over the head with the butt of his pistol. They collapsed. The empty shotgun clattered onto the floor. A middle-aged man groaned weakly on the ground. Vincent grabbed him by the collar of his shirt, hauling him to his feet before he could stutter. He slammed the man against the wall.

"Mister Sylva, you and I need to have a little chat," Vincent growled.

"About what?!" the man snarled. His dark hair was going grey and his clothes were well-made but old.

"Your hospitality, for a start," Ferro joined the conversation, stepping neatly towards them. "And an accident that occurred a few blocks over from here this morning, for a second."

"The car bombing," Vincent growled. "We know it was you. If you want to survive today, you're going to tell us everything."

Sylva spat at his feet. Vincent thumped him against the wall. Ferro placed the barrel of his pistol under the man's jaw.

"We're going to require a much larger vocabulary than that…" Ferro threatened.

While the other two began their interrogation, Owens stepped into the room Sylva had just occupied. It was an office of some kind. There was a large desk and well-stocked bookshelves. Some of it looked like legitimate business – relatively speaking. There were shipping manifests on the desk, with a glass and pitcher. Yesterday's teacup. Collections of Lewis Carroll and A.A. Milne. They were significantly less suspicious than some of the occult books lining the walls and the black hooded robe hanging on the wall behind the broken door. Owens checked the engraved metal clasp.

"*Le culte de la sorcière de sang...*" he murmured.

A low growl started behind him, deep and fearsome. Well, fuck. He turned slowly, catching the beast just out of the corner of his eye. It was across the room. Even if he could get around the door and into the hallway, slamming the door behind him would barely be any use with the bloody great hole in it. He took a deep breath. He could feel it readying to pounce.

"Vincent!" he bellowed the warning and slammed the door shut.

The monster leapt. Owens threw himself in front of the closed door, snatching the robe. He threw it over the dog's head as it lunged him. Owens pulled the robe tight, sidestepping the attack. Barely. The hound smashed headfirst into the door. Its mutant elongated head was wrapped in the robe, and it jammed in the hole. Owens leapt back. He ran for the other side of the desk.

Outside the room, the other three men jumped. The hooded black head burst, snarling, through the hole. Even covered, it was recognizable as another of the creatures from the back yard. It wasn't the only distraction. Vincent heard another growl. He saw mutant clawed paws coming down the stairs.

"Don't let him go anywhere!" he growled at Ferro,

drawing his sword in one hand and picking up the empty shotgun in the other. Vincent stalked back toward the staircase. The next mutant dog was padding down from the third floor. Nearly a dozen eyes across its body looked his way. Three separate mouths growled at him. He hung back, forcing it to be the one to move. It lunged for him, claws out, jaw wide. Vincent shoved the barrel of the shotgun straight down its throat, forcing it down. He tried to aim his sword between the barrels of the shotgun. They had to wound it from the inside to kill it. It slashed at him. He couldn't get a good angle. It began to bite and chew the gun, piercing the metal with its fangs. Its claws raked the bottom of his coat. He kicked it down the stairs.

In the office, Owens stood over the water pitcher, muttering in Latin. The dog was stuck in the door. It thrashed and scrabbled, trying to break free. More wood splintered in the hole. The cloak was shredding. It kicked and pulled, tearing free. All around its neck a ring of fangs opened where the splinters had torn its skin. It whirled, snarling, for Owens. He grabbed the pitcher and threw it as the dog jumped for him. It screamed and yelped, hitting the ground and pawing at its flesh. Everywhere the water touched it burned and sizzled. The creature batted its own face. Owens cleared the desk, shoving his gun into the mouth at the back of the creature's neck. He angled it and fired. Once. Twice. Straight into the monster's brain. It collapsed.

The other dog lunged up the stairs. Shrapnel flew from its mouth as it destroyed the shotgun. Vincent dodged its attack. He leapt and rolled, dragging his sword down the side of its body. Fangs ripped the graze open. Vincent drew his pistol as he spun to his feet. The giant mouth roared at him. He fired into it. Starting at the shoulder, Vincent unloaded his pistol down the beast's body into the gaping maw. The sound of his bullets ricocheted off the walls. Dark blood squirted from the wounds, splattering the hallway. The dog flinched at each bullet. Its legs quivered, then gave out.

Vincent stood, panting, leaning heavily on the remaining railing of the stairs. He watched the beast for a moment, but it didn't move again. The broken door in the hall opened and Owens stood in its place, smoothing his suit. Of course. The boy had always been slick. Vincent had heard more shots. Owens would have taken care of the other dog. Apparently, he wasn't the only one taking care of things.

Ferro stood with Sylva, holding him partially upright by his collar. Sylva's knees had been shot out and were bleeding all over the hall rug. He was pale and trembling, his face a mask of agony. Vincent gave the gangster a sharp look and Ferro returned it unapologetically.

"You told me to make sure he didn't go anywhere," Ferro reminded. "I made sure he couldn't."

Vincent crouched down to meet Sylva's eye.

"I hope, Mister Sylva, that you are starting to appreciate your situation," he said.

"I was just doing what I was told..." Sylva whimpered. "I didn't know it was Mafia..."

"Who told you what to do?" Vincent demanded. "Who are you working for?"

Sylva shook his head. His eyes were weeping from the pain, but he didn't look like torture would make him budge. Vincent felt Owens step up beside him. The younger man held something out to him. Vincent took the silver clasp, scraps of black fabric clinging to it, and regarded the engraving.

"The Cult of the Blood Witch," he noted. "Your mistress doesn't appreciate the attention we've been giving her?"

"Our Queen ordered the execution of the young mage and his Hunter," Sylva spat. "You will never find her. You will never catch her."

Ferro laughed. It was not a humorous sound. He jammed his gun violently under Sylva's jaw.

"Do you know who this is?" he implied Vincent. "Do you know how many of your kind he has killed? How many cults he has wiped out? Do yourself a favor, *Signore*, and don't make yourself another."

"There is nothing you can say that will make me betray my Queen!" Sylva declared between clenched teeth.

"Mister Sylva…" Owens interrupted softly. "Where is your son?"

Everyone paused. They all looked to him. The young man's attention wasn't swayed. He kept his serious eyes on their bloody hostage. Sylva pinched his lips together.

"My associates, Mister Sylva, are angry," Owens continued in the same patient tone. "You tried to kill their children. They are, as you can imagine, unshackled by their wrath. I have no horses in this race. I am merely working. While doing my job, I have discovered several signs that a child was recently living here. Your son, if I'm not mistaken." Owens paused to push his skewed glasses back up his nose. "Mister Sylva, *le culte de la sorcière de sang,* or the cult of the blood witch as they are more commonly called up here, are infamous for murdering children and draining their blood in the name of their queen." Owens crouched beside Vincent to meet Sylva's eye. "Where is your son, Mister Sylva?"

Silence reigned. Sylva didn't look like he wanted to speak, but no one else was going to break the silence in the wake of that statement. The wounded man kept his lips pinched, but they were trembling. His whole body was trembling, possibly from more than the pain in his legs. Finally, he gave a shivering, tortured sigh.

"She said if I ever wanted to see him again, I had to kill the mage and his bride," Sylva whispered, eyes downcast. "She said they were threats to the cause. They had to be removed."

"So you bombed the car," Vincent nodded. "Tell me who she is, Sylva. Give me a name and I will get your son back."

Sylva shook his head.

"You really think she will let him go?" Vincent pressed. "She murders children to use their blood for magic. I know you have every reason not to trust me, but I am your boy's best hope right now. Whatever grudge I might hold for the attempt you made on my family, I would never let an innocent child get hurt. Not if I had a choice. Help me help your son – give me a name."

Sylva looked up and met his eye. His expression was torn. His lips parted. His eyes rolled back. He began to seize. The three men descended on him. Sylva's mouth was turning black. His tongue swelled up, blocking his throat. Blood began to stream from his nose and eyes. Owens handed his knife to Vincent to cut a hole to help him breathe, but it was no use. He was dead before the blade bit his skin. Ferro had lowered him onto his back, and blood was pooling under his head, dripping from all his cranial orifices. It was thick and sticky and dark like treacle. All three men sat back from the body, grimacing at the sight.

"That's a blood magic curse for you…" Vincent muttered.

"He was going to tell us," Ferro lamented. "Why else would the curse have killed him? He was going to give up the ungodly dame who took his boy."

"Probably," Vincent sighed. "But I've got no way of speaking to the dead, and I'm all out of friendly demons to ask, so we'll have to do this the hard way."

"You've been trailing the cult?" Owens asked. "What have you found so far?"

"Too many dead children," Vincent glowered. "I put Lucy on research – she's got an entire folder on this, and a lead suspect. Crippled gentry so we've been light on pursuit, name of Lady Diana Rogue."

Owens jumped to his feet and dashed back into the office. The other two watched him go, but didn't move. Ferro frowned at Vincent's claim.

"Lady Rogue is extremely philanthropic aristocracy," he commented. "And with her condition she's not getting around without help. She seems a most unlikely suspect."

"From the outside, maybe," Vincent shrugged. "But I trust Lucy's work, and I promised her we'd move once she had enough solid evidence." He pulled a face. "Might have moved sooner if we were getting on better with the law."

"Don't look at me," Ferro protested. "I like working with you, Doctor, but you chose this. If you have police throwing you dirty looks for hiring us and marrying into the family, that's your business."

Owens rushed back out of the office, paper clutched in hand.

"I saw this when I was solving the dog problem in the next room," he offered it to Vincent. "It wouldn't be hard to track down."

Vincent flicked through the paper. It was a travel itinerary. A one-way trip for Lady Diana Rogue and her aide Ezra White.

"You found this on his desk?" Vincent asked. "You just happened to remember it?"

"I pay attention to things, Vincent," Owens replied.

"When it suits you..." Vincent muttered under his breath. Owens let it slide.

"Your lead suspect, Chancellor," he changed the subject, "is connected to the dead man on the floor, and has a ticket booked for Germany. It would not be the first time someone pursued by Hunters has fled their country."

"No it would not..." Vincent agreed. He continued to peruse the document. For all that he couldn't seem to help the occasional snipe at his old colleague, he was grateful for the help. This was exactly what they needed.

FORTRESS OF THE SHADOW REICH

3

Lucy was out of her wedding dress. Instead, she had donned an apron over her sweater and trousers. She had several pieces of alchemy equipment on the desk in front of her, along with her notebook. The chair at the desk was pulled out, and she was sitting crookedly, with one leg pulled up, half facing the notebook, and half facing Tony who sat on the end of her bed. Their bed, she corrected herself with a smile. He was still in trousers and his singlet, with his suspenders hanging loose.

"Do you think adjusting it like that will work?" she asked, tapping the notebook with the end of her pencil.

"Only one way to find out," Tony suggested. He grinned at the face she pulled. "Don't give me that look." He stood and kissed her cheek. Then he took a deep breath, held his hands out, and closed his eyes. When he opened them again they were completely black. A golden arcane circle was writing itself around the items on Lucy's desk. Tony exhaled slowly, focusing.

The circle flickered, glowing brighter. It began to pull in, shrinking and condensing. It sparked as it shrank. Some of the runes popped and vanished. The items on the table rattled.

Tony gasped and let go. The magic went out. He shivered, hugging himself and blinking his eyes back to normal. Lucy was on her feet in a second. She held him by the shoulders, her gaze searching his face. He shook his head fiercely.

"I can't do it!" he gasped. "I can't make the spell small enough."

"It's okay," Lucy insisted, touching his face to calm him and kissing the corner of his mouth. "We'll get there. It doesn't have to be today."

He nodded slowly. There was a strong agreement in his action, but a distant vagueness too, as though he wasn't all there.

"Tony…?" she called his attention.

He blinked and focused back on her.

"Where do you go when you're not all here?" she asked.

"Nowhere permanent," he smiled, kissing her softly.

She slipped her arms around his waist, holding him close, and rested her head against his chest.

"You know I trust you," she whispered. "I know you know what you're doing… I just don't like seeing you like that."

He rubbed her back soothingly and kissed the top of her head. They'd had that conversation before. There wasn't much more to say. She wasn't going to tell him to stop using magic, and he wasn't going to tell her she had to be okay with him looking possessed. His head jerked up at a sound outside.

"Is that a car in the drive?" he asked.

She let go of him. He quickly snapped his suspenders over his shoulders and threw a shirt, haphazard and unbuttoned, over the top. She untied her apron and tossed it on the chair. They both went for the door. They rushed through the house and kept pace on the stairs. His legs were longer but she was faster.

Vincent and Owens were coming through the front door as they came down. Fred was already there. She flicked the bloody hole in Vincent's sleeve the second it was in reach.

"Sir, this is why we can't have nice things," she sighed.

"What did you find?" Tony demanded urgently as they joined the others.

"Your uncle managed to get a shade of vengeance for your cousin," Owens admitted. "For whatever comfort that might be worth."

"What have you two been up to?" Vincent looked them both over.

"Sex mostly," Lucy answered, explaining the outfit change before anyone else could offer an alternative response. It wasn't even a lie. She had certainly had her husband's help getting out of her dress.

Vincent's expression remained dour and unimpressed. Owens raised an eyebrow and a single corner of his mouth.

"Good for you," he stated, mostly because he seemed to know it would annoy the old man at his side. "So, Miss...us... Temple... Junior...?" He addressed Lucy and then realized he was stuck with her new name. So was everyone else. Miss Lucy was not going to cut it anymore. "Lucy," he settled on with more conviction. "Vincent tells me you have some research on Diana Rogue and the Cult of the Blood Witch? We need to see it, please."

"That's who bombed the car?" Fred queried. "The Cult?"

"It looks like it," Vincent nodded. "The bomber died before he could tell us more, but he was a member of the cult and succumbed to one of their curses. They are the most likely culprits so far. He admitted he was ordered by the queen of the cult. You told me Rogue was your best suspect."

"That's a stretch," Lucy muttered reluctantly. "But I'll get the file."

She ducked off down the hall to Vincent's office. Tony pulled a grim face and did not follow her. He never went in the office. Not for anything. No one talked about it. Owens gave him a nod and politely followed after Lucy.

"You should get that arm looked at, Doc," Tony advised.

"I'll sort it out," Fred insisted. "I've still got your cousin in the reading room, Seg–" she stopped short, nearly falling prey to the new name dilemma as well. Tony grinned at her. She grinned back. "Giovanni is in the reading room, Tony," she stated. "You can let him know his mentor's back."

"Will do, Miss Winifred," Tony smiled at her, shoving his hands in his pockets and letting her know nothing had really changed.

She gave him a look because she knew better, and

then dragged her old man off to patch up.

* * *

Vincent's office was a mess, but it wasn't Owens' place to comment. His own office had seen worse. This place looked like it was unofficially being used by more than one person. Lucy grabbed a brown folder off one of the shelves and opened it over the desk, pushing aside some of the clutter.

"This is all I have so far," she told him. "There are reports on each of the children we've found, but separate reports for the ones still missing. They have all gone missing from city orphanages which have connections to Lady Rogue. To be fair, she is a noted philanthropist, and she donates lots of money to orphanages. Even holds fundraising galas."

"These are detailed reports," Owens approved, flicking through the paperwork.

Lucy glowed at the praise. "Vincent says I have a natural talent for slaying monsters, but if I want to be a good Hunter I need to know how to be a decent detective, work a case and such."

"Hm." A bitter smile touched his face. Lucy was watching it. Her eyes were curious. He noticed her noticing. "He said a similar thing to me once," he admitted. "The old man must be getting soft with age. He's a lot nicer to you."

"Why?" Lucy inquired, remembering some of her mentor's less affectionate comments. "What did he say to you?"

Owens was quiet a moment. He continued flicking through the file, focusing on the contents. Finally, after a few seconds, he began again.

"Vincent was always one of the best," he commented. "The Order has been in awe of him for years. They certainly were the entire time I was a member. When I was just coming up, ten – maybe fifteen – years ago, they tried to get him to apprentice me. I wanted him to. I wanted to learn from the Hunter everyone said was the best. I was good enough the Council were taking notice. It was enough that they managed to convince him to watch over my work for a couple of months. Whatever he saw in me, it wasn't enough to persuade him to train me, but he told me I had a gift for murder."

Lucy watched the sour twist at the corner of his mouth. He watched the notes flicking over in his hands.

"That's probably a compliment, coming from him," she pointed out.

"Probably," he agreed. "It's still not a particularly nice thing to hear about yourself, even in our line of work. I think he knew though. I think that's why he said it. He knew I was gunning for his title. He knew how good I'd be, and he didn't trust it. Heh, I swear he trusted me more – liked me more – after I was thrown out."

"That sounds like Vincent," Lucy agreed drily. "He doesn't trust the Order, so being in their good graces wouldn't have done you any favors."

"And now he runs the ship..." Owens commented.

"I'm sure he'd hire you back if you wanted to rejoin,

now that Whitehall's gone…" Lucy offered.

Owens laughed. He laughed properly and looked up at her over the frames of his glasses.

"I wasn't fired, kid," he smiled. "I was excommunicated. I was damned. It's only thanks to Vincent that I kept my life and my university job. If the rest of the Council had their way, I would have been looking at prison or the gallows. They would have hung me off a tree and set me on fire. They wiped their records and pretended I never existed. In the past years since your old man took over, he's added nearly a dozen women to the ranks. The olds are spitting over that, you can believe, and Vincent is gearing up to name you too. He has enough trouble with the trees he's already shaking. If he petitioned to bring me back, he'd have a revolution. They ignore that he speaks to me, but if he brought me to them they'd lynch us together."

"What could you possibly have done to make them react like that?" she asked.

"Inappropriate conduct," Owens quoted his own dismissal.

"They never managed to get Vincent with that," Lucy pointed out. "What could you possibly have done that was worse than his backlog?"

Owens was very still and quiet for a moment, transfixed by the paper in his hands. He flicked it up and pointed to a piece of writing.

"It says here Rogue is terminally ill and wheelchair bound," Owens changed the subject.

"She is, yes," Lucy nodded. "Another reason she's not an ideal suspect. She would have to have help to commit any crimes, and most of them she isn't physically capable of. She couldn't have taken the children herself."

"But that's what a cult is for," Owens pressed. "To serve their leader. I would argue her condition makes her a more likely suspect. She might have her minions doing the heavy lifting, but the desperate are often the ones driven to dire action. She would not be the first terminal diagnosis to turn to black magic to save herself."

"Then it sounds like we need to pay her a visit," Lucy suggested.

"Urgently," Owens agreed. "Another child was taken not long ago. Gather the team and I'll run this address by a map so that we know where to find her estate."

Lucy gave him a nod and moved to the doorway.

"Lucy," he called to her.

She paused in the doorway.

"I betrayed them," he answered her earlier question. "I was caught committing a crime by some of the acolytes, and I tried to destroy the evidence."

She gave him a polite nod of thanks for answering, but he wasn't finished.

"Lucy..." there was a hesitant urgency to his voice. "I wasn't in the wrong. Vincent might disagree, but I know I wasn't."

"I believe you, Stuart," she smiled, and stepped out of the office.

Owens watched her go with a strange bewilderment. Her blind trust felt naïve, but she was Vincent's apprentice. There was no way that was the case. That meant something else was going on.

* * *

They took two cars. It was the easiest way to fit all the people and the gear. Vincent had taken the lead with Owens and Fred. Lucy was riding with Tony and Gio. Her husband's cousin was relaxing in the back seat, spinning a pistol in his fingers. He had thanked them for the invite. Apparently he'd been worried he might get bored on holiday, or worse: rusty.

Rogue's estate wasn't too far away. The cars pulled up in front of a large manor under the dark grey sky. Everyone piled out quickly. Tony staggered as soon as he was out the door. Lucy looked over to him. He was pale and shaky, almost doubling over, with a wince creasing his face. She moved towards him, but he waved her off.

"Weapons out, people!" she ordered.

Everyone followed her advice. Tony was basically a dowsing rod for magic and only an idiot ignored his tells. Vincent approached them.

"They got away on us last time. We can't have that happen again, but even with extras we don't have enough people to cover all the exits," he warned.

"We can take it slow," Lucy assured him. "Scout around and see where everyone is. We might be able to pin them in one place…" she trailed off, watching Tony violently shaking his head. He wasn't breathing properly. His eyes were squeezed shut. He bent over the hood of the car, resting his forearms on the metal, his face screwed up like he was in pain.

"Now!" he wheezed. "Go now!"

"Everyone be careful!" Fred ordered as they raised their weapons. "We're storming the front and someone in there is using a lot of magic. Come here, Tony," she coaxed him off the hood of the car and led him after the others.

Vincent went first. Owens followed right behind him, and their apprentices backed them up. Fred and Tony brought up the rear. She kept an arm around his ribs, keeping him upright. The plan had been for stealth, but with Tony reacting like that... All Vincent could think of was the kid inside. They couldn't be too late. They couldn't. He shot the lock out as he ran up the stairs. The sole of his boot kicked the front door in. It shuddered on its hinges. The entrance hall was empty. He went left and Owens went right.

"Back!" Tony called to them, his voice strained. He could barely get words out.

Vincent took this as guidance towards the back room, but he was glad he and Owens cleared the sides first. They raced to the back, busting through the door. It was a private library. Massive drapes blocked the bay windows. Books lined the walls and the nooks all around the room, floor to ceiling, with a ladder on runners for the higher shelves. All other furniture had been pushed to the sides.

In the center of the room sat a ring of a dozen cultists, all in black robes. An arcane circle marked the floor with chalk and candles. In the center of the circle lay a bowl and a book. The cultists were chanting in unison. None of them stuttered or flinched when Vincent burst into the room. They were absorbed in their ritual, eyes closed.

He paused, gun raised. This wasn't what he'd been expecting. Not entirely. Where was the queen? Where was the sacrifice? The child? This was just—

A blow knocked him off his feet. Something thick smashed into his stomach. It tore the wind from his lungs and crashed him into a bookshelf. He hit the heavy shelves with a grunt. Still no one in the circle moved. He blinked reality into focus. There was nothing there. He couldn't see what had hit him.

Owens moved into the room and leapt. He dove sideways, skidding across the ground. His gun was pointed back, but he didn't fire. Alarm stained his face. Finally, Vincent saw what Owens did. Shadows. They stretched back from the candles in the circle, and they moved. Not with the movement of the flickering flames, with their own consciousness.

One raised itself from the ground, twisting and distorting. It dove for him. Vincent fired at it. His bullet passed clean through the darkness and rained plaster from the ceiling. He lunged away. His shoulder hit the ground and he rolled. The shadow swerved. It snatched him. A tentacle of pure darkness caught him around the ankle. He barely had time to curse before it whipped him into the air. Vincent drew his sword and slashed at it. The blade cut the limb. He hit the ground. So did the shadow. It flattened against the floor and wriggled away.

Vincent groaned and pushed himself up. The cultists were still chanting. None of them had noticed anything happening. It would be easy enough to take them out, but Vincent wanted them alive. Owens was climbing to his feet as the kids followed them in. They must have glimpsed part of the action through the doorway.

Everyone gave the circle a wide berth. Fred helped Tony into the room. The boy was white as a ghost. Sweat sheened his brow. He was visibly shaking. His eyes were fixed on the center of the room. Fred saw it first. Her hold on him tightened. She snatched him, tackling him to the floor. Vincent and Lucy caught on. She moved first.

Like a leopard, Lucy ran and jumped the cultists. She pounced into the middle of the circle, snatching the book, and leaping away again. No one moved to stop her. Their heads were bowed and their eyes closed. They weren't even aware of this plane of existence anymore.

"Fred!" she called back.

"Kinda busy!" Fred yelled. She was struggling to keep Tony pinned down. Vincent ran to help her. The boy was thrashing on the floor. His eyes were black. He roared in tongues. Owens and Gio looked on in open shock.

"Lucy!" Owens yelled, glimpsing something her way.

She jumped back. The darkness snatched for the book. A sliver of shadow shot up from the ground and latched onto the book. Lucy kicked at it. Her foot passed straight through it. She stumbled. It pulled.

"No!" she cried, as the book was snatched from her fingers. Behind her, a larger shadow rose and shoved her. She crashed into a bookcase. Then Gio was beside her. He rushed over, snatching the book back. He caught it under his arm, pulling against the shadow. It tugged. He tugged harder. He pulled a vial from his pocket, ripped the cork out with his teeth, and upended it over the shadow. The water spilled through it and splashed over the floor, but the shadow reared back and let go. The thing twitched and flailed like it had been burnt.

Lucy staggered to Gio's side.

"We have to burn it!" she ordered.

He fumbled in his pocket, pulling out cigarettes and a book of matches. Lucy ripped off a match. She lit it and held it to the book. The shadows dove for them. Darkness rose up like a ring of snakes. It burst from the circle. Owens was there. His gun had been holstered and he had two short blades in his hands. He slashed through the shadowy limbs, but there were too many. The book hit the floor. The fire went out. All three of them were smashed against the wall. Muffled cries were punctuated by falling books. The shelves behind them rocked from the force. The shadows pummeled them.

Lucy gasped as blows rained down. She fired her pistol. The bullet hit the wall harmlessly. A shadow knocked her gun from her hand. She couldn't move. Her arms shielded her head. Still the blows rained down. She kicked out. It hit her in the knee. She felt the pop.

Beside her, Owens was slashing at the shadows

where he could. The blades could catch them, but there were so many. One hit him in the side of the head. The force drove his brow into the bookcase. Blood dripped down the side of his face. He gritted his teeth and stabbed back.

Gio shoved against the darkness. He was a solid man who looked like he knew better than the rest of them how to take a beating, and he was after that book. The shadows could pry it from his cold dead fingers, but not before. He ripped a flask from his coat pocket and upended it over the book, splashing liquor over the floor. The shadows grabbed him and shoved him against the bookcase. He ripped an arm free. They banged him again. He lit a match and flicked it at the book.

It caught. The book went up in flames. The shadows drew back, writhing and screeching. Gio touched the side of his face where a bruise was blossoming. He grimaced, then he ran for the side of the room.

"Let's show you how we deal with this shit *a casa*," he cursed, ripping the curtains from their rails. The last of the evening light spilled into the room. It lit up the space and tore the appearance of night from the shelves. He stood, panting, with the book burning on the floor and the sunlight framing him in a halo.

"Good work," Lucy gasped, tears glistening in her eyes as she popped her knee back. She whimpered in pain as she struggled to her feet and moved to collect her pistol.

"*Oui*," Owens agreed, wiping blood from the cut on his forehead. "Not bad, Mister Amarti, not bad at all.

Except…" his eyes watched the other side of the room.

The sunlight stretched the shadows of everyone in the library. The cultists, the Hunters, even the furniture. Darkness stretched long and vivid from all of them. It pooled, growing larger and larger. Then it began to morph, twisting and building, pulling itself solid and real from the wall.

"Light might be the only thing that can kill a shadow…" Owens muttered. "But it's also the only thing that can birth it."

FORTRESS OF THE SHADOW REICH

4

The shadow monster grew and stretched, filling the room. It was completely black, with empty wells for eyes. The enlarging body was something not quite man and not quite beast in shape. It pulled and melted, as though it was dragging itself there from another realm. A large torso with snaking arms hauled itself from the wall. The head shifted lazily, like an antlered reptile, looking over the room. Everything below the waist became a melting pool of darkness.

Vincent stood and fired. This time the bullet pierced one giant meaty shoulder. The creature felt it. It started, turning sharply towards him. Behind him, Fred was still crouched over Tony, who was lying limp on the floor. Vincent kept his gun pointed at the monster's head. He fired again. The shadow beast raised its hand. It reached towards them with long midnight fingers. Vincent's bullets filled its giant palm. The holy bullets lit small particles of light in it, sizzling away the dark flesh, but they didn't slow it down.

Fred raised her hands, getting to one knee. Magic glowed up from her wrists. Fire spurted from her fingers. The hand drew back as Fred's shield of flame erupted over them. The fire in the rest of the room grew.

All the candles flared up. The book became a roaring blaze. That drew the creature's attention. There was no saving the tome now, but that didn't mean it wasn't prepared to try. It ignored the fiery mage and trigger-happy Hunter, growing even larger and sharper in the firelight.

It began to reach for the ashes of the book. Lucy and Gio opened fire on it. The hail of bullets only slowed its movement. Owens dashed into the circle and began pinching out the candles. If they could upset the magic it might banish the creature. Its hand came down over the book. Lucy leapt away. Her injured leg protested the treatment. She yelped in pain, catching herself on the ladder and gliding it down the wall of shelves.

Gio backed up to the window. The hand came down on the book. It crushed out the flames. The remains of the book scattered to dust. Owens shoved one of the cultists, but they didn't budge. The people sitting in the circle stayed like statues, caught in the spell. The monster was aiming for Lucy again. It could see she was the weak one. The ladder slid to the end of the row and she jumped off it, ducking around one of the nooks into cover. She unhooked her rifle from her shoulder and fired back around the corner.

The bullets erupted through the shadow monster, but its darkness oozed closed over the bright wounds. Its movement was creeping, glacial. Vincent took his chance. While it hunted his apprentice, he went for it. He leapt up one slow arm, running from its fingers to its shoulder. It straightened up. He ducked beside its neck as it tried to knock him into the ceiling.

"Vincent!" Owens called. He tossed one of his blades up. Vincent caught it. He drove it into the base of the monster's neck. It lurched and snatched for him. Lucy and Gio shot at its hands. Vincent ducked and dodged across its shoulders. Owens ran in. He jumped the circle and slid towards the beast, driving his other dagger into its abdomen. Vincent slid from the arm and leapt from the elbow. He crashed next to Lucy, helping to tuck her back behind cover.

"Now, Fred!" Owens yelled. He tried to roll out of the way, but the back of a shadowy hand smacked him into a shelf. It raised its palm to crush him.

Fred stood, hands glowing red, and focused her magic. Red lightning exploded between the two blades. It crackled and arced, connecting the metal and tearing through the center of the creature. The shadow twitched and flailed, as though confused. The light inside it began to dissolve it. With one slow hand, it reached towards the blade sticking out of its stomach.

"Boss!" Gio called to Owens, motioning him over. He was ducked down behind a small pile of stacked furniture by the window.

Owens grimaced, nodding, and staggered towards him. The shadow pulled the dagger out, severing Fred's lightning. It looked for its threat. It threw the blade.

"Stuart!" Fred yelled at him.

Owens dove. The throw was strong. He got lucky. It caught his sleeve, pinning him to the ground, but the blade barely nicked his arm. He grabbed the handle and pulled. It was stuck. He pulled harder, struggling against the dagger. He had to get free. The shadow was already raising a fist above him. Bullets rained into the giant dark hand, but it would not be stopped. It wasn't enough. Owens squeezed his eyes shut as he failed to haul himself loose.

The shadow was forced back against the wall. Ropes of golden light bound it down, slowly burning away its body. Tony stood in the center of the circle. His eyes were black. Golden light lit his fingertips and etched itself around the cultists' circle, wiping away their chalk design. He stared at the creature with a serious expression, but a vague distance to his gaze, as though looking beyond the room.

"*Te video,*" he said softly. Then his gaze shifted. He looked around the circle as his light dissolved the darkness, letting the shadow drip naturally back to where it should be. "*Revenite.* Wake up." he ordered. The light faded out. The black drained from his eyes.

"Tony!" Lucy cried. She rushed over, catching him under the arms as his knees gave out. He buried his face against her neck, holding on around her shoulders.

All around them the cultists shifted. They began to collapse as they woke, groaning and shivering. Then it hit them. Some vomited, others just choked and gagged. Many began to cry. Bodily fluids were mixed with a dark ooze and some were tainted with blood. A few didn't wake. They keeled over, still and unbreathing.

Owens finally ripped himself free, climbing to his feet with a grunt. Vincent reached his side first, offering him a hand and helping him steady his feet. Gio and Fred watched the carnage with expressions of disgust from the safety of cover.

"What the hell was that?" Owens asked quietly. The look he gave Vincent and the room spoke volumes. He was asking about Tony.

"The boy's our golden goose," Vincent replied just as softly.

"I've never seen magic like it," Owens commented, straightening his glasses. "Where did he learn that?"

"Somewhere best not investigated too thoroughly," Vincent answered.

Owens gave him a deadly look that told the old master it was the worst answer he could have given. Vincent knew how bad it sounded. There was nothing they were supposed to leave uninvestigated. That was how terror spawned. If they didn't know how or why, it could lead to apocalyptic danger. He hoped Owens could take a hint and save the questions for later.

"Help me tie this lot up," he requested. "They might not be going anywhere in a hurry, but best keep it that way until we can alert the police."

Together, the group bound the cultists, but questioning them proved fruitless. They were too far gone. Vincent knew why. He'd known why since he'd entered the room, but he had refused to admit it to himself. Now, standing in the circle, he couldn't help but inspect the bowl. The smell hit him first. It was so fresh and raw, as strong as ethanol. The fumes stung his nose and throat. His mouth tingled, and his body instantly yearned for the sharp burning sensation. He dipped a finger in the liquid and dropped it on his tongue, just to be sure. He remembered the taste. It was awful. He wanted more.

The bowl caught fire. He started, nearly dropping it, as he saw the match sail in, hit the tonic, and burst alight. He looked up and saw Fred handing Giovanni back his matches. The woman had good aim. She was looking at him with patient but judging eyes as she wiped sweat from her face. He set the bowl on the ground again and waited for the contents to burn out. It didn't take long. He didn't begrudge her the action. Sometimes he needed the help.

"Now what?" she asked, like nothing had just happened.

"Search the house," Vincent ordered. "Rogue isn't here, neither is her aide or the missing child. We need to find them."

Everyone nodded and broke off into pairs to search. Vincent took silent note of the close attention Fred paid him as they explored. He wondered if he should say something, but he wasn't sure how. Instead, he let her stay attentive without any of his characteristic frustration. He appreciated her concern, and he wanted her to know that, even if he didn't know how to say it. They'd been friends long enough now that he felt she could tell. She even smiled at him while they were rifling through a bedroom.

Drawers had been emptied, but that wasn't wholly unsurprising. Still, Vincent had been hoping for more incriminating evidence. He was nearly ready to call the search done, albeit unsatisfactorily, when he heard Owens yelling for him.

"Vincent!" the younger man's voice rang out, echoing through the halls. "Vincent!"

They raced back towards the yelling and found Owens searching at the top of the stairs.

"Doctor Temple," Owens retained his urgent tone, although his voice became more measured at the sight of the old Hunter and his mage. "Sir, you need to see this."

Owens led on towards one of the upper back rooms. Lucy and Tony joined them in the hallway, having also come running to the noise. Owens led them all to a study where his apprentice was perched on the edge of the desk. Gio appeared to be looking straight at them as they all entered. He gave an indicative nod and they all turned to follow his gaze. The long wall stretched out behind the door, and words had been painted, dripping across it.

"Is that blood?" Lucy asked.

"Sure looks it," Gio commented. "Professor says it's Latin too."

"It is," everyone else confirmed.

Vincent read over the words slowly, and then translated them under his breath.

"When the door to dark stars opens and the master of all universes comes hither, then the King of Hell shall sit upon the throne of God, and his Queen shall bathe in the blood of the masses. Thus shall the world be baptized and the true faith restored. Thus cometh the old ones to their rightful rule."

"Oh goody," Fred drawled. "Just when I was worried things would quieten down with the kids on their honeymoon. Now we have to find this mad bitch before she ends the world."

"That's alright, Fred," Owens smiled at her. "I can spare the time. Besides, she might not be here, but we know where she will be." He pulled a folded sheaf of paper from inside his coat. "Her itinerary puts her on a ship first thing tomorrow morning. It might not be as hard as you think."

* * *

Vincent got Fred to take the kids home. He wanted to scout the docks, check the ship, and if possible, speak to the Captain and the Harbor Master. Their best chance was going to be taking Rogue by surprise. He didn't want to give her any reason to hurt her hostage.

The sky was dark with winter but it was not yet late. The sun had sunk behind the city, and the lights of the harbor blinked out of the darkness. When they pulled up at the docks the police were already there. The two men climbed from the car slowly, taking in the scene. Police tape had cordoned off the area and uniforms were keeping everyone back. Vincent saw a man in a long coat look their way from the other side of the barrier. Detective Wilcox. The man raised his cigarette and waved it at them as soon as he saw Vincent, leaving a trail of smoke in the air.

Vincent gave him a nod and approached. Owens followed. Wilcox was a tall man with a long forehead and greying curls. He stuck the cigarette back in his mouth as he waved Vincent and Owens through the barrier. Vincent felt his stomach sink as they walked closer. A cold dread clutched his heart.

"That's some time you made, Doc," Wilcox commented. "Didn't think my guys would get to you that fast."

"They didn't," Owens answered bleakly. "We were already on our way. Just left some of your people at one of the big houses outside of town."

"Think I heard someone radio that in," Wilcox nodded. "You are?"

"Professor Stuart Owens," Owens shook the man's hand. "I work with Vincent, although I'm usually based down south."

"Good to have you here, Professor," Wilcox greeted him. "Did Doc Temple call you up to help with this one? I ain't seen anything like it before. This is the eleventh one we've found now." He led them around behind a stack of crates. A sheet had been laid out to cover the shape of a small person.

Owens looked to Vincent, but Vincent's eyes stayed on the silhouette of the body. His grim face was drawn and tight. Murder glistened in his eyes.

"Harbor Master found the poor thing and called it in," Wilcox continued, motioning to a man sitting away from the scene with an officer. "He's a bit shook up, unsurprisingly. As soon as we heard it I knew it must be another one of yours. Only things in your department can do that to a body. Don't know how to identify it, but I presume you've got a list of the missing kids."

"His name is Bobby Sylva," Owens said quietly. "His father died this morning. No sign the mother was in the picture. We'd been trying to track him down."

"Then I'm sorry to be the bearer of bad news," Wilcox sighed. "You got any idea who's doing this to these kids? I know you said it was a witch, but without starting a city-wide panic I need more to—"

"Diana Rogue," Vincent answered cuttingly, finally breaking his silence. "All our evidence points to Lady Diana Rogue as the witch responsible for these killings."

"The highborn cripple lady who donates to the orphanages?" Wilcox raised an eyebrow.

"I think those payments might prove to be unwilling bartering on the part of the orphanages, rather than selfless donations," Vincent growled. "That woman is killing children by draining their blood for her magic. She's supposed to be getting a ship in the morning and we came here to catch her, but if the body has already been dumped..."

"You think she's left?" Owens surmised.

"I personally wouldn't dump a body and then wait around to get caught," Vincent commented. "But there's one way to find out."

He strode over to the Harbor Master with the other two in tow and had Owens produce the itinerary again to check Rogue's ship with the man. The itinerary was out of date. They had changed things around last week. The ship sailed this afternoon. If Rogue had been on it, she would have been sailing out during Lucy and Tony's reception. It was taking all of Vincent's strength not to punch a wall, but hurting himself wouldn't get them any closer to justice.

Owens and Wilcox were watching him carefully, like

they could tell from the throbbing vein in his temple that he was a ticking timebomb of fury. These were not the people to be taking out his wrath on. The people who deserved it were Rogue and her assistant White, who were somewhere out in the Atlantic. His thoughts were whirling, and he gave them a moment to churn before he spoke. Eventually, he addressed Wilcox.

"The good news, detective, is that your city should be safe from this threat for now," he grated.

"Our city, Doc," Wilcox insisted. "I gather the bad news is that this witch got away, but is that so bad? Don't get me wrong, I wanna see whoever did this swing, but maybe this time we can let it be a Kraut problem?"

Vincent and Owens shared a look. The old Hunter was more concerned than he let on about the writing on the wall of Rogue's mansion. Owens was a mystery, but his eyes were creased with deep concern. If Rogue and White were on an apocalyptic mission from a dark god they couldn't be left to run free. Besides, Vincent was determined to make the evil that had drained those children pay.

* * *

Lucy was in the drawing room, lounging in a chair, with her foot up on a stool and a towel of ice on her knee. The pain had mostly worn off now, but she didn't want to move. Tony was resting upstairs, probably asleep, and Gio was sitting across from her, nursing his own bruises. The drapes were pulled across the window and a fire was crackling in the grate. It wasn't doing the medicinal ice any favors, but it had cut the winter chill from the house.

Fred entered with a tray of steaming mugs and handed them both hot cocoa.

"*Ah grazie,* Miss Winifred!" Gio thanked her. "Gee, this is decadent."

"It's a special day," Lucy smiled.

"It's been a long day," Fred sighed, sinking into a chair herself. "Between the wedding and the bombing and the cult. Hard to believe that was just this morning."

"You certainly know how to throw a party," Gio smiled. "I was worried when the Professor said we were staying here. Thought I might do better crashing with family, but the old man keeps me busy."

"Watch who you're calling old, Amarti," Fred warned.

"He's older than he looks, *Signora,*" Gio insisted. "There's a lotta years in those eyes."

"He's younger than I am," Fred replied.

"No!" Gio exclaimed. "No way!"

"Nice save," she grinned. "Stuart's not that old. He's just had a rough time of it."

"He doesn't seem old," Lucy commented, sipping her drink. "Within a year of Fred, and easily less than a decade on you, Gio. Maybe a dozen years on me, if that."

"You work for Doctor Temple," Gio laughed at her. "No one seems old to you. That man is a grizzled relic, tougher than grilled goat meat."

The women laughed. Their amusement didn't quite drown out the sound of the car in the drive. As though invoked, Vincent and Owens returned. Lucy removed the sodden towel from her leg as they set their drinks down and went to meet them. When the men came through the front door Lucy could see what Gio meant by the age in Stuart's eyes, but to her it looked more like weariness than actual years.

"So, when are we setting our trap?" she asked.

Vincent ignored her and went straight for his office. He brushed by them all without a word. The bleak expression on his grim face spoke volumes, and no one stopped him. Stuart removed his coat and scarf and hung them by the door. He checked the hole in the sleeve as though trying to decide if it was worth attempting to wash out the blood tonight. The suit was a much direr situation.

"What happened?" Fred asked him.

Owens turned from the coat with a sigh. "Itinerary was out of date. She's gone and the boy's dead."

"Fuck," Fred cursed. "So what now?"

"That's for him to decide," Owens replied. "He hasn't shared his thoughts with me."

"He'll have to make calls and send telegrams and letters to see if someone else can catch her at the other end," Fred muttered. "Lord knows he hates having to ask the Order to pick up after him."

Lucy left the conversation and followed after her mentor. The corridor stretched dark and oppressive, like his temperament. The entire house reflected the old man, a clutter of oddities in a wealthy rough shell. He hadn't shut his office door. She reached the doorway and looked in just in time to see him thump the desk like it had wronged him. He was lucky it was so sturdy, although that was certainly by design. Weaker desks had probably failed their tests over the years. Besides, he needed something that could hold the weight of all his junk.

She waited in the doorway until he acknowledged her. Just a glance her way was enough. You took what you could get with Vincent. Once he looked at her, she stepped gently into the room. Now he was looking anywhere but her. His eyes scoured the shelves of occult paraphernalia and hardback tomes. He rubbed his stubbled jaw wearily, probably missing the beard. It was still strange to see him without it.

"We should have gone to the docks first," he muttered. "As soon as we had the itinerary we should have gone down there and waited for her."

"How were you supposed to know?" she asked. "Your proof before searching her house was weak, and you were trying to save that kid."

"But I didn't!" Vincent exclaimed. "If I had gone straight to the docks we might have had a chance, but he was probably dead before I got to her house. If I had just–"

"'If' doesn't change anything, Vincent," she advised the same way he'd told her before. "You're not psychic. There was no way to know what she was doing or planning."

A grim darkness settled in his eyes. Lucy knew that look. She'd been fielding it a lot recently. He was thinking about that goddamn tonic. He was dwelling on the lives he could have saved if he'd been drinking it and dreaming of things before they happened. Rogue would never have beaten him if he was still using and all those children might still be alive. Forget the fact that he would have died from overuse by now and couldn't have helped anyone. A small frown settled on Lucy's face. Vincent saw. His glower melted into resignation. She couldn't stop him from being angry. He had every right to be angry, but his penchant for self-destruction wasn't helpful, and he knew it. Her eyebrows were telling him so. She reinforced them verbally.

"I know you're upset, Vincent," she began, "but cursing all the 'ifs' in the world won't change anything. You were trying to save that kid. You had every reason to believe she was sailing out tomorrow, and that she would have taken the boy back to her lair as a hostage. Based on the information you had, you were doing the right thing. It's important to remember that. No matter the way things played out, you did everything you could to try and save that child."

Vincent nodded slowly. He sank down in the chair by his desk, leaning heavily on the polished wooden tabletop. She watched him process everything. He knew she was right even if that did nothing to diminish his frustration. Finally, he sighed in agreement.

"You always know how to set my priorities straight, kid," he muttered.

She nodded. That was certainly true. She'd been shot for it. The Prince had said she was too good an anchor for Vincent and Tony. He had shot her in the chest. It was a miracle she'd survived. Now, she sought to return the favor. Ever since then Vincent had gone straight and stopped drinking tonic. That decision had saved his life and his sanity. But it had made the Prince elusive and Lucy could tell that sometimes Vincent regretted his decision.

"Come on," she patted his arm. "Fred made cocoa. Have a drink and we'll work out what to do next."

"If I say no you'll just bully me into this, yeah?"

"Yes," Lucy confirmed. "I will. It's my wedding day. You have to be nice to me."

Vincent laughed despite himself. He gave a conceding nod and pulled himself to his feet again. Lucy took his hand and led him back to the drawing room. She dragged him back down the dark corridor of gleaming glass cabinets. One day she was going to be responsible for all these trinkets, and she still only knew what half of them did. At least Vincent only owned one thing Lucy considered truly dangerous, and he kept that book locked in his safe. They couldn't risk Tony touching it again, and he in turn did his best to avoid the office.

Back in the drawing room, the fire was still crackling warmly. Gio was reclining in his seat with his drink and Owens was waving Fred off as she tried to check the bloody scratch on his arm.

"I'm not undressing for you, Winifred. You're just going to have to use your imagination," he quipped.

She slapped his injury in retort and he gave a muffled yelp of pain.

"What if you need stitches?" she demanded.

"He'll stitch himself up like he always does," Gio commented.

"Leave him be, Fred," Vincent urged. "He's not bleeding anymore. He'll be fine."

"It's not that bad a wound," Owens insisted. "The suit has had a worse time of it than I have."

Fred shrugged them all off and turned her attention to Vincent as he and Lucy entered the room.

"Can I help you with anything, Sir?" she asked.

"Lucy says you have spare cocoa?" he ventured.

Fred arched an eyebrow at him, but obligingly poured a mug of hot cocoa from the pot on the tray. She handed it over and he settled on the couch with it.

"Are you going to need any help contacting people, Sir?" she asked.

Vincent sipped his drink quietly in thought. Everyone waited on him. It was standard Vincent behavior. He wasn't trying to be rude, and he wasn't ignoring her, he just didn't have an answer yet. Lucy watched him, but he was thinking slowly. Owens got there first. The younger man frowned behind his square-framed glasses, and rubbed his chin thoughtfully.

"We're going to Germany, aren't we?" he mused.

"We?" Vincent echoed.

"You don't have anyone to contact, do you?" Owens pressed. "That's why you didn't race back to start making calls. You don't know who to go to."

"You have Hunters all over the world though," Lucy protested. "You must have plenty in Germany."

"But do you have any spare?" Owens pressed. "I

don't know if any of you have picked up a newspaper recently, but things aren't exactly going well in Germany. They've been in trouble since the war. You think the Depression was hard here... you're talking about a country that never got the boom we had last decade. Those people have been struggling for a long time. It's a powder keg over there. I might not be a part of the Order anymore, but things were hard for the German Hunters when I was a member, and I do not imagine anything has improved."

"As astute as ever, Owens," Vincent nodded. "I do think I will need to head to Germany. I can't ask my people over there to drop what they're doing. Their new government is giving them grief, and I can't make my problem theirs. If Rogue and White are as dangerous as their prophecy suggests, I have to get rid of them. I have to finish it."

"So Stuart's right?" Lucy reinforced. "We're going to Germany?"

Everyone stared at her. Her gaze was utterly unapologetic. She tossed her hair back primly and stared them all down.

"Tony said we could honeymoon anywhere we wanted. Germany sounds interesting."

Fred gave Vincent a sidelong glance. "You were never going to get away without us, Sir. You need a mage, and the kids will want the mission."

"I was talking to the Harbor Master at the docks," Owens offered. "There's a ship we can take to Calais leaving in two days. We can train to Germany through Belgium from there. It's our best shot. How do you feel about Germany, Amarti?"

"I understand the nagging persistence of my family," Vincent grumbled, cutting off any reply from Gio. "Why in God's name are you pushing this, Owens?"

"How many of you speak German?" Stuart replied. An awkward silence filled the room. He let it hang there for some time before he finished politely. "*Ich bin froh, dass wir uns einig sind.*"

"Guess we're all going to Germany," Gio commented, slurping his drink.

FORTRESS OF THE SHADOW REICH

5

The big mainline steamer could cross the Atlantic in less than a week, but time wasn't on their side. Lucy was still calling the trip her honeymoon, so she and Tony had splashed out to afford a nice room on the ship, even if they weren't staying long. It was certainly a vast upgrade from their last adventure. They had a private room with a large, shared bed. It was the morning after their first night on the water, and she snuggled up to him under the blankets. The feeling of his skin on hers was warm and soft and she yearned for it. He pulled her into his arms.

"Are you cross I requested Germany for our honeymoon?" she murmured.

"No," he smiled, resting his lips against her hair. "But don't think I don't know why you did it."

She propped herself up on an elbow, pulling away slightly and looking down at him. Her hair spilled over her shoulder. He was still smiling at her, but there was a cautious warning in it. He traced the scar against her ribs with his thumb, gently brushing her skin.

"We're not ready, Luce," he warned. "I wanna help you, you know I do, but we haven't got it right yet. If this takes the turn you're looking for, we're not ready."

"We will be," she assured.

He gave her a wry grin. "I could have conquered the world by now if I had your confidence."

She grinned, cupping his cheek with her hand and kissing his lips. It was a nice compliment, even if he was saying it to caution her. Her smile faltered and the pause reached her kiss. The memory of the mansion flared in her mind. The darkness in his eyes and the way he had thrashed trying to get at the book. The absolute hold it had taken over him.

"Lucy?" he whispered, sensing something was wrong.

She didn't answer. She didn't know how. Instead, she kissed him firmly, climbing on top of him and straddling him. She didn't know how to talk to him about his magic. She didn't know enough about it. Every time she tried, every time she raised her concerns, he brushed them away. He always insisted he knew what he was doing, that he was the one with the power, even to Fred. Besides, he'd saved their lives. More than once over the years. Significantly more.

Her lips traced down his neck as she pushed herself against him. It wasn't difficult to get him aroused, and she'd swear she always got there first. A hot, pleasant blush spread between her legs as she ground against him, hungry for the feeling of him.

"Are you going to answer me or just distract yourself?" he whispered in her ear, letting his lips brush the soft cartilage.

"Can't I just distract us both?" she sighed.

He didn't stop her and he didn't fight it. He

squeezed her breasts and kissed the hand that still caressed his face. Her finger traced his lips. He took it in his mouth and sucked it gently. His hands clutched her body and pulled her closer. That made her answer worse somehow. It made her feel like she was keeping secrets. She took her hand from his mouth to direct him inside her. He pushed up with his hips as she slid down onto him. The sensation made her want to scream.

"I'm worried about your magic!" she gasped sharply.

"I know," he grunted. His hand pressed firmly on the small of her back, pushing her down as he thrust up harder. He moved his hands to her hips, sliding them behind her and squeezing.

She couldn't speak. She could hear her own voice gasping and panting with an urgency that sounded like she might cry. It sounded like her, but it seemed so far away. She felt like she was riding fire. Her whole body was hot. Sweat glistened across her skin. The pressure between her legs tightened every muscle in her body. An explosion was building. Every time they collided the force was like jolt of elation. Over and over and over.

Detonation. She didn't relax. She tensed. She couldn't move. Everything froze as her entire body stiffened. She curled into him, over him, burying her face against his neck.

"Lucy?" he panted.

Nothing. Her fire was spreading and she couldn't move, even if she'd wanted to. He grabbed her tightly and lifted her just enough to gain momentum. He thrust rapidly beneath her, pounding roughly until she couldn't contain her scream. It slipped from her lips as a muffled cry of ecstasy. He kept going. She thought she might actually explode. He groaned and shuddered beneath her, stopping as the strength left his grip. His hips sank back against the mattress. His upper body stayed half risen, and he pulled himself up, taking her with him, until they were sitting on the sheets, tangled in each other.

Sitting like this, her legs wrapped around his body with him still pressed deeply inside her, they shifted. He brought one arm beneath her, his hand tightening on her behind, and adjusted her on him, pushing deeper still. Her back arched. He rested his face against her breasts, kissing her skin. They were both still gasping. His lips traced her sweat down to her nipple as she held on around his neck. She pushed her fingers through his damp sweaty hair, enjoying the way he sucked on her.

"What do we do if you go somewhere you don't come back from?" she asked.

He stopped. Now it was his turn not to answer. The question hung over them, but she didn't wish she hadn't asked it. It had haunted them much longer than this, unspoken. His breath crashed in waves against her chest. She kissed the top of his head. They stayed locked in each other's arms, both fooling themselves with the knowledge that distractions were easier than answers.

* * *

Days on the ship seemed to pass slowly. Vincent was primed and ready for danger. He expected it around every corner. So far, the most dangerous things he'd encountered were Tony and Gio's intensifying accents and telegrams from the Council. He had informed his people of the situation. The Council generally were apprehensive about his behavior. They always had been. He could sense the careful hesitations in their messages – although none of them had the nerve to challenge him for the position of Chancellor. The general European Hunters were grateful. As suspected, no one had time to drop what they were doing to chase a new threat.

They were helping where they could, however. Provided the location of Rogue's itinerary destination was still correct, she was heading to a castle maybe half a day's travel down the Rhine from Koblenz. Apparently, the Hunters had a safehouse on a farm near there. It was currently unoccupied, and they were more than happy for Vincent and his team to make use of it as a base of operations.

It was a sunny, still day on the water. All of them were out on the deck gathered around a table. Fred was playing cards with the kids while Vincent flicked through his telegrams and Owens perused a newspaper. The card game was getting loud. Someone was cheating. The Italians were growing heated.

"*Mamma mia!*" Gio exploded. "Antony, ya grandma oughta be ashamed of ya!"

"Of me?!" Tony bit back. "*Sai* we got the same grandma, Gio! An' the only *bugiardo* she oughta be ashamed of is sittin' across from me!"

"*Come osi!*" Gio exclaimed.

"Ain't on me that ya blowin' this," Tony scoffed.

"Either you cheatin' or ya wife is," Gio accused.

"*Riprenditelo!*" Tony cried. "Dishonorable s*tronzo!* Making accusations just 'cos ya getting sore!"

The longer those two boys were together the more they reverted to their family's vernacular. Vincent held back a frustrated sigh and an eyeroll. A soft chuckle caught his attention, barely audible. He looked up. Owens caught his eye over the newspaper. The man was an avid follower of more than half a dozen papers from around the globe. He'd stocked up on the most recent editions he could before they left. This one was in French. He gave Vincent a discreet smile and dropped his gaze back to the words.

"Your upper class is showing, Sir," he cautioned gently.

"My upper class?" Vincent raised an eyebrow at him. Everyone ignored him and he glared at the man behind the newspaper. "Rich of you, Owens. Everyone thinks you're British."

"*Bêtise!* They do not!" he scoffed, folding down his paper irritably.

"Please," Vincent grinned. "We can practically smell the Empire wafting 'God Save the King' off you."

"Calm down, Yankee," Owens retorted. "Being born into the British Empire doesn't make you a monarchist."

"You're Canadian?" Lucy turned to Owens curiously, catching on and ignoring the card fight.

"I was born in Canada," Owens admitted, folding his paper neatly. "I left a long time ago."

"You were driven out," Vincent snorted.

Owens looked like he was about to snap, if Fred didn't jump to his defense first, but Lucy held her conversation with him while ignoring her mentor.

"I didn't realize you were from up north," she commented. "I guess because I knew you from Louisiana I just assumed you were from there, even though your accent doesn't sound southern, but I figured that was just the French coming through or something."

"Not quite," Stuart sighed. "I speak several languages though. English and French, *de toute évidence.* German, Italian, Spanish, Latin, a little Portuguese."

"You can see why everyone thinks he's British," Vincent scoffed.

"No one thinks that, Vincent," Owens sighed. "I don't sound British; I just enunciate properly. You should try it sometime."

"Enunciate?" Vincent echoed. "Half of everything you say is in French – they've never pronounced a whole word."

"Now who sounds like bickering schoolboys?" Fred groaned loudly.

"*Pardon*, Fred," Owens implored. "You know he can't resist ragging on the Europeans – even if his best shot is through me."

"You weren't there," Vincent pointed at him. "You don't know. You were all children. Those two weren't even born!" he indicated Lucy and Tony.

"No one's saying the war wasn't a catastrophe in every direction," Owens soothed. "But your dislike of everything British and European is infamous – and rumor has it the loathing began with Whitehall in Egypt, not the Great War."

"When you see humanity at its worst, it helps to stay wary afterwards," Vincent growled.

"No," Owens disagreed. "When *you* see humanity at its worst, Vincent, it helps to have someone to blame."

"They started it," Vincent stated. "More than fourteen million people died, the worst horrors I've ever seen were brought forth, armies were massacred, the Darkness got as close to consuming this world as it has ever done, and it all happened because a bunch of entitled Europeans decided to go fuck themselves. Because their honor and their greed were more important than the safety of this world and the lives of millions."

Owens patted his newspaper with his fingers.

"They're paying for it now," he reminded.

"Everyone has been," Vincent sighed. "Believe me, I know. If you'd been there... if you'd seen what I saw... time hasn't erased that anger. Perhaps it never will. They threw the world into desperate times, and our Order has been picking up the pieces and mopping up the blood. We've been doing it since time began, but... but it feels worse. It feels like it just keeps getting worse."

Lucy reached out a hand and placed it on Vincent's shoulder. She gave him a reassuring pat.

"We'll fix it," she promised. "Even if we have to take you back to Germany."

"Hm," Vincent grimaced darkly. He didn't want to shut her down. They needed her optimism. But some things were too big to fix. The human condition was one of them. "I've never actually been to Germany," he admitted. "We never made it that far. The German Hunters were the ones who took care of most of the cults and magic there, and a few of the French went down to help. Most of the Darkness followed the death..." he trailed off.

The air coming off the water was cold, but the light glinting from the ocean was bright. It was strange to feel memories of necromancers on the Western Front conjuring themselves on so peaceful a day. Maybe that was a problem. Maybe Vincent brought the Darkness with him, even if he wasn't using anymore, even if he wasn't bound to the Prince, maybe he still carried the horror like a wet blanket, dripping tension everywhere he went.

"Sorry, Owens," he sighed and tapped the telegram scraps on the table. "I'm on edge. I shouldn't rile you."

"We're on the same side, Sir," Owens assured. "It's alright."

Vincent nodded appreciatively to him, trying to convey his gratitude. He'd taken some shots at Owens that the man didn't deserve. Whatever wariness Vincent might still carry for him after his expulsion, he had paid his dues. He had done his time. Now, he had offered to help without Vincent having to ask. He had packed up and come with them because they needed him. Perhaps he was trying to pay Vincent back for the help he had received in the last five years. Perhaps he was trying to get experience for his apprentice. Whatever the reason, Vincent knew he was lucky to have him. Now if only he could drive off the constant weight of unease.

* * *

Night on the ocean was peaceful. The sky was bright with stars. The hum of the ship's engines and the sloshing of the endless waves was like a lullaby, while the roll of the ship was like a hammock rocking everyone to sleep.

Vincent lay in his bunk, warm and comfortable and sleepy. It wasn't a bad way to travel. Maybe one day he'd get himself a boat, learn how to sail properly. Perhaps he could even retire. That wasn't something Hunters usually got to do, but it wasn't impossible. Maybe one day.

He wasn't someone who had given much in the way of thought to the future. The future had usually meant staying alive to see the next day. Lucy had changed all that. More so than Fred or her baby Toby. Lucy had become his legacy, even before they'd planned her wedding, before they'd talked about her taking the Temple name. When he had agreed to train her, he had known what he was doing. He was making sure there was someone to take over when he was gone.

This was the first time in his life it had occurred to him that 'gone' didn't have to mean 'dead'. Still, even as he thought it, he wasn't sure he believed it. Hunters never died in their beds. He'd had that conversation with Owens five years ago. The Brotherhood had thrown Stuart out. Vincent had made them swear not to take action against him. Abandonment was enough. That way, he would keep his territory safe and they wouldn't have to find a new Hunter for the area. If they'd killed him or arrested him things might have been very different.

Vincent had defied the Council's orders not to aid or supply Owens. Maybe he believed in second chances. He liked to think he did. Contemplating his treatment of the man now that he was in his company again, he had to wonder if he'd just been making things easier for himself. It had been easier to tolerate Owens and give him another chance than it had been to replace him – to let him go free, because Fred wouldn't have tolerated anything else. But that wasn't how it worked. Hunters never die in their beds.

His insides squirmed as he dwelt on it. They weren't the only things squirming. He started as he felt it. His body jerked. He threw himself from the bed, hitting the floor. He stared down at his bare arms. Something was moving under his skin. Dozens of writhing worms shifted like risen veins under his skin. He could see them squirming. Burrowing. He tried to grab one. They were in the backs of his hands. His flesh writhed. With one hand, he pinched a worm in his other arm. He shoved his thumbnail into his skin, drawing blood, cutting an exit. He pinched the worm, dragging it, bloody and thrashing, from his body. It was white and fleshy like a maggot, nearly half a foot long.

The sight of it on the ground made him want to vomit. He crushed it, but it didn't help. His body was full of them. He began to rip at his skin. He cut and scratched, ripping worms from his body. He could feel them as he pulled them out. The hideous slippery sucking as he dragged them from his veins. Blood covered his fingers. It was oozing down his hands, dripping from his wrists. It made the process harder. They were so slippery. There were so many. Too many. He couldn't get them all. They were burrowing into his flesh. He could feel it. His skin still squirmed. Nothing could make it stop. He screamed, ripping at his arms as though trying to remove his skin and expose the worms beneath.

He jerked awake, choking and throwing himself from the bunk. He hit the hard floor with a thud. His skin was perfectly fine. Old and weathered and scarred, but fine. Nothing moved. Just a nightmare. He hadn't even realized he'd fallen asleep.

"Sir...?" Fred's sleepy voice came from the bunk above his.

Vincent sighed and pulled himself back onto the edge of his bed. He sat hunched, rubbing his arms gently as though trying to massage away the feeling of writhing evil beneath his skin. It had felt so real. He almost thought he could taste the bitter touch of the tonic where he had dropped it on his tongue in the mansion. That had been days ago. Still, the Dreamlands were the realm of the Prince. He had always been fond of giving Vincent presents. Maybe this was a new one.

"Just a nightmare, Fred," he sighed. "Go back to sleep."

"Are you okay?" she asked.

He watched the infinite blackness out the window.

The midnight sky of stars and endless waves. Did the Dreamlands reflect reality? Or did reality reflect the Dreamlands? When he looked out at the night he could see places he had been in the other world. Memories stronger than many of this world. Which realm was more real? When night fell and darkness swallowed this world, it could be hard to tell them apart.

"I will be," he answered. "Just unsettled. I'll be alright."

"Do you want to talk about it?" she asked.

"No," he replied gently. "It was grotesque. I'd just as soon forget it."

"Okay, wake me if you need me," Fred yawned, but he could tell from her voice she was already drifting off again.

He didn't lie down. He didn't want to sleep again. There was no way of knowing what was waiting for him. Another nightmare? Another vision of the Prince seeking vengeance? Both were equally possible and neither would do anything to help quell the dread plaguing him. Still, he couldn't stay awake forever.

* * *

The afternoon that met them in Calais was bitterly cold and dreary. Not exactly sightseeing weather. They disembarked from the ship and Vincent took it upon himself to engage in reconnaissance while the rest of them found lunch. Lucy watched in soft awe as Owens fluently chaperoned them, and was surprised how adept Fred was. Her own timid murmurs of *'bonjour'*, '*pardon*', and '*merci*' felt deeply inadequate.

She sat in a café, nursing a bowl of hot soup and watching the light rain trickle down the window. The door banged and Vincent clattered in with the grace of a buffalo. He strode to their table and pulled up the chair at the end, shaking out his old coat.

"She's left town," he announced before anyone could ask what luck he'd had. "Heading for Germany, so for now we assume the itinerary was correct and pursue her there. There's an overnight train to Cologne via Brussels. Owens, can I get you to sort us tickets after lunch?"

"*Oui*," he was struggling to switch back. "They're proving easy to track then?"

"Not as easy as I was hoping," Vincent glowered. "I'm starting to think the wheelchair was a disguise. She was feigning her illness back home so that no one would look at her too closely. By the sounds of things, when she got on that ship, she was walking."

"Could that have been what the blood magic was for?" Lucy asked.

"It's certainly possible," Vincent agreed. "But it's not the only possibility. For now, I'd rather assume she was tricking everyone and keep an eye open for what other dangers the magic may have been spent on."

"You found her trail pretty quick for a broad who's been changing it up," Gio commented.

"She still has a modicum of distinction," Vincent replied. "And I'm finding it easier to track White. I remembered, when Lucy and I met them briefly at the start of our investigation, something about Lady

Rogue's aide seemed off. It was hard to place at the time, but it's easy enough to track. Ezra White unsettles people, and he wears dark glass all the time, even at night."

"Sounds like a fella with something to hide," Tony remarked. "Something wrong with his eyes?"

"Could be a mage who tapped into some powerful black magic and couldn't make it all the way back?" Owens suggested.

"We don't know what it is or why he does it, but if it's going to make them easier to track, I'm not going to complain," Vincent sighed.

No one disagreed with him. They got Vincent fed and finished up their lunch before heading to the station. Lucy was surprised by the afternoon crowds there. The dismal weather was keeping people indoors, but indoors included the train station. It wasn't packed but it was crowded. Clusters of people gathered together out of the cold.

They queued as a group for tickets, even though Stuart was doing the talking. As they were crossing borders it was possible their papers would be checked here as well as at boarding. Lucy waited at the back of their clique with her hand tucked in Tony's elbow. He was chatting and smoking with Gio but she wasn't following their conversation. Her attention was elsewhere. Specifically, her eyes were scouring the crowds. She could feel people watching them, and she wasn't wrong.

Catching Vincent's eye failed, but she managed to get Fred's attention. Fred gave her the usual stern eyebrow lift and leant towards her.

"I think we're being watched," she warned. "Is it possible Rogue left spies?"

"Maybe," Fred whispered back. She gave Lucy a cautious nod and moved back to Vincent, murmuring something briefly in his ear.

Reassured that her mentor was aware, Lucy went back to making mental notes of those she thought might be watching them. It was possible she and her companions simply stood out as a tourist group, but they weren't the only ones. An entire boat of Americans had just been unloaded onto the city. Still, it was them people were watching.

Her suspicions were confirmed as they were walking away from the ticket line. Owens was shuffling through the papers he'd just collected and handing them out when one of the women who had been watching them strode up and inquired something of him. Lucy watched her play coy, but had no idea what they were saying. Stuart's responses were all helpfully polite. Just like that the woman's eyes washed over them all and she sashayed away.

"What was that?" Lucy demanded.

"*Elle a demandé l'heure,*" Owens answered automatically, pointing to his watch.

"She asked the time," Fred translated almost over the top of his reply. Her brows were furrowed and her tone suspicious.

"What? With that big clock on the wall?" Tony pointed his cigarette at the large station clock. His disbelief echoed Lucy's own, and Fred's expression matched them.

Giovanni started to laugh. "You get used to it," he grinned.

"Get used to what?" Lucy asked.

"All the attention," Gio nodded his head at Owens. "Women love him. You should hear Renée back home – all the older ladies – every mother in New Orleans wants to marry him off to their daughter." He adopted a faux accent and waved his cigarette dramatically, clutching his heart. "*S'il vous plaît, Monsieur Owens!* You must stay for dinner! Gabrielle will be devastated! Lucille and Viviane missed you last week! You break an old lady's heart!"

Stuart had gone bright red and was nervously adjusting his glasses. Lucy noted the severe frames did nothing to detract from his thick dark hair, strong jaw, and dimpled chin. He looked like he was searching for an uncovered manhole to jump into. Pointless – even covered in sewage there was a good chance he'd still be ridiculously handsome.

Tony was grinning openly at the situation, enjoying his cousin's dramatization. Even Vincent was struggling to hide a wry, pitying smile.

"Oh Stuart," Fred kissed his cheek sympathetically. "We can't take you anywhere, can we?"

"He makes more of it than it is," Stuart dismissed through his blush. "*Monsieur* Amarti likes to throw me in harm's way to distract Renée from his own intentions."

"Uncalled for, *Capo*," Gio pointed his cigarette at his boss. "I ain't never had to throw you nowhere. You got dames lining up just to ask you the time standing under a giant clock."

"And you've been stepping out with Renée's daughter, Dot, and hoping no one will notice you taking up with a jazz singer," Owens sighed like this was a matter on which he'd tried to counsel his apprentice before.

Gio gave Owens a dark look as surprised glances were thrown his way, most notably Tony's.

"You just gonna throw me under the coach like that?" he glowered.

"On récolte ce que l'on sème," Owens quipped at him.

Giovanni didn't speak enough French to know what Owens had said, but the Professor's expression spoke volumes. Gio glared at him. Owens was unmoved. He slapped his apprentice playfully in the chest with their train tickets.

"Come along, *aprenti,*" he coaxed. "Stop teasing me about pretty French ladies and find me my train." He strode off across the station, looking for their platform. The others followed along, with Gio muttering irritated grumbles around his cigarette.

Lucy continued to watch the crowd, but now that it had been pointed out to her it did mostly seem to be women watching them, and they did seem to be watching Owens. His broad shoulders and tailored coat cut a striking figure in the crowd. Lucy had always known her mentor's estranged friend was attractive, but it had never properly struck her before now. She had a sudden onset of worry that her profession had made her blind to normal life. Here was a handsome man attracting attention and she was looking for spies.

It then occurred to her that she wasn't necessarily wrong, and she begrudged him a little for making the spies harder to spot. That wasn't fair either.

A few hours later they were on their train with their bags packed safely in their cabins and her concern had proven unfounded. If anyone had been watching them with ill intent at the station they hadn't made a move. Owens had parked them to wait at the platform two numbers down from the one they needed until the train actually arrived, just in case they were being followed. At least Lucy hadn't been alone in her paranoid vigilance. She might be worried about what the Hunter psychology was doing to her, but they'd been doing it longer. Of course they had it worse.

* * *

Night fell fast in the depths of winter. The grey countryside dissolved into darkness. Lucy sat on her bunk, reading by the dim light, and listening to the rattle of the train as they raced along the tracks. This felt more like the travel she was used to. She and Tony had stacked bunks in the same cabin as Vincent and Fred. Owens and Gio were based in a different room. Currently, Tony was off wandering with his cousin. Fred had gone to see Owens. That left Vincent on the bunk across from her.

He was hunched over new telegrams, scribbling rough replies to send when he next had the chance. He did that a lot these days. Once upon a time Lucy couldn't have imagined the grumpy recluse as the Chancellor of the Brotherhood of Hunters, now more commonly known as the Order of Hunters thanks to his updated recruitment conditions. He was taking the position very seriously.

"What are you looking at, kid?" he grumbled without glancing up.

"I'm reading," Lucy replied.

Now he glanced up, and met her gaze directed his way. He only held it long enough to make his point. Then his eyes returned to his messages.

"I hear you got a letter from Fajr before we left," he commented.

"I did," Lucy smiled. "With a wedding gift. It was extremely kind of her. She's doing well."

"And what have you been doing?" Vincent inquired.

"I don't know what you mean," Lucy replied. She really didn't. She could tell he was niggling for something and she had no idea what.

"Ship we were on let me know there were scorch marks left on the writing desk in your room," Vincent told her. "I'm used to you two trying to get yourselves in trouble, but I'm curious as to why scorch marks were involved."

"We were experimenting," she admitted. "I told you we were working on something."

"And that something involves setting fire to desks?" Vincent queried.

"No," Lucy sighed. "The magic just got a bit hot. We're trying to make something, something with our alchemy and his magic."

"What kind of something?" Vincent growled, looking up at her.

"I'm not going to tell you," she replied, turning back to her book. "We haven't gotten that far yet."

"Lucy—"

"It's our business," she insisted. "We will tell you about it when we get a bit further, but I don't want you butting your nose in and trying to take over."

"You could be messing with something dangerous," he warned.

"We're always messing with something dangerous!" she exclaimed. "That's all we ever do, Vincent. This is our project. It's his magic. He knows what he's doing and I trust him. I don't need you coming in and telling him not to try just because we don't understand what he's got. You're more than happy to let him help us when we're in peril, so let him try something to keep us out of it." She turned back to the book again in a huff, and ignored his lingering eyes and heavy silence.

"You told him about your curse yet?" Vincent asked.

"No," Lucy grumbled. "And I don't want to. He won't take it well. All he'll hear is that I'm cursed. He won't think about the fact that it kept us safe for two years."

The judgmental silence grew, filling up the cabin like a giant balloon. Lucy sat there, staring at her page, taking nothing in, and ruminating in the quiet. The pressure of it intensified until she shuddered like someone had walked over her grave.

Vincent was on his feet in an instant. She looked up at him, but he wasn't watching. His eyes were on the door.

"What?" she hissed.

He didn't answer. The door rattled and was hauled open from the outside. It rolled along its hinges so hard it bounced. Tony and Gio stood in the doorway. They both looked serious.

"I felt it," Vincent stated to Tony before he could say anything. Tony nodded.

Lucy wanted to ask what, but now that they mentioned it she could feel it too. Something cold. Colder than the normal chill of winter. It wasn't just the silence oppressing the air. She was about to ask what it was when the light went out. Her question turned into a squeak. The train jarred sharply, bumping and rattling. Then came the scream.

6

A scream tore sharply into the night. It was cut short by the sound of shattering glass. An uncomfortable silence followed. Vincent was standing in the doorway of the cabin with Tony and Giovanni. Lucy was curled up on the bed. The door next to them banged open. Fred appeared in the half-darkness with Owens at her shoulder. Every light in the carriage appeared to have gone out. The faint glow of the outside world left them all little more than silhouettes.

"What was that…?" Fred whispered.

"Something's here," Tony muttered back. "Something cold and dark. Something dead."

Vincent slowly drew his pistol. He might not have Tony's gift for defining the Darkness, but he still knew it when he felt it. So the kid said it was something dead. That would help narrow it down. With one arm he ushered the boys into the cabin with Lucy. Then he started quietly up the hallway towards the sound of the scream. Each step was carefully placed, silent under the bang and rattle of the train. They were going fast. Too fast. The train jostled. Vincent barely kept his feet as he stalked down the carriage. He picked up the pace.

The acceleration was too sharp to be normal.

Something had happened to the engine. As he raced down the hallway, something cold brushed down his spine. He whirled. A flicker of movement caught his eye in the window. Fred was following behind him, but nothing else moved. The scenery whooshed by too fast to see anything, and it was pitch black.

"Vincent!" Fred started, pointing.

He spun back. A pale glint disappeared into the cabin beside them. Vincent hauled on the door. It was locked. Fred lifted a hand, sparking red. The lock flashed scarlet. Vincent ripped the door open. A cry sounded, but Vincent couldn't see anyone in the dark. Fred lifted a red light and illuminated two startled women. Nothing supernatural. Something dead that could pass through walls.

Vincent hated ghosts. How the hell had one gotten on a train?!

"Where is it?" Fred demanded. The women stared at them in horror. Fred rolled her eyes and pulled a face as she tried to work out how to ask. "*Où est-il allé?*" she tried.

One of the women pointed at the wall across the room, in the direction they'd been going. Vincent left them and hauled open the next door down. A sharp cold breeze hit him. This was the window that had smashed. Fred's light creeping up behind him glinted off shattered glass strewn across the floor. It looked like glimmering drops of blood in the red light. The effect was amplified by the dead body sprawled on the ground. The man stared blankly at the ceiling, throat slit, eyes empty.

Vincent kept his weapon out as he stepped into the room and crouched to check over the body. He patted down the pockets for clues. Something hit him. The force was like a cannon ball. He was smashed off his toes. Pain exploded through his body as he crashed into the metal bunk frame. Everything was dark. Spots flared in his vision, tainted by a faint red glow. Vincent raised his pistol and fired. He had no idea if he hit anything. He shook his head to clear it.

Fred screamed. Glass cracked. Vincent lunged upright. He staggered and tripped, but he forced himself up. Red light marked the doorway. He threw himself at it. Fred was pressed against the hallway window. She had hit the glass hard enough to crack it. The spiderweb pattern spread from behind her shoulder. Red lightning crackled from her hands as she held the creature back. A wraith. It was tattered and ghostly, like the memory of a decomposing killer. It was solid enough to hold a short blade in its hand, and it was trying to force it to Fred's throat. Her magic held it at bay, just. The two of them struggled, grimacing, trying to force the other back.

Vincent couldn't shoot it from this angle. If his bullet went through the wraith it could wound Fred. Or worse. He swapped weapons. With a steely rasp, he drew his sword. The monster heard it. It released Fred, letting her magic blast it back. Red lightning exploded down the hallway, rattling the windows. The wraith was forced down the passage. It vanished through a wall.

"You okay?" Vincent panted, grabbing Fred's

shoulder.

She nodded. The train screeched and wobbled. He stayed holding onto her, but he wasn't sure if he was comforting her or holding himself upright.

"We shouldn't be going this fast," she warned.

"No. Something's wrong," Vincent agreed. "We have to get to the engine."

She nodded again and they continued up the passage. They needed to hurry, but every step was cautious. That thing could come out of anywhere, vanishing and reappearing. They couldn't even see or hear properly in the dark with the sound of the rocketing train.

Vincent reached the door of the carriage, bumping roughly into it. He grabbed the wheel and twisted, forcing it open. The icy wind beat him mercilessly. His eyes watered from the cold and the force. Even with gloves, the metal was bitingly cold. He planted his foot firmly on the link between the carriages, trying to lock the heel of his boot against it. If he was thrown at this speed he wouldn't survive. Fred helped hold him steady as he opened the door to the next carriage. The two of them tumbled through. The wind howled behind them, but it was a blessing to be out of it.

Until the wraith struck. Vincent shoved Fred forward, raising his sword behind them to block the blow. The wraith's blade struck his own with a ghostly clang. It screamed at him with a chilling rattle. Goddamn things were usually incorporeal, and they still always tried to stab people in the back. He shoved with his sword, forcing the wraith through the door. It hovered over the carriage links, ready to leap back and attack.

Fred cried out. Red lightning flashed down the hallway. A second wraith had risen up through the floor. Fred blasted it with magic, but they were pushing through, blocking both ends. She raised her hands as she stood back-to-back with Vincent, shielding them with red light.

"Two of them..." she muttered through clenched teeth.

"Means they've been summoned," Vincent replied. "Two or more means they didn't occur naturally."

"There's no such thing as a 'naturally occurring' wraith, Sir!" Fred retorted. "Dark magic is always involved somewhere."

He gave the statement a small frown and a nod. It was not wrong. It also wasn't helpful. They needed a way out of this before those things worked out how to get past Fred's barrier.

"Any ideas?" he queried.

"One," she muttered as the wraiths closed in. "You remember Vermont?"

"I do..." Vincent recalled, slowly drawing his pistol again. He tensed, waiting. It had been a while since the two of them had gone it alone like this, but some things still came naturally. She pushed. He fired.

Fred ripped her barrier in half. She forced both sides in either direction, charging down the corridor. She slid down, shoving the barrier before her up like a shield. The wraith shot up to the ceiling, pinned high, but easily able to glide over. Vincent shot it twice straight through the head. He'd aimed exactly where he knew it would have to go. Holy bullets ruptured golden light through the ghost as it tried to slash Fred's shield, causing explosions of magic where they struck. It writhed and screeched once as it dissolved.

They bolted. The other wraith had been forced back out the door by the second half of the shield, but there was no telling where it would appear again. Vincent and Fred raced down the carriage. They sprinted for the door. The engine wasn't far now. If they could just—

The wraith rose up through the floor. Vincent cursed and raised his sword. They were going too fast. His feet pounded along the hallway, unable to slow. The wraith went for them. Vincent's sword hit the wraith's blade with force. The clang echoed down the hallway. Vincent twisted as he hit it, letting himself fall sideways so as not to collide with the blades. He brushed past the ghost. Everywhere they touched felt suddenly cold and sickly. He shuddered. His sword grated against the wraith's, grinding the steel unpleasantly. Neither gave an inch. They shoved, the force driving them apart.

A red barrier sprung up around the wraith. It slashed at it. The blade glanced off the magic. The wraith became translucent as it attempted to pass through its containment. That didn't work. It scrabbled desperately at the walls, confused by anything that could imprison it.

"Vincent!" Fred grated, shuddering from the effort it took to bind the creature. "Shoot it!"

Vincent aimed his gun at the barrier. He'd seen her do this before. One-way barriers. He shot into the containment. Two bullets, just like before. They passed inside the barrier, then ricocheted madly off the walls. The wraith stayed transparent. It settled, waiting, only becoming corporeal again when the bullets lost momentum and hit the floor. It snarled at them. Vincent reloaded his pistol, straining his brain for a new idea.

"Get the door!" Fred grunted.

He understood. He ran the last few steps to the end of the carriage and ripped the door open. Icy wind blasted down the corridor. It tore the breath from his lungs. It was so cold. So sharp. He rushed back and put an arm around Fred, guiding her to the door while she held the spell. He could feel her panting from the effort. He kept his sword raised towards the barrier with his other hand. If that thing got out he wanted it to think twice before charging them.

They were nearly at the engine. The only thing between them and the head of the train was the coal car. A ladder ran up the side of it. It would be easy enough to climb, but Fred couldn't do it while she held the spell. Vincent got her to the doorway before she let go. As soon as the barrier vanished, so did the wraith. Fred clambered up the ladder. Vincent followed. It struck.

He lashed out. Their blades clanged in the air. It had tried to stab him in the back again. At least they were predictable. He hung onto the ladder with one hand, swinging back to slice at the ghost. It left him, swooping up to the top. He heard Fred yell. Vincent launched himself up the ladder. He scrambled up on top of the coal pile. Fred was curled up, encased in her own barrier. He opened his mouth to yell at her to blast it, but realized why she hadn't. If her magic went wrong up here it could set the whole cart alight.

The wraith could sense her weakness too. That's why it was targeting her. Rookie error. Vincent aimed his pistol carefully. He waited until it was corporeal, beating against Fred's shield. He shot it straight through the temple. Ghost brains erupted from it in a spray of golden light. One more bullet through the chest for good measure to help it dissolve. Vincent stumbled to Fred and helped her up.

An ethereal cry went up from deep within the train. They both turned back.

"What the—" he started.

"Don't wanna know!" Fred replied.

That was a problem for after they slowed the train. They clambered faster over the coal and down the other side. Even before they opened the door the heat radiating from the engine was stronger than a Mediterranean summer. Vincent smashed the door open, letting the hot air crash over them. It was a blessing after the cold. The furnace was roaring, and the engineer lay covered in blood on the floor. Fred jumped in first, her hands already glowing with red light, as she began to pull the heat from the engine and kill the fire.

Vincent went straight to the fallen engineer. He was alive. Stabbed in the back, and it didn't look good, but he wasn't dead yet.

"Sir!" Vincent called to him, trying to gauge his alertness. "Sir, how—" He abandoned English. His French wasn't good, but this was probably the one thing he'd always remember how to say. "*Monsieur, ça va?*"

The man groaned weakly.

"Okay," Vincent muttered to himself, turning the man back over and inspecting the wound again. Not as bad as the trenches. Nothing could be. Even if he was back to dealing with bloody and wounded Europeans. He ripped up the man's shirt, scrunching some of it into padding and applying pressure. He could feel the train slowing under his knees as Fred's magic worked. The engineer wasn't going to be doing anything for a while, provided Vincent could keep him alive. That meant it was Fred's job to get them to the station safely. Fortunately, there was no one he trusted more.

* * *

It was a long trip to Koblenz. Owens and Giovanni came to find Fred and Vincent after the fight. It turned out more wraiths had come after them, but Tony had done his thing, glowing like a star, and blasted them all to dust. He spent the rest of the trip unconscious with Lucy watching over him. Owens had helped Vincent patch up the engineer, and Gio had shoveled coal and helped Fred get the train to Cologne. They had been in rough shape by the time they got there, and swapping trains to Koblenz had been done out of necessity, even if none of them knew where they found the energy.

Vincent and Owens took turns staying awake on that trip. They were both expecting another attack, and the rising stress of its absence almost felt worse. When they reached the station they were all still exhausted. Luckily, Vincent had made plans.

A man in a thick knobby woolen coat and matching hat was waiting for them. Vincent wasn't sure how comfortable he felt about the distinctive attire, but figured that people who had never seen each other before, meeting in a train station, needed something to distinguish each other by. He shuffled over as the man came to meet them.

"*Doktor* Temple?" the man checked.

Vincent nodded. "Oskar?"

"*Ja, guten Tag, mein Herr,*" he replied. "*Brauchen Sie Hilfe?*" He indicated their bags.

"*Nein danke,*" Owens answered, stepping up, shaking the man's hand, and making introductions in German. "*Sprechen Sie Englisch?*"

"*Ja,* a bit," Oskar gave them a crooked smile. "Vorking vith Hunters, you got to learn somezing from everyvere." He waved them on. "*Komm.* I take you vere you staying."

He led them from the station. Vincent was so tired he could hardly walk, but his mind was fizzing with tension. His eyes darted everywhere, looking for any sign of Rogue or White or their magic. He was certain they were responsible for what had happened on the train. When Lucy had been concerned about being followed in the Calais Station, she'd had a point. They had all been expecting something. Vincent had been expecting the witch to act when she disembarked in France and discovered no one waiting to attack her. At that point she would have known Vincent was coming after her himself instead of sending his people.

When he thought about the events that led them here

he couldn't help but wonder if the entire affair had been designed to force him to track her here. She had organized the bombing of the car, which meant she probably thought Lucy and Tony were dead – reason enough for Vincent to come after her himself. She would have no idea about Owens or Giovanni. She probably knew about Fred, so she was probably only expecting one old Hunter and his mage. The notion comforted Vincent. He had been worried ever since he'd gotten off the ship.

Some kind of trap had been an inevitability. Just one attack on one train made him worry that he'd missed something. He was used to more things trying to kill him. Still, half a dozen wraiths on a train was a decent effort for someone targeting a single Hunter and mage.

A faint sliver of stress slipped from his shoulders as they left the station and Oskar took them to a horse-drawn carriage across the street. It was snowing. It wasn't heavy, but the sky was dark grey and small flakes were drifting lazily down to the slush on the road. They stashed their bags and clambered inside. So much of Vincent's body wanted to warn him that everything could be a trap, but at this point he was almost too exhausted to care.

Once they were settled, Oskar set off. Vincent lounged in his seat and watched the scenery go by in a haze of grey. The city was grey. The countryside was grey too. He wasn't even sure he'd noticed where one stopped and the other began. The snow became thicker and the sky darker as they travelled. It felt like night by the time they pulled up. Vincent was dozing, watching the flecks of white drift by the dark window. He'd barely noticed they'd stopped, until the door opened and Oskar was standing there with a lantern.

"Ve here," he announced.

They climbed from the carriage and grabbed their things. Once he was outside Vincent could see the farmhouse. There was smoke rising from the chimney and light in the windows. They were parked right outside the front door. Oskar led them inside and gave them the key. It was a simple place, but spacious. The front door led to a large main room that seemed to serve as some kind of combined kitchen and living space with a large roaring fire, and a small hallway running off it that led to sleeping quarters. Quaint, was the term that sprang to mind.

"I had ze ozers come and light ze fires and make ze beds for you," Oskar indicated. "Zere is food in ze cupboards, *ja*, and some in ze icebox out back. You help yourself to anyzing you need. Ve are house just down ze lane if you need us."

"*Ich danke Ihnen sehr. Das ist so lieb von Ihnen,*" Owens thanked him sincerely in German.

"*Sehr gern geschehen,*" Oskar replied, shaking his hand as he headed back out. He paused at the door and looked back that them seriously. "You came at good time. Ve are glad you here. Zings... not good. Zere have been tremors – shakes – and strange happenings. It good to have Hunters here again."

"We'll sort it," Vincent promised.

"*Ja, danke,*" Oskar thanked them again. He opened the door and as he went out someone else came in. A small furry tabby someone padded into the room. Oskar stuck his head back through. "Also, zis is Tobias. Don't mind him. He keep ze rats out. Can smell demons. Very good boy. You like cats, *ja*?"

Fred made a sound, small and involuntary. Oskar flashed them a smile and disappeared into the night. As soon as the door was shut, Fred's bags were on the floor and she was crouched down letting the cat sniff her fingers. He seemed to approve. She scooped him up, burying her face in his snow-flecked fluffy side. Tobias purred.

"Heh," Owens smiled at them. "Not only do they give the witch a cat, they name it after her son."

Fred was making cooing noises as she snuggled the cat. Tobias approved of the chin scritches.

"The Germans are known for being a generous people," Vincent replied wryly.

"Since when?" Gio scoffed.

"Try all the people you've met since we arrived," Owens warned his apprentice curtly. "The people at the station in Cologne were extremely understanding of the situation when we showed up with a broken train and wounded engineer. They didn't keep us for further questioning, they took over the situation, and helped us get our next train. Here, Oskar and his people have been more than generous."

"Don't get ya knickers in a twist, boss," Gio grinned at him, lighting a cigarette. "We all know ya got a soft spot for Krauts."

Owens did not look impressed. He pushed his glasses up his nose, glaring at Gio. Lucy drew back innocently towards the fire, dragging Tony with her so they were out of the way.

"Anyone who calls themselves a Hunter must be above prejudice," Owens enunciated like chalk striking a board. The Professor was in, and his tone only became sharper. "They must be above race and sex and creed. They must be above nationalism and religion. It's the only way the system can operate. Everyone deserves to be saved. Once we begin to judge who is worthy of our help, once we decide to let some parts of the world fall while preserving others, the Darkness wins. It grows wherever you let it. You let it grow somewhere... you might not have the power to cut it back when it begins to encroach. Everyone counts. Everywhere is important."

Silence hung in the air, except for the crackling of the fire and the purring of Tobias. And Vincent, who was rummaging in the cupboards. He pulled out a loaf of bread and some leftover cooked sausages. Looking quite pleased with himself, he ravenously bit the end off a sausage. Then noticed everyone was looking at him.

"You kids listening to him?" he asked, pointing the sausage at Owens. "Man knows what he's talking about."

"Thank you, Sir," Owens replied.

"You're very good at articulating these things, Owens," Vincent complimented him. "I know as a teacher myself I spend more time on the practical side of things and not enough on the theoretical. Now, you lot come help me eat this food, and then I'm going to bed. If the world ends, someone come get me."

7

The world didn't end that night, although the entire group was prepared to admit that was no thanks to them. While the trip halfway around the world on a ship hadn't been so bad, the twenty-four hours from Calais to Koblenz had been rough. Most of them managed to sleep it off. The only one who still looked worse for wear at the breakfast table was Tony. He was pale and strained, even more so than usual.

"You look like shit, *amico*," Gio grinned at him. "Tell me she let you sleep last night."

Tony gave him sour look.

"He slept, but it was restless," Lucy replied, rubbing Tony's arm comfortingly. "He was muttering in his sleep half the night."

"Muttering anything useful?" Owens asked over his most recent newspaper. It had yesterday's date and it was in German. At least he was trying to keep up.

"Does anyone ever mutter useful things?" Lucy asked.

Owens shrugged and folded away his paper. "Young Antony is more in tune with the workings of the universe than most of us," he reminded. "Oskar warned us that strange happenings are afoot here. It's possible he can feel them. The place Rogue is supposed to be staying isn't far from here. Her magic could be affecting him."

"It's not," Tony muttered, shaking his head. "I can't even feel her."

"Well, you should come out with us later when we go to poke around and see if you can sense anything closer," Owens encouraged. "The new German Chancellor has an unsavory interest in all things occult, and rumor has it he has hired Rogue for one of his projects and lent her a castle for her stay."

"What does that mean?" Lucy asked.

"Means there's a big fortress of Nazis up on the hill working with a blood witch," Vincent growled. "And I don't have enough dynamite on hand to fix the problem."

"So, we're doing it the old-fashioned way," Fred smiled, scratching Tobias behind the ears as he rested on her lap. No one had told her she couldn't have the cat at the table. No one dared.

Outside, the morning was grey, but the snow had stopped. It lay in thick white blankets everywhere, yet there was an atmosphere of unease the snow couldn't quieten. Something was wrong. They all knew the feeling. Except it was broader here. There wasn't that specific pull of Darkness. That meant they were going to need to employ some extensive reconnaissance.

After breakfast they split up. There was a black car in the garage that Vincent insisted Owens take, along with Gio and Fred. It made sense for his team to be the one that went further afield, as he could effectively communicate with the locals. Vincent took the kids and went down the lane to borrow horses from Oskar. Just because they'd have less luck asking around didn't mean they got to sit on their asses and do nothing.

Tony had never been riding before, and it showed, but Lucy stuck by him and he seemed to perk up a bit out in the fresh air. Vincent related. Everything was cold, but it was invigorating. The great black stallion he rode was no Brendan, but it almost felt like being home again. Poor Brendan was getting on in years now. He didn't take to adventures like he used to. Vincent wasn't the only one thinking about him. Lucy had already affectionately dubbed her mare 'Little Grey'.

They took the path down by the river and followed the bank. The valley of the safehouse seemed a peaceful one. Even with the strange tension hanging over the region, the landscape was too picturesque to be foreboding. Patches of ice had formed over the river, they could see where the snow had settled on it. Vincent didn't feel like testing the sturdiness atop a roughly fifty stone horse. Besides, they could see just fine from here.

They rode around a bend in the river, with the hills around them twisting in and out like ribbons of white. There, on the clifftop in the distance, stood the castle. There were a few around, and no doubt they had passed more on their drive to the safehouse yesterday. This one was the one they had been warned about. That was where Rogue was hiding out, doing God only knew what for the Nazis and their new Chancellor. Vincent didn't read as many newspapers as Owens, but he'd read enough for the entire political situation to make him nervous.

"That place is a fortress," Tony commented, eyeing it like an eagle.

"Hence why we haven't tried to storm it ourselves," Vincent replied.

"Yet," Lucy grinned at them.

"Yet," Vincent grinned back at her.

Tony rolled his eyes.

"We need to know what we're up against," Vincent insisted. "If our current intel is correct, they've got half an army up there, but no one knows what they're doing. It's heavily guarded, heavily fortified, well-resourced. Most cults I've come across don't have strong military minds behind them."

"I'm still not getting anything," Tony muttered, watching the castle. "Unless… just a big void of static, like a bunch of radios that ain't finding a channel. Wait–" He stopped suddenly, pulling up and turning his head.

Everyone paused. They all waited. Silence. Then Tony winced and clutched his head. The ground began to shake. The horses spooked.

"Tony!" Lucy stepped Little Grey closer and grabbed Tony's reins to keep his mount from startling. It wasn't a big earthquake, but it was noticeable. Loud snaps filled the air like gunshots as the ice on the river cracked. The whole world shivered. Then it stopped. Tense silence filled the air again.

"Ooooh, what the hell was that?" Tony groaned, rubbing his temples.

"I would say an earthquake," Vincent commented.

"But given your reaction it's more likely something is actively trying to destabilize the region."

"Rogue's magic couldn't do that though, could it?" Lucy looked at him nervously.

"I wouldn't have thought so. Not on its own…" Vincent muttered. He hoped, and then realized that he was hoping for something worse than a blood witch. Maybe it was better not to hope.

More cracks came from the river beside them. The sounds were startling, but Tony had control of his mount again – insomuch as he ever had. The horses still seemed spooked. Vincent didn't begrudge them that. Animals were wise. They had instincts for things like this. Still, these three were well-trained not to bolt. Vincent turned his stallion back down the path. He was about to tell the others they should continue on when something happened to the water.

He knew something was wrong before he could work out what it was. The river wasn't moving right. It wasn't flowing beneath the cracked ice. It was building, ballooning.

"MOVE!" Vincent roared, kicking his heels down and taking off down the path. The kids gave chase. So did the water. It exploded up from under the ice, a giant hand of freezing river snatching for them. Vincent veered off the path, racing up through the twisted saplings and bramble. The banks of foliage weren't high. Vincent and his horse busted out the other side, small twigs and ice flying everywhere. The kids were just behind him. Tony was holding on for dear life, hunched over his saddle. Vincent paused and looked back. The river was still swelling.

"I don't wanna alarm anyone," Tony panted. "But I don't got enough fire magic in me to take out a whole river."

"What was that?" Lucy asked.

"I don't know yet," Vincent admitted.

"Old legends? Old gods?" Tony offered. "Maybe it's always been like that?"

"The Rhine is not infamous for eating people," Vincent replied. "And Oskar would have warned us if anyone had encountered this before, or if drowning numbers had risen."

"That's a cheery thought," Lucy muttered. She was slowly and carefully backing Little Grey away from the water. The field behind them stood open and inviting, but running away from this would put others in danger. That wasn't the way of a Hunter. "So how do we fight a river?" she inquired. "Anyone ask Achilles?"

"I would," Vincent quipped, watching the water rise, "but I think I left his phone number back home."

"Drat," Lucy commented softly.

They had all been watching the river, slowly backing their horses away, tense and waiting. It attacked. All three of them whirled their mounts and raced back. Fingers of water clawed up the bank. Plants were crushed. Snow melted. Dark stains bled into the landscape everywhere it touched. Vincent drew his sword and turned on it. He slashed through a whip of water coming at him. His sword passed straight through it. It crashed against his chest like a wave, nearly knocking him from his horse. The icy water stung as it drenched him. He felt his lungs tighten with the cold.

Lucy fired at the rising mass of water. The rifle hit true, even while she rode, but the bullets did nothing. Their weapons were enchanted to fight the supernatural, but the magic didn't seem to be enough to counter whatever this was.

Tony pulled up to focus his magic. He did it just like Fred taught him. He conjured lightning. The red lightning Fred always used. His couldn't help but be flecked with gold, but it worked just the same. He fired it at the heaving mass of water. It flinched. Finally, something worked. If only for a second. The water monster recoiled when Tony struck it, but the lightning dispersed through the river.

It shivered. Multiple arms began to burst up from the surface. They clawed up the bank like the hands of drowned lost souls. The limbs strained. The mass pulled, dragging itself from the river. It was all water. Water and darkness. Something about it was haunted. Lost. It reached for them again.

Tony pulled up in front of Lucy. He raised his hands and summoned fire. It wasn't enough to cause damage, just enough to hold it back. What Vincent wouldn't have given for a bottle of tonic to light and throw right then. Not that there was any guarantee that would work. His flask wouldn't explode like a glass vial would, but it gave him an idea. He quickly pulled it out and poured a trickle of spirits down his blade. He swapped the flask for a lighter, and set the blade on fire.

With a grunt of force, Vincent drove his horse

towards the creature, flaming sword aloft. It shied away from his attack, but only barely. Vincent swung mercilessly at it. The section he attacked seemed to sink back into itself, trying to avoid the fire. Then it tired of its fear. A hand of water smashed into him like a wave. The black horse reared, and Vincent barely held on. His sword was doused and his body soaked. He could feel his clothes starting to freeze to his skin.

The creature used the same attack on the kids. Vincent blinked freezing water from his eyes. He watched in horror as the hand slashed at Lucy and Tony. Tony's fire went out. Lucy whirled Little Grey, dodging away from the attack. Tony wasn't so lucky. His horse reared and he was thrown. He barely hit the ground before the water snatched him. Icy dark water closed around him like the jaws of death and dragged him back to the river. Lucy galloped for him.

"TONY!" she screamed, giving chase.

Vincent rode up beside her, cutting her off.

"Get out of the way!" she yelled. She tried to barge past him, but he held fast. He caught her as she tried to push through, and nearly pulled her off her horse.

"How would it help?" Vincent demanded. "How will riding into the water help?!"

"TONY!" she screamed again, loud enough to make him wince. She struggled, but he held her tightly. She didn't have access to reason. It was a miracle he did. He was vaguely aware that the only reason he could hold her back from this was because he wasn't thinking about what he was doing. They were both moving on instinct. He couldn't lose her too.

But he didn't know how to get Tony back. The boy had been dragged into the river, and that long under water that cold could be fatal. His own health was suffering just from getting wet in these temperatures. Right now his desperation to protect the girl in his arms was the only thing keeping him going.

Then the river rose again. Vincent watched it swell up, horror blossoming in his gut. They wouldn't survive another round, and there was no way he could make her flee the monster that had just eaten her husband.

The darkness inside it had grown. The icy water was blue and black, flecked with white like a deadly midnight sky. Too many arms writhed from its body. It twisted and warped before them, rising up like a tower of water. The river drew low as the water became vertical. At this size they couldn't even outrun it. Lucy had stopped struggling as she watched it rise above them.

Then it ripped in half. The horses startled again as they were all sprayed with water. Lucy cried out. They all flinched back. Vincent wiped his eyes a second time and looked up. He froze. The darkness and the water were separating. Water sprayed every direction, dousing the banks, melting all the snow. Black earth spread from the river, seemingly adding to the visual size of the creature. Vincent wasn't sure if he could still call it a creature, but it looked like one.

Tony was at its center. His eyes were completely black, and the darkness had begun to stain his veins. He didn't move, but he hung in the air with darkness pouring from his body. It ripped and shredded and tore the river spirit, devouring the other entity. Tony's darkness grew as it consumed the body of the thing that had tried to drown him. It made quick work of what had been a deadly enemy. Then it twisted, shifting, ravenous, on the landscape.

"Back!" Vincent ordered, guiding Lucy away and turning his mount. She was edging back on her own. Neither could tear their eyes from Tony. He shivered and spasmed in the air, his head tipping back to look at the sky. Shadowy black arms reached out from the darkness, groping at the land. The earth was already dead with winter, but they could see what little life remained being sucked from the ground everywhere the darkness touched. Spindly trees were drained white into cracking bones; snow steamed and hissed where the black fingers touched it.

Vincent slowly drew his pistol and aimed it.

"DON'T!" Lucy bellowed at him, smacking his gun down.

Tony jerked at the sound. Everything about him swiveled towards her. The darkness began to fold in on itself at the sound of her voice. It rushed back inside him like a vacuum. He fell. With a soft thump he landed face first in a drift of snow. He wasn't moving.

Lucy dismounted instantly and ran to him. She fell to her knees at his side and pulled him into her arms.

"Tony?" she whispered, touching his face. "Tony? Baby? Are you okay?"

Vincent dismounted and followed her over, leading the horses by the reins. The animals seemed to understand something had happened, but they also seemed to understand it was over. They had no hesitations about approaching. Vincent found it a comfort, but he didn't holster his gun.

Tony was frighteningly pale, yet his veins no longer looked black. He still wasn't moving. The first breath he took was deep and shuddering. Lucy looked like she was about to cry with relief.

"Tony!" she gasped, clutching him to her. He raised one hand weakly as though to hold her, but the strength wasn't there. He patted the front of her coat as she held him, their breath steaming in the cold air.

Vincent stood over both of them, looking down on the mess. Finally, he holstered his weapon.

"What the hell was that?" he demanded.

Tony half turned as though to answer, but no words followed. He didn't meet Vincent's eye. Part of him looked like he needed to curl into Lucy, and there wasn't anything powerful enough to resist that need. He was still panting for breath and the only answer he could muster was a weak shake of his head. Vincent watched. The kid didn't seem to be dangerous anymore, but that didn't make Vincent feel any better.

"Come on," he ordered them up. "We have to get back to the farmhouse before we freeze to death."

* * *

They returned the horses to Oskar before hurrying home to bathe and change. The fire was still going Vincent thawed himself out with relative ease after making sure the kids were going to be alright. Lucy had taken it upon herself to care for Tony. He looked awful. He looked worse now than he had when he'd woken that morning. There were shadows under his eyes and a grey tinge to his skin that made him look half dead. All things considered, Vincent was concerned that the boy might be.

The kids were in the main room when Vincent came back out. Despite being inside with the fire, he'd layered up warm, and was pulling on a woolen sweater when he walked though. His head poked out through the hole, and he glimpsed the collection of items Tony was stacking on the table.

"Would you like a tea, Vincent?" Lucy called from the kitchen. "I'm boiling some water."

He could hear her filling a kettle and setting it over the fire, but his eyes were on Tony and his ingredients. A hiss came from under the table.

"Get out of it, cat!" Tony muttered, trying to shook it away.

Tobias growled a deep and low rumble of displeasure. Vincent did not like the warning in the little feline's voice, and he knew Fred would disapprove too.

"What are you doing?" he growled.

Lucy turned around. "Tony! I told you to leave it for now! You just used all that magic!"

"I don't feel tired," he told them. "I can do this."

As far as Vincent was concerned that was most of the problem. Tony didn't even look tired. He looked half dead, but there was a spark in his dark eyes. There were also traces of black around the tips of his fingers, like he'd been playing with charcoal. No wonder the cat was hissing.

"You told me once that the power was yours…" Vincent reminded slowly. "This… whatever you're doing now… this isn't yours."

"No," Tony admitted. "This is borrowed. I might as well use it while I've got it."

"You are not using any magic ever again until Fred tells you that you can," Vincent ordered. "I don't know what's going on with you, boy, but what I just saw you do isn't the kind of magic our side uses. That's the kind of Darkness we take down."

"And what would you have done if I wasn't there?" Tony retorted, glaring up at him. "If I'd gone with Gio, would you still be around? Would you have gone out there and gotten my wife drowned? Some bullets and a sword against a river? That's how you fight the Darkness?"

"Tony–" Lucy tried to placate him.

"You asked for my help with this, Luce," he reminded, turning to her and indicating the alchemy on the table. "You need a way to fight back when I'm not there. I've been trying… for over a year now we've been trying… and I just haven't been able to get it. But I can now. I know I can. I can use whatever this is to just push it that little bit further…"

"Raise your hand, kid, and I'm putting a bullet through it," Vincent warned.

"Vincent!" Lucy snapped.

"This isn't a maybe, children," he told them firmly.

"Don't test me."

They both paused. Vincent stared Tony down, forcing the boy to concede. As soon as Tony dropped his gaze, Vincent let himself settle. He turned to Lucy.

"Tea would be real nice, sweetheart. Thank you," he told her. Then he looked back over his shoulder at Tony. "When Fred comes home she can have a look at you. She gets the final say on what you're allowed to do, but I just watched you pull something truly evil from I don't know where and I don't know how. That means you're on time out for a while."

They didn't fight him about it again. Lucy cleaned up the ingredients for the spell and convinced Tony to take a nap. Tobias hissed him from the room, but settled when he left. Lucy frowned at the cat. She tried to sooth him with scritches, which he appreciated, but he clearly didn't like her husband. Vincent sat with her while they had tea. He watched the nervous way she fidgeted with her mug and the way her eyes darted around.

"You doing okay?" he asked.

She gave him the 'what do you think' look. He gave her the 'do you want to talk about it' nod. She sighed. Her eyes rolled heavenwards, but it was a despairing action rather than a sarcastic one, like she didn't know where to begin.

"I don't know how to tell him about the curse," she muttered. "You asked on the train, and I told you to butt out of it. I think... I think part of me always thought that once we were married I'd get Fred to lift it and he'd never have to know... but now..." she trailed off.

He didn't fill the silence. As far as he was concerned

she hadn't finished, so he waited for her to pick up again.

"Now I just don't know how to tell him," she sighed. "Fred told me it was the simplest curse. All witches know how to cast spells to make things barren – people, cattle, land. It's witchcraft 101, easily reversable, and the kind of curse that she said would unravel if anything happened to her. It wasn't permanent. She promised."

"Fred is a mage of her word," Vincent agreed.

"So I thought it wouldn't matter, and I could just tell him I'd taken precautions, and then lift the spell when we were married, and never get into the gritty details..."

"Somewhat dishonest, but fair," Vincent nodded. "It is more your business than his, and marriages survive on hidden truths like that, but he does have a right to know. He is a mage himself, and he's sharing his bed with a curse."

"Do you think the curse is affecting him?" Lucy panicked.

"I very much doubt it," Vincent replied. "Although, I know almost nothing about magic."

"Me neither," Lucy pouted. "I have no idea what I'm doing and I don't know how to talk about it."

"And you don't want Fred to remove the curse even though you're married now?" Vincent asked.

Lucy gave him a look. "A just over a week ago I nearly got blown up on my wedding day; we're investigating the ritual sacrifice of kids, which had led to us chasing a blood witch to a Nazi castle; and my husband nearly just turned into some kind of evil dark spirit/eldritch horror creature. Forgive me if I'm not ready to bring a child into the world just now."

"I would have put at the top of that list the fact that you are still a child yourself," Vincent offered.

"I'm not a child!" she protested.

"Lucy, you're not even twenty," he retorted. "You are most definitely still a child. You'll be a child for at least another ten to fifteen years."

She laughed at him. It seemed a strange time to be laughing, but it was such a dad thing to say. She enjoyed the way that he made the problem seem simple. The way he made it sound like a problem any girl her age would be having. It wasn't though, and the dread crept back up her spine.

"I'm scared, Vincent..." she muttered. "I'm scared the magic is corrupting him."

"The notion is concerning me too," he admitted.

"Tony always says it's his magic," Lucy said. "Whenever I worry about it he explains that even if none of us understand it, he does. It's his magic, he draws it forth, and he understands how it works, even if he doesn't have the vocabulary to explain it to us. I believe him. The things he does... the things he's saved us from..."

"Agreed," Vincent conceded. "However, what he did today was not normal magic. He hasn't been normal since we got to Germany. I didn't see what he did on the train, but it sounded normal, and he reacted like he always does. But he was off this morning, and then we took him out and he pulled... that stunt. I don't even know what to call it. He channeled more magic than I've ever seen, none of it good, swallowed the Darkness back, and then had energy spare when we got home. I've been concerned about his unique brand of magic for years, but today took the cake."

"He's right though," Lucy muttered. "What would we have done without him?"

Vincent sighed and rubbed the short beard growing back across his chin. That was his usual response when he didn't have an answer. He wanted to say they would have found a way, because they always did, but throwing out something like that wouldn't get him far with his protégée right now and he knew it.

"What if there is no right answer?" Lucy whispered fearfully. "What if the magic is destroying him, using him as a gateway, but we'd all die without it? What if there is no lesser evil?"

"Then it would be a perfect example of life," Vincent sighed with the practiced pessimism of one who had seen decades of measured evils. He paused at the heartbreak in her eyes and sighed again, more deeply than before. "Don't borrow trouble, kid. Let Fred check him out before we start worrying about exorcisms."

She nodded, but it didn't stop her from fretting for the next few hours. If Vincent was honest with himself he didn't know how to comfort her. He was as worried as she was, even if they showed it differently.

When the others finally returned, the Darkness seemed to have drained from Tony. His skin was no longer marked by it, and he was back to looking exhausted rather than possessed. He even had the sense to look ashamed as Vincent described to the others what had happened. He sat on the couch with his head bowed like a disobedient schoolboy.

"You did what?!" Gio demanded, cuffing him over the head and cussing him out in Italian.

"*Via*! We all woulda drowned if I hadn't!" Tony smacked him away. "That thing wasn't like anything I ever seen before. Nothing like the stuff Lucy talks about neither! Monsters and horrors are one thing, but this was something else. This was..." he trailed off.

They all stood around watching him like a wall of judgement. Gio and Fred loomed over him like he was their responsibility. Lucy, Vincent, and Owens watched on with concern. Tony rubbed his face angrily, like he couldn't find the words. Like he knew things he didn't know how to explain, and he knew too many of them now, and years of being unable to explain the building blocks of reality as he saw it was doing his head in.

"I can't describe it," he despaired again, shaking his head helplessly.

Lucy sat down beside him and rubbed his shoulder. He massaged his temples, screwing up his face as he thought.

"When the Darkness comes through, it comes through," he explained to the floor. "It don't belong here, it pulls in from somewhere else – from the deepest oceans and the coldest moons and the darkest stars. Souls of Others pull through and are given some kinda form – some body – some physical manifestation of themselves. We can slay those. We defeat them or banish them, and then the soul returns. Most of the time only the body is destroyed. The... thing... the entity goes back where it came from."

"Not a bad explanation," Vincent nodded approvingly at him. He had known this theory for some time. It was why multiple cults around the world could summon the same old gods time and time again. Their magic brought forth a manifestation. Tony even knew the word. Vincent felt a strong urge to praise Fred's teaching.

"That wasn't the way it happened earlier," Tony looked up at him. "Something got called though, somehow, somewhere, I didn't see it happen, but some Other pulled through without a body and used the water instead. You can't slay that. You can't banish it. At that point, it belonged here. Whatever is happening up on that hill, we're in real trouble. If they're bringing souls in and binding them while refusing to let them manifest… they're trying to make monsters that belong in our world. I don't know if that's what they intend, but if it is they nearly succeeded today."

"So what did you do to counter it?" Fred demanded. "That's all very alarming, Tony, but we're far more concerned by whatever stunt you pulled. Lord knows we got no problem with you going all shiny and blasting monsters to bits, but Vincent made your ordeal sound a lot scarier than a big haunted river."

"I just…" Tony started weakly. "I dunno… I just had to… so I did."

Vincent's eyes narrowed. It wasn't just the vague non-answer that the kid gave, it was the way Lucy looked at him, as though she could tell he was lying even though he'd barely said anything. He could feel the warning rebuttal rising up his throat, but Fred got there first, and she'd decided to be gentler about it.

"Okay," she told him with a slow nod, looking over both kids on the couch. "I'm going to have a poke around and see if anything came back with you, alright?"

Tony nodded, albeit reluctantly.

"Come through to the bedroom and lie down. I don't want you collapsing and hurting yourself," she instructed. "Lucy can come too."

"You're not leaving me out if you're poking around in his head," Gio added.

Fred nodded and motioned them all down the hallway. Lucy took the lead, dragging Tony with her. He didn't look thrilled by the prospect, but he didn't look like he was going to fight it either. Vincent stood back and watched them all go. It settled his nerves to see Fred handling the situation, not to mention that Tony himself looked much better than he had when he'd been floating twelve feet in the air with shadowy tentacles flowing out of his chest.

Beside him, Owens was checking his watch.

"You find anything to add to all this?" Vincent asked him.

"Maybe." Owens pushed his glasses up his nose. "Your information so far seems to have been correct. We were able to verify that an American philanthropist and her aide arrived at the castle a few days ago. She's holed up there with a small army by the sounds of things. They're working on a top-secret project for the government – extremely hush-hush – but possibly in league with a university, although I couldn't get a name out of anyone."

"Delightful," Vincent drawled. "How do we get in there, shut it down, and burn the witch?"

"Those questions are harder to answer," Owens admitted. "The place is a heavily guarded fortress. There is no way on God's Earth we're storming the place and I don't see us sneaking in anytime soon. We will need time to come up with a plan to infiltrate it. However, if we can't get to her, there's always the option of getting her to come to us."

Vincent raised an eyebrow. Owens grinned at him and tapped his watch.

"There's a trainyard about an hour's drive from here. Apparently, Lady Rogue and her entourage will be meeting some sellers there at 8pm tonight. I can't help but think that the polite thing to do would be to make sure we were there to greet her when she arrives."

Vincent grinned wolfishly at him. "Recon or assassination?"

"Start with the former, possibly evolve to the latter," Owens replied. "Again, I don't want to walk into something we can't walk out of." He glanced down the corridor after the others. "And I don't think we should take anyone else. I know it's remiss of me to suggest going after a mage without bringing a mage of our own, but–"

"You don't need to explain it," Vincent waved him down. "I agree. I don't want Tony going anywhere at the moment, and I want Fred to keep an eye on him."

Owens nodded. "So we lean towards

reconnaissance."

"Yeah," Vincent agreed. "I wouldn't mind knowing more about this 'top secret' project the Nazi government has decided it needs a witch for. But if we get the shot…"

"Oh yes," Owens nodded. If they got the shot, they would take it.

* * *

The night was dark as they drove through winding country roads. There wasn't much in the way of traffic, and the unfamiliar, lonely terrain was a ghostly landscape of black and white. The snow had stopped falling, and the drifts across the ground were thinning in patches. Owens sat in the passenger seat, digging through his satchel and triple-checking his supplies. Bottles kept clinking.

"You carry a lot of holy water with you," Vincent commented.

"It's just so useful," Owens replied. "Imagine if you'd taken some with you today."

"It was a river, Owens," Vincent sighed. "It would just have made it more wet."

"You don't know what it would have done to that thing, but I meant you could have thrown it on the young Mister Temple," Owens quipped.

Vincent gave the night a wry grin and shook his head slightly, keeping his eyes on the road. He was not getting used to the idea of the kids using his name, and he had no idea what pouring holy water on Tony would do. What if it did burn the boy? What would they do then? For now it was Fred's responsibility to deal with her apprentice, and anything else could be saved for emergencies.

They pulled up a safe distance from the railyard with plenty of time to spare. The snow was patchier out here than it had been back at the farmhouse. They made the most of it to scope out the area, doing their best not to leave any tracks. The last thing they wanted to do was spook Rogue and lose her before they got what they needed.

Owens heard the voices first, and raised a hand to alert Vincent. One of the warehouses at the yard was being used. A lantern was on inside, through an open doorway, and the discussion of two men drifted out. Vincent looked to Owens for translation, but the Professor's eyes widened and he motioned Vincent away. They crept out of the area and hid behind a stack of containers.

"That's them," Owens whispered. "They were talking about meeting an American woman. Those are her contacts."

"Let's get on top of these containers," Vincent suggested. "We'll have a better view of what's going on."

"And a better vantage point to take action from," Owens agreed.

They clambered as carefully and quietly as they could up the wooden crates, staying hunkered down in the dark and watching for any sign of their quarry. They heard her before they saw her. The long sleek Mercedes that pulled up several minutes later had a deep throaty growl in its engine. It pulled up alone. The car stopped outside the warehouse, its engine grumbling idly. The back doors on both sides opened. Vincent watched the people they were waiting for exit the car.

White stepped out first, coming out of the door facing them. Vincent recognized Rogue's strange aide. He was a tall man in a neat suit with a sharp face. Even in the black of night he was wearing his trademark dark glasses. He turned and helped Rogue out the same door. She looked healthier than the last time Vincent had seen her. She was walking on her own two legs for a start, and there was a rosy blush to her cheeks. On the other side of the car an umbrella opened out, even though it wasn't currently snowing, and another suit stepped out. Vincent didn't get a good look, but the man seemed similar in build and dress to White. All three of them were wrapped up tight in winter coats and gloves. If they were carrying weapons it wasn't obvious, but that meant nothing. He knew from experience how easy it was to hide weapons in winter clothing.

"If that engine doesn't shut off we won't hear a thing," Vincent muttered.

"Honestly, if it's just the witch, her driver, and two suits... we could probably take them," Owens hissed back.

"Hold," Vincent warned him. He wanted to know more first. Besides, Rogue was a powerful mage and there was something about White that was setting off warning bells in Vincent's head. He appreciated the initiative Owens was showing, but he knew there was something important they were missing.

For a moment they simply watched as the two men from the warehouse came out and spoke to Rogue and her cronies. The engine of the car made it impossible to hear the conversation. At a guess from their gestures Vincent figured they were talking about moving cargo. That made the most sense. His suspicions were solidified when Rogue started motioning and the two men from the warehouse began loading up a nearby truck with crates from inside.

It was now or never, but Vincent felt a strong urge to hold off. Every time he glanced at White his stomach flip-flopped. The man was fairly ordinary. All the right limbs in all the right places, and yet something about him was just fundamentally *wrong*. Vincent could feel it under his skin.

Rogue turned her orders to the men at her sides. They moved to the truck and opened a crate to check it. Vincent noted the way White popped the lid on the crate with his hands. He could see the nails pop up, no crowbar no nothing, as White levered it open. That confirmed that suspicion. The men inspected the contents. Vincent saw the gleam of metal, but couldn't make out any more detail.

When they turned around he finally got a look at the other man beneath the umbrella. It wasn't someone Vincent recognized, possibly the German academic Owens had hinted at earlier. He was well-kempt with perfectly combed dark hair and an angular face that seemed to be made up of severe edges. He glanced up. His piercing dark eyes stared Vincent directly in the face.

Vincent froze. There was no way the man hadn't seen him. The stranger had stared straight back through his eyes all the way to his soul. They were made. He was sure of it. But it must have been darker than he thought, because the man turned away with no sign of alarm. He went about his business as though he had seen nothing. He raised no alarm. Didn't point them out to anyone. If anything, he turned up his collar and tightened his hold on the umbrella as though staving off the weather.

Vincent turned to Owens. His guts didn't just flip, they vanished. Owens stared at him, his eyes wider and his face paler than Vincent had ever seen. He'd heard people talk about someone looking like they'd seen a ghost, he'd even used the phrase himself, but all previous instances paled in comparison to the expression on the Professor's face. Owens didn't just look like he'd seen a ghost, he looked like he'd turned into one.

Things began to click together in Vincent's head faster than light. Owens might look like he was grief-stricken but Vincent was the one rapidly charging through the five stages. He settled on anger and grabbed his partner by the collar, dragging him off the crates under what he hoped was the cover of the growling engine. A sound he was just realizing wouldn't do much to save them.

8

Vincent dragged Owens all the way back to the car.
Every second he expected to be attacked. He kept
waiting, tensing, expecting something to snatch him
and rip him apart. Nothing happened. There was no
sign they were followed. Owens stumbled along behind
him, completely devoid of his characteristic grace. His
feet scuffed the dirt and snow as Vincent hauled him
away. The man looked like he was in shock. Vincent
sure as hell wanted to give him one. He dumped Owens
in the passenger seat before climbing in the driver's side
and slamming the door. His blood was boiling.

They sat there in silence for a moment. Vincent could
hear his breath mixed with the pounding of blood in his
ears.

"He saw us," Owens blurted finally. "He saw us. He
knows we're here."

"Maybe not," Vincent cautioned through gritted
teeth.

"He saw us," Owens insisted. "He... he didn't say
anything. He didn't tell them... but he did see us.
There's no way he didn't. He probably knew we were
there as soon as he got out of the car."

Vincent turned his head sharply to look at the man

sitting beside him. Owens was shaking. He was staring out the windshield, eyes fixed in front of him. He looked tortured.

"That was him then?" Vincent checked.

Owens nodded numbly.

"Couldn't possibly have been some—"

"It was him," Owens confirmed.

"Fuck, Owens!"

"Vincent—!"

"No! No, *Goddamnit*, Stuart!" Vincent thumped the steering wheel. "Of all the abandoned railyards in the world! Of all the small villages on this God-damned continent! Seriously?! This is where he shows up? Working for them?"

They both stayed silent again for a while, until Owens broke it a second time.

"He didn't out us. He didn't betray us. Maybe I could— I should—!"

Vincent started the engine and pulled off onto the road.

"Vincent! What are you doing?!"

"Stopping you from doing something unbelievably stupid," he growled. "Again."

* * *

When they pulled up at the farmhouse Stuart was sweating. His mind was whirling and he couldn't think straight. Everything was a blur. His heart was still pounding in his chest like it was trying to bruise his ribs. Vincent hadn't said much else, but there was so much that needed to be said. The old Chancellor was angry. Maybe he had a right to be. Mostly Stuart couldn't help but think that was wrong. Vincent killed the engine, but neither of them moved.

"What are you going to tell the others?" Stuart asked softly.

"I have no fucking idea," Vincent grated.

"He's not on their side," Stuart tried to defend.

Vincent gave him one of the most scathingly contemptuous looks he'd ever seen, and that was saying something.

"I'm serious," Stuart insisted. "If he'd wanted us dead, we never would have made it to the car. We never would have made it off the crates."

"Well, that just fills me with confidence," Vincent drawled.

"It means he didn't want to hurt us!"

"It doesn't mean anything right now, Owens!" Vincent growled him. "We are putting a pin in all of this until I work out what to do. Your faith in his abilities is–"

"It's not faith, Vincent. It's experience," Stuart cut him off. "I have witnessed what he can do. He was better than I was even before I trained him. The things I tried to teach him… Vincent, he knew them instinctively. Every skill, every tactic… he could pick it up easier than breathing. If he had wanted to stop us, we wouldn't be here. He let us go."

The glare on Vincent's face was venomous. Stuart couldn't out-stare it, and he didn't try to. That was the first time he had ever admitted out loud what he'd actually done. He had denied training the man, no matter how hard the Council had pressed him. They'd never had real proof, and Stuart had never confessed to that particular crime. He knew Vincent had known. They'd all known, even if they'd never been able to prove it. Disclosing the truth to Vincent now wasn't improving the situation.

Vincent opened the door and climbed from the car. Stuart gulped air and followed him out. He was starting to feel that Vincent was trying to walk away from the conversation. He didn't blame him, but that wouldn't fix anything either. Vincent stormed back to the house and Stuart followed him. Vincent burst inside like a thundercloud. Stuart hurried after him. The others were all still up and they watched them enter with piqued curiosity.

Fred was at the kitchen table, and the kids were lounging on the couches. Stuart could feel their eyes on him. Everyone's gaze had started on Vincent, but he just looked like his usual angry self. They all slowly turned on him, and whatever they saw was notable. He didn't know what was different, but something was, and it made him deeply uncomfortable.

"What happened?" Fred asked.

Vincent didn't answer. He hovered in the middle of the room like a churning storm, unbothered by the eyes of everyone else darting between them. Stuart didn't understand how he could ignore the weight of expectation. People were staring at him like they could see his sins. It was unbearable.

"We saw Rogue collecting construction supplies," he

answered nervously. "She was working with a couple of men. One we knew as her aide, Ezra White, and the other…" he trailed off. He couldn't bring himself to say it. He felt like he was about to have a heart attack.

Vincent turned on him with that expression again. The scathing one. The one that told him if he didn't say something Vincent would, and by God Stuart would be sorry if he did. Before he could say anything, Fred's chair creaked. He saw her face, the dawning in her eyes as she started to stand.

"You gotta be shitting me," she said.

"His name is Hans Wagner…" Stuart admitted in the smallest voice he'd ever mustered.

"Jesus Christ Emmanuel, Stuart!" Fred exclaimed. "Of all the towns in all the–!"

"We've already done that bit, Fred," Vincent cut her off.

"He's here?!" Fred continued. "He's working for Diana Rogue?!"

"I don't know," Stuart spread his hands helplessly. "He was with her, looking over the merchandise, but he saw us and he never gave us away."

"What are the odds you didn't die tonight because you were with him?" Fred asked Vincent.

Vincent just shrugged. He'd probably been wondering the same thing. Stuart hated that they were contemplating it, but it wasn't wholly unfair. He didn't want to think of Hans as a killer, but if he was working for Rogue and White…

Stuart ran his fingers through his curls for what felt like the dozenth time since they'd left the railyard. It wasn't helping him think, but he felt it should. That was when he glimpsed the light out the window and froze. Lucy was watching him. She saw him freeze. Then she looked for what he'd seen.

"That's weird," she commented. "There's a light on in the barn."

"It'll just be Oskar," Gio shrugged.

"Not at this time of night it won't be," Fred disagreed. She looked between Vincent and Stuart. "Any chance you two were followed?"

"No," Vincent shook his head, but he didn't sound sure.

"Yes," Stuart disagreed. "Easily." He was already starting towards the door. He heard Vincent draw his pistol behind him, and he felt the tension flare in the room. He stopped with his hand at the door but didn't look back. "Shoot me or let me go, but be quick about it," he ordered. "If you don't kill me, I'm going to hear what he has to say."

"Vincent!" Fred scolded, aghast that he would have drawn his weapon on their friend.

Stuart didn't care. He was used to that kind of treatment from the Order. He'd had worse. Not wanting to give them a chance to stop him, he snapped open the door and headed into the snow.

It was freezing outside and he turned up his collar against the cold. Not that it helped. He was a bundle of nerves and that was half the agony. It made him drag his steps. He had no idea what he was going to say. What could he possibly say after the last five years?

He reached the barn. The door stood cracked open

and footsteps led inside. He followed them. It was warmer inside the barn, and the air was filled with the dusty scent of hay. A lantern was sitting on the ledge of a frosted window. A tall man in a pinstripe suit was warming his hands by its flame. His coat and gloves lay discarded across a hay bale, and a shiny briefcase sat beside it. He didn't look up when he spoke.

"I alvays knew Hunters vould come for us," he murmured softly. "I have been vaiting for zem to arrive for montz." He finally looked up, meeting Stuart's gaze across the room. "I never zought it vould be you."

Stuart stood inside the door, staring. He couldn't move and he had no idea what to say. He felt like he was time travelling. Everything about Hans looked and sounded exactly as it had five years ago, just before Stuart had forced him on a ship back to Germany.

"You look vell," Hans offered, possibly to fill the silence. There was the tiniest sliver of hesitance in his voice and actions. He was nervous. Stuart swore it barely showed, but that meant it was bad. Possibly as bad as he felt. Hans picked up the briefcase and held it out. "Zis is everyzing ve have," he continued. "I made sure I had it ready to go. I knew zat vhen Hunters came knocking it vould help to have ze plans available. I have been sabotaging ze project for montz now, vaiting for someone to come and stop it."

Stuart could feel his feet closing the gap between them like an out of body experience. He walked numbly forward, reaching Hans and the briefcase.

"If you need any help viz it, just say," Hans extended. "I am sure you vill have no trouble, but, obviously, if you need anyzing..."

Stuart took the briefcase. He was vaguely aware that he still hadn't said anything. Not even 'thank you'. The freezing cold leather of the briefcase felt alien in his hands. His fingers were numb, but not from the cold. It wasn't that kind of numbness. He tossed the briefcase aside. There was no rude intent, he just didn't care, and cast it into a nearby pile of hay. Part of his mind had been under the delusion that he would make better life choices this time around. The rest of him knew that was idiocy talking.

"Stuart—" Hans started.

Stuart cut him off. He threw his arms around Hans' neck, silencing him with a kiss born of terror and exhilaration. It was foolish. They hadn't seen each other in five years. Hans had clearly moved on with his life. But Stuart didn't care. He didn't care if this was what finally got him killed, because he'd cared once before, a long time ago, and he'd regretted it ever since.

Hans caught him. He pulled Stuart into his arms so tightly he nearly lifted him off the ground. Stuart held on around his neck, his hands touching Hans' face, messing his hair. Hans was so cold. It felt like kissing snow. His lips were freezing and his fingers icy on the back of Stuart's neck. Stuart couldn't stop kissing him. He didn't know how.

"Hans..." he whispered, hearing the pain in his own voice. His breath was steaming and his heart pounding. He knew Hans could feel it. His lips pulled away from Stuart's, but he didn't let him go. Even so, Stuart clung tighter. Hans' freezing lips brushed his cheek.

"I never zought I vould see you again..." he whispered.

Stuart buried his face against Hans' neck, feeling his glasses dig into his face.

"I never should have made you leave," Stuart apologized heartbrokenly.

"You should have come viz me," Hans insisted.

He slipped his hands inside Stuart's jacket, under his waistcoat, the way he always used to when he pulled him close. Stuart could feel how cold Hans' fingers were through his shirt. He shivered at the touch.

"I zought about returning," Hans admitted softly. "I zought about coming back to find you, so many, many times... I vould zink zat Louisiana has much better veazer..." he chuckled. The humor didn't stay. It dropped away like an avalanche of grief. "I couldn't. I couldn't do it. Ze Hunters, vhat zey do is important. *Ja*, zeir vork staves off ze end of ze vorld. Ze vorld needs Hunters." Hans pulled back slightly, leaving his hands still tucked under Stuart's waistcoat at his sides, and looked him in the eye. His slim face was so serious. So devastated. "If I had come back and found you gone, if zey had killed you like ve feared zey vould, I vould have viped your Order from ze face of ze earz. Zere vould have been no place in ze vorld your kind could have hidden from me if I found zey had hurt you. It vas easier to believe you had chosen zem. It vas safer to zink you had sent me away and stayed a Hunter."

"I didn't," Stuart choked. "I didn't stay a Hunter. I would never pick them over you. I was terrified they'd kill you if they ever found you. I knew it would be safer to stay and give them someone to punish. I... I never meant... I'm so sorry, Hans. *Es tut mir leid.* I wanted you to be okay. I wanted you to be safe. I never meant for you to fall in with witches and Nazis."

"*Ja,* zere are lots of zings ve never intend," Hans smiled.

"Are you alright? Are they hurting you? Blackmailing you?"

"*Nein, nein,*" Hans shook his head. "Zey treat me very vell, actually. Zey keep me paid and fed and clozed. Zey keep a roof over my head – I have my own room in *das schloss.*" He gave Stuart a shy look. "It is not easy for someone in my position to find vork, but zey are good to me." He shot a tentative glance at the briefcase. "Still don't mean I vant ze vorld to end zough. Pity only ze *Verrückten* vant to employ me."

"If you want them stopped, say the word and I'll stop them," Stuart promised.

"Vhy do I find zat so easy to believe?" Hans smiled at him. He traced his lips down Stuart's cheek.

Stuart felt like an ice cube was being brushed across his skin. He wanted to suck on it. He turned his head, directing his mouth back to Hans', kissing him again, wanting nothing else in the world. He kissed him with a burning intensity, yearning to taste him. Hans tightened his grip, pulling Stuart up into his arms again. He lifted him easily and tipped him back onto the hay behind them, following him down. His lips traced Stuart's neck, kissing him hungrily and loosening his tie.

"I have a strong urge to pick up vere ve left off..." he

whispered.

"I don't know where the nearest library is," Stuart admitted, remembering where they'd been caught last time. Hans was already unbuttoning his clothes.

"Ve vill have to make do," he replied.

Stuart slid a hand around the back of Hans' neck, pulling him down into another kiss. His lover's fingers traced down his skin, bitingly cold. The kind of cold that hurt. He could feel his body trying to flinch, but it just made him want it more. He pulled Hans firmly on top of him, pushing back against him. Everything was freezing, but he felt like fire. His chest heaved as he gasped. His hands tangled in Hans' clothes as he fumbled to undress him. Hans dragged his lips down Stuart's neck again, across his chest, kissing him as he went. His hand went further, sliding between Stuart's legs and massaging him through the fabric. Stuart groaned longingly as Hans touched him. Hans ran his tongue along Stuart's sternum.

"I've missed the vay you taste…" he whispered.

"How badly?" Stuart asked, lying back against the coat spread over the hay. Hans was already unbuckling his belt. Stuart still remembered the ways Hans had liked to taste him.

* * *

Lucy was on her feet with her arms folded in outrage. She was vaguely aware that it was probably a mannerism she had learnt from Fred. Still, she had to do it now because Fred was busy at the stove. The boys were doing what they always did and taking a vested interest in their cigarettes so that they didn't have to get involved in this.

"I cannot believe you pulled a gun on him!" Lucy exclaimed.

"It's not the first time, and I'd do it again," Vincent growled.

"Lucy, darling, slap him for me, would you?" Fred called.

Lucy did not slap her mentor. She didn't have it in her. But she glared at him vehemently and he knew Fred had said it, so that was good enough. She didn't know what had gone down during the stakeout, but she was piecing it together and, as usual, it was Vincent's behavior she was finding fault with. Vincent had come back angry. That was normal for him, but Lucy had noticed a streak of cruelty in his recent interactions with Owens. The more she dug into it, the less impressed she was with her old man.

Owens had come back disheveled. Certainly, for most people it wouldn't have counted, but for him it had been noticeable. The Professor was always so perfectly put together. He even stepped out of monster fights with barely a hair out of place. When he'd come back through the front door his curls had been rumpled and his tie was loose. The man's tie was never loose! Then Vincent had pulled a gun on him for saying he was going to go and talk to someone!

"I can't believe you," Lucy huffed. "The way you've treated him after the decency you've shown Fred ..."

"What?" Vincent turned on her with genuine

confusion.

"She means the double standard," Gio offered, deciding to involve himself after all. "Look, color us naïve or whatever, but piecing together what I know about the man, I'm guessing that guy in the barn that everybody's getting all worked up about is the reason Owens got himself kicked out of the Order?"

"You'd be about spot on with that," Fred told him.

Gio shrugged helplessly. "Figures. Look, don't get me wrong, I like the Professor. He's a good guy, and a great teacher, but you spend enough time with 'im you start to realize he's a cake-eater. I ain't here to judge, just saying. Then rumor has it you got all kinda freaks living in that big ol' mansion of yours back home – no offense."

"A little bit taken," Fred told him.

"I mean it with the utmost respect, Miss Winifred," Gio deferred. "But my girl Lucy's not wrong. You got the time and space for all those wackos, why not this one?"

"We're definitely going to work on your phrasing, Gio," Lucy told him. "But thanks for summing that up."

Gio shrugged at Tony who shrugged back. Neither looked like they knew what was wrong with the language, although if Tony had thought about it, he would never have had it in him to imply Fred was any of the words his cousin had just used.

Vincent scratched his cheek with the muzzle of his pistol.

"You lot think that my issue with Owens is that he's homosexual?" he checked.

The kids went quiet. That was exactly the line they'd been going down until Vincent had put it so plainly. His expression was clearly asking if that really sounded like him, and if Lucy was totally honest, it didn't.

"Is it because he's German...?" Lucy hesitated.

"Girl, I don't care what nationality anyone takes to their bed," Vincent growled. "If Owens and Oskar decided they wanted to run off together, I'd buy them a damn cottage. My problem is that the man Owens fell for isn't even a man. At least, it's certainly not human."

* * *

Stuart was sprawled over his coat on the hay bale. His fingers tightened in the folds of the wool. He could barely move. Hans was still knelt with his head between Stuart's legs, licking him clean. He sucked harder. Stuart could barely breathe. Each breath came shallow and shivery, crashing through his lungs. He was panting. Another moan escaped as Hans moved his head, dragging his lips away to kiss up the inside of Stuart's thigh.

"Do it," Stuart ordered.

Hans licked the cold sweat from his skin, ignoring the instruction. His hands pushed forcefully along Stuart's legs, groping him, toying with him. With gentle fingers, he brought one hand back to start massaging Stuart's penis again. Stuart groaned.

"Hans... please... I want this. Do it."

Hans brushed his lips against the cluster of scars on Stuart's inner thigh. He set his mouth, taking a second for the shift, and bit down. Stuart felt the sharp pain like a refreshing splash. An instant rush exploded through him as the fangs pierced his flesh. He could feel Hans drinking, sucking greedily on his leg. Stuart let his back arch, opening his body further, offering it up.

He sighed blissfully, reaching down and running his fingers through Hans' soft black hair. Everything felt so hot where Hans drank from him. Stuart bit his lip, fighting another moan.

"I've missed you so much…" he whispered.

Hans retracted his fangs and let out a deep cold breath. Stuart could feel the wound clotting and sealing. The cold exhalation sent a shiver through his spine. Hans stood over him, crawling back over his body and kissing his cheek. His naked skin was freezing against Stuart's bare flesh, but he was putting the gifted blood to good use. Stuart pulled Hans down tighter against him, ensnaring him in his legs and kissing him passionately.

"You vant–?" Hans began.

"*Ja*," Stuart insisted. "Take me. Right now."

* * *

The wind had been quite firmly taken out of Lucy's sails. She had retreated to the couch with her husband and was watching the smoke trail from Giovanni's cigarette. It hung limply in his hand as he gawped.

"A vampire?" he repeated again.

"Yep," Vincent glowered.

"Like an actual blood-sucking, bitey, can't go in

sunlight..."

"The whole shebang," Vincent nodded.

"Still a person," Fred commented from the kitchen. She hadn't changed her tune at all, but then, she'd always known the whole story. The rest of them were trying to catch up.

"You can see my problem," Vincent growled, ignoring Fred. "We're monster hunters. That's what we do. That's our calling. The entire purpose of our Order is to protect the world from creatures like that. And that idiot–!" Vincent waved his pistol at the window, "–is off in a barn getting sodomized by the undead!"

Tony took a long drag on his cigarette. He'd already had a rough day, and now bore a look that suggested the conversation had ventured into extremely unsettling territory. There were phrases being used that he could never unhear. Lucy patted his hand reassuringly.

Gio was frowning contemplatively across from her. He tapped his cigarette in a nervous frantic pattern against the ashtray.

"Do ya think he's alright?" Gio muttered, biting his thumbnail.

"Who can say," Vincent grumbled. "He goes out of his way to protect that thing. Lied to everyone. Told us to stay out of it. I tell you, if I find his body in the barn tomorrow morning, I'm chopping it into pieces and burning them separately."

Fred cuffed him around the head. Vincent barely acknowledged the rebuke, but he did turn to look at her.

"I'm not trying to be mean, Fred," he insisted. "I'm

trying to be safe. Vampires are malicious, bloodthirsty psychopaths. Owens…" Vincent sighed wearily. "Owens, bless his soul, is the kind of person that the world is unjustly cruel to. That makes him extremely vulnerable, and my concern is that this monster preys on that. Owens prostitutes himself to this creature, trading blood for sex–" Vincent stopped with a sharp glance at Tony.

Tony was leaning back with his head tipped against the couch, letting the longest stream of smoke Vincent had ever seen pour out his nose. He looked like a dragon having a panic attack.

"Stuart is a smart man," Fred defended. "He was the best Hunter in your entire Order and he judged Hans to be nonthreatening – that has to count for something."

"Stuart's an idiot," Vincent scoffed. "I don't care how academically brilliant and physically gifted he is, the man was caught having sex with a vampire in a public library!"

"He what now?!" Lucy and Gio exclaimed, while Tony choked on his cigarette.

"It was a private Hunter library," Fred corrected firmly. "In the middle of the night, after hours, when no one else was supposed to be there. The acolytes who caught them arrived while they were distracted, using a borrowed key they shouldn't have had."

"Fred, the acolytes are not the ones who are at fault in this story," Vincent insisted.

She didn't counter that. Whatever wrongs may have developed from the situation, it was hard to see an angle where Stuart hadn't been doing something a little bit wrong, or at least doing something that should have been private in the wrong place.

Gio gave a low whistle. "Didn't know the old man had it in him..." He quickly raised his hands defensively at Fred. "Not old! Just..."

"We get it, Gio," she sighed.

"So that happened five years ago and that's what got him kicked out?" Lucy checked.

"Yeah," Vincent nodded grimly. "It wasn't just a fling. It came out that he'd been living with the thing for months, more than half a year, I think. He'd been training it and disclosing all kinds of Hunter secrets, although we could never prove any of that. You can understand there were people on the Council who wanted him dead. Everyone assumed he'd be thrown in prison, possibly executed after. They wanted to know the extent of the damage. That's when they brought Fred and I in. We were the ones who had to investigate the situation. They needed someone he'd actually talk to..." Vincent set his gun on the table and sat down wearily, scratching his new beard. "We had to check him. That's when we realized how far and how long it had been running. You shoulda seen the scars... Boy's covered in them. Bite marks all over his body. Clusters of them on his wrists, thighs, throat... Goddamn mess."

"How did you sweep it under the rug?" Lucy asked softly. "Why did you...?"

Vincent rubbed his tired face. Fred took her sizzling pan off the heat and came over to kiss the top of his head fondly. Whatever disagreements they had about the situation, this clearly wasn't one of them.

"The Council didn't care about the vampire," Fred told them. "They cared about Stuart's sexuality. Most of those old bastards have had a succubus or two in their closets over the years. I told Vincent, if Stuart had been caught with a vampiress they'd all have laughed about it, maybe slapped him on the wrist. I told him to fix it."

"I *did* care about the vampire," Vincent glowered. "But by then it was long gone. Owens smuggled it out of the country and wouldn't tell any of us where he'd sent it. He wasn't a threat to anyone but himself... and Fred wasn't wrong. The persecution of Owens wasn't right, so I got myself involved. I made sure our Order and the law never went after him, stamped out the rumors, negotiated with the university to keep him. He couldn't stay a Hunter, but he could still do the work. I got him resources and such when he needed them. In return, he promised to do the work and not take up with anymore monsters."

"And now his vampire is here in Germany working for Rogue and White?" Lucy said.

"So it would seem..." Vincent growled. "They are nasty, dangerous creatures. I'm not surprised a blood witch would keep one."

"But this Hans saw you two spying tonight and didn't say anything?" Lucy checked. "He followed you here to see Stuart without alerting our enemies?"

"We don't know that yet," Vincent warned. "We don't know anything for sure."

"So you don't know he's a nasty evil monster?"

"Lucy–"

"Have you ever met him?" Lucy pressed.

"Excuse me?"

"Have you ever met Stuart's vampire boyfriend?" Lucy asked.

"No," Vincent admitted reluctantly.

"So how do you know he's an evil monster if you've never even met him?" she asked. It felt important to contest the assumption. She did trust Vincent, but she also trusted Fred and Stuart, and surely it was only fair to investigate before condemning someone. Besides, not all things that were touched by the Darkness were evil. She resisted the urge to look back at Tony as she thought it.

Vincent, meanwhile, looked like he wasn't hearing these questions for the first time. He turned back to Fred, whose expression of triumph and pride was positively maternal.

* * *

It had started to snow again. A faint swirl blew in through the barn door. Stuart and Hans were cuddled up naked in their makeshift blankets of coat. It wasn't good weather for improvised shelter. Stuart shivered in the cold. His feet were going numb, but he didn't want to move.

"You're freezing," Hans whispered, pulling the coat tighter around him and holding him close.

"You're colder," Stuart reminded. He could feel Hans insulating him from the cold, but only using Stuart's own body heat. When they shifted and Stuart brushed against the parts of Hans he hadn't been touching it was so cold he had to bite down a yelp. Hans nestled in closer, resting his face by Stuart's and letting Stuart's breath steam between them. The shivering was getting worse.

"You need to get back inside before you make yourself sick," Hans insisted.

"I don't want to," Stuart chattered.

Hans laughed and kissed him gently. "You have to. I have to go anyvay."

"Where? Why?"

"I have to get back before zey notice I am gone for too long," Hans replied. "Rogue and Vhite vill be moving ze new parts back to ze basement. I must be zere to help zem reconstruct ze machine." He touched his nose to Stuart's and traced his fingers down Stuart's cheek. "You have to show zose plans to your people. Ze Hunters need to stop us."

"We will," Stuart promised.

"Dame Rogue said she suspected a team of American Hunters on her tail. I assume zey are your friends?" Hans checked. "I vas hoping for ze cavalry. She said she had provoked ze Chancellor."

"She has a bit," Stuart admitted. "New Chancellor. They had a change of leadership a few years ago – for the better. The man who took over was the one who saved my life from the Council. I might not be a Hunter anymore, but I owe him one, and Rogue went after his kids. That's why we're here. I don't mean to disappoint you, but we are the cavalry."

"You could never disappoint me, Stuart." Hans kissed him again.

Stuart tightened his grip, pulling Hans closer, kissing him harder, as he felt him start to leave. Hans let him have the moment, let him have the kiss, but he was significantly stronger than any human, and when he eventually tore himself away Stuart couldn't stop him.

"I have to go," he repeated reluctantly. "Get drezzed before you freeze." He bundled Stuart's clothes onto him even as he said it.

On top of being impossibly stronger than any human, he was also faster, and it never ceased to amaze Stuart how quickly Hans could get them in and out of their clothes. The vampire was dressed again like nothing had ever happened in seconds. Stuart hurried, but he was taking longer. His fingers jittered on his shirt buttons as his whole body spasmed with cold. Then Hans was there, taking the front of Stuart's shirt in his hands and nimbly feeding the buttons through. Stuart wished it was going the other way again.

"I don't want you to go," he begged.

"I'll come back," Hans promised. He rapidly slipped Stuart into his waistcoat, suit jacket, and heavy overcoat. His icy fingers brushed against Stuart's cheeks. "*Ich liebe dich.* If you'll be here tomorrow night, I vill come back."

"I'll be here," Stuart assured. "*Ich liebe dich mehr.*"

Hans handed him the briefcase again, placing it firmly in his hands. He kissed him again, once in farewell and once for good luck, and then once more just because he could. Hans smoothed his hair down, turned up his collar, and disappeared into the night. Stuart watched him go feeling strangely heartbroken all over again. He stood in the barn, as numb as he'd felt when he'd arrived. A shiver racked his body. It broke him from his trance. He checked the barn over, making sure he wasn't leaving anything behind, and strode out into the snow. It blew lazily around him and he hurried to the front door, trembling the whole way.

He could feel his teeth chattering as he shoved the door open and stumbled inside. Everyone was where he had left them. It would have been nice if they'd had the decency to move on. Unfortunately, not only were they there, but they were looking at him like Vincent and Fred had disclosed personal information to the kids. Everyone was staring at him. He realized he must look a complete mess. His collar was open and his tie was simply draped around it. His waistcoat was still unbuttoned and his hair was a scruffy mess. He glanced over them but couldn't bring himself to meet anyone's eye. He handed the briefcase straight to Vincent.

"What's this?" Vincent asked.

"Plans for whatever machine the German government has commissioned them to build," Owens replied. "Hans said he's been waiting for months for Hunters to show up and stop them. He's been quietly sabotaging the project and biding his time. He wants us to destroy it."

"So he claims…" Vincent mused, clicking open the fastenings.

"Sir, don't make me come over there and slap you," Fred warned, grabbing Stuart by the shoulders and directing him away. She herded him to the other side of the table and sat him down in front of the fire. A plate of hot diced steak and liver was set in front of him. "Eat," she instructed.

"I really don't need–" he started.

"Eat!" Fred ordered.

Stuart picked up his fork obediently. If the world had been different Fred would have made the army's best drill sergeant. He supposed it was nice that she cared. He hadn't lost that much blood though. Not that he felt inclined to admit to the room that he'd lost any. He felt Fred pluck some straw from his hair and toss it into the fireplace. No one said anything. He didn't know what was worse.

Vincent was leafing through the files in the case and beginning to spread them across the table. Some of them had diagrams sketched across them. All the notes were in German. Even though he clearly couldn't read them, Vincent had yet to dismiss them. He was scrutinizing them carefully. The diagrams were easy to read in and of themselves, and the symbols marked on them were occult runes. They were what Vincent spent most of his time looking at.

"This is his handwriting?" Vincent checked.

Stuart glanced at it. "*Ja*– uh, yes. Yes, it is."

"He's bragging..." Vincent muttered. "He's built this thing and he's rubbing it in our faces..."

"I just told you he's been–!" Stuart started.

"This is a doomsday device, Owens!" Vincent yelled at him. "Look at it!" He picked up a sketch and waved it in Stuart's face. They'd both gotten to their feet across the table, glaring at each other. "Look at this! Do you know what this could do?! The magic it could channel!

If I'm reading this right, this thing could destroy the world, and these plans are complete! He designed this!"

"He's been sabotaging it! Are you deaf! He has to fool witches and Nazis, of course it has to look like it would work!" Stuart retorted.

"You idiot," Vincent scoffed at him. "You'll believe anything that thing says. It's a monster, Owens. It was born of the Darkness. Of all the creatures that have slithered into our world, their kind are the most malicious – the most manipulative. It has you wrapped around its finger, which I suppose was more useful when you were a Hunter–"

Stuart snatched Vincent's pistol off the table. Now everyone was on their feet. The entire room froze. Stuart clicked open the chamber and tipped the bullets onto the table. They hit the wooden surface, clicking together like tiny heavy bells. Holy bullets had more in them than regular bullets. Hunters didn't carry anything else. Stuart set the gun down again, aware that he had the room's undivided attention, but he didn't mind that now. It was better the two of them didn't have a loaded weapon in reach if that was the way this argument was going to go.

"It's funny..." he said, ever so softly over the crackling of the fire, knowing the room hung on his every word. "I always thought, Sir, that of everyone I knew, you would be the first to tell me that how a man's born isn't what defines him." Stuart looked up from the bullets to meet Vincent's eye again. "What makes a good man?" he asked.

No one answered. The rest of the room were all

watching Vincent, but the old man stayed silent and stone-faced.

"I found him on a job," Stuart continued quietly. "On a farm much like this one. Something had been spooking the cattle and they were worried it was some kind of demon. I went to investigate and I found him. He was dying, Vincent."

Vincent still didn't respond. It was almost as though he was trying to outstare Stuart. It wasn't going to work though. Not this time. Everyone else was listening intently.

"You're so quick to demonize him for what he is, but he's never killed anyone for food. Never attacked or hurt anyone to feed. He barters and trades for blood."

"So he claims," Vincent sneered. Stuart glared at him so fiercely Vincent's sneer faltered.

"He was dying, Vincent, because he'd been feeding off animals to survive," Stuart stated in the same sharp voice he reserved for education. "Despite not killing anyone, Hunters found out about his existence living with a traveling circus. They chased him out of Europe. He fled to America, hiding his trail by feeding on animals, starving himself, and when I found him on the farm he was dying. He wouldn't feed on the people there, even though it would have saved his life."

"You want to give him a medal for that?" Vincent drawled.

"I want you to remember your own code of ethics! The one you tried to pass onto me!" Stuart bellowed. "You remember when we met, Sir? Back when you wouldn't apprentice me? You warned me that humans were the greatest evil we would ever face. I found a man dying because he wasn't willing to hurt others, and he – along with everyone else from our Order – expected me to kill him just because of what he was. Does that sound like you or I, Vincent, or does that sound like Chancellor Whitehall?"

The temperature in the room dropped a couple of degrees. The question hung damningly in the air. Stuart sighed deeply, trying to release some of his anger.

"No one chooses how they're born, Sir," he reminded. "We don't get that luxury. We don't get to pick how we come out, we just have to learn to deal with what we are. If the world had its way, I would be in a prison cell. For some reason, you don't think that's where I belong. You still think I'm a good man, or at least, a good enough man to save. That's why you stood up for me, despite what I am. How can you then support the Hunters trying to kill Hans just for existing? He is a good man, Vincent. A better one than any of us. He's killed fewer people than you or I. Hell, he might have worked with me for six months, but he's almost certainly killed fewer people than your little girl has!"

"You're talking about cultists!" Vincent countered. "You're talking about lives spent in order to save the world!"

"But they are still lives!" Stuart argued. "They are the cost your Order deems necessary. Doesn't that make the Hunters just another cult? A cult that kills in the name of Justice instead of some other old god. Those cultists – as we are so quick to label them – are the human sacrifices our Order offers to the altar of salvation, same as anything our enemies would do. Hans wasn't hurting anyone. He was simply living the best life he could, and the Hunters decided he needed to be sacrificed for the good of the world. How can we make calls like that and then declare we're any better than the people we remove?"

"We're trying to save the world, not end it," Vincent retorted. "It's completely different."

"But how many innocent people have to die for us to win?" Stuart countered. "Doesn't that defeat the purpose? My whole life, Vincent, you have been telling the Council that we need to be better than what we hunt. How can you condemn Hans and claim you're better?"

"Maybe check he walks the talk before you appeal to his sensibilities," Tony chimed in from across the room. The boy was standing like everyone else, but he wasn't really watching the fight. He had dark circles under his eyes and he looked unwell. Most of his attention seemed focused on finishing his cigarette. "You're talking to the guy who shot his boss, after all," he added. "Last Chancellor's death was no accident."

No one spoke. Half of them already knew that. Tony clearly assumed they were in safe enough company telling the others, and nobody wanted to be the one to suggest they weren't. He wandered slowly past the table to the fireplace.

"'Course the same probably goes for your vampire too. Been my experience, people tend to say what'll serve them best. Gotta check they act on it." He tossed the butt of his cigarette into the fire. "But, hell, this ain't my fight. Not my damn business at all. I'm going to bed." He started towards the hallway, passing the plans and pointing to a piece of them as he went by. "Those symbols won't work."

Stuart didn't see the exact part the boy pointed at. No one did. No one stopped him and asked him to come back and explain himself either. They all knew Fred had checked him out earlier and given the all-clear, but he still looked like something dark was hovering about him. It just wasn't as obvious as it had been. He disappeared down the hallway. The crackling fire did little to fill the quiet he left in his wake. Vincent broke the silence first, clearing his throat uncomfortably.

"Kid's right," he muttered. "It's late. We should all get some rest. This will still be here in the morning. We can plan what to do with it then." He didn't say anything else. He just turned and followed Tony from the room.

The heat had been sucked from Stuart's indignation. With Vincent gone there was no one left to be angry with. He stood, leaning on the table, with no idea what to do with himself. He didn't have to make the first move. Fred approached him slowly. She slid a tender arm around him and kissed his cheek. He sighed and hugged her back.

"*Merci*," he whispered.

She rubbed his back comfortingly, but let go of him to answer the scratching at the back door. When she stood back from him her eyes were full of support. She wanted him to know she was on his side, and he appreciated it. He gave her a nod and she went to let the cat in. That left him in the room with Lucy and Gio. They were both still standing and watching. He didn't know how to look his apprentice in the eye, but he knew he had to.

"Well?" he asked them with more indifference than he felt.

Gio puffed a couple of smoke rings at the ceiling. "Well what?" he shot back.

Stuart didn't have a retort. He had been trying to train the casual gangster out of the man in his tutelage. Right now he didn't have the usual superiority complex to back it up.

"I won't lie," Lucy raised her hands. "The vampire part was a surprise. I didn't see that coming."

"You an' me both," Gio agreed. "The rest... *eh*, maybe not so much."

Stuart knew they were trying to make him feel better. He didn't know if it was working. Somehow it didn't surprise him that Gio knew. It did surprise him that his apprentice wasn't alarmed or disgusted. He had expected a bigger reaction. Instead, Gio was busy playing it too cool for school. The kids basically ignored him as they descended on the plans across the table.

"That's it?" Stuart couldn't help but ask.

"*Cosa vuoi?*" Gio shrugged at him. "We got a doomsday device to stop, Professor. You want to help or not?"

"You don't–?" Stuart stuttered. "You're not–?"

"Give Tony and Vincent some time to come around, Stuart," Lucy encouraged. "They'll get there. They're just a bit stubborn."

"Hey," Gio looked him in the eye. "*Non preoccuparti.* Lord knows sometimes the world don't got it right."

The pin fell into place. Of course – Dot. Of course Gio felt that way. Of course he understood. Stuart gave him a nod. He didn't know if the action was sympathetic or grateful. Maybe both. He wasn't sure what emotions he was feeling right now. Too much had happened tonight, and his brain needed time to catch up with all the chemicals it was releasing.

"So, *Capo*, what is this thing?" Gio tapped the paperwork.

"It looks like a rift gate," Stuart answered, helping them rummage through it. "And Vincent isn't wrong... it looks like it should work."

FORTRESS OF THE SHADOW REICH

9

The house was cold and dark. The moon shone through the windows, but the glint on every reflective surface felt ominous, like eyes watching from the walls. The ripped lace curtains did nothing to hinder it. It was a sinister pale light that made the shadows look haunted. They stained across the rotting wooden floor, hiding the real stains. Vincent could smell mold and feces and blood. Even holding his breath, the stench was deep in his nostrils.

He was too terrified to breathe. He couldn't move. If he so much as shifted his weight, the floorboards might creak. A creak here meant death. Worse than death. The pole across the ceiling stretched wall-to-wall like a giant coat rack. A slaughterhouse rig. The bodies hung from meat hooks, spread all the way across. Some of them were fresh. Some had been decomposing for a while. It seemed they were kept for a long time. Each one could be used again repeatedly before it completely fell apart.

Vincent could see the suffering in each shriveled twisted little face. The children had died in excruciating pain. Who knew how long they had been tortured before they had succumbed. He hid between the bodies. Pressed in against the dusty dead. Each one completely drained of blood. He could see bite marks on their bruised, desiccated flesh, human and otherwise.

The shadows stretched and moved. Vincent could barely suppress his terror. Part of him wanted it to be over, wanted to die just so the horror would end, but death was a long way away. If he was caught he would not be lucky enough to simply die. No. He would follow after the children.

Their ghostly laugher sounded through the halls. The thing that had stolen their voices was looking for him. It would find him. That was inevitable. It still came to play with the bodies. It would find him in there, hiding in the rack. It would play with him too.

There was a table beneath the window. Small dusty bottles glistened on it. He needed them. He needed them more than he'd ever needed anything in his life. If he'd just had access to the tonic none of this would have happened. If he'd just been able to drink… if he'd just been able to see… There was a cough building in his throat. It hurt. The itch was building. Burning. He needed it. If he didn't get it soon…

But the light glinting off the bottles was too dangerous. If he disturbed the light it would find him. If he breathed it would find him. That thing was searching for him. It had been looking for so long. It just didn't know to look in its own house. Floorboards creaked. Shadows swayed. He couldn't hold anymore. It was impossible. He coughed. The sound was soft and weak, desperately suppressed. Not enough. A child-like giggle sounded between the bodies near him.

"Hello Vincent…" the Prince's deep voice

whispered in his ear.

Vincent tried to bolt. His whole body tried to throw itself from the closet of corpses and take off running. He was stuck fast. Trying to pull away only ripped his skin. He felt it tear. A scream exploded through his lungs. The Prince had him. The Lord of Darkness held him fast. Every inch of him was bound as his skin was slowly peeled from his flesh. The Prince oozed around him, the acidic sticky goo burning and seeping, forcing its way inside his body.

It was agony. Vincent couldn't scream enough. No scream would do it justice. He couldn't think. He couldn't talk. There was nothing but pain. He wept in the throes of excruciation. The Prince held him tighter. Vincent did not believe the pain could get worse, but it did.

"I'm coming for you, Vincent…" the Prince whispered lovingly. "I will find you. Don't worry, no time or space can stop us… No distance will separate us for long…"

The Prince sank his fangs into Vincent's throat. They pierced his neck like serrated needles, tearing and ripping. He gushed blood. He could feel the life leaking out of him. He could feel the Prince drinking it. The creature sucked hungrily, draining him. Wet, slurping, guzzling sounds rang in his ears as the children's corpses began to giggle all around him.

Vincent woke with a cry. He half threw himself from his bed, face wet with tears, body shivering in terror. His throat felt raw. He would have given anything for a bottle of tonic, for a way to see what was coming and stave off the unknown. His breath rattled as he gasped weakly.

But the room was warm and the darkness soft. He recognized the bedroom of the German farmhouse. He could hear someone snoring in the next room over. As his panic eased, the desperation for the tonic settled. He wiped his face, hands still trembling. It was just a nightmare. Things would be okay.

Still, it was strange how the thoughts didn't make him feel any better.

* * *

Morning dawned bright across the fresh snowy landscape. It promised a beautiful day, not that any of them knew what to do with the good weather. Lucy was tired after poring over the rift plans with Gio and Stuart last night, not to mention Tony muttering in his sleep every hour after she went to bed. He still looked terrible and she couldn't stop worrying about him. Vincent didn't look much better. They might have had a mission to complete, but most of them looked like they needed hot bowls of chicken soup and a day in bed.

The worst part was the tension. Vincent and Stuart were still fighting. Lucy had a strong urge to bang their heads together. She was pretty sure if she asked Fred for permission she'd get a helping hand. But the men butting heads was causing the problem in the first place. It was unlikely more of the same would help. What she needed was a way to make them work together on the plans. Her first thought had been dragging Tony in to expand on his comment from the night before, but when he finally came through later in the morning he had already donned his overcoat and satchel.

"Where are you going?" she asked.

"Out," he shrugged.

"Out where?"

"I dunno. Just... out..." he replied aimlessly. "I just wanted to go for a walk."

"On your own in the snow?" she pressed.

"You're managing to make something very normal sound odd, Luce," he sighed.

"She has a point, Tony," Fred agreed with her. "After what happened yesterday, it might be best to keep you here where we can make sure you're okay."

Tony looked between them with a kind of helpless desperation. He scrunched his wool cap in his hands.

"I just... I just want to get some air. I feel like fresh air would do me some good. I... I won't leave the property. I swear. I'll stay on the farm. I just..." he trailed off as Lucy approached him. She kissed his cheek.

"It's okay. I'm just worried about you. Stay close, yeah?" she told him. Her voice dropped to a whisper. "Don't go anywhere you can't come back from."

"Of course," he promised. "Just wanna stretch my legs and pump my lungs. I won't be gone long, *mi amore.*" He kissed her gently. The kind of kiss that settled her nerves.

She watched him head out the door, setting the cap over his slicked dark hair and trudging out into the crisp winter.

"It is stifling in here," Fred muttered. "I don't blame him."

She wasn't talking about the heat. Lucy rolled her eyes in agreement. Vincent and Owens were taking turns coming and going in the main room. Their avoidance of each other was designed to ease the discomfort of the situation, but it just expanded it to fill the entire house.

"How about," Fred began, "we tie them back-to-back with some rope and toss them into the woodshed? See how long it takes them to work together to get free?"

"I love the way you think, Fred," Lucy approved.

"I don't," Vincent growled, stalking back into the room.

"Profoundly untrue, Sir," Fred contradicted. "You tell me you love the way I think all the time."

"Can't recall a single one," he lied.

"Aww... is someone still feeling grumpy this morning?" She tickled his chin.

Vincent had the look of a man ready to go out and murder a lion with nothing but his hands. Lucy busied herself with the rift paperwork again to avoid meeting his eye. She didn't know where Fred found the bravery to provoke him, but she personally did not want to poke that bear. Vincent could be a little scary when he wanted to be, and there was a threatening seriousness to him this morning.

Owens chose that moment to reappear, as though the two of them had forgotten which of them was allowed in the kitchen at that moment. The Professor was back to his usual pristine self as though nothing had ever happened last night. The only difference was the cold shoulder he was showing their leader. Lucy decided it was time to try bridging that gap.

"Stuart," she called to him. "Would you please help me translate this stuff we were looking at last night for Vincent?"

The whole room held its breath. Nearly. A deep meow came from under the table.

"Oh Toby," Fred huffed and scooched down to grab him. The cat had been giving Tony the stink eye before he left, and had clearly wanted to see him gone before making himself known.

That left Lucy standing between the men, looking at them with the biggest eyes she could muster. Owens sighed.

"Of course," he replied, coming to join her. "What bit do you need help with?"

"This bit here," she pointed and both men looked curiously over her shoulder. "You said last night that this combination of technology and magic is unusual. I thought it might give us a clue."

"Mm…" Stuart mused, tracing the scribbled notes with his finger and muttering in German as he read. "…*die Verbindung zwischen den Welten*… *Ja*, it's a strange kind of alchemy not usually employed by cults. Most run-ins I've had with mages… none of them use stuff like this."

Fred stood back up with the purring cat in her arms, peeking at the notes from the other side of the table. Her eyes were focused on the diagrams rather than the writing.

"No..." she agreed. "We're more about the raw power channeled by casters. That looks like the work of imbuing machinery with magic."

"*Genau!*" Owens pointed at her. "Exactly! Yes! Rather than having a mage cast the spell they are placing the spell inside the machine so that it will cast it for them."

"So that literally anyone could turn it on..." Lucy muttered. "You wouldn't have to be a mage... anyone could use it..." A cold dread welled up in her gut as she said it, and she felt the horror sink over the room. There was a solid thud as Vincent's hand hit the table.

"That's Hunter technology..." he hissed. They all looked to him and he glared. "That's the kind of tech we use to make our weapons – our holy bullets! Alchemy bound with spells."

"This is far more advanced than a sword or a bullet," Owens tapped the paper. "It's the evolution of Hunter tech. Crazy to think it's the Nazis who came up with it."

"Except they didn't, did they?" Vincent growled venomously. "Your vampire did. The vampire you were training when you were betraying our Order..."

"Vincent!" Fred snapped at him.

"Shut up, Fred!" Vincent roared.

His bellow scared Tobias, who ripped himself from Fred's arms and bolted for the back door. Even Lucy felt herself cowering. Vincent was still glaring at Owens, who hadn't flinched at all. He was staring Vincent down with no remorse. Vincent's eyes flickered to the woman at his side, who still clutched her chest where the cat had pounced from.

"I am sick and tired of listening to you defend what he did because you have empathy for his situation!" Vincent yelled. "You think I lack sympathy here? I went out of my way, I bent over backwards to help him, and you know what he did?! He lied! He fucking lied and he taught a monster – a blood-sucking creature of Darkness who happens to be aligned with Nazis – how we make our tech! How we slay their kind! He taught our enemies how to beat us!"

"I did nothing of the sort!" Owens retorted. "I worked with a man who was helping root out cults in my area. I trained him to work with us!"

"Are you kidding me?" Vincent exclaimed. "Did he fuck your brains out or did you casually forget where we found him last night? Who we found him working for?!"

"*Va te faire foutre!*" Owens roared at him.

"AE!" Gio bellowed from the doorway. Everyone froze and turned to him. He was louder than they were, and the look he was giving them was deeply reminiscent of his uncle Ferro. The disapproval was palpable as he stood in the entrance to the hallway, glaring over at them. "*Teppisti incivili...* You use language like that in front of the ladies?! *Mamma mia...* you oughta be ashamed!"

"If it's all the same to you, Mister Amarti, this is none of your Goddamn business. You're not exactly the model citizen I want to be taking etiquette lessons from," Vincent warned.

"Well, I oughta be," Gio clapped back. "The ghosts

of ya mothers would be horrified."

"*Mi dispiace*," Owens muttered.

"Don't say sorry, Boss, *be* sorry," Gio insisted.

"I can't," Owens sighed. "I can't be sorry, because I'm not. I didn't do anything wrong. Vincent will *never* give Hans a chance, not even when he is doing everything he can to help us." Owens glared at Vincent. "You condemn him for working with Rogue and White, but who else would have hired him?"

"My point exactly," Vincent drawled.

"No, Vincent!" Stuart snapped. "If he had come to us, to your Order, you would have cut his head off before he could have said *'warte ab'*. You would never have heard him out – you won't even do it now."

"He built a doomsday device for the Nazis–" Vincent started.

"And gave us the plans to stop it!" Owens interrupted.

"–or just to rub it in our faces!" Vincent yelled. "Have you, in fact, found any way to stop this device, Owens?"

"Tony said it wouldn't work," Fred reminded, rubbing her arm where Tobias had left a startled scratch. "He said some of the runes were off."

"And have any of you been able to verify that?" Vincent pushed.

No one said anything. Lucy wanted to chase the cat outside and frolic in the snow where it was safe. This was not the outcome she had been hoping for this morning. Gio was the first one to sigh.

"I'll go find him," he muttered, grabbing his coat and

swinging it on as he headed for the door.

Lucy was half tempted to follow him, but she didn't want to leave Vincent and Owens alone, and she didn't want to abandon Fred to deal with them on her own. She leant on the table and gave the next deep sigh.

"How about, for now," she began slowly, addressing Vincent, "we take Stuart at his word, trust him, and you keep some extra bulbs of garlic in your pockets, just in case?"

* * *

The snow outside was light and crisp. Everything about the scenery was perfectly picturesque, from the distant hills to the white fields and their lonely dispersed dark trees, topped with fluffy clouds of snow. Even the farmhouses were iconic fachwerkhaus style buildings with painted crossbeams that gave them their quintessentially German look.

Gio strolled from the house lazily, glad for an excuse to be out. That place was starting to feel toxic. He'd been able to feel something twisting in his gut, and it wasn't just Miss Winifred's cooking. Something was wrong. At first he'd assumed it was the nastiness bleeding over from the old fellas fighting, but it was more than that. He was only just realizing how much more.

The footprints were the first clue. He saw them and instantly stopped fumbling for a cigarette. He shoved everything straight back in his pockets and took off, jogging for the barn. He could see the footprints disappearing inside. Straight from the front door to the barn. No detours. The little frosted window was already flickering. Gio could feel the sickening dread hit his heart.

"Tony!" he yelled, busting through the door. "Ae! Kid! Tony!"

The wind hit him as soon as he was through the door. Outside it was beautifully still. Inside was a damn hurricane! He clung to the door like a shield. His coat whipped up around him, viciously smacking his legs. His hair felt like it was trying to rip off his head.

In a clear space in the middle of the barn, a large arcane circle shone golden from the floor but it was tainted with shadow. It was the heart of the storm. In the center floated Tony. His eyes were completely black. The darkness was staining his veins, his lips, his fingers. Golden lightning crackled in the whirlwind around him. Everything was stained with inky black clouds.

"TONY!" Gio bellowed at him. "TONY!"

He lunged forward, trying to reach his cousin. The wind knocked him down. He caught himself on a bale of hay and pulled himself forward, gaining mere inches against the hurricane battering him. He couldn't yell again. He could barely breathe. The storm was tearing the air from his lungs. He hauled himself over the hay. The bale buckled, but held. Gio collapsed on the other side. He reached into his pocket, fingers closing around the cold vial. He pulled out the small bottle and threw it as hard as he could. It shattered across the edge of the circle. Holy water splashed across the magic, making it flicker.

Tony whirled to face him. Gio leapt. He took his

chance when the magic sparked and dove for his cousin. He hit him full in the ribs, tackling him straight out of the air. They hit the ground hard. Gio emptied a second bottle across Tony's face. The kid choked and writhed, trying to shake the water out of his eyes.

The magic went out. The darkness dissolved from Tony's features and the circle dispersed beneath them. Gio parked himself on the skinny boy's chest, using his weight to keep the kid on the floor. Tony wriggled under him like a startled worm. Holy water dripped from his hair and trickled down his face.

"G-Gio...?" he stammered.

"*Pazzo bastardo...*" Gio shook his head. "You crazy bastard! What the hell were you doing?!" He smacked Tony up the side of the head.

"Ow! Hey!" Tony protested, still unable to go anywhere with Gio sitting on him. He wiped the water from his face, but at least he looked close to healthy again.

"What kinda mad bullshit are you pulling, Antony?" Gio demanded. "*Sei Fuori!* Don't make me get your wife out here! That wee dandelion can be scary when she wants to."

"Don't tell Lucy!" Tony panicked. "Please, don't tell her!"

"Tony, *amico*, you really think you should be doing something if it's a thing you don't want anyone telling ya wife?" Gio pointed out.

Tony collapsed back against the ground, panting for breath and abandoning his struggle. Gio let him lie there for a moment, waiting for reality to kick back in.

"What the hell you doing, kid?" he asked again.

Tony just shook his head, rolling his hair back and forth in the dust and hay. Gio climbed off him and held out a hand. Tony took it and Gio helped him up. Tony got to his feet and scrabbled in the mess, grabbing some small items off the floor. Gio perched himself on the end of a bale and fished in his pocket for a cigarette.

"What did you throw water in my face for?" Tony asked, drying his eyes with his sleeve.

"Holy water," Gio mumbled around his smoke as he lit it. "The Professor always makes us carry some. Never know what you might need it for." He looked up from under his eyebrows and saw Tony watching him. He pulled out a second cigarette and offered it. Tony took the smoke and the light, and perched down on the bale opposite Gio. For a moment they smoked in silence, then Tony held out one of the things he'd picked up from the floor. Gio took it and turned it over in his fingers. He raised an eyebrow.

"A holy bullet?" he asked.

Tony nodded. "Yep." He blew out a trail of smoke. "You know how they make 'em?"

"Alchemy and witchcraft," Gio nodded. "Made my fair share. Think the old fellas were fighting about that just before."

"I'm trying to upgrade one," Tony admitted.

"You what now?" Gio gave him a look.

Tony sighed a stream of smoke at the floor, trying to cool his nerves.

"A few years ago now, when we went and helped Vincent in Egypt... we came across this... this thing," he took a shivering breath. Gio saw his cousin's lip tremble. "Vincent calls it the Prince. I guess like the Prince of Darkness or something. Not our first run in. Not our last, I'm sure." He paused.

Gio waited. He didn't mind waiting. Something was up with his boy, and he had nothing but time on his hands. Tony started up again slowly, a faint warbling crack in his voice.

"That was the thing that shot Lucy," he admitted. "It tried to kill her. The Prince's got something about the Doc, yeah? It's got some hang up about him that makes him a target. Said Lucy was getting in the way. Said she was too good an anchor for the old man and was getting between them, so it tried to kill her. Thing is... that nasty gooey motherfucker sunk dozens of holy bullets. It didn't take any damage. It was like its power was so much greater than anything we had, there was nothing that could kill it, nothing that could slow it, it was just playing with us all, and there was nothing we could do."

"How'd you get out alive then?" Gio asked.

Tony gave him a look. Gio knew that look. They both got it from their mothers' brother.

"You did your thing, huh?" he asked.

Tony nodded. "What I got... it comes from the same place. It has the same kinda power. It can hit back." He reached out and Gio handed the bullet back. Tony held it up between his thumb and finger. "These things work by combining ingredients monsters are weak to with a holy incantation, and condensing it down into a bullet. But it works because it's just a little spell. You can fit a little spell in here."

"You're trying to fit some massive spell inside a tiny bullet?" Gio checked.

"I know I can do it," Tony sighed. "We... we've been trying for months, me and Luce, I know that it's possible. When it comes to magic, size is just an illusion... the trick is explaining that to the spell."

"Not playing ball, huh?" Gio grimaced.

"Nope," Tony sighed. "*Non funziona.* But... but I touched onto something yesterday... it has the answer. It can help me do this. I know it can."

"You talking about that shadowy shit ya keep spewing?" Gio glared warningly.

"It talks to me," Tony explained. "It comes from the same place. It's part of the gateway and it knows how to make it work. If I can just—"

"You got darkness talking to you and messing with ya head?" Gio interrupted. "Antony, tell me, how long you been listening to angry black shadows?"

"Since we got here," Tony waved his cigarette towards the house. "It talks to me in my sleep. But it knows me! I know it!"

"Nothing about that is making me feel better," Gio warned. "You're not touching that shit again."

"But it can help me—!"

"No, Tony!" Gio shut him down. "*Basta!* No more of this. Not until we've talked to the others about it. There's a reason ya been keeping this from us. You knew we wouldn't approve. You know it's wrong."

"You're going to lecture me on what's right and wrong?" Tony exclaimed. "After the stance you took last night?!"

"*Cosa intendi?*" Gio replied in a soft warning voice.

"Your boss–" Tony started but fell sharply silent at the look on his cousin's face.

Gio's glare was warning him to back down. It was warning him because the set of his frown stated very clearly, in multiple languages, that if Tony said something offensive about the Professor he might find himself getting his nose reset. Gio took a long drag on his cigarette, forcing Tony to stay silent and contemplative, except that wasn't always the kid's strong suit.

"How can you be okay with it?" Tony asked.

"What about you and Miss Winifred?" Gio replied.

Tony was silent for a while. Gio got the impression that Tony had been forced to come to terms with that and had been given years to adapt. Not to mention, the concept of ladies was probably easier on his unquestioning little brain. While Tony thought, Gio reached out and tapped his cigarette over the bare dirt. He crushed the ashes with the sole of his shoe and kept them well away from the loose dry hay.

"You ever think that maybe the world's doing it wrong?" Gio asked.

Now Tony just looked alarmed. Gio sighed and tried to head off his cousin's dangerous imagination.

"I got a girl back home," he said. "Finest lady I ever met."

"The jazz singer..." Tony recalled.

"Dot," Gio nodded. "Stuart knows, but he ain't unkind about it. Quite the opposite. I wasn't shocked by the news last night because I've known for a while that he's the kinda guy who knows what it's like to be in trouble over who he steps out with – not that I imagine he ever got to step out with anyone, but you know what I mean. He looks out for us, but there're a lot of people not happy about me and her. Haven't even thought about trying to tell the family."

"Your girl's colored?" Tony asked.

Gio nodded. "Most beautiful lady I ever seen. Voice like an angel. Owens got me into the music, wasn't really my jam before I went south, but they don't do it back home like they do in New Orleans. Professor got friends in all the strangest places. He frequents jazz clubs, and I started tagging along. That's where I saw her. Figured a lady like that would have nothing to do with a mug like me, but I got it bad. Never been so lovesick. Owens took me back there every night for a week." Gio grinned wryly. "Don't think it took 'im too long to work out I wasn't just going for the music. He tried to warn me off, but that didn't last long. Figured he knows what that's like. Instead, he changed his tune, started to advise me how to play it careful."

"You owe him," Tony nodded.

"It's not about owing, kid," Gio smiled at him. "That man is my mentor, my teacher, and my friend. He's a good person. One of the best. And, y'know, I got some sympathy for him. We might not be in the same boat, but we both know what it is to have the world telling us we're not allowed to love who we love. You've never had to live with that, but I tell ya, Tony, it hits ya like a goddamn freight train. It makes ya start thinking – how can society be right if this is wrong? And if it's wrong about this, what else is it wrong about?"

Tony hugged himself and smoked deeply, trying to hold down a shiver. His expression was profoundly troubled. He had the look of someone who had been taught an unwavering black and white version of right and wrong as a young kid, and now couldn't wrap his brain around how his world had changed in the past few years. How his world was still changing now. He looked like he was trying to comprehend a world where someone had told him he wouldn't be allowed to love Lucy, and Gio half rose from his seat in concern that the darkness was about to swallow the kid again. Tony looked up at him with pained eyes, drawn by the movement.

"I think I get it…" he muttered. "But I'm not sure…"

"You don't have to get it," Gio patted his shoulder. "You just have to trust us and support us."

"Okay," Tony nodded. "*Bene*, okay, I can do that." He finished his cigarette and crushed it out in the cold dirt. "What about Doc Temple?"

"Oh, that is not my circus," Gio waved his hands defensively. "It's funny. When Temple got me the apprenticeship, he had a firm chat with me about morality before he put me on the train. I thought it was the weirdest thing until I met Owens. That was when the first seeds of suspicion began to sow themselves. I figured the old coot looks after his own, he knew Stuart swung a little different, and wanted to be sure that wouldn't be a problem if I ever found out. I didn't think the Doc had a problem with it. Now…"

"*Si*," Tony sighed. "He probably didn't have an issue with it when it was just dealing with Owens being a cake-eater. You know what he's like. Only thing Vincent cares about is killing evil and saving the innocent."

"Not a bad stance," Gio shook his head. "I wanna side with Owens. I trust him completely, but the vampire thing was very much news. I've never met a vampire before. No idea what they're like, and you can bet your ass Owens never taught me about them."

"What if he's being manipulated though?" Tony muttered. "What if Vincent is right?"

"Then it's a damn good thing my man Owens is living with a house full of Hunters," Gio finished.

* * *

The sun set orange and pink that night. It reflected off the snow in shades of hot coral and Lucy thought it might have been the most beautiful thing she'd ever seen. There was a frozen pond out the back of the farmhouse, and the light reflected off it so sharply it was hard to tell where the sky stopped and the earth began. Everything was just one huge sunset.

She stood on the back stairs and watched it, comfortably rugged up with Tony's arm around her shoulders. He looked better since his walk with Gio. Apparently the fresh air really had done him some good. She'd decided to get some herself, and the afternoon trek around the property had been peaceful. It was still peaceful. Everything about this was so peaceful she didn't want to go back inside. She had absolutely no faith that Vincent and Stuart would have managed to agree on anything.

God, the old man was so stubborn. Weren't they all, she supposed. The best of the light began to fade, and the dark blue of night crept in to dull the bright pinks. With an almost tragic sigh, Lucy turned from the scenery. She stole a quick kiss from Tony and stalked back into the house. He took the wicker basket from the step at his side and headed for the wood shed.

It was easy enough to hear the yelling coming from the other room. The only reason they weren't hoarse was Fred's intermittent separations. She had been firm about those. When she couldn't stand it anymore, and when she was worried about them spooking the cat, she sent them to their rooms to cool off like misbehaving children. The behavior was not inspiring confidence.

"I just need you to think about it, Owens!" Vincent insisted. "If things were different maybe I would have more patience for this, but you must be able to see how this looks! Rogue is a blood witch. She uses blood for her magic. She does… *unspeakable evils* to achieve her ends. You didn't have to see those children, Stuart. You didn't have to see what she was prepared to do when she drained them of life. But you must be able to see how her employment of a vampire doesn't look like a coincidence! They are the same brand of evil."

Lucy entered the room but no one took any notice of her. The men were back at the table and Fred was back at the stove. Tobias was on the bench beside her, getting fed tidbits as she cooked. Lucy despaired for them all.

She wasn't the only one. Stuart was pinching the bridge of his nose like he'd run out of patience years ago and was ready to switch sides.

"I don't know how many different ways I can tell you that man isn't evil," he sighed.

"If you are right then I am unfairly unjust," Vincent conceded. "But if I'm right, Owens, if I am, then I cannot risk the safety of my family. I just can't. If your vampire turns out to be like every other vampire I've ever encountered, he will trick and manipulate and then kill us all. He will tie us up and bring us to his mistress, who will slit our veins, drain our blood into her spells, and probably offer him a share as payment. You can see why I can't risk that!"

"No, Vincent, I can't," Stuart replied. "Because that is all in your head. That's your tale, not his. The worst that happens if you're wrong is that you're unfairly unjust? No. No, I don't think so. The worst is that we turn away our best chance at stopping people significantly more powerful than us, and we lose, because you can't get over your own racist bigotry."

"My w–" Vincent started.

"Don't get offended when it's true," Owens told him disgustedly. "I know that's been your cry against your own Council for longer than I've been alive, but that's what makes this whole ugly situation so ironic." Owens wasn't yelling anymore. He looked exhausted. The fight had gone out of him and his body looked heavy with resignation. "You despise Hans simply because of the body he was born in. You've never met him. His race is the only reason you hate him. But he is a good man. The best. He deserves this chance. The chance I tried to give him – to let him try and be more than the monster the whole world tells him he is!"

"And that there is half the problem," Vincent pointed.

Owens looked at him with disinterest, as though he couldn't care about Vincent's arguments anymore. Vincent sighed heavily.

"I can't imagine what you've been through, Stuart," Vincent sympathized. "You attacked me earlier with the sentiment that I've never felt the way you do... maybe I haven't. Maybe that isn't on the cards for me, but I do care. I do love my family and my friends. I do care about you. I worry about the harsh hand you have been dealt in life, and the idea that you might see a monster when you look in the mirror – I worry that is the reason you are so desperate to see a good man in this creature, but it's not the same. You're not the same. You're as good a man as any I've met, and I am not trying to hurt you, Stuart. I'm trying to protect you. You are not a monster, and no decent person who has met you could ever say otherwise. You and this vampire are not alike."

"What if we are?" Stuart asked. "What if your sentimental parallels do run deeper, and we are exactly the same?"

Vincent just sighed and rubbed his face. They both looked like they'd wasted energy on this for too long. Lucy watched them patiently. At least they'd mostly moved away from name-calling and slapping. Vincent was trying. She was proud of him, and she did understand that his heart was in the right place, but she was still on Stuart's side. She wandered over and placed a comforting hand on Vincent's shoulder.

"Why can't we give him a chance?" she asked. Everyone looked at her, but no one answered, so she continued. "I know you're trying to do right by us, Vincent. I know you want to take care of us, but think about the stance you're taking. Stuart isn't wrong. Why can't we meet Hans and decide for ourselves instead of surrendering to fear? You were the one who told me that the worst monsters in the world were men – that they made the monsters and brought them into the world. Why can't one of the monsters then be a man? Why does it always have to skew to the side of darkness? Why can't it go our way every now and then? Where's your optimism?"

Stuart sighed deeply and turned away, rubbing the back of his neck. He wasn't going to tell her not to help, but he clearly felt like the ship had sailed and there was nothing more to be said that they hadn't screamed at each other five different ways already.

The back door sounded and Tony and Gio came in, hauling the overfilled wood basket between them. Everyone got out of their way as they ran it from the back door to the fireplace and parked it down. Tony chucked another couple of logs on the crackling blaze. Both of them seemed determined to ignore any signs that they had interrupted anything. It was easier to pretend the fight hadn't been happening all day.

Gio wandered between them all with casual disinterest, heading for the couches, but he stopped before he got there. He paused, staring out the window into the starry twilight. It was too dark to see much now, but it was still pretty.

"There's a light on in the barn…" he announced softly.

The room tensed again. Everyone waited to see what would happen. No one was surprised when Owens broke first, heading for the door.

"Owens," Vincent called.

"What?" he snapped, swinging on his coat and pulling the door open. A small gust of snow blew in and melted on the doormat. Stuart glared over his shoulder at Vincent, who gave Lucy a long and mysterious look.

"Invite him in," Vincent instructed.

FORTRESS OF THE SHADOW REICH

10

It was cold in the barn, and the lamp did so little to ward off the chill. Hans had been waiting by the window in the castle for the sky to darken enough to be safe. As soon as the last rays had been swallowed by night, he had swooped down from the hill. The farmhouse looked warm, cozy even. Stuart was in there. In a warm house with real people. The sharp stab of longing Hans felt as he went by it was so painful he could almost believe he was alive for a moment. But he wasn't and there was no point dwelling. He hid in the barn with his lamp and waited in the cold.

He didn't have to wait long. He heard the front door and perked up, turning towards the barn door and waiting. He could hear footsteps crunching across the snow. They approached, growing louder. Stuart's footsteps. Hans recognized the gait. He couldn't believe he'd found him again. The barn door opened and Stuart stood in the open space, but he made no move to come inside.

Hans felt his hands tighten anxiously on the handle of his briefcase. He could hear Stuart's heartbeat from here. It was pounding wildly.

"We don't have to stay out here," Stuart called. "You

can come inside."

Hans didn't move.

"Hans...?" Stuart called to him.

"You... you vant me in ze house?" he checked weakly. "But... viz ze people? Are you sure?"

"They said it was okay," Stuart replied. "We've been going over the plans you gave us. They want to meet you."

Hans raised a dubious eyebrow. Stuart smiled at him. His hesitations dissolved under that smile. He'd had several, but he couldn't remember what they were now. He crossed the barn and met Stuart in the doorway. He could feel the warmth of him draw near as he approached. Stuart waited. Hans reached him and resisted the urge to slip his arms into the warmth of Stuart's coat. Stuart reached up and touched his face. His fingers were practically hot on Hans' icy skin.

They kissed in the doorway of the barn, and Hans was half tempted to drag Stuart back in with him and forget the imminent end of the world. Everything about him was so deliciously warm. His hands, his lips, his breath. The hot salty scent of his skin. Hans kissed him harder, one hand sliding around his waist and pulling him in. The other hand nearly dropped the briefcase. Stuart pulled away. His fingers still traced Hans' face, but his distraction was short lived, for now.

Hans risked a quick glance at the house. The windows were bright, but he saw no faces in them.

"Zey know...?" he asked.

Stuart nodded. He was apprehensive. No. Terrified. Hans could hear it in his pulse. Stuart was afraid of what was going to happen next. Hans shared his fear. It was all well and good for Stuart to speak well of his people, but the Hunters had driven them apart. They had sworn to kill Hans if they ever found them. Besides, it wasn't like there was a world they would be welcomed in by people who knew. Still, Hans trusted Stuart, and did not believe there was any way Stuart would lead him into a trap. He slipped his free hand into Stuart's and held on tightly.

They walked hand in hand to the front door. Stuart paused when he reached it. Hans had been watching his lover's breath steam in small shallow gasps. When Stuart took his hand back he wasn't surprised. He wasn't even disappointed. He knew it was safer. They'd played things much safer than this back in America all those years ago. Well, mostly.

Stuart opened the door and led Hans inside, inviting him in. He ducked through the doorway and was struck by a wall of heat. It was bliss. The fire roaring in the fireplace heated the space like a hot summer day. Instantly, the world felt like a better place. The cold that always seemed to sting the edges of his nerves vanished. There was no tingling of blood flow as in the living, for he had no blood flowing, but the pain of the cold disappeared.

Everyone was staring at him. There were five other people in the room. Two young Italian men with a fug of cigarette smoke about them so thick you could walk on it. A young lady with them who was watching with the strangest brand of curiosity Hans had ever seen. A severe dark-haired lady with a spark of magic in her eye and a cat in her arms, and a dangerously angry older man with a short grey beard who looked like he'd rather shoot people than talk to them. Hans stood before them holding his briefcase nervously in front of him. Stuart shut the door behind them as Hans raised an apprehensive hand in greeting.

"*Guten Abend*," he started.

"*Guten Abend*," the woman at the bench smiled at him.

Before anyone else could say anything, her cat gave a chirp and bounced from her arms, trotting over to investigate the newcomer. He gave Hans' shoes a good sniff, and rubbed against his legs, purring.

"*Hallo Kätzchen*," Hans smiled at the cat, bending over to scratch it behind the ears. "*Wie geht es dir, mein pelziger Freund?*"

"Aw…" the young girl made a soft sound. "He likes you!"

"*Ja*," Hans gave her a nod. "Cats like me usually."

"That's a promising sign," the older woman smiled. "They're good at driving off demons."

"*Ja absolut*," Hans agreed. "Zey extremely territorial. Never let ozer demons in zeir space."

Stuart made official introductions, now that they had Tobias' blessing. Hans gave each of them a polite nod and they returned the gesture. He wasn't in a hurry to close the gap between them though. A room full of Hunters made him nervous, and he was fairly sure Vincent was toying with weapons. That was made apparent when the old man pulled out a knife and pointed it at the pages still scattered over the table.

"You're responsible for this?" he growled.

"*Ja bin ich,*" Hans admitted. "Ze plans are half mine, half from an international Professor one of ze Generals hired. I have not met him, but ve have corresponded a couple of times. Mostly all ze orders come zrough Rogue and Vhite now. Truz be told, zey have been running ze operation much longer zan zey have been here. Zey vere hired long before zey came to Germany."

"And we just take that on good faith?" Vincent asked.

"Take it on vhatever faiz you like," Hans shrugged. "Doesn't make it less true."

The strange look he'd noted on Lucy's face slipped away slightly and was replaced by a sweet smile. She was nearing, slowly, and she had absolutely no hostility about her. He didn't know what to make of that.

"So, can you tell us more about what we're dealing with?" Lucy asked, approaching the table and drawing the others in her wake. "Vincent says the plans are functional, but my husband said some of the symbols are wrong and they won't work."

Hans shot a look at the young man who was keeping the most distance from them.

"You are very perceptive…" he commented. "Even Dame Rogue has not noticed yet."

"I don't know why it don't work," Tony shrugged, shoving his hands in his pockets. "I just know it don't."

"Zese symbols here," Hans pointed, setting his briefcase down on a chair and shuffling through the plans on the table. "I have done zem ever so slightly incorrect. Zey are responsible for ze gravitational pull.

Zis means zat every time zey turn ze machine on, zey nearly pull ze fortress down on top of zemselves. Ve have been vorking in ze caves under ze basement. Zey haven't vorked out vhat keeps going 'rong yet. But ve are running into a problem."

"What, only just now?" Gio commented.

"*Ja*," Hans nodded. "Specifically now." He clicked open his briefcase and pulled out some new papers, placing them on top of the old ones. "Zis is Doktor Maximilian Schmitt. He is one of ze new Chancellor's mad scientists, and he is on his vay here as ve speak. Rogue has hired him to come and fix our problems. He is vell versed in ze occult, and if he sees ze machine he vill know vhat is 'rong..."

"I have a question," Fred raised.

"*Fortfahren*," Hans invited.

"It's my understanding," she began very diplomatically, "that vampires can be unbelievably deadly when they want to be. So why are you bringing this matter to us? Couldn't you just kill Rogue and White and destroy their machine? Burn the plans? If you want this done, why not do it yourself?"

Hans looked back at Stuart who stood loyally at his shoulder. Stuart gave him a shrug as though he thought the question fair. Hans smiled at him.

"I'm flattered you zink so highly of my skill, but I could not vin zat fight. Perhaps against just one of zem I could vin in a fair fight, but zey are not ze kind to play fair, I zink."

"One of them has as much power as you do?" Stuart asked in alarm.

"*Ja*," Hans nodded, surprised they were surprised. A dawning suspicion began to creep up on him. "If zey vere mere humans I could have removed zem and half zeir army using zeir machine like a shovel. As it stands, ve are all in grave danger."

"Why do I hate everything about that sentence?" Fred muttered.

"If they were mere humans?" Vincent echoed sharply.

"We were under the impression Rogue was a blood witch and White was her aide," Stuart elaborated, adjusting his glassed nervously. "You might need to start at the beginning…"

"*So scheint es*," Hans sighed. He pulled up a chair and sat down. No one seemed to mind him making himself at home, and most of them got comfortable as well. He crossed his legs and linked his fingers over his knee. "You vere not 'rong zat Rogue is a blood vitch. She is. In fact, she is *ze* blood vitch. She is ze Queen of *der Kult der Bluthexe*."

"The Cult of the Blood Witch," Stuart nodded. "Sylva told us as much when we ran into the cult back home."

"*Nein*, Stuart," Hans pressed. "She is ze one. Ze same one. Across all languages and countries. She is millennia old, ancient to zis vorld even back vhen I vas born. Ze *Kinder* sacrificed by her cult keep her young – zat is vhat ze blood magic is for. To keep her immortal." He gave them a moment to let that sink in before he continued. "Ezra Vhite is her pet demon. It gives ze illusion of a man – a good illusion – but only an illusion.

It cannot get ze eyes right, hence ze glasses to hide ze demon's silver eyes. It is an unusual creature, unlike any I have seen before, and I do not know vhat spell she uses to keep it bound. I do know zat its strengz and speed rival my own. Vhatever zat zing truly is, it is a match for me."

Hans' bombshell was clearly news to everyone in the room, as they all sat in dreadful silence. He could hear the fire crackling hot nearby and was tempted to go and stand by it. The echoes of a room full of stunned heartbeats was a strange and quiet space.

"Well, we're fucked then," Gio announced. "Who wants to get drunk and wait for the world to end."

"*Nein!*" Hans scolded him. "Vhat kind of Hunters are you? Your kind did not chase me halfvay around ze vorld and back again just to run avay from zis fight!" He tapped the new paperwork. "Zis is vhere Doktor Schmitt comes in. His train is travelling up to Koblenz from Southern Germany. You need to make sure he never gets off zat train. You help me viz zis, I vill have more time to vork out how to smuggle you in to help me take out the operation in ze castle, *ja?*"

"*Ja,*" Stuart nodded gently. "We can do that."

"Zese papers contain all ze details I have – vhich trains, vhere zey stop, everyzing on ze Doktor, and a photograph of him, etcetera." Hans held them out. "Have a look now. If zere is anyzing else you need, let me know. I vill see vhat I can do."

"And why should we trust you?" Vincent demanded.

"Vhat choice do you have?" Hans replied coolly,

meeting the old man's eye. He gave the weathered Hunter a grim smile. "I can tell you don't like me, Chancellor. Zat is not my problem, and I don't care, but I live in zis vorld and I don't vant it to end. Zere are zings in it I care about. I vish to protect zem, and you are my best chance. I can put my dislike for your kind aside to make zat happen. If you cannot, I vill come up viz a new plan."

"And how many of us end up drained like cattle in that plan?"

Hans laughed and stood up. He knew the action would spook Vincent, and he rather enjoyed watching his pupils dilate and listening to his heart race. Vincent's hand was on his pistol, but it took such a long time to get there. Hans could have snapped him in half and thrown him out the window before any of them realized it was happening. He wanted Vincent to know that, and he got the impression he did. No one else had moved as though he was a threat, but the Italian boy across the room was still trying to keep as much distance as he could without being called out.

"I see none of you as food, Hunter," he replied. "I don't know vhat Stuart has told you, but I vould never drink from anyone vithout zeir consent. Besides, no one vould vant to eat you anyvay. *Entschuldigung*, I do find it amusing zat ze two of you zat fear me ze most are ze two not even ze most insane of my kind vould drink from."

"What's that supposed to mean?" Fred asked.

"It means your men have tainted blood, *Fräulein*," Hans answered. "Zose two," he pointed at Vincent and

Tony. "Zey have darkness in zeir blood. Zey reek of it. You can smell it a mile avay. Zey have been *zere...* to ze ozer vorld. It never leaves ze flesh. You cannot vash it out. Zey are practically poisonous. Your young one is very sick."

"What do you mean very sick?!" Lucy demanded.

"Zere is evil in his blood, fresh, nasty," Hans shook his head in distaste.

"If it's all the same to you, I'm not going to take health checks from a vampire," Tony scoffed darkly.

"*Was immer du wünschst,*" Hans shrugged at him. "I'm not ze one sveating around ze eyes, viz ze heart palpitations, and ze blood coagulation. You're ze one hiding somezing."

"I don't like what you're implying–!" Tony started, pushing forward. Lucy stopped him, placing a hand on his chest and holding him back. She wasn't the only one. The cat placed itself between Hans and Tony and hissed at the boy. Hans noted the way Tony's hands itched to ball into fists. The veins throbbed in his throat and temple. He was not well, and he was trying hard to hide it. He was actively hiding something. Right now. Hans decided it wasn't his problem and turned away.

"Ze train job?" he raised, turning back to the table.

"We'll get it done," Stuart assured.

Hans smiled at him. If Stuart said they'd do it, Hans believed him. He didn't have it in him to doubt his love. The man had never failed him before. He had a serious expression on his face as he started to flick through the new papers. His brows creased above his glasses and his lips pouted slightly as he frowned. It was so cute

Hans thought he might be swooning.

"Do you know what kind of security Schmitt will have?" Fred asked, joining them at the research table. "If he works in the occult, is he a mage?"

"I do not zink so," Hans replied, tearing his attention from Stuart. "Based on ze information I have gazered in zese files, if he does practice ze arcane arts, he is not adept. He is an academic and a scientist, more zan a cultist. Zat said, it is my understanding zat he is coming here on ze orders of ze Chancellor himself, so I vould prepare for trouble."

"That's something we're good at," Lucy smiled grimly, also joining them.

"Unfortunately, he is due to arrive late afternoon," Hans sighed. "Zat means he travels during ze day, and I cannot help you."

"So that's a thing then?" Lucy asked curiously. "You'll catch fire?"

"*Ja*," Hans grimaced. "Very slowly, very painfully, *ja*, I vould burn. I have seen it. Once. It took some time."

"You saw a vampire burn to death?" she exclaimed. "You didn't help them?"

"*Nein*," Hans chuckled darkly. "I killed zem."

He had the room's attention again. He was almost getting used to it, although he still wasn't sure he liked it. Then there was the girl, the very sweet, very curious young lady who kept looking at him with big eyes.

"You are full of questions," he sighed. "I can tell."

Stuart gave a very soft snicker behind his paperwork. Even Fred was hiding a smile. The men were holding back, but only the youngest one was still more hostile than intrigued.

"What was it like to die?" Lucy asked in a small voice.

Hans glanced at her. She was biting her bottom lip like she was scared the question was rude, but she'd never had a chance like this before. She bore all the marks of the Hunter trade, but none of the darkness Hans had come to associate with it. He wasn't yet ready to admit to himself that he was curious about her too, but he was prepared to humor her.

"I have no idea," he answered. "I don't remember."

"He has no memory of any life before this one," Stuart elaborated gently. He glanced over, his eyes inquisitive, as though checking it was alright he had said it. Hans gave him a nod. He didn't mind.

"My first memory is digging myself out of my grave," he admitted. "All I know of ze man I was before zis is vhat vas on my gravestone: Hans Wagner 1801-1832. I barely even remember zat. I vas a bit feral vhen I first came into ze vorld."

"You look amazing for someone who's been dead more than a century," Stuart smiled at him.

"Zat never gets funny, Stuart," Hans warned.

"You mean it never gets old," Stuart grinned.

"I zink your sense of humor gets lost in translation..." Hans mused.

"No," Vincent shook his head. "It's not you. He's not funny in any language."

"*Comment peux-tu le savoir?*" Stuart preened.

"Because he knows you," Hans grinned. "Vhen God made you he had to give you a flaw, just one, and he made you like bad jokes."

Stuart rolled his eyes. Hans loved him, if possible, even more.

"You speak French too?" Lucy asked.

"I'm a hundred years old and I spent most of zat time traveling Europe. You pick up enough," he replied. "Alzough, most of zat time was spent in ze east viz a Romani family. I lived viz zem for generations." He could feel his eyes growing soft at the memories. "Zey vere good people. It vas a peaceful life, until ze Hunters came."

"And chased you to America…" Lucy recalled like she'd heard some of the story before. "Where you helped Stuart hunt monsters? Is that where you killed the other vampire?"

"*Nein*," he shook his head. "Zat vas in my first days, back here, in Germany." Half of him wanted to leave it at that, but he knew the girl's curiosity wouldn't be sated, and why not tell her? She might as well know. Besides, something about her wanted to give him a chance, why not make the most of it? "I mentioned before zat I vas feral for a brief period vhen I first avoke, but as my sanity returned I met one ozer of my kind… Count Ludwig Beck." He glowered just saying the name.

Lucy was leaning forward on the back of a chair, hanging on his every word. The last person who had cared about any of his life was Stuart, and Hans couldn't help but give the girl a small smile.

"Beck vas vile," he continued scathingly. "Ze vorst man I ever met. He took me in and tried to teach me his vays, I don't zink he ever realized zat I hated him, but I did. I lozed him from ze first moment I saw him. He vas vain and smug and cruel. I learned vhat I could from him, but vhen I could stand it no longer, I took him by surprise. I took off his head, cut up his body, and impaled ze pieces separately to ze hillside and vaited for ze dawn to find zem. It took most of ze day for zem to burn completely to ash."

Everyone was staring at him again.

"Vhat?" he shrugged. "Ze man vas evil, and if nothing else his deaz kept *die Fräuleins* of Wurzen safer."

Stuart glanced up from the report to look over the tops of his glasses at Vincent.

"Told you he was as good as we are," he commented smugly.

Hans felt Stuart was in the privileged position of being one of those kind and beautiful people who managed to look unfairly attractive even when they were being smug. Perhaps he was biased though. He'd never thought Stuart was anything but stunning. He still remembered the first time he'd seen him. It had been in a barn not too dissimilar to the one outside, although the temperature had been much hotter. The summer air had been scorching and dusty.

Hans had been dying, but pondering that at least he might die warm. He had been starving himself for months and was nearly too weak to feed. He had fled Europe, knowing the Hunters were after him, desperate not to die, but knowing it was inevitable. Hiding in pain under piles of hay and hoping for a merciful death hadn't become much of a life.

Stuart had walked in and Hans had recognized him as a Hunter instantly. The steady heartbeat, the smooth suit, the weapons... he didn't belong on the farm. He'd been hired. Hans had assumed that was it. He had finally met his match, and it took Stuart no time to find him – almost as if he had known Hans was there before he walked in. He was good at his job.

Hans had begged for a quick death, promising that he hadn't hurt any humans in the hope that the Hunter would grant him mercy. He had never in his hundred years expected what had followed. Stuart had checked his condition, verified how long Hans had been trying to sustain himself on animal blood, and then unbuttoned his cuff and rolled up his sleeve. At first it had seemed like a trick, but it wasn't. Stuart had let him drink from his own wrist, just a little, not enough to make himself sick after so long without human blood. Just enough to sustain him a little longer.

Stuart had told him to stay hiding and that he would come back for him at night when it was safe. And he had. He came back just as he said he would and smuggled him away to his small university funded apartment where he had nursed Hans back to health. The entire situation was completely surreal, unless you knew Stuart. He had been adamant, through all questioning, that he could never kill something harmless and defenseless in cold blood. He was the first Hunter to ever see Hans as a person rather than a monster.

The second was watching him right now. She had

the biggest eyes Hans had ever seen, they were far too innocent for a Hunter. Something about her reminded him of Stuart. She had the same kindness, the same sense of justice. How utterly bizarre.

"Are you alright?" Lucy asked, touching his shoulder.

He stared at her hand. She took it back nervously, but he shook his head politely at her concern. She had nothing to fear from him.

"I'm fine, *danke*, vhy do you ask?" he replied.

"Oh, you just looked a bit... intense..." she answered.

"You get used to it," Stuart told her, still browsing the file. "It takes a while, because you can tell something isn't quite right – he doesn't breathe, he forgets to blink, all that jazz – but you do get used to it."

"I don't mean to unsettle you," Hans apologized. "I can simulate breazing."

"Don't," Stuart chuckled. "Vampire breath has some interesting properties, I'd rather not find out what happens if we all start breathing it."

"Probably very good for you," Hans suggested.

"Quite possibly, but let's leave the testing for later. I don't want anyone starting to think they're bulletproof and coming off the high mid-job tomorrow." Stuart was starting to spread the files across the table in neat little stacks. "Do you have more information about the terrain in this area? We haven't been here long and I'm not sure what our best plan of attack is."

"I could maybe sketch somezing," Hans offered. "But I'm sure you vould have better maps in ze library."

"Do we have time to get to a library?" Stuart asked.

"Your library," Hans specified. "Ze one in ze basement."

Everyone stared at him like they had no idea what he was talking about.

"Ze library. In ze basement," he repeated, pointing. He walked over to the light fitting in the wall by the corridor and pulled it across, grating open the hidden door in the wall that led to a dark musty set of stairs. "Ze library," he pointed again like it would help.

"I don't think any of us knew that was there…" Stuart stated slowly.

"One of you knew," Hans replied, looking straight at Tony. "You knew, didn't you? You didn't know how to get down zere, but you knew it vas zere."

Tony was glaring at him. Dark shadows hung around his eyes. The whole room was holding its breath. Hans could hear it. He had started something. All the humans had frozen. The moment shattered. They moved as one. He watched it unfold as though in slow motion. They all moved as fast as they could, but it was easy enough to follow.

Tony lunged for the door, but Gio caught him around the waist. Lucy had leapt towards him too, pushing him back. The adults had all leapt the table to block the doorway. The cat was hissing like a firecracker. Gio brought Tony crashing to the floor. As soon as he was down, Fred changed tack and knelt by the boy, trying to get her fingers to his temples. Hans knew a possession when he saw one.

"Ah," he stated delicately.

Lucy had backed away to give them room. She was still backing up towards the others, hugging herself tightly as she watched them pin her thrashing husband to the ground.

"Let me go!" Tony bellowed, struggling against Gio and Fred. "I'm only doing it to help you! You're all lost! You're all lost, stumbling helplessly in the dark! But I can help you! Let me answer its call! I can save us!"

Lucy whirled around to the three men standing by the library entrance.

"We have to find the book!" she cried. "We have to get rid of it!"

They all nodded, but it was Vincent and Hans who went down with her. Stuart stayed by the door, just in case something went wrong. Hans could sense the Darkness as they descended. The room itself was surprisingly well insulated to protect the collection. The door was connected to a generator that powered buzzing strings of flickering electric lights around the room. It was a good space for research. The Hunters who used this space were well-resourced.

There was a small desk, and shelves packed to the brim with items. Many books, but also scrolls and maps. There were weapons and bottles that looked to contain potions. There were old arcane relics and holy crosses. Some things looked like they were probably confiscated contraband.

One shelf, down the back of the room, tucked away, had a distinct smell to it. Hans noted the way Vincent was drawn to it, as though he could sense it. The girl didn't know what she was doing. She was following them. She didn't have that sense. The old man did. He had enough of the Darkness in him to feel when it pulled.

They stalked to the shelf and found it. A complete collection, bound in human skin that had been stained pitch black. One of the originals. Vincent hissed sharply when he saw it. Hans simply watched. The old Hunter reached out to take the book, but drew his hand back sharply before he'd even touched it. Lucy reached for it, but Vincent threw an arm out to hold her back.

"We have to destroy it!" she insisted.

"We do," Vincent agreed, although there was a trace of reluctance in his voice. "See if there are some tongs up in the kitchen—"

"Don't bozer," Hans told them. He plucked the book from the shelf before anyone could stop him. It was a cold heavy tome and it smelled evil, but he'd touched worse. He gave the troubled Hunters a nonchalant shrug. "It does not affect ze dead."

He carried the book from the library and the other two chased him hurriedly up the stairs. They came out the doorway into the main room. Tony shrieked when he saw the book.

"Don't!" he screamed as he saw Hans heading for the fireplace. "DON'T!" His eyes flickered black, stuttering with darkness.

Hans gave him a curious look. He had expected a stronger manifestation of possession. Something in the voice perhaps, or even the energy of the boy, but it wasn't there. The one screaming was Tony, not his Darkness. Hans tossed the book into the fireplace.

Tony gave an unholy scream, but the old dry book caught like a log and began to burn. Gio kept a tight hold on him, pinning him to the floor with his arms twisted behind his back. Tony's struggles slowly became weaker.

"That thing was underneath him that whole time," Vincent muttered bleakly. "Probably talking to him in his sleep. That's why he was getting so bad."

"Will he be okay now?" Lucy asked desperately. "He doesn't get like that at the house and you have a copy of that book in the safe."

"My one isn't the same as that one," Vincent sighed. "That one was more powerful."

"I'm not sure it's ze book..." Hans warned, watching Tony whimper.

"What makes you say that?" Lucy asked.

"Zat is not possession," Hans pointed. "He is villing, not coerced."

"We appreciate your help," Vincent muttered. "But the boy is a special case. Unique. Best leave him to us."

Hans shrugged. As long as the team could do the job and their situation wasn't putting Stuart in unnecessary danger, it wasn't his business. He turned back to his lover, who stood watching the ordeal with concern creasing his perfect face. Hans stepped by him, brushing against him and letting his fingers trace against the inside of Stuart's palm. It wasn't the same as holding his hand, but it was comforting to know he was there.

"Ze maps you vant," he murmured privately. "Zey look like zey are on ze first shelf on ze left. Do you vant me to retrieve zem for you?"

"*Danke,*" Stuart thanked him softly. "I'll make sure we're ready for tomorrow."

FORTRESS OF THE SHADOW REICH

11

The train bounced and rattled down the tracks. Outside was another fine winter's day and the landscape chugged by in smears of blue, grey, and white. Vincent sat in his cushioned seat and let the motion of the train rock him gently as he measured all the distances in his mind's eye one more time.

Fred had the window seat beside him and gazed out patiently. Lucy and Tony were sitting across from them holding hands, heads together. Tony looked much better to be out of the house again. Vincent still couldn't believe it had taken them so long to work out what had been messing with him. There had been a strong reluctance to take him anywhere, but Fred had pointed out it was almost more dangerous to leave him, so here they were. He trusted Lucy to keep an eye on her boy.

Owens and Gio were sitting across the aisle. Owens was lost in whatever newspaper he'd picked up in Frankfurt. Gio was jittery, nervously tapping a cigarette he hadn't lit yet. Vincent thought about what was coming and didn't blame him.

They had gone to Frankfurt in the morning to meet Schmitt's train when it stopped. Having now scoped it out and boarded it, the plan was looking daring. A carriage up near the engine had been notable for its honor guard of conspicuous black uniforms, tinted windows, and elite private access. There had been no way to get to Schmitt at the station. Now they were improvising.

Vincent stood. Owens noted the signal and folded away his paper, rising to join him. They were followed by Fred and Gio. Once they left, Tony stuck a leg out, blocking the aisle with his foot behind them like a warning. Not that anyone was paying them much attention. The only seats between them and the front of the carriage were empty. It wasn't far. They walked straight to the door and stepped through. The train had decent bridge links and the four of them huddled between the carriage doors.

"You alright with this, Amarti?" Owens asked.

Gio grinned at him. "You think this is hard? I'm Mafia, Boss. This is a piece of cake."

Owens raised an eyebrow at him, but he opened the hatch in the roof anyway.

"*Grazie, Capo,*" Gio smirked, bouncing up and hauling himself through the hole in the ceiling.

"*Buona fortuna!*" Owens called to him and closed the hatch after him. He met Vincent's eye. "Ready?"

"Now or never," Vincent looked to Fred.

She cracked her knuckles and turned to the door. Her hands began to glow. Vincent and Owens drew their blades and shared a nod. They were going to take things quietly where they could. Lucy and Tony were responsible for keeping the ordinary passengers out of harm's way and making sure no one followed their team. The kids weren't the right fit for an assassination. The rest of them…

Fred unlocked the door and hauled it open. Owens moved like lightning. He was through the gap as soon as the door started moving. Short blade in each hand, he struck as he entered the carriage. The two guards either side of the door had daggers through their temples before they realized they were under attack.

Vincent followed. The carriage was partitioned into multiple rooms. There were three other guards in this section. He ran one through, clamping a hand on the man's mouth before he could scream. The other two were hauled, writhing, into the air. Red light choked them, tightening around their throats. Their necks snapped. They hit the floor with loud thuds.

Owens and Vincent both looked back at Fred warningly. She gave them a shrug. They were, after all, supposed to be a distraction. However, they weren't supposed to be obvious about it. Distractions never worked if you ran in screaming 'distraction!'. You had to make people believe it was a real attempt. Besides, as long as the Doctor died… who cared who killed him?

They stormed the next room. A line of guards raised their rifles as soon as they entered. There was no way to surprise them. Fred raised a glowing red shield as the guards shot at them. Vincent and Owens drew their guns. It was time to make some noise. They fired through Fred's one-way shield. Six men dropped as the Hunters fired with practiced precision. They were trained to defeat ancient gods – a few Nazi soldiers weren't exactly challenging. That was the point, provided they only drew the right attention.

They waited. No one else came busting through to attack them. Vincent felt it before anyone said anything.

"Something's wrong..." Owens muttered.

Fred took the lead, keeping her shield up. She opened the next door. The room was dark. The tint on the windows was thick and stained the faint available light a dark red. They edged into the room. Vincent had a sudden and horrifying realization that he didn't know what species Schmitt was. These were the same people who had hired Hans, after all. Both men hung close to Fred, staying behind the shield. A peal of laughter came out of the darkness, light and sugary. A woman's laughter.

An electric bulb sparked into life above them. The room was bare, but two people stood before the door at the other end. A woman in a long red dress smiled at them, her lips painted a scarlet that matched her skirt. She wore a thick, black fur coat, and her pristine orange curls were perfectly styled around her cheeks. She looked like a Hollywood starlet, now that she had completely abandoned her disguise of sickly invalid. They all recognized the tall man in the dark suit and glasses behind her.

"That's a cute trick," Rogue purred at Fred. "You know any others?"

The sorceress lifted her hands and made a ripping motion. Fred cried out as her shield tore in half, destroying the spell. Rogue grinned at them.

"I don't know how you found out about this, Chancellor, but I'm not surprised," she declared. "I was wondering how long it would take you to finally catch me up. How are the children?"

Vincent aimed his pistol at her. There was a flicker. Something grabbed his arm. His own face was reflected back at him in two mirrored pools of dark glass. A window shattered as his bullet went through it. White's hand tightened on his wrist. Vincent flinched. He nearly dropped his gun. It felt like his bones were about to snap.

"Vincent!" Owens barked. He fired. Vincent felt his body jerk. A bullet grazed his skin. He felt the heat of it burn past his cheek. He kicked. His foot caught White full in the chest. The beast didn't budge, but Vincent tore himself free of the demon's grip. Owens caught him and pulled him up. Fred was ahead of them, facing off against Rogue. The mages began to circle each other warily. Both women's hands sparked with red light.

Sunshine was spilling into the room from the broken window. Vincent paused, sword in one hand and pistol in the other. Owens was still helping to prop him up. White watched them with an expressionless face. Vincent could see himself hesitating in the demon's glasses. He tried to catch it off guard. It dodged his bullet again, lunging for them. Vincent raised his sword. The blade nicked the demon across the arm and it leapt back. Owens fired. White leapt through the broken window.

Beside them, Fred struck at Rogue. Lightning crackled from her hands, but Rogue caught it. The energy dissolved in Rogue's fingers, making her own light brighter. She fired it back. Fred smacked the blast into the ground, grunting with the effort. Rogue attacked. Light burst from her hands. Fred roared as she caught it. They both stood, hands raised either side of their heads, locked in a fierce struggle of power.

The window on the other side of the train shattered. Vincent lunged, but he wasn't fast enough. White swung through the gap. He kicked Owens in the back and sent him flying. Vincent caught the edge of White's boot against his hip. The glancing blow threw him off balance. He staggered. The demon moved too fast. It was impossible for the human eye to follow. Black blood stained its arm where Vincent's sword had caught it, but it didn't seem troubled.

Owens rolled onto his back and fired. White flickered away from the bullets, dodging them without a scratch. He came in swinging. He kicked Stuart in the stomach, flinging him into the wall. He kicked him again. Owens grabbed one of his daggers from inside his jacket and stabbed it into the demon's ankle. White grabbed him by the collar and threw him with one hand. Owens flew the length of the room and smashed into Fred.

Vincent lunged for White. The demon turned faster than Vincent could follow. It caught the blade of Vincent's sword in the air, pinching the metal between two fingers. Vincent pushed down with all his strength. The blade didn't budge. White smiled. He snatched the sword and stabbed at Vincent. Vincent barely dodged. The blade stabbed through his jacket, scratching his side and pinning him to the wall.

White jerked his head sharply, his demon ears

sensing something. He leapt out the window again. Vincent hauled himself free, yanking the sword from the wall. He glanced between the broken windows. Sunlight did nothing to the demon, so that was no help. He waited for it to lunge back through the side. Nothing. What else…?

Gio! Vincent ran to the window and hauled himself through the gap, grabbing for the roof of the carriage. He struggled up, feeling the wind tear at him as he pulled himself onto the roof of the speeding train.

Beneath him, Owens and Fred both roared with pain as Rogue took the opportunity to zap them. Fred threw a hand out, still tangled in a mess on the floor with Stuart, and set the floor beneath Rogue alight. The sorceress leapt away as the carriage caught fire. Fred pushed Stuart off her. He was struggling to his feet. She got up and tightened her fingers, flaring the fire. Rogue extinguished the flames from the hem of her dress. She threw another blast of red lightning. Fred dodged.

Owens fired at her. Rogue yelped as a bullet caught her hand, blasting across her palm and destroying her spell. Owens fired again, but Rogue had learnt her lesson. She threw up a shield. Stuart's bullets ricocheted off the wall of light. One caught him in the shoulder. He snapped back with cry, clutching the wound.

Rogue went for him. The blast looked lethal. Fred jumped in front of him, raising her own shield. She staggered as the spell hit her guard. The force nearly knocked her over. Stuart propped himself against her to help hold her up. Rogue's magic exploded across hers, adding to the fire filling the room.

"We have to fall back!" she told Stuart. He nodded.

On top of the train, Vincent was struggling to his feet. The wind battered him relentlessly and the train rocked under him. He could see White heading for the young gangster.

"Gio!" he bellowed, firing at White.

The demon paused, dropping down and hitting the roof. Gio turned. He was crouched low, making his way carefully along the roof to drop down at the other end and strike. He froze when he saw White coming for him. Gio drew his pistol and aimed it at the monster. He fired. White lunged back. A bullet nicked his shoulder, but he didn't even flinch. His hand stabbed down. Claws the size of butcher's knives erupted from his fingers, stabbing into the top of the train and pinning him in place.

"Oh shit…" Vincent heard himself say.

Claws extended on White's other hand as he prepared to lunge. Vincent bolted. He threw caution to the wind and raced down the carriage, catching White around the middle and tackling him down. The surprise caught the creature off guard. He crashed into the top of the train with Vincent on top of him.

"Doc!" Gio yelled, rushing back and drawing a bottle from his pocket.

White snarled and turned on them. He jerked Vincent off his back and whirled, claws outstretched. The glasses fell from his face, one lens cracked. Vincent saw the demon's glittery silver eyes catch his, the tiny slitted pupils focusing. Vincent swung his sword, catching the blow of White's claws. It was like trying to hold back a sledgehammer. Gio ran in and threw the contents of the bottle. Water splashed down White's back. For a moment it seemed as though nothing had happened, then it soaked through the suit.

White hissed as his flesh began to smoke under his clothes. Gio lined up his shot. White went berserk. He slashed his claws across Vincent's sword, hitting him hard and driving him back. Vincent crashed to his knees under the blow. The demon whirled, knocking Gio's gun away and stabbing him in the side of the leg. Gio yelled as the claws pierced his flesh.

Vincent forced himself up and swung at White. The demon dodged away. It gave Gio time to escape him. He staggered and slipped on his wounded leg, hitting the roof and sliding further down the train. White attacked again. Vincent defended the strike with his sword, grimacing from the effort. He felt like his elbows would crack or his shoulders would pop.

"Get down to Fred!" Vincent yelled back over his shoulder, ordering Gio to safety.

The gangster used his belt as a rough torniquet, trying to stop the bleeding from his thigh. He slipped further down the roof, leaving a smear of blood as he headed for the hatch. As soon as he opened it, smoke poured out. Something was on fire. He disappeared inside.

Vincent held his ground. There was nothing else to do, but deep inside he knew he couldn't win this fight. White knew it too, but he wasn't smiling anymore. They'd annoyed him. His fangs were bared at Vincent, whether in a snarl of frustration or pain Vincent didn't know. He slashed, once, twice. Vincent couldn't hold him off. His knees buckled. He didn't have the strength. He slipped. White kicked him in the side. Vincent lurched. White kicked him again. His foot connected with Vincent's ribs and fired him off the side of the train. Vincent fumbled for a hold. There wasn't one. He couldn't catch himself. He flew towards nothing.

* * *

Gio collapsed back through the hole. Smoke swirled around him, but he couldn't see the fire. He coughed and wheezed, struggling against his injury.

"Fred!" he called desperately, trying to get help for Vincent.

She staggered into view. Owens was dragging her with him, with her arm pulled over his shoulders. They were both bleeding.

"Vincent's on the roof!" Gio exclaimed, not sure what else to do. He could barely stand.

Owens kicked the door open into the next carriage. Everyone who saw them started in fright. Lucy and Tony leapt to their feet.

"Kids–" Fred choked. "Vincent!" She motioned to the roof.

They were already moving. Lucy ran up first. She was leaping for the hatch when they heard it. Vincent's yell. Something blew past the door. Something human sized. At this speed–

Fred screamed. Lucy paled like she was going into shock. Tony started to glow. Darkness filled his eyes.

With a small gesture, the door ripped clean off the side of the train and crashed in their wake. Tony lashed out. He leant out the door, holding tight to the guard rail. Golden light flashed from his hand. Ropes of it snaked from his grip and whipped behind them. They pulled taut. He'd caught something. Caught Vincent. The ropes he used to bind monsters began to pull Vincent back to the train. Tony grimaced as he pulled Vincent up with one arm. Something banged behind them.

"We have to move!" Fred grunted.

Tony was still trying to pull Vincent close enough to reach. Red lightning crackled through the doorway.

"She's going to catch us," Owens muttered. He shoved Fred off his shoulders and propped her against the wall. "Take the others, I'll hold her off."

The whole train rattled. The bump and rumble changed as they went over a bridge. All the bangs echoed through the beams. Below them the river sparkled blue and freezing.

"Jump!" Fred cried.

"What?" Lucy turned on her.

Fred was already herding them, grabbing Stuart by the collar before he could do anything stupid.

"We can't outrun her!" Fred yelled. "JUMP!"

She shoved everyone out the door, pushing Tony and Vincent with them. Rogue burst into the room. Fred glimpsed the sorceress over her shoulder. She grinned a vicious and bloody grin. Then jumped.

FORTRESS OF THE SHADOW REICH

12

The castle gates were drawn open and a long black Mercedes pulled into the courtyard. Hans set his umbrella carefully and stepped out into the afternoon to greet it. He watched the guards' reflections drift across the polished body and dark windows. He, of course, didn't feature. The courtyard was warm underfoot from the sunshine. It wasn't the kind of warm humans noticed. They were too vulnerable to winter due to their own heat. It was that impossible distant warmth only the sun could provide, but that Hans could never truly partake in.

The car stopped and the doors opened. Hans felt his throat tighten as he watched Rogue and White climb from the vehicle. At first he had feared them unscathed, and it had left him nervously thirsty. Then he smelt the smoke coming from Rogue's coat. He saw the crack in White's glasses and the bloody tear in his sleeve. Somehow that made it all so much worse.

"I did not realize you vere going to be gone today," he said.

"We decided to go and meet our guest at Frankfurt and travel with him the rest of the way," Rogue announced, checking her lipstick in the reflective window.

"A good thing we did, too," White added darkly, holding the door open for their guest.

"Oh pet," Rogue purred at her demon. "It was just a bit of fun." She grinned at Hans and placed a delicate hand on his chest. "Be gentle with the dear this afternoon," she bid him. "I think he's in a bit of a mood. A few pesky Hunters came out to play. He didn't get to eat anyone and I think they got a few good licks in. He's a bit sore."

"Vhat happened to ze Hunters?" Hans asked, trying to keep the urgency from his voice.

"They're not our problem anymore," Rogue shrugged, turning to face the man climbing from the car.

Doctor Schmitt was a slight man with thinning blonde hair and a friendly smile. He looked deeply out of place between Rogue and White, more like their snack than their associate. Hans greeted him politely in German and Schmitt responded in kind. They shook hands. The Doctor had a warm firm handshake that wanted very badly to be friends with everyone.

Rogue watched the two greet each other with sultry amusement. She turned her face to White as he reached her and whispered something. Hans was very aware that she intended the statement to be private, but he could still hear her at that volume, even with Schmitt talking to him. She was commenting that their consultants were 'very German'. Hans ignored the obvious quip and privately held that the Americans were 'very American', even the one that technically came from some different hell pit.

With the pleasantries out of the way, Rogue invited them all inside and led on, dragging Schmitt in her wake. Hans and White followed behind, with Hans carefully stowing his umbrella as they went inside. He was painfully aware of White trailing extremely close at his shoulder. Too close. The demon tended to do that.

"Look at you, up and about in daylight," he smirked. "Did you miss us?"

"I zought it only polite to get up early to greet our new colleague," Hans muttered. "Especially given zat he and I vill be vorking togezer so closely." He paused, feeling his chest tighten. He had to ask, but he didn't want to. "Vhat happened on ze train?"

White gave him a strange look. His dark glasses reflected the hallway and hid his expression. Hans could feel fear curling through his insides. He had no idea if it showed. The demon was a mystery and he had no idea if it could sense his terror, but it was only getting worse. He had to know.

"We ran into the Hunters Diana's been baiting," White admitted. "They're more of a nuisance than I anticipated. Also... the mage is still alive. The one we were supposed to kill before we left America. He and his bride were on the train today. They escaped... again. Our benefactor will not be pleased..."

Hans felt the pressure begin to ease. He did all he could to hide his relief.

"You let ze Hunters escape?" He tried to layer the judgement thick.

"Doctor Schmitt was the priority," White muttered

defensively. "It's not like you were offering to come help."

"Zere's nozing like one of my kind blazing in ze midday sun to interrupt a train heist," Hans quipped.

White chuckled. "Don't worry, Wagner, you'll get your chance. A car bomb didn't manage to end those kids. I can't imagine they have the decency to give up and die after falling from a train. We'll make sure to bring you back a snack next time."

"*Wunderbar,*" Hans commented. "At least viz Schmitt ve may be able to gain ground on ze project. He seems a decent man and an adept occultist. Hopefully he vill be a notable asset."

"What glowing praise," White mocked.

"*Ja,*" Hans replied, ignoring the demon's tone. "Civility is important. Ve are not animals, Herr Vhite."

White grinned viciously. "She's right. You are so German."

"*Nein!*" Hans exclaimed sarcastically. "Vhat gave it avay?!"

White just kept grinning that same grin at him. On another creature it might have been pleasantly handsome. Hans took it to mean the demon liked him, but that wasn't a comforting thought. He was used to being the apex predator of his world. Living in the same building as something that looked at him like food was deeply disturbing.

* * *

When they made it back to the house they felt lucky to

be alive. The river had been freezing. Fred had used her magic to help dry them out and warm them up enough to make it back home. It had taken most of the effort they had left. Some were worse than others. Gio's leg didn't look good. Vincent had been beaten around a bit. Fred was exhausted and had a rough cut on her forehead. Stuart had some serious bruising around his ribs and a bullet hole in his shoulder. Lucy and Tony were doing what they could for them, but it wasn't ideal.

The all crashed in the main room to start patching themselves up. Lucy got the fire lit and brought through dry clothes. Tony started handing out medical supplies. The sun was already sinking down below the horizon. The day felt worse than wasted. It felt like failure.

"It would be great to learn how to mend stuff with magic instead of just destroying it," Tony commented, checking on Gio's leg.

"You're tellin' me," Gio grimaced.

"Magical healing is incredibly rare," Stuart told them, grunting in pain. His face was alarmingly pale as he tried to dig the bullet out of his shoulder. He sat at the table shirtless, with his chest mottling like a midnight blue and purple Monet, and used a long set of tweezers to dig through the bloody hole. "Ugh– but wouldn't it be great if it wasn't."

"Here, stop," Lucy bid him. "Let me help."

"I've got it," he grunted.

"You don't," she disagreed.

His hand was shaking and she could see him losing his grip. They all could.

"Let her help, Owens," Vincent muttered. "God knows you're a masochist, but maybe keep it private."

"Oh, bite me, old man!" Stuart retorted, letting Lucy take over.

"Not interested," Vincent replied. "Besides, I understand you've got someone else to feed that fetish, in return for selling us out."

Lucy chose that moment to push for the bullet. Stuart gave a cry of pain and his face screwed up in agony as she fished the metal pellet out. The entire time she muttered apologies, but he looked like he could barely hear them. She dropped the bloody bullet on the table with a clunk. Stuart turned straight to Vincent, his eyes watering in pain.

"What is that supposed to mean?" he demanded.

"What do you think?" Vincent scorned. "It was a trap! A Goddamn trap, Owens! For us! The only people who knew what we were planning were us and the thing that sent us!"

"He didn't set us up," Stuart insisted.

"You don't know that," Vincent grated.

"I do," Stuart argued. "I know you'd doubt the word of Christ himself, Chancellor, but Hans did not set us up. He wouldn't do that. He's not that kind of person, no matter what you want to believe."

"The problem, Owens, is that I'm not taking anything on faith," Vincent snapped. "You can *believe* whatever you like, but the indisputable facts are that we were sent on a mission that turned out to be a trap, and the only other person that knew about it was your bloodsucking vampire who works for our enemies. I know you're lovelorn to the point of idiocy, but surely even you can see how that looks."

Before Stuart could fight him further the door burst open. Vincent was on his feet, sword in hand, in an instant. Just as quickly, his sword was stabbed forcefully into the wall and he was abruptly shifted.

"*Bewegung*," Hans ordered, physically lifting Vincent and setting him out of the way like he was a child. He was across the room faster than the human eye could follow, kneeling by Stuart's chair, his hands on Stuart's arms and his wide eyes taking in the damage. "*Oh mein Gott, Stuart! Was haben sie dir angetan?!*"

"It's not as bad as it looks," Stuart winced. Hans grabbed his chin and looked him in the eye.

"Lie to me again and I vill fold you up like a paper ball and kick you halfvay to Mexico," Hans warned.

"That's a long way from here," Stuart smiled.

"*Verdammt richtig!*" Hans huffed. His hands cupped his lover's cheeks and he kissed the top of Stuart's damp and ruffled curls. "I vas so vorried..." he sighed. "I had no idea Rogue and Vhite vould be on zat train. Vhen I found zem gone I almost tried to pursue... but..." he looked tortured. "I have never been so terrified as vhen zey returned... I feared ze vorst."

"Why set us up then?" Vincent growled, hauling on his sword. It was stuck fast and he couldn't get it free.

"I did no such zing," Hans replied. "I zought ze plan vas for zem to collect Schmitt from ze station at Koblenz. I zought zey vould get zere and find him dead. It never occurred to me zat zey vould go and meet him partvay zere."

"I'm sorry we didn't get him," Stuart apologized. Hans was touching his face again.

"You have nozing to be sorry for," he breathed. "If I had known Rogue and Vhite vould be on zat train I never vould have asked you to go."

Hans stroked Stuart's cheek lovingly. His eyes dropped to the wound in Stuart's shoulder. His lips followed. The room tensed, neither of them noticed. Hans breathed deeply on the ragged hole. It slowly began to clot and seal. He blew slowly on the cut like it was hot and he was trying to cool it down. The skin began to fuse back together until the hole was nothing but a dark scar.

"Does it hurt?" Hans asked, pressing it gently.

Stuart shook his head. "*Nein*, it's much better. *Danke.*"

Hans gave him a nod and rested his forehead against Stuart's. They stayed like that a moment, willfully oblivious to everyone's eyes on them. Lucy broke the silence.

"You can heal people?" she blurted. She'd been rinsing Stuart's blood off her hands and drying them on a towel.

Hans nodded to her. "*Ja*, vampire breaz has ze strongest healing properties in ze known vorld. It makes sense in some vays, when you zink about it. It is how ve heal vounds after ve drink. Ve do not leave people bleeding out, zat vould be terrible. Somezing happens to ze air vhen ve imbibe it in our lungs. Ze same energy zat keeps us alive – against all forces of nature – combines viz ze air and zen ve breaze it back out and it contains ze same power ve use to regenerate – an instantaneous ability as long as ve have access to fresh blood."

"Can you help heal Fred?" Lucy asked.

Hans gave a willing nod but looked to Fred for her permission. She gave a halfhearted shrug of consent. Hans stood and approached her slowly. The cut on her head was already scabbing over. Hans placed a gentle hand on her hair, lowered his mouth to her forehead, and blew carefully on her cut. It sealed up instantly.

"Oh, you have cold breath," she startled slightly.

"*Es tut mir leid,*" he apologized.

"No, don't be sorry," she waved his apology off. "Thank you. I'm grateful, I just didn't know what to expect." She raised a characteristic sharp eyebrow across the room at Gio. "What are we thinking, Amarti? You want that leg patched up?"

"At this point I'm prepared to try anything," Gio gasped painfully. "If Mister Wagner's up for it."

"Really?" Tony exclaimed. "You'd let him–" He stopped mid-rant, aware of the eyes on him, but the disgust had been evident in his voice.

"Tony, *amico*, one day I'm gonna set you straight on how the world works," Gio sighed. "In the meantime, find me some damn opiates or let the vamp have me."

"If it's all ze same to you, Giovanni, I vill not be 'having' anyzing," Hans told him, appearing at his side. "Your blood is zick and you smoke too much. I vould lay off if I vere you. Zat said, I can spare some breaz if you vant zat leg fixed."

"Please," Gio begged, clutching his leg.

Hans knelt down and inspected the wound through Gio's shredded trouser leg.

"Hm," he mused. "I see you met Vhite. Charming fellow, *ja*?"

"Actually thought he was kinda an asshole," Gio muttered, fishing a cigarette out of his pocket like Hans had just reminded him of them.

"Put zat down!" Hans ordered. "If you light zat zing vhile I'm beside you I vill leave you to bleed."

Gio pulled a very sad face and tapped his cigarette anxiously. Hans breathed deeply across his leg. When he really tried it was like an outside draft pouring straight from his lungs. Gio tried not to squirm, but the effect it had on his leg was almost instant. It took several good puffs to set his flesh right. Then Hans stood and gave him a reluctant shrug, because it was probably going to take some other good puffs to set the rest of him right.

Hans went back to Stuart and eyed up his bruised ribs.

"Zat doesn't look good..." he commented, giving the injuries a gentle prod. "But I don't zink anyzing too serious is injured. Zere doesn't appear to be any internal bleeding."

"No," Stuart agreed. "Nothing's broken or cracked... although I don't know how. That thing moved like you do. He should have broken half my ribs."

"Hm..." Hans mused. "He is extremely dangerous. His skin is not veak to sunlight like mine... but he can't heal like I can. Zat is probably our only saving grace."

He sighed deeply. "*Es tut mir Leid.* I am so sorry... I should never have put you in danger like zat. I truly had no idea..."

"It's okay," Stuart took his hand. "We believe you."

They looked around the room and most eyes fell on Vincent. He still hadn't gotten his sword out and he was glaring at the room like it had mortally offended him.

"Please don't kick me halfway to Mexico..." Stuart whispered.

Hans smiled and kissed his brow, unconcerned about any audience. He left Stuart's side and retrieved the sword from the wall. With a single sharp tug, he yanked it free and handed it back to Vincent.

"Sorry about zat," he offered.

Vincent took the sword, but he didn't look ready to accept the apology. Hans met his eye with all the honesty he could muster, but the look was guarded with mistrust.

"I know you still don't like me," he acknowledged. "Zat is vhat it is, but I really am sorry. I never vanted you or your people to come to any harm. I just vanted Schmitt safely out of ze vay."

"Too late for that now," Vincent glowered. "He's your problem."

"Actually... zere is a chance he is more ze artist of our second chance zan he is a problem..." Hans smiled. "My concerns vere not unfounded, yet he has not your boy's knack for ze magic and runes."

"What are you saying?" Fred asked.

Hans linked his fingers with a cunning smirk. "Zey laid a trap for us... I zink it's time ve lay a trap for zem."

"You have something in mind?" Stuart checked.

Hans nodded. *"Ja,* Schmitt and I had a play viz ze machine *diesen Nachmittag.* I expected him to out my mistakes, but *nein.* Instead, he uncovered ze problem but not ze source. He confirmed zat ze issue ve are facing is ze gravity, but he hasn't corrected my runes. Ze solution ve are discussing is setting up an outdoor test in a secure location avay from ze castle..."

"What secure location?" Vincent growled.

"I am currently scouting for it as ve speak..." Hans smiled. "I told Vhite I vould find us somevhere appropriate. Zere is a small railyard in a valley near here zat I zought ve could use..."

"And you want us to lay a trap?" Tony joined the conversation.

"It is ze best plan I have been able to come up viz," Hans shrugged. "My largest problems vere zat Rogue and Vhite vere too powerful for me alone, and ze machine vas hidden beneaz ze castle. I designed it to destroy itself by bringing ze castle down on it vhen it vas turned on. Alas, it has never been left on long enough for zat."

"That might be a blessing..." Stuart commented.

"Ja stimmt," Hans agreed. "If ve can take out our enemies and zeir device vizout destroying landmarks and endangering the region, zis vould be ze preferred outcome."

"So what do you actually want us to do?" Lucy asked. "Or are we brainstorming the plan now?"

"I am open to ideas," Hans began. "But I vas zinking zat you could take some of ze old var mines you have stored in ze basement, set zem up in ze clear space vhere I vill instruct ze ozers to set up ze machine, and zen detonate zem vhen ze time is right. I am zinking zat vhen zey try and turn ze machine on vould be best. Carnage erupts. Zen ve can set upon zem vhile zey are still trying to vork out vhat vent 'rong."

His plan met silence, save the opinions of the whistling wind and the crackling fire. They seemed supportive.

"I love it," Lucy announced. "Maybe a little biased, but I do like blowing things up. Quick question, how do we set up the mines before you guys come in without having your team set them off during your assembly?"

"Zey vill have to be buried shallow and left inactivated," Hans replied.

"So they work... how...?" Lucy coaxed.

"Your mages vill have to be able to detonate zem vhen ze time is right," Hans admitted.

"That's not impossible..." Fred mused. "Hypothetically we could do that..."

"Easy," Tony folded his arms. "Especially if we set them up in an arcane pattern. You can write a spell around it that means when you set off one the others will join."

"I don't have my books with me to check the best method for that," Fred admitted. "And everything I've found downstairs so far is in German."

"I can do it on the fly," Tony assured her. "Don't know how much good I'll be after ignition, but if it goes right I can just have a short rest in the dirt without anyone biting my face off."

"I'll look after you," Lucy promised. "I'd never let anyone eat that pretty face but me."

Tony's air of disapproval and distrust stuttered at his wife's declaration. He couldn't help himself and cracked a grin, losing the scowl of displeasure and struggling to get it back.

"Then we're settled," Stuart nodded. "We know how we're recovering from today's mishap. Unless anyone has any objections?" His words opened the question to the room, but his eyes were directing it to Vincent.

The old Hunter hadn't come down on the plan at any point, but he didn't look happy about it either. Truth be told, it was a good plan. The only reason to say no to it would be a dislike and distrust of the man who had designed it.

"I like a good fight," Gio quipped. "And I prefer doing it on our terms."

"Agreed," Vincent finally chimed in. His eyes hadn't left Hans. "You designed that machine and you know how to bring it down. We'll be relying on that."

"I vill make sure ze sabotage does not fail," Hans swore. "I have already discussed viz Schmitt zat ve must perform ze tests tomorrow night so zat I can be zere." He shook his head. "Zey zink zey need me, and I vill not have anozer debacle like ze train. You vill have my aid zis time."

"Then I best check the collection of mines and see what we have to work with tomorrow," Vincent sighed.

"We're doing this, Sir?" Fred checked.

"I guess we are," Vincent nodded.

* * *

The moon hung sickly and bright in the dark sky. Everything around it shifted and distorted, as though the stars were drawing nearer. They swirled and twisted, the entities within them bursting to life, hatching from fire and darkness, and drawing ever closer.

Vincent stood at the edge of the circle and watched. Pillars stood either side of him. A circle of stone ran atop the pillars around the altar and shaded his face. The pillars went all the way around, with figures standing between each of them. His brethren. They watched the center. It was different, but the same. The great tree. It was dark and cold and shadowy. A sacrifice was brought forth and dumped at the foot of the tree. Something small and weak and wounded.

A girl. She struggled up, whimpering in agony. Lucy.

Vincent felt something shift inside him. A desperate, powerful horror. She couldn't get away, and he couldn't move. Something dark snaked out of the tree. A large shadowy tendril. As it reached for her, a large, fanged mouth opened at the end.

Lucy struggled harder, weeping with terror and the effort of pulling her mangled body across the polished stone ground. The mouth snatched one of her legs and bit down. She screamed. Her bloodcurdling scream of pain ripped through the air. The fangs pierced her flesh, her bones. It began to eat her alive.

Vincent fought against his binding. His body would

not move. It refused to move. Lucy kept screaming as the tree continued to bite, tearing her apart. Blood splattered across the ground, dripping from the tendril's teeth, dripping from Lucy's mauled body. Her legs were gone. She dragged her butchered torso inches across the ground. Still screaming and weeping.

Vincent felt a shift. He poured all of his soul into making his body move. It couldn't end like this. Cold fingers closed around his throat, grasping him by the jaw. That deep smooth voice whispered in his ear.

"No, no, my love, you just get to watch."

The tree was eating Lucy's body. It had made it to her lungs by now, but still she screamed, fresh and raw, as though the sound of her pain came from somewhere more profound than her eviscerated flesh. The Prince held Vincent fast and made him watch. He could feel himself struggling as though encased in stone. There was nothing to be done now. It was much too late. That didn't stop him from fighting. When the Darkness ate her head she finally stopped screaming. There was nothing left of his little girl but the dark ocean of blood smeared across the ground.

The Prince began to laugh in his ear. The pleasure was so real, so utterly delighted. Vincent ripped himself free with an apocalyptic fire. He could feel the flames inside him, consuming him. A rage and terror and grief so strong that he would end his captor and take the world with him. There was nothing left to save anyway.

Vincent tore himself from the arms of the Prince, and lurched from his blankets. He was awake, in his bed in the farmhouse in Germany. His heart was pounding.

He felt sick. His face was wet and he didn't know if it was tears or sweat. He wanted to puke. His whole body was shaking, shivering. The bruises from the train fight ached.

He gulped air and still didn't feel calm. He couldn't sleep. He knew he needed to. They were supposed to be setting a trap in the morning. It didn't feel that late, but there was no way he could lie down and close his eyes again.

They were losing, even with Stuart's supposed spy helping them out. If Rogue and White worked out what was wrong with their machine and turned it on, it was game over. Vincent was exhausted. His bones were tired. They creaked. He was old. His prime was so far behind him he couldn't remember exactly when it had been. Everything had always been a struggle. He needed a way to make it easier. He needed to know what he was up against instead of floundering along like they had been these past few years.

Something glinted sharply in his recent memory. Something he had seen just before he went to bed. Something he had tried to actively ignore.

There had been bottles in the basement. He had noticed them when he had been going through the weapons. He had recognized the bottles and the liquid within. He had also made a point of turning away from them. But perhaps that had been the wrong call. Perhaps that was what had been missing this whole time.

He climbed from his bed and stalked down the hall.

* * *

The room was too small to warrant its little wood stove and with the door shut the space became hot very quickly. Its occupants did not mind. The sweltering heat had caused the ice on the window to melt, and the glow from the coals gave the room an atmospheric light. A simple single bed was tucked into the corner of the room. It wasn't designed to fit two, but they made it work.

Hans and Stuart lay tangled in the sheets, pressed together. Stuart lay on his side, half asleep, while Hans held him close. The vampire had his arms tucked around his lover, pulling him back against him. His lips rested in the crook of Stuart's shoulder, warm against his skin. He could feel the heat radiating off him and the pulse of his blood like a heartbeat everywhere they touched. He traced his fingers gently against Stuart's ribs where he'd been feeding off his bruises, trying to help heal them. He kissed his neck again softly.

"You have to go…" Stuart murmured sleepily.

"*Ich liebe dich so sehr,*" Hans whispered.

"But you still have to go," Stuart sighed. "That's what you were about to say, wasn't it? I think I can tell when you're about to leave."

Hans kissed him again apologetically. "*Ja,* I do."

Stuart rolled over in his arms, turning to kiss him and slipping his hands around Hans' face. He hooked a leg over Hans' body, futilely pinning him in place.

"*Bitte bleibe.*" Stuart begged Hans to stay in his lover's native language.

"You said zat twenty minutes ago," Hans reminded.

Stuart pressed himself heavily against Hans, half straddling him and using his weight to pin him between the wall and the small bed. He opened his lips against his, sliding his hot wet tongue into Hans' cold mouth. Stuart kissed him, pressing him down into the bed like he actually had the strength to make him stay. Hans kissed him back longingly, tasting him warm and sticky. Stuart drew his lips back with a hot breath that tingled across Hans' tongue.

"You could stay another twenty minutes," he suggested, starting to kiss down Hans' jawline.

"If you keep convincing me to stay, dawn vill rise, I vill have been gone too long to explain my absence, and you von't have slept all night…" Hans warned.

"I can think of worse things…" Stuart whispered into his ear.

Hans smiled and tightened his grip on Stuart's body, thrusting against him, listening for the small catch in his breath that came when he pushed for it. That tiny shiver of longing in his throat, and the quiet way he moaned in pleasure when Hans got rough with him. Stuart kissed the corner of his jaw, sucking on him and dragging his teeth across his skin. Hans rubbed himself between Stuart's legs, feeling Stuart's heart race faster and his blood pound. He turned his face back to his lover, nuzzling him. He licked the sweat running down Stuart's neck.

Stuart was panting and it made Hans hungry for him. A different kind of hunger than the one he'd felt around other humans. An intimate lustful hunger. The scent of Stuart's body filled his nose. He could almost taste the blood already. His mouth itched. He wanted to bite him. He wanted to push himself inside Stuart's hot tight body and ride him hard and fast, the way that made Stuart cry for him. The way that made Stuart beg him not to stop before his breath was broken into short shallow gasps and he couldn't form words. The best he could manage was the occasional '*schwerer*' that made Hans worry he'd break him. Stuart made love like he wanted to get his bones shattered. Hans had to be careful he didn't oblige. His beautiful human was so fragile, but so fierce. Hans could feel his fangs extending. Stuart moaned longingly, grinding himself against him.

Hans stopped. His fangs retracted. He tipped Stuart onto the mattress as he climbed from the bed.

"Hans–?" Stuart gasped in confusion.

"Somezing is 'rong," Hans answered. "Vait here." He reached a hand back to bid Stuart to stay, stroking down the inside of his thigh. Then he flickered away. In seconds he was half dressed. It took less time than Stuart blinking himself back into reality. Hans was out the door. He strode down the corridor in absolute silence. His bare feet and soft steps made no sound. He'd been able to smell it from the bedroom. The Hunter didn't even realize he was there until it was too late.

Vincent was sitting at the kitchen table. He had folded away all the papers and set out candles. There was a rough chalk pattern around them. An open glass bottle was set on the table with a cup beside it. Vincent poured a shot from the bottle into the cup. Anyone watching might have thought the old man was drinking spirits. In a way he was. Hans was at the table in a flash. He set his hand on top of the cup before Vincent could lift it. The Hunter froze.

"Don't do zis, Chancellor," Hans bid him.

Vincent looked up at him. The vampire loomed over him like a statue. His white shirt was unbuttoned over deathly pale skin and dark trousers. He almost seemed to hover as he stared down, unblinking, with eyes full of warning.

Vincent's face twisted into a snarl at the sight of him. He lunged. Hans shoved him back into his chair with one hand. Vincent snatched for the cup. Hans tossed the contents over the smoldering remains of the fire. It flared into life. The old Hunter yelled in fury, drawing his pistol. Hans smacked it out of his hand. Vincent leapt at him. Hans felt the old man catch him around the waist, but no human had the strength to bring him down. He grabbed Vincent and forced him to his knees, twisting his arm behind his back.

"Let me go!" Vincent roared.

Doors were banging and lights were coming on. Vincent struggled against Hans, bumping the table and knocking over one of the candles. It tipped and went out, drowning its flame with wax as it spilt all over the chalk circle. Hans stood fast and unrelenting. He held Vincent tightly and wouldn't budge an inch, no matter how hard Vincent fought him.

"Stop it, Chancellor," he bid gently.

"Let go!" Vincent screamed.

"You know I can't do zat," Hans sighed. "I need you to calm down."

"Calm?! I am calm, you beast!" Vincent raged. "Let go of me, you monster! You'll kill us all!"

"I am trying to save you, Chancellor," Hans replied, his voice tinged with tragic pity. "Your blood is already so toxic. Zis could kill you if you drank it."

The others were gathering in the hallway. Owens had thrown on a dressing gown. Fred and Lucy were piling in behind him in their pajamas, and Gio was sneaking up at the back. They stared at the sight before them. Hans stood patiently, holding Vincent down as he struggled like a man possessed. Vincent hissed and spat and cursed, almost frothing in fury.

"I am sorry, Chancellor, but zis is for your own good," Hans insisted. "Ve cannot afford to have you die on us, or vorse. I know it is hard. I know ze struggle of compulsion, but zis is not going to make anyzing better."

"What the hell is going on?" Fred demanded.

"This thing is trying to kill me!" Vincent screamed. "Get it off!"

"I found him trying to drink ze Gatevay poison," Hans sighed. "Ze toxin of ze ozer vorld. It is too dangerous. Even if zat place vasn't deadly alone, he is still too sick from a lifetime of abuse to guarantee ze poison itself vould not kill him."

"I need it!" Vincent cried. "I have to know! We need it to find out what's happening! We'll all die if I don't!"

"Oh Vincent..." Lucy lamented, pushing through and approaching them.

"Lucy!" he cried. "Kill it! Kill it and I can find out what Rogue and White are really up to! We can stop them!"

Lucy kicked Vincent's pistol further away and knelt in front of him, taking his face in her hands.

"I'm not going to kill him, Vincent," she sighed. "You promised you'd stopped."

"Addiction doesn't work like that," Stuart commented softly from the doorway.

Fred strode into the room like the queen of Hell and picked up the bottle from the table. They all saw her go.

"Fred..." Vincent pleaded.

She walked to the fireplace and held the bottle out.

"No!" Vincent implored. "Fred! No! No! Don't! Please don't! Fred! FRED! STOP!" He yelled at her as she slowly tipped the liquid into the fire. It flared up like she'd just upended a bottle of whiskey over it.

Hans could see the tears in her eyes as she resolutely stared away from them. He could see the pained set of her mouth and the infinite exhaustion in her face, like this wasn't the first time she'd done this. Vincent was becoming limp in his hands. The old Hunter had lost, and he knew it, he was giving up the fight.

"Sorry Vincent," Lucy sighed at him. "But they're right. You know they're right."

"You've doomed us all..." he muttered. It was quiet and slurred. Hans didn't know if anyone else had heard it. He let Vincent go and the old man slumped on the floor.

"I am sorry," he repeated.

"Don't be," Fred told him coolly, unable to keep the

anger from her voice even though none of it was directed at him.

Hans stood there awkwardly. He knew he'd done the right thing, but it didn't feel good. The only consolation was knowing that it would have been worse if he hadn't, if someone else had found Vincent dead and poisoned in the morning. At least this was something the rest of them could pull back from. However, something still didn't feel right. He'd stopped the old man from drinking the tonic. It had all been destroyed. Why did it still feel like the Dreamlands were pushing through?

Stuart approached him, linking his hands around his waist and holding him close. Hans placed a warning hand between them, half holding Stuart back. He could sense something else. It wasn't over. Everyone was tense, even the cat. Hans had seen the fluffy little creature slink into the room. Tobias had his tail puffed up. His fur stood on end and he bared his teeth at the front door, hissing.

Hans turned his head, his heightened senses identifying the real source of the cat's contempt.

"Vhat is happening in ze barn?" he demanded.

13

Beneath the ghostly moon of the nightmare sky, the center called. Tony recognized it with a familiarity beyond home. He knew this place better than anywhere in the real world. He had been living here for years now. In all his dreams, waking and not, part of his soul always resided in the center.

A ring of pillars rose up in a circle around the altar. Tony saw figures standing between the pillars. The seven guardians. They served the Prince. They ruled the Dreamland. They were children of the Darkness. Tony couldn't see their faces. Just their silhouettes between the pillars. The circle that ran atop the pillars cast those beneath in shadow. Everything in his body told him not to look. Every fiber screamed at him to look away.

He looked closer. Tony stepped forward, approaching and seeking. He peered into the Darkness. He saw their faces. He stared them down and they stared back. His eyes met theirs and he committed each unique face to memory. They didn't smile. Their expressions were neutral as someone finally saw them as they had seen others. There was no terror, no madness, only truth. Tony accepted this. So did the seven.

Finally, he turned to the center. Inside the center grew the altar. The giant tree of flesh. Skin and muscle and tendon twisted and throbbed and pulsed together, growing and stretching up like a trunk, and then branching out in thick, ropy tendrils. Roots had cracked through the stone that had otherwise been polished smooth within the circle.

Tony stared at it numbly. He remembered all his interactions with the altar. He remembered the first time he had encountered it. He remembered the pain and horror. He remembered the feeling worse than death. So much worse than death. The altar was a mark of recycled pain and existence so visceral it withered the soul. Tony stared. He felt nothing.

"You have returned," the tree spoke in a thousand voices.

"I have," he replied.

"You always would," the voices intoned. "You always must. You belong to us. You are ours."

"No," Tony disagreed. "Maybe once you had claim... but you don't anymore."

"That is not possible. It was made. It was done. You belong here."

"I always feared that," Tony nodded. "I don't fear it now. You'd be surprised what's possible."

"You returned once. You will return again. You will always return."

"I don't think that's the victory for you that you seem to think it is," Tony smiled.

"You... think..." the tree intoned.

"Yeah," Tony nodded. "The notion would shock my

cousin, but I think. I'm a singularity. I have thoughts."

"You are part of the we," the tree insisted.

"So is everything," Tony shrugged. "Every 'I' is part of some 'we'. I'm sure there's a fancier way to say that. Lucy would know, or Miss Winifred, or the Doc. I think I get my point across just fine." Every time Tony referred to himself in first person the tree flinched. "I just wanted to come and see you again. I needed to know how it works. I get it now. I'm better at working things out if I can see them. My wife made me promise never to go somewhere I couldn't come back from. I needed to be certain I could make good on that promise. I needed to know what I was doing wrong. Now I can fix it."

Tony was aware of people beside him. The seven had left their posts. They had entered the circle and they stood with him in a ring around the tree. Tony looked either side to his strange brethren and gave them each a nod. They were not alone. Tony turned to look at the Prince as the Lord of the Realm joined them. Tony glared at him; the Prince, dark and faceless and shadowy, grinned back. Tony wondered how it was possible to know the Prince was grinning, but he was, and Tony knew it.

"I should have known you'd be here," he glowered.

"You did," the Prince smiled.

Tony glared. He tried to outstare the Prince's smirk. The smirk faltered. For a moment Tony caught a glimpse of his reflection in the Prince's face. He saw his own eyes. He saw exactly what was bothering the Prince. Suddenly, their expressions were reversed. Now

Tony was the one grinning, and the Prince's blank face turned sour.

"I'm coming for you," he warned.

"Not if I come for you first," the Prince threatened. In a flash, his frown flew upside down. Manic glee stained his face as he lunged at Tony, arms outstretched.

* * *

Something was flickering in the barn. Once Hans pointed it out they could all see it out the window.

"Where's Tony?!" Gio demanded.

"In the bathroom..." Lucy answered. The tiniest hint of terrified doubt tinged her voice.

"Na, he ain't," Gio shook his head, grabbing a shotgun from inside his bedroom door. He threw on a coat and boots and ran out into the snow. Everyone followed suit.

They were too late. The door to the barn stood open, and an electrical storm flickered inside. Dark clouds roiled in the center, punctuated by golden lightning. They all recognized Tony's magic, or what had become of it. Something was pulling itself from the center. Something made of shadow and darkness. Thick ropy tendrils shot out, grabbing the edges of the barn, snapping the icicles from the guttering, clutching at the snowy ground. They pulled and heaved and oozed as something tall and straight with branches and roots of pure black hunger hauled itself into the world.

"TONY!" Lucy screamed for him. There was no sign

of her husband.

Gio ran forward, face as grim as death, and blasted the massive entity straight down the middle. He braced himself and served it both barrels. The holy bullets scattered shrapnel across the twisted trunk. It looked like golden fireworks in the darkness. The thing didn't flinch or slow. It took the injuries without note and lashed out. A thick dark branch swept across the snow. It smacked Gio like a slingshot. He went flying.

Lucy drew her pistol from her coat pocket. She moved closer to fire. Vincent rushed forward and caught her around the waist.

"No!" he grunted, pulling her out of the way.

"Let go!" Lucy cried.

"Can't," Vincent muttered. "Gotta get you safe."

She struggled against him as he hauled her back towards the house.

Fred's hands were glowing red, but her magic was struggling to take hold. The thing seemed to feed off it. She swapped to her handgun, and stood shoulder to shoulder with Stuart as they clustered their shots. Each golden bullet sparked as it hit the trunk, ripping and exploding through the darkness. Even it the dim light they could see that the thick ropy texture of tree grew back where it was wounded, sprouting new flesh to replace the old.

It was hard for some eyes to see. One pair could see everything. He could even see the arcane circle still burning gold on the floor of the barn. A branch lashed out at Fred and Stuart. They flinched. Hans caught it. They hadn't seen him move, but he was suddenly ahead of them. Both pale hands gripped the writhing dark appendage.

"Get back," he warned them coldly.

Stuart grabbed Fred by the arm and pulled her away. He knew that tone of voice. For most of them it was hard to follow what happened next. It occurred faster than human eyes could process. One second Hans had been holding the monstrosity back. The next it was coming apart in pieces. Branches tore and snapped and ripped from the trunk. They fell thrashing to the ground and dissolved in the snow. It whipped and flailed, crashing into the barn as it tried to dislodge its attacker. Hans took no pity. He ripped it apart with his bare hands. He moved faster than it did. He was stronger than it was. Pieces of evil tree flew into the night like he was chopping firewood.

It caught him. A matter of unfortunate coincidence. He had stepped quickly across its sticky body, and a tendril had snared his ankle. It snatched him and smashed him into the ground. The icy earth cracked beneath him. A small crater. Enough force to kill a human. He'd certainly felt it. He grabbed the branch and ripped it, but the roots were already swarming him. They bound his arms and drove him under. He struggled against them.

"Take this!" Gio yelled.

The boy was back on his feet and running in fast. He threw a clear bottle and splattered the tree. It recoiled as the holy water smoked and hissed across it. Hans ripped free, wincing as the water splashed his hand. He clutched it to him reactively, smoke sizzling from his skin.

"Oops," Gio muttered so quietly only Hans heard it.

"Hans!" Stuart called.

The vampire turned. One of Stuart's daggers flew end over end towards him. Hans snatched it out of the air. He leapt towards the tree, stabbing it in the center and yanking the blade sideways. The whole tree shivered as he split the trunk. He slipped his hands into the wound and tore. His arms strained. Tendons stood out on his hands. The sleeves of his shirt pulled against his muscles. The tree split further. Dark sap sprayed out in a mist across him. It was trying to grow back as fast as he ripped it. He could feel the veins of it worming around his wrists, trying to patch the wound with his hands inside it. He tightened his grip and pulled. The tree tore in half.

The crack split the air like cannon fire. Hans flickered. The next bottle Gio had been holding ready vanished from his hands. Hans stood over the halves of the monster and pulled out the cork. He poured the water very deliberately through the center of the tree. It shivered and writhed. The vines stopped trying to grow back. It withered helplessly.

"Alcohol!" Hans called sharply.

Gio ran over to him and handed over his hipflask obediently. Hans upended that over the remains too. He handed it back and Gio was already holding out his matches. Hans flicked one into life and dropped it to light the tree. It caught instantly. The writhing sped up for a few seconds and then faded. The darkness began to melt. Hans stood over the husk of the dark tree. He carefully watched it burn, making sure nothing escaped into the night. Whatever that danger had been, it was over. He lifted his eyes to the barn.

The storm was gone, but the arcane circle was burnt permanently into the ground. Tony staggered from the barn. He looked like he could barely walk.

"Tony!" Lucy called to him. She still hadn't managed to get free of her mentor, who was trying to haul her over his shoulder.

"Tony, what in God's name–" Fred joined in, hurrying towards him.

Gio got there first, and he was cursing in Italian.

"*Porca puttana!* Antony, *cazzone! Sei fuori!* Why I oughtta–!" He smacked his cousin in the side of the head.

Tony stumbled, but he looked like someone who was used to getting hit by his family. Fred reached them and waved Gio down. Her expression stated violence wasn't the answer. Hans followed behind them and he wasn't so sure. His bare feet crunched through the snow as he walked slowly to the downtrodden kid. He stood over him, looking down severely. The only one whose breath didn't steam the air. No one else had noticed what the boy was carrying. He looked up at Hans, and thrust the singed papers into his hands.

"There," he stated roughly. "I'm done. Now you can burn them."

Hans held the scorched remnants of the book he had tried to destroy. It was too late now. The kid had already used them to achieve his ends. Hans looked down on the remains of the thing that had crawled through him into this world. He thought of all the things he knew about Hunters. He thought what might have happened if he hadn't stayed, if he hadn't been here.

"Zis is vhat I'm risking my life for…?" he asked numbly, discarding the pages into the flaming tree and letting them burn together. "I have been fighting zis battle since long before you got here. I have been holding off ze Darkness alone, vaiting… praying… for Hunters to show up and help me save ze vorld. Zis is vhat I get? I have set in motion a plan to take out two of ze most dangerous people I have ever met, trusting zat you lot vill do your part. Now I am forced to vonder! Stuart, how did you fall in viz zese people? How am I supposed to trust zat zis vill vork?! Look at you all! Anyone capable of action is rendered inept caring for an addict and a dark sorcerer! You are… vhat is your American vord…? Fucked. You are fucked. Zis is a disaster. I vould not trust you to make yourselves breakfast, let alone take down Rogue and Vhite."

"Hans…" Stuart appeared at his side and placed a calming hand on his bare chest. His fingers were starting to go cold but his hand was still warm.

"I'm sorry, Stuart, but I just…"

"It's been a bad night," Stuart conceded. "But when I promise that we can do this, I mean it."

Hans placed his hands on Stuart's cheeks and looked him in the eye.

"I believe zat you zink zat," he sighed. "But I am vorried."

"You have every right to be," Fred agreed coolly. She

had Tony by the collar and she was dragging him back. She touched Hans' shoulder with her free hand. "You're not wrong. This is an utter clusterfuck – another American term you might like. Believe me, I will deal to these two. Stuart isn't wrong. We can do this."

"You said you veren't sure about ze magic," Hans reminded. "Ze one zat said he could do it just summoned a dark entity!"

"It was a shadow," Tony retorted. "I did it making sure I had the magic to execute your plan!"

"If you didn't have ze pover you should have said!" Hans yelled. "I do not intend to consort viz vorlocks! Look at zat zing! Look at ze danger you just put your family in!"

"The danger he put our family in?!" Vincent snapped, joining the fight. "You don't want to throw that stone, vampire."

"I'm standing by ze vreckage of somezing zat disagrees…" Hans warned.

"They're Hunters!" Tony cried. "Killing things like this is what they do! It was barely a danger, and better a small fragment like this now than floundering in the unknown until we hit the real thing!"

"Zis is vhat you call barely a danger?!"

"Is anyone hurt?!" Tony yelled. "Seriously, did anyone get injured? Vincent is right! Your assassination plan came closer to killing us than that mere reflection did, and it turns out you didn't even need us to do it!"

"He was trying to help!" Stuart argued. "He's the one on the inside helping us find out what's going on! We were trying to eliminate the risk!"

"You don't want to throw your hat in this ring, Owens," Vincent warned. "He could be biting us and you'd still be sticking up for him."

"*Va te faire foutre!* You have no ground to stand on right now, Chancellor! He just saved your life twice in ten minutes!"

"I didn't need saving!" Vincent roared.

"ENOUGH!" The bellow shattered the argument. It silenced everyone and brought a still and somber icy rattle to the night. They all looked to the girl who had made the sound. Lucy stood grounded, heavy boots splayed in the snow. She had her thick woolen coat on over her nightdress. Her curls were escaping her ponytail and springing around her face. Her pistol still sat in her hand like she was on the brink of a duel. Her breath clouded the air in angry gasps. None of them had ever seen her so furious.

Vincent opened his mouth but Lucy glared at him so sharply they worried she might shoot him.

"Shut it!" she warned. Her eyes rolled over all of them and none of them dared speak. "Tomorrow," she began very slowly and softly, forcing them to listen, "I will go to the railyard and set up those mines. I will take anyone I think might be able to help. We will meet Hans tomorrow night and make sure his plan works. We are not going to fight each other. We're here to remove Rogue and White and any danger they pose. If anyone tries to start anything else tonight, I'm finishing it."

"Luce–" Tony started. She ignored him and cut him off.

"Stuart," she turned to him. "Take Hans inside and

get him cleaned up. Gio, please take Vincent back to bed and get him to stay there. Fred, can I get a hand with your apprentice?"

Fred nodded. A cold sick tension settled over them all at Lucy's choice of language. They traipsed slowly back inside, Lucy waving them all in with her pistol. No one said anything until they were back in the house. She shut the door with an imposing slam. The main room crowded as everyone paused, torn between doing as she said and wondering if there was anything they could say to settle the atmosphere. They didn't need to. Someone else had an opinion.

Tobias gave a curious chirp from the corridor. He padded over, winding between Hans and Stuart, and blinking at the room. He meowed at them. No one wanted to lose their temper at the small fluffy creature, but tensions were running high. He responded to it in a typically feline manner. He gave a big yawn and a stretch, extending his front legs then back, standing tall, fluffing his tail, and then strutting over to bunt Tony's ankles.

"Hey little guy," Tony sighed, bending over to scritch his chin. "You're not normally this friendly."

"Not to you..." Fred agreed.

They all watched. Tobias nuzzled Tony and purred. He'd never done that before. Tony looked... healthy. More so than he had the entire time they'd been in Germany. More so than he had in a long time. The shadows were gone from around his eyes, and some of the color had come back to his cheeks. He stayed crouched, smiling at the cat as he tickled its chin. Tobias hadn't shown him affection before. He'd always hissed at Tony until now. Now, the little fluffy beast was rolling on his shoes, looking to get his belly rubbed.

"Tony..." Fred said softly. "What were you doing in the barn?"

He looked up at her, hand absentmindedly fluffing Toby's tummy. When he blinked there was a clarity to his eyes that had been missing for years.

"I was getting rid of the ghosts," he answered.

Stuart and Hans looked confused. Everyone else looked quietly awed. Lucy and Fred shared a glance like they wondered if it was even possible. There was no evidence to prove it wasn't. Tobias was certainly writing him a clean bill of health. The cat rubbed his cheek on Tony's shoelaces.

"I think he likes me now I don't got demons," Tony grinned.

"Good," Lucy nodded. "He can share the couch with you."

Tony's smile faltered, but he didn't fight her. She didn't give him a chance to. She turned on her heel and stalked back to her bedroom. No one knew what to say. Hans and Stuart were the next to follow, and Fred was right behind them. Vincent and Gio were the last to go. Gio got some blankets and a spare pillow from a linen closet and brought them back to his cousin.

"*Grazie amico,*" Tony thanked him.

"*Figurati,*" Gio shrugged at him. He paused, giving Tony an extended sidelong glance. "You really did it? You really got rid of your ghosts?"

Tony nodded. "Looks like it."

Gio shook his head impatiently. "Why didn't you wake us? Why didn't you warn us or ask us for help? Why didn't you tell us?"

"You never woulda believed me," Tony shrugged. "Any one of you saw me with bits of that burnt book, you woulda assumed the worst."

Gio sighed and scratched his head. "Your old lady is sore as a drunken sailor in a bar fight."

"That's my problem," Tony told him. "I'll fix it."

"Guess it's a tomorrow problem too," Gio gave him a wry smile. "I'm glad you're doing well."

"*Grazie,*" Tony smiled. He tossed the bedding on the couch and kicked off his shoes as Tobias tried to claim the pillow. Tony ignored the cat and waved Gio off. "Come on, if we're all going to spend the night staring at the ceiling and contemplating our failures we might as well get started."

* * *

When Hans got back to the castle he went straight to the basement. He'd cleaned himself up at the house and Stuart had lent him a shirt without dark stains on it. They weren't sure it was blood, maybe evil sap, but whatever it was it was going to take some experimenting to remove. The loaned shirt smelt like Stuart and Hans felt warm wrapped up in it. It was the only part of him that felt warm. Outside was cold. He was cold. He was full of fear. It had settled in his gut like bad blood his body couldn't process.

He kept his coat pulled tightly around him. The

room he was going to was kept quite warm, but that wasn't any immediate help. It took him a while to warm up anywhere. He reached the door and entered quietly. The room was dark. He could see just fine. It was a simple bedroom with a large bed and closet. An elegant writing desk and bookshelf covered one wall. Someone lay asleep in the bed. Hans moved silently so as not to wake them. He snuck to the wardrobe and quickly changed shirts.

His heart ached with reluctance, but if he could smell his love on his clothing then so could the demon. There was no point taking more unnecessary risks. He was already risking it all on Stuart's people. He wanted to trust them, he wanted so badly to trust them and believe Stuart was safe with them, that the world would be safe, but they were such a useless mess. It was infuriating.

The spark of despair and irritation caused him to shut the wardrobe door a little too hard. The figure in the bed started.

"*Hans?*" a soft voice came out of the darkness.

"*Sorry Greta. I'm just changing. Go back to sleep,*" he apologized in German.

"*Do you need anything?*" she asked, also in their native language.

"*No, I'm done. I need to get back to work. I will return in the morning.*"

She gave a sleepy noise of acceptance and buried her face back in the pillow. Hans watched her a moment. He thought about telling her about the plan, about letting her know that he was putting things in motion to free them, but he didn't want to risk it. He had promised he would get her out of here. It was the first thing he had promised her, in return for her silence. Although, her silence frequently involved a lot of screaming. He smiled.

He left her to sleep and remembered to close the door silently, before heading down to the caves beneath the castle. When he had been given the kidnapped young lady as a gift he had struggled to hide his distaste. It was Count Beck all over again. He was fairly sure most people had expected him to kill her, but he liked to argue there was no point destroying the buffet if it refilled itself. People seemed to buy it. As far as they were aware he had a toy he was happy with.

In reality he had a deal. He would work on a plan to destroy their captors and the machine and find a way to get her home, and in return she would keep that secret and feed him as required. A grin tugged his lips as he thought of Greta and the dramatic way she had declared, upon their pact, that she was going to be an actress. He was now her coach. Screams of horror were required to sell the illusion to Rogue and White. Sometimes he felt she required direction when she wasn't quite conveying the expected anguish. Many an early morning had been spent, after a quick snack from her wrist, patiently reading the newspaper while she shrieked and destroyed furniture on behalf of them both.

"Having fun, Wagner?" a voice purred in his ear.

Hans didn't startle. He never startled. But he was prepared to admit he hadn't been expecting it. He hadn't realized White was hiding in the tunnels. The rough rock passages were poorly lit and his mind had been on other things. He cursed himself silently. He couldn't afford to be this clumsy.

"I don't often see you with a cute smile on your face," White continued at his ear.

The smile was already gone. It had vanished as soon as White had appeared. Hans didn't slow his pace, but the demon kept up easily, hovering at his shoulder.

"I found ze perfect place to run tomorrow night's test," Hans answered coolly, stepping out into the cavern they used as a workroom. "It is private and secluded, but still appropriately open. I zink it shall vork nicely."

"Nearby?" Rogue called out, her voice echoing through the rocky chamber.

"*Ja*, close enough," he called back.

The cavern was a massive space beneath the castle that had been rigged with lights and cables. Multiple tunnels from above led down to the jagged terraced floor. The edges of the room had been set up with huge generators and conduits to feed their masterpiece in the center. Giant circles of steel, six meters high and etched with arcane runes, fitted together and crisscrossed each other like a gateway. Rogue was sitting on a crate nearby carefully reapplying her lipstick with the aid of a pocket mirror. Doctor Schmitt was at one of the machines hooked up to the apparatus, reading a feedback report from the device.

Hans stepped down into the center, near the machine, and straightened his cuffs patiently, waiting for permission to continue. White followed at his shoulder. He stopped even closer. Hans could feel the demon sniffing at him.

"Dame Rogue," he called disapprovingly. "Heel your *Köter*."

"Aw... but he likes you," she teased.

Hans did not look impressed.

Rogue chuckled and clipped her mirror shut. "Ezra, darling, come here. I think our precious Hans might be a cat person."

"It shows," White grinned, slinking past him.

"*Herr Wagner*," Schmitt called to him without looking up from the report. "Come look at zis."

Hans flickered across the room to his side. No one in present company looked impressed with his pace. Schmitt was going back through old reports Hans had written. None of it was new to him. It was all in German and he switched languages to speak with the Doctor. He reached Schmitt and stated as politely as he could that he would need his help disassembling and packing the machine before morning.

"*Yes, but look at this,*" Schmitt agreed in German. "*This is talking about the gravity issues – seemingly unavoidable when trying to connect multiple worlds with this much energy – and it discusses the possibility of time dilation.*"

"*Yes, that's a real possibility,*" Hans nodded.

"*I won't lie, Herr Wagner, gravitational effects are not my area of expertise.*"

"*That's what I'm here for,*" Hans shrugged. "*Although, my education was not as formal as yours.*"

"*If we turn this thing on tomorrow night and the world*

jumps a month ahead of us while Germany seemingly freezes, we will have big problems," Schmitt warned.

"Don't worry," Hans consoled him. *"The generated field will not be large enough to encompass the entire country. Possibly just the valley, worst case scenario maybe a couple of neighboring towns."*

Schmitt laughed. *"Oh well, that's fine then. If we disappear for a month the wrath of the Chancellor will pale in comparison to my wife's fury."*

Hans glanced at Schmitt's wedding band. *"Where is she?"*

"Back home in Munich."

"Children?"

"Two," Doctor Schmitt smiled. *"Boys. One nearly four, the other eighteen months."*

"You miss them?" Hans asked softly, thinking about his plan and making some snap decisions.

"Very much, but we must do the good work, must we not?" Schmitt queried with his earnest and friendly expression.

"What are you two jabbering about?" Rogue called.

"Time dilation," Schmitt called to them in English. *"Herr Wagner* here vas asking about my Alida and ze boys."

Rogue arched an eyebrow. "You? Making small talk?" she commented.

White looked like he was about to be handed a treat. His body swiveled and began to tense beneath his suit like he was ready to pounce. Hans ignored them both.

"You seem surprised," Schmitt grinned at them, folding away the report. "He has a perfectly varm collegial disposition."

White grinned like he'd forgotten he didn't have fangs in this form. Rogue's eyebrow didn't lower.

"You've met him, right?" she checked. "Warm isn't how I'd describe him."

"Nonsense," Schmitt chuckled. "Look at him, he is a man of extreme depz. Zose are ze eyes of someone who has been in love."

Rogue and White both laughed. Hans didn't. He continued ignoring them all as best he could and got to work. He stepped down to the machine and slowly began unscrewing it by hand. The laughter slowly subsided, and he didn't like the way it dropped off. It felt like Schmitt was giving them a look behind his back.

"Hans...?" Rogue's voice called coyly.

"Vhat?" he replied.

"Oh, this is too good..." White purred.

Hans could feel his chest tightening. If that evil creature came sniffing him again right now he would rip it to pieces, and damn whatever it managed to do to him in return. He focused his super-human strength and gently twisted a large section of metal ring apart.

"Vhat happened?" Schmitt asked. There was genuine concern there. The strange man actually cared. Hans could hear his heart flutter sympathetically. He wondered if Schmitt would be so sympathetic if he knew the truth. He wondered if anyone would. It was a good thing his own heart didn't beat, otherwise it would have betrayed him utterly. They'd brought it up, and the scent of Stuart was still on his skin even though he'd discarded the shirt. His beautiful Hunter was all he could think about. He could feel his jaw tighten, but no one else was filling the silence. He was going to have to, and his mind was empty of everything but the truth.

"Hunters," he answered finally and curtly. "Hunters vere vhat happened."

Schmitt's sympathy deepened. Even Rogue and White shared a curious look. The answer gave their imaginations plenty of space to fill in the blanks. Some of it probably wasn't even wrong.

14

Nobody felt better in the morning. Weary tension hung over everyone. The sky was thick and grey and the light was weak. Tony had sketched out a plan for how to lay out the mines and write the spell around them. He looked tired, but his eyes were brighter and clearer than they'd ever been, and Tobias still seemed fond of him. Lucy agreed to take him with her, but the cold shoulder between them was visible to all. She also agreed to take Gio and Owens. Vincent wasn't coming, and no one was prepared to leave him alone, so Fred was staying to watch him. They agreed to talk to Oskar about the barn.

The other four carefully packed away the mines and drove out to the abandoned railyard Hans had chosen. It was easy to see why he'd picked it. Nestled in a small valley, with a few broken and rusted rail cars providing cover, was a neat clear space that would be perfect for assembling a portal machine. The ground was nice and flat and the snow had killed all the grass. Tony used magic to burn a path and clear the ice and snow where they would be working.

"Hans said if we can make the area we work in look like a large obvious space that's been cleared he'd take the credit for it," Owens told them. "He said he would tell his people that he'd left a space cleared for them to set up the machine."

"Perfect," Tony nodded, wandering into the center of the area he'd cleared. "I was not looking forward to trying to cover this with snow again. You lot all good if I just mark out where to dig? We only got thirteen mines and we're gonna have to be specific with them."

"Only mind if you don't help with the digging," Gio replied. "Brought four shovels, kid. Pull your weight."

Tony flashed him a grin and began marking out the spell that would bind all the explosions. Lucy watched him, noting that the magic he'd been using this morning didn't jitter. It was all golden light, no traces of the red magic Fred taught him. It was sure and constant. He'd marked out the entire circle within five minutes. Everything about him was unwavering. It reminded her of their wedding day. That was the only other time she'd seen him so certain. She could feel Gio and Owens watching her, and didn't want the attention.

"How are you two doing today?" she tried shifting focus.

"Better than I thought I'd be," Gio admitted, firing a stream of smoke into the air. He gestured his cigarette at Owens. "I didn't think I'd be able to walk on this leg yesterday afternoon, but I was running on the damn thing last night. Your boyfriend really blows some magic, Professor."

Owens went scarlet. A hot blush rose in his cheeks despite his resolutely defiant expression.

Lucy chuckled at him. "Yes, he's quite impressive. After seeing that fight outside the barn I'm surprised you can walk today."

"I was barely involved," Stuart replied quizzically. "The monster didn't hurt me."

"No," Lucy conceded. "But we all saw Hans rip it apart. He's faster than light and stronger than God, which explains the noise."

"The noise?" Owens was obviously confused.

"We can all hear your bed rattle, Stuart," Lucy sighed. "It sounded like you were getting nailed by a jackhammer."

Gio choked on his cigarette as he failed to stifle his laughter. The sound turned into a hacking cough. Owens stayed frozen for a moment. Seconds passed as he realized he had walked into that, there was no point trying to talk to the kids about propriety, and the only thing left to do was go and dig a hole. He picked up his shovel and walked away.

"Do we bully him?" Gio wheezed quietly to Lucy once he got his breath back. "Are we the bad guys?"

"We're the annoying younger siblings," Lucy smirked.

"You might be," Gio patted his chest like he was thumping his lungs. "He's still my Master. Apprenticeship ain't finished yet."

"Ain't that the truth," Lucy sighed, thinking of her own Master.

They picked up their shovels and moved off towards the spots Tony had marked. He was coming back as they moved out and Lucy could see him trying to get her attention. She didn't want to acknowledge it, but it was impossible to ignore.

"Luce–" he murmured imploringly as she passed him.

She paused with an impatient look. She couldn't spare more, and she still wanted to yell at him. He moved in closer and she felt her throat tighten. The certainty was wavering on his face. Nervous hesitation was creeping back in. He was so cute when he was anxious. She was so angry, but he was so earnest, and the bed had been so cold without him.

"I'm sorry about last night," he apologized.

"Which part?" she demanded, clipping the words out through her constricting throat.

"All of it..." he replied uncertainly. He bit his bottom lip like he didn't know what to say. This was usually the part where she knew what he meant even if he couldn't get the words right, but she wasn't offering that kindness right now. She was forcing him to struggle through, and he was stuck.

Lucy sighed deeply, trying to find her own words without hitting him with a shovel.

"Tony... you summoned a monster last night..." she began.

"I know! I'm sorry!" he interrupted. She shut him up with a look.

"We kill people for doing that," she continued bleakly. "We murder them or lock them up to keep others safe from that kind of horror. What you did..."

"I didn't mean to!"

"We know," she nodded. "We know you're not that kind of person, but..." she sighed in frustration. "You did something awful last night. Something none of us believed you'd ever do. Something I always defended against anytime someone got worried about your magic! Tony, what you did was stupid and reckless and dangerous, and that's not even why I'm angry! You didn't tell me! You didn't talk to me about any of it! You didn't say what you were trying to do, what you were planning to do. I woke up with Vincent screaming at Hans in the living room and suddenly you were summoning monsters in the barn, that just–!" She tightened her hands on the shovel like she was trying to throttle it. "I need space right now. I know it sounds nuts – I'm mad at you for not talking to me and now I don't want to talk to you – but I just need some time. I need some time to be less angry."

Tony nodded slowly. "I can do that…" he admitted. "I know I messed up. I need you to know I'm sorry. I'll be waiting when you're ready."

"Thank you," she sighed.

He nodded again and began to turn away.

"Tony," she sighed.

He stopped. She quickly tiptoed up and kissed his cheek.

"I still love you," she whispered. "Now go sort out those mines before I hit you with this shovel."

"Yes ma'am," he smiled.

He hurried off. The threat of violence was not a real one, and they both knew it, even though she had a strong urge to beat something with the shovel. Hopefully the expended energy digging holes would suffice. There was also the promise of an evening full of explosions to temper her mood. Nothing like blowing up some Nazis to settle the soul.

* * *

Vincent was down in the basement listening to the electric hum of the lights and the distant buzz of the generator. The night had been long and lonely and difficult. He hadn't been able to explain his panic to Lucy. He hadn't been able to tell her of his nightmare, of the delirious fear that had gripped him when he had seen the monster from his dream haul itself out of the barn, straight out of her husband's magic, towards her. His terror had been visceral in a way he hadn't experienced in years. Everything had felt so real, more real than everyday life.

When he had agreed to Lucy and Tony's marriage, his deepest fear had been what the boy's magic would turn into. The Tony he knew would never do anything to hurt her, would never let any harm come to her, but what happened when they woke up one day and that boy wasn't there anymore? What if they'd already gotten there? The darkness he had shown on the banks of the river had been more than a warning, and they'd done nothing to stop it escalating. Tony had done the unthinkable and instead of addressing it they were trusting the word of a cat! Fred's stupid cat was the rule by which they were measuring evil. It signed off a damn vampire!

Vincent sighed, straightening in his chair and turning the page of his ledger. The cat had signed off a vampire, and that was his problem, wasn't it? He was sitting at the desk with books from the private library spread out around him. Fred was sitting nearby reading. No one was letting him down here alone just in case there was another bottle of tonic they hadn't found yet. The memory of last night was burning a painful hole in his stomach.

He pulled the dictionary close again and started translating what he could. Of course the Germans kept all their records in German. He wondered if he could declare a rule as Chancellor to have everyone make copies of their records in English or Arabic or Hindi or Latin or something he could actually read, just in case he stopped by to check things. He knew what he was looking for, and if it had been in one of his learned languages it might have taken him an hour or two of research. He was worried it would take all day. Maybe it would take all week and he'd never find it. Maybe what he was looking for didn't exist. The memory of last night floated real and awful in his mind, and he knew he was right. He knew he could find it.

Fred brought him a cup of tea and a sandwich in the middle of the day. He still hadn't moved, and the others were yet to return. Aside from the brief conversation he'd had with Oskar this morning, he'd been at this table all day, trying to ignore Fred watching him. He wanted to say something to her, but he wasn't sure how to. Vincent had spent a lot of his life with both feet firmly planted in the belief that as long as he was doing the right thing he didn't have to find the words to justify it to anyone. Now he didn't know how to explain the parts that he was doing right when it was painfully obvious that he was no longer infallible. He watched her as she went back to her book. Her bookmark was a photo. A small black and white square with a picture of Helen and Toby. She saw him looking.

"I'm sorry," he said quietly, hoping that these words would be the right ones. "I'm sorry we dragged you away from them."

Fred folded her hands contemplatively over the book and thought a moment before replying. Her voice was soft and pensive when she finally spoke.

"I feel like everyone here is afraid to die," she began slowly. "I know that's normal, I don't begrudge it, but there is a strange fear hanging over this house. A reluctance." She touched the photo. "We aren't fighting this fight for us. We're fighting for all the people in the world who need us to win, for all the lives that will be taken if we lose. We used to be good at that. I don't know what we're doing wrong this time, but it feels like we're only doing this for our immediate survival. I need to remember that's not what it's about."

Vincent sighed and rubbed his face. She was right. She was always right.

"I don't know when I stopped trusting..." he muttered.

"I don't know when you started," Fred sniped.

"You know what I mean, Fred," he grumbled. "That's what we're doing wrong this time. That's what keeps getting in the way. I don't trust everyone else to do what I'd do."

"Thank God they don't," she replied cuttingly.

He dropped his gaze. "I deserved that..." he

admitted.

"You promised, Vincent," Fred shook her head. "You *promised!* And you never deliver. You always swear you've stopped and then I find you with it again. You're an addict, and I don't know what to do. I don't know how to help. I thought you'd been doing so well the past two years. Now I feel like a fool."

"You're not. I was. It..." he sighed. "I... I've been having nightmares, Fred. Bad ones. They never really left. I suppose in our line of work they don't. I suppose given my tonic abuse they never will... but they... fuck, they're bad, Fred. Last night I dreamt something ate Lucy. I was so scared... I was so terrified it was real. I needed the drink to check. I needed to know how to stop Rogue and White without losing her. Then Tony summoned the same goddamn thing straight out of my nightmare! I just..." he was panting as he trailed off. The fear was still real, even now. His hands were shaking.

Fred came over. She stroked his hair and kissed the top of his head.

"We're just going to have to trust them, aren't we?" Vincent sighed. "I'm getting too old. I'm getting too frail and unstable... I have to trust the kids to do this..."

"Don't say it like you're only other option is to walk out into the snow," she chided.

"My days are numbered," Vincent insisted. "I'm too tired for this work now. Too broken."

"Hunters never die in their beds," she recited to him. "Sir, knowing you as I do, I firmly believe you would climb from your own grave to keep working. That's just the way you are."

Vincent laughed. Fred gave him a surprised look, like she didn't know why that was so funny. She probably didn't. It shouldn't have been funny, but given what he'd been pouring over all day it was.

The front door sounded upstairs. Footsteps plodded over the floor above them. The others were back. Fred patted his head and went up to check on them. Vincent thought about following, but then decided to turn back to his work. It was the right call. It only took him another quarter of an hour to find what he'd been looking for.

Footsteps sounded on the basement stairs and he looked up to address Fred. It wasn't Fred. Owens ducked into the room. He looked as professional as ever. Sometimes Vincent found it hard to reconcile what he knew about the man with the figure he saw. The slick suits and severe spectacles, that handsome elitist expression, the dignified posture, were all so far from the man he'd seen ruined and naked in the aftermath of one of their Order's biggest scandals. The man that Vincent had pitied. Now it looked like Owens was the one pitying him.

"Fred says you're doing better now, Chancellor," Owens addressed him.

Vincent nodded, watching Owens glance at the notes in front of him.

"Old German records," he stated, flopping the dictionary on top of them all. "Might as well see how they do it, given that I'm responsible for it all now."

"If you need help translating..." Stuart offered.

"No," Vincent shook his head.

"We're on the same side, Chancellor," Owens insisted frustratedly.

"How can you say that?" Vincent asked.

Owens pinched the bridge of his nose, taking a deep breath to hold back what was clearly a screaming rant.

"How can you say that when I've been so awful?" Vincent finished. He sat back in his chair, linking his fingers and looking up. Stuart's expression softened with confusion. Vincent continued. "I've been a complete pig, Owens. A bigot of the highest order. Years ago, the Council were looking to shoulder-tap you. We all agreed you were the best of us. Then the acolytes came screaming that they'd found you with a vampire and everything imploded. While the rest of them were all wringing their hands over perceived moral perversions, I was desperately worried you were a complete idiot and we'd somehow all missed it."

Owens lowered his gaze bashfully and Vincent realized, for the dozenth time that year, that he was terrible at apologizing.

"Here was I worrying you were foolish, like I had a leg to stand on," he sighed. "Like I'm not the same or worse. I won't pretend I understand you and Hans, or Fred and Helen, or even Lucy and Tony. Maybe I don't know what that means, but I love my family, Owens. I'd do anything for them. I truly believe that. So why did I dig that bottle out last night? Why did I lie to Fred about the tonic I was drinking for years? Why do I keep doing this? Why do I need it?!" He sighed gruffly. "I don't know the answers, but I do know I was wrong. I was wrong about me, I was wrong about you, and I was wrong about Hans."

"He was just trying to help," Owens agreed.

"I know," Vincent nodded. "I realize that now. He's a good man. He stopped me from doing something awful last night, even if I couldn't see it then. He protected us, and I treated him like garbage just because he's not human. You were right and I should have trusted you. I think I began to realize... but I was too busy being the monster to see that someone else was being the hero. I'm sorry, Stuart."

Owens contemplated that for a moment. He pulled up a chair across the desk from Vincent and sat down. Owens tapped his fingers on the table in an absentminded morse H.

"You're a good man too, Vincent," he commented. "Good men are wrong sometimes. No one is perfect. Trying to be is how we become fixated. Becoming fixated is how we become bigoted. You were so obsessed with being right about vampires being evil that you ignored that Hans was good. I appreciate your apology, but we both know he's the one who deserves it."

"You both do," Vincent sighed. "I'll say something to him tonight. Provided our plan is still going ahead?"

"We're all set up," Stuart nodded. "With any luck they will arrive this evening and assemble their device over the mines. We can sneak up outside their perimeter and detonate."

"Is there something we have to do to warn Hans first?" Vincent asked.

Stuart shook his head. "He'll be aware of us and our signals. If he needs to, he can move faster than the explosion."

"He can what?!"

"How did Lucy put it..." Owens mused. "He's faster than light and stronger than God."

"She has a way with words," Vincent nodded. "Be careful, that sounds like she's smitten."

"I rather doubt it," Owens frowned. "She was asking how I was able to walk today..."

Vincent snorted with laughter. Owens glared at him. Vincent grinned in return.

"You're the only one who isn't going to find that funny, Owens," he warned.

"You are terrible at apologies," Owens glowered.

"It's possibly my greatest shortcoming," Vincent nodded. "And that's saying something."

* * *

The view from the castle was majestic. The sun set red and gold across the snowy landscape. Hans watched it with a strange longing from the shadows of the building. Apprehension had settled in his stomach. Things were already going wrong, but there was no way to call it off. They were just going to have to do the best they could. He set his umbrella and walked to the trucks packed in the courtyard. Schmitt had already climbed up into the back of one, and he turned and offered his hand to Hans. Not wanting to be impolite, Hans took the Doctor's hand. He didn't need it, and he was careful not to squeeze. The last thing he needed was to explain the man's broken fingers.

There were benches along the interior sides of the truck, and the center was full of crates. Schmitt and Hans found seats and Hans set his umbrella away. It would be dark by the time they reached the railyard. That had been the deal. Five trucks full of machinery and troops were heading down to the designated area to set up the machine and run a test. Rogue and White were not coming. They said they had something more important to do. Hans was not privy to what might be more important than this, but his imagination fathomed the worst. If his stomach had still worked he might have puked from nerves.

'*Is everything alright?*" Schmitt asked in German. "*You seem nervous.*"

"*I assure you, Doctor, I'm not holding my breath,*" Hans replied.

Schmitt chuckled, nodding his head and smiling his sweet genuine smile. He twisted the wedding band on his finger as though fidgeting. Hans looked away. He didn't need to see that right now. The engines started and the trucks rolled away.

"*You seem perturbed that Dame Rogue and Herr White are not joining us,*" Schmitt continued. "*However, if they do not attend the test, we do not have to share the success. They are little more than muscle to keep out enemies at bay as it is. We have the soldiers. We do not need them.*"

"*The sorceress is supposed to be helping with the project,*" Hans covered stiffly. "*I am no mage.*"

"*The entire point of the project is not to need her magic,*"

Schmitt encouraged. "*I have seen your work, Wagner. You sell yourself short. It is an absolute marvel. I have faith this will succeed — you should too.*"

Hans shook his head in disbelief. He couldn't help himself.

"*Why are you doing this, Doctor? What is the birth of a new age to a man like you?*" he asked.

"*It is progress,*" Schmitt shrugged. "*It is a safer, better world for our children, cleansed of the filth that corrupts it now. We can open the door and bring in the angels to save us.*"

"*The angels...*" Hans drawled. "*That the six-winged seraphim do dance and cry about the throne of the Holy, as the mindless flutes do play about the center of the universe, and we see salvation there for we know no better.*" He shook his head again. "*Those who have truly looked upon an angel don't hope to do so twice.*" He didn't know how he knew that, but it was ingrained in his bones from a time before this life. He knew in a way he could not explain that the Darkness had found many ways to express itself and convert humanity to its embrace.

His cynicism wasn't winning him any friends, but Schmitt still smiled at him gently, as though touched by pity now rather than kinship.

"*Why then?*" he asked. "*Why do you do what we do? You do not strike me as an evil man, there is nothing malicious or cruel about you, why serve the cause if you think it is wrong? Why do the work if you do not believe?*"

"*I wanted a job...*" Hans answered softly, vaguely aware why he was being so honest with the man and not liking the dark thoughts that accompanied the realization. *"I wanted to work, to do something with my time. I was tired of struggling, of starving, of being cold and alone. Here I could put my skills to use, have a roof over my head, clean clothes, I do not have to beg for food... that is why I did what they asked, and risked opening the door to darker places we could never escape."*

"We won't open the doors to darker places, Hans," Schmitt assured, clapping him on the shoulder. *"We will open the doors to Heaven that the righteous shall be saved. The world shall be cleansed."*

Hans wondered who had fed what delusions to Schmitt and how long it had been going on for, but he didn't argue. Opening the doors of Heaven. Everyone who threw themselves into magic and sought to conjure a portal to other worlds thought they were seeking Heaven – it just looked very different to different people. It always opened to the same place. Hans had seen a remnant of that world crawl into theirs last night. He had ripped it in half with his bare hands. If things didn't go well tonight he was worried he'd have to do it again.

It didn't do to dwell on those fears, and he tried to push them from his mind as they drove down from the castle and away to the ambush. Unfortunately there wasn't much to distract him from his thoughts, rattling in the dark in the back of a truck. The weight of the mission before him was starting to push him down. It was supposed to be over. He was supposed to destroy the machine, kill Rogue and White, and run off into the future with Stuart. Elope somewhere. France maybe. But that wasn't happening. Not tonight. Rogue and

White weren't here, and he didn't like the way plan B was shaping up.

They pulled up at the test site and the trucks were unloaded. Night had fallen and Hans steeled himself. He'd had time to adapt to what had to be done and there was no point getting squeamish about it. The soldiers were already unloading the crates and setting up a perimeter. Hans could see where the Hunters had laid their traps. It was subtle, but his eyes were better than human eyes, even in the harsh lights of the trucks. Schmitt followed him from the truck and began directing the project. There was no sign of the Hunters' return yet. Hans moved quietly through the chaos, observing and waiting. Either they were better than he thought or the setup was more distracting than he realized.

Schmitt was organizing the final pieces and the machine was nearly ready to go when Hans heard the whisper. It was distant, away from the circle they were using and safely behind the rusted railcars. It sounded like Lucy muttering that there were more than fifty troops around. A whisper returned, the older Italian man, pointing out that was less than ten each provided no one died in the explosion and Hans didn't want any. The vampire smiled.

Then Schmitt gave him a sign they were ready to begin. He hadn't realized the Doctor could do it without him. He needed the Hunters to blow it up but he didn't particularly want to be standing over the mines when it happened. He hurried over. The Hunters needed to be warned, but there was no way he could tell them directly. He needed to alert them to the situation without blowing their cover. This was going to have to be done in German and Stuart would have to translate for his people.

Hans took his place at Schmitt's side and addressed the troops. *Perhaps Rogue and White couldn't be here tonight, but they were about to make history nonetheless. They were about to witness God.* Schmitt flashed him a proud smile. The man really believed. Hans placed a hand on his shoulder.

"Perhaps we should stand back," he advised.

"Nonsense," Schmitt grinned happily. *"This is what we've built our entire lives towards, I want a front row seat!"*

Hans couldn't stop him. Schmitt grabbed the lever and shoved it over. Electricity sparked. Hans fled. He moved faster than the machine did. Behind him he could hear the metal turning in slow motion. He could hear the flare of the magic igniting. He could see the light of the portal sparking, reflecting off every truck and soldier in attendance.

In a flash he was on the other side of the railcars. Or he would have been. The portal was open. Gravity was increasing. He couldn't move as fast. No one could. His eyesight was still extraordinary. He saw the spell weave across the ground. A normal human might have seen a flicker of light. Hans saw the symbols flash across the earth.

Everything exploded.

The force smashed him straight into the railcar he was nearing. He hadn't quite made it. Behind the ringing in his ears he was vaguely aware of screaming and gunfire. His shoulder hurt where he'd crashed. At least he didn't bruise. He'd had worse. He shook his head to clear it. Just a second. His body recovered quickly. He blinked reality into focus.

Fire. The mines had been concentrated in the center beneath the machine and at the perimeter where the guards had been stationed. They had planned well. The machine was broken. Everything was burning. Soldiers were scattered, some trying to take cover behind the remaining trucks as shots picked them out from the darkness, some screaming and mutilated on the ground. In the remains of twisted metal, a bright spark flickered. The portal was still trying to take hold, even though the rings to hold it were sprayed in pieces across the ground.

A hand grabbed his shoulder. He startled. The explosion must have disorientated him.

"Hans, geht es dir gut?" a familiar voice asked if he was alright.

"Stuart..." Hans smiled, blinking him in sight, wondering why the world was still spinning. He placed a hand against Stuart's cheek as the Hunter leant over him, eyes scouring his body for damage. He was fine. Things were starting to steady and his hearing was coming back. He was sprawled against the old railcar, and he wanted to pull Stuart over him and kiss him, but it was the worst possible time. His mind was spinning and he couldn't focus on what was important. There was something desperately important he was ignoring. There was a battle going on. There was–

The portal sparked. Eerie pale blue light burst aflame

in the ruins of the rings. It ripped open, spinning and cold. *Scheiße.* Portal magic was fueled by sacrifice. That was why cults made human sacrifices to bring forth creatures of darkness. The machine was dead, but so were nearly fifty people. The portal was designed to draw off electric power to fuel the magic, but in its absence...

Schmitt's adjustments had worked. He had succeeded. It went exactly where he wanted it to. From the depths of cold blue ether floated a six-winged veiny eyeball. The iris swiveled around in curiosity. The wings flared out, pristine feathers on display. The Hunters poured out of cover, guns blazing, at the sight of the abomination. They all fired at the creature. Golden sparks lit up the night as holy bullets ripped through the wings. Feathers sprayed into the sky. The monster didn't falter. It began to vibrate.

Hans watched it quiver, hovering, expressionless. Stuart dropped his gun. He fell to his knees beside Hans. Hans grabbed him, half catching him, and holding him close. Stuart had his hands pressed to his ears, his face twisted in agony. Hans couldn't hear it. Across the ground the already injured soldiers began to leak blood from their cranial orifices, their bodies shivering in pain. Hans could feel Stuart's blood convulsing in his body. He didn't understand what was happening, beyond the creature trying to kill the man he loved. He set Stuart gently on the ground, kissing his temple and taking his gun.

In a flicker he was back in the center. Standing before the eye it was as tall as he was. He unloaded the clip into the center of the pupil. Goop splashed from the wounds. A soft blue glow began in the depths where the bullets had struck. Hans dashed away. A beam of light shot from the eye, zigzagging across the path of its vision. It blasted across the ground, exploding one of the trucks and carving the earth like lightning. The thing didn't move fast, and Hans was nowhere near its attack. That didn't mean others weren't.

"*Hans...*" a voice choked near him.

He looked down. Schmitt. The doctor was still alive. Although Hans was prepared to admit it was a slim technicality – Schmitt's legs had been destroyed. So had some crucial internal organs. He was choking on his own blood. He was smiling.

"*We did it,*" he coughed. "*We found them.*"

Hans didn't have the will to pander to his delusions. He picked up a broken shard of one of the rings, quickly glancing at the runes to make sure he wasn't going to make the situation worse, he threw the metal spike like a javelin. It stabbed straight through the eye. The metal made a sick wet sound as it pierced the gelatinous flesh. The attack didn't bring it down. The wings quivered and it began to turn.

"*What are you doing?!*" Schmitt cried.

Hans ignored the Doctor. Stuart staggered to his side. He looked dizzy and pained, but he was on his feet again. Hans handed back the pistol for Stuart to reload. Schmitt was watching them. Hans couldn't help but risk a glance at the dying man. Schmitt's smile was gone. His face looked strangely bleak without it. There was a deep comprehension in his eyes.

"*Hunters happened...*" he rasped weakly. "*You will burn in Hell, Wagner.*"

"*Only if you get there and warm it up for me,*" Hans replied, grabbing Stuart and flickering away.

The eye blasted where they had been standing. The ground erupted like another mine went off. Schmitt was eviscerated. Hans paused, setting Stuart down carefully.

"Stay safe," he instructed.

Stuart was too busy wincing to reply. Hans left him in the shelter of one of the trucks and rushed back to the monster. It was emitting some kind of sonic frequency that attacked the living. He had to stop it. The gun was reloaded, but bullets alone weren't doing enough. It saw him coming and blasted. Hans dodged. Barely. He felt his sleeve scorch as the beam brushed it. There was no time to assess damage.

He grabbed the metal spike still lodged in the monster and ripped it out. Strange luminescent goo bled from its body. The rough edges of the broken ring grazed his fingers. He grabbed the makeshift blade tighter and swung it down. The metal sheared through one of the wings. It hit the wing beneath and stuck fast. Hans pulled. He couldn't get the metal free. The pupil swiveled directly at him. It was already glowing. There wasn't time to move. He realized he was going to meet Schmitt in Hell a lot sooner than he'd planned.

Everything became light. It was warm, but not painful. Hans stayed frozen. Then he realized he hadn't been struck. The light was golden. He stepped back. A massive arcane circle of golden light separated him from the eye, protecting him like a shield. The blast had reflected off it straight back into the monster's eye. A large hole bled more pale goo out the back of it. Still the eye didn't fall.

Ropes of golden light lashed out and snared the wings. The ropes pulled back, driving the monster down, halting its vibrations. He leapt out of the darkness. The mage from the barn. The young Italian one. Each fist clutched a handful of ropes, binding the creature. His hands glowed with golden light. Symbols danced in it, flashing and changing. The same light flared in his eyes. It was warm, so warm, and Hans wasn't burning as he basked in it – yet. But it felt like sunlight.

"You doing alright, Mister Vampire, Sir?" Tony grunted, hauling on the bindings as the creature fought back.

Hans nodded numbly. He didn't know what to make of the situation. He didn't know what to make of the boy. How could the same kid from the barn do something like this? He'd just saved Hans from annihilation. Tony gritted his teeth, struggling against the force of the eye. Human strength had nothing on this monstrosity. The magic was doing most of the work. Hans shrugged away his stupor as he saw Tony struggle. He grabbed the broken shaft again, ripping it from the damaged wing. Lining up his strike carefully, he raised the blade. With a single mighty swoop he brought it down, slicing straight through the eyeball. It split in half, collapsing to the ground and spilling ooze across the carnage beneath.

Tony's light went out sharply. Hans felt the winter cold rush back like he was getting stabbed by ice. He moved quickly, dropping the sticky blade and catching the young mage. Tony trembled in his arms. He was trying to stand, but he was exhausted. Hans recognized the sensation. For him it usually meant he was in dire need of fresh blood. For this kid it probably meant he was in dire need of some good *sauerbraten*.

The others were hurrying over. Hans scooped Tony up and carried him over to meet them.

"Tony!" Lucy exclaimed, pulling him from Hans' arms and checking him over.

"He's not hurt," Hans told her. "Give him a good meal, he should be fine." He watched the others fuss over the boy and commented. "I've never seen anyone do somezing like zat before..."

"None of us have," Stuart sighed, placing a hand on Hans' back. "Young Mister Temple is an anomaly. Completely unique." His touch was warm through the fabric of Hans' suit. Hans wanted to curl into Stuart's arms and stay there, but he couldn't. He had something much less pleasant in store, and he probably had to hurry.

"You need to go," he sighed, "but I need you to do somezing for me first."

"What's wrong?" Stuart asked, knowing instinctively that something wasn't right.

"Rogue and Vhite did not come viz us," Hans stated. "Our mission is not over, ve still need to lure zem out to a fight ve can vin, and I am more useful as a spy in zeir castle." He grabbed a large section of broken ring and balanced it carefully on the wreckage, directing the sharp point of the sheared metal at the group. "I need you to hold zis steady vhile I impale myself on it."

"*Nein!*" Stuart exclaimed.

"It vill not kill me," Hans assured. "If you hold it steady it vill completely miss my heart, but ve must do zis. It is ze only vay to convince Rogue and Vhite zat I am on zeir side. If I vas truly vorking for zem, zere is no vay I vould return vizout your heads after zis attack unless I vas seriously injured."

They were all staring at him aghast. Stuart was pale and drawn, and he hadn't stopped shaking his head the entire time Hans had been speaking. Hans wasn't surprised by that, but he was surprised that the others looked equally horrified.

"You can't ask him to do that," Vincent grumbled.

"I have to," Hans insisted. "You know I'm right."

"But you can't ask him to help you," Vincent replied. "You can't ask him to watch. I'll hold it for you."

"No offense, Doc, but that's worse," Gio commented.

"I owe you," Vincent stated. "You saved my life last night and protected my family. I was wrong about you and I owe you more than an apology. If you need someone to do this, let it be me."

"You have changed your tune, Chancellor," Hans replied warily.

"I was wrong," Vincent shrugged. "I know I was, and I'm sorry. Owens was right about you all along, and I was too stubborn to see it, but I'm not too stubborn to admit my faults when I'm forced to see them." Vincent fished in his pocket, striding over and handing over something small.

Hans let his curiosity get the better of him. He held out a hand. Vincent dropped a little metal object into his palm. It was warm from being in the old man's pocket. Hans tipped it gently, letting the light glint off it. He laughed when he realized what it was.

"A Hunter's pin?" Hans chuckled. "You vant to recruit me, Chancellor?"

"No," Vincent shook his head. "No need. It's yours."

"Vhat do you mean...?" Hans asked.

Vincent looked like he was trying to decide how to answer before he settled on the longer explanation.

"When Owens said that training you had been all but pointless because you knew how to do everything already, I wanted to hit him back to last Tuesday," Vincent started. "Then I saw you fight last night and I realized what he meant. So I looked you up. I spent the day digging through the old records the Order is required to keep, and I found you. Hans Wagner, born 1801, initiated 1818, presumed dead 1832. Last seen hunting known vampire Ludwig Beck, mission considered successful. Neither seen again." Vincent gave him and the pin a nod. "It's rightfully yours. You were a Hunter, long before the rest of us. At a guess, I would say Beck won the first round. Probably thought it would be hilarious to keep a turned Hunter as a disciple. Never realized there are some things not even death can train out of a man. Guessing you won the second round. Doesn't sound like there was a third."

Hans was staring at him. He was vaguely aware that

he wasn't remembering to blink and that such things were unsettling to humans, but no one else seemed to be blinking either. They were all staring. Hans assumed he looked as dumbstruck as the rest of them.

"Anyway," Vincent gestured at the pin. "Keep it, throw it away, sell it, melt it down, do whatever you want, but the pin is rightfully yours. I'm not initiating you into anything, because technically you never left. Like it or not, Hans Wagner, you are a Hunter."

Hans looked up. He met Stuart's eye. Stuart hadn't known, but Hans could see the surprise wearing off fast. In a strange way it all made sense. He smiled, just a little, and dropped the pin into his pocket.

"Very good," he gave a slight nod. "I vill accept your help, Chancellor. Please hold ze ring."

"Hans, there has to be another way–!" Stuart insisted, coming forward to intervene.

Vincent took the ring off Hans and steadied it with a grunt, trying to balance it as straight as possible. Stuart took Hans by the shoulders and tried to direct him away. Hans held him briefly and kissed his cheek.

"I have to do zis," he whispered. "I vill be alright."

"Fred!" Vincent grunted. "Take Owens and the kids back to the car. They don't need to see this."

She nodded, reluctantly, and came and took Stuart by the shoulders, directing him away. Hans gave her a grateful nod as he watched her put an arm around Stuart and guide him from the railyard. Vincent and Hans watched the rest of them leave, and once they were sure they were alone with the dead, Vincent braced himself and gave Hans a nod. Hans returned the nod and lined himself up with the point of the ring. This was going to hurt. It was now or never. He steeled himself and ran at full speed. Full speed was like a flicker to most eyes. One minute he was standing away, the next there was an awful sound of tearing flesh and cracking bone.

15

Hans had anticipated it would hurt, but he had never been injured this badly. He had seen Vincent's face pale as the Chancellor beheld the damage. His punctured lungs struggled to move the air required to make sound. It left his voice weak as he ordered Vincent to leave and not say anything to Stuart. The Chancellor had nodded obediently and fled.

Hans was left lying in the mud, impaled on a piece of broken machinery, surrounded by the dead and the mangled remains of the device and its monster. He was intensely aware that on any other creature this would be a mortal wound. His body knew it should be dead. He kept blacking out in flashes from the pain, and he wasn't completely sure how long he'd been lying there. At least it would look authentic. He just had to get himself off the metal and get back to the castle.

And he had to do it before dawn.

That had seemed so much easier as a hypothetical situation. In practice, he could barely move. There was no blood on the ring segment. Vampires didn't bleed, they were dry creatures, which was why they needed blood. He needed blood now. He grabbed the metal protruding from his chest. Merciful God, it was huge.

The steel beam took up half his torso. He pulled. The pain flared where the twisted metal caught his broken ribs. Everything went dark.

When he came to, he could hear footsteps. There weren't supposed to be people here. He grabbed the metal again, grunting and whimpering with the effort. Some human tendencies still came naturally. He pulled again. It was all he could do not to scream, but some tortured sound escaped him.

"Hans?!" a voice called his name.

Suddenly, someone was kneeling beside him. He could feel hands on his body. His vision swam, blurry with pain. A man in a dark suit, combed black hair.

"Stuart...?" Hans mumbled weakly.

"Who's Stuart?" the voice asked cheekily.

Reality hit Hans like another metal spike. The accent was American, not Canadian. White. Ezra White. His silver eyes drifted in front of Hans' vision. He wasn't wearing his glasses.

"Hold still, honey, this is going to hurt," White grinned at him, one hand grabbing the spike.

Hans nearly blacked out again as the metal shaft was ripped from his body. He was vaguely aware of his own cry of pain, but it was not a priority. He needed blood. Fresh blood. He grabbed White's arm and snatched it to his mouth. The smell made his stomach turn, if he even had a stomach left. Just as quickly, he pushed the demon away and flung himself on the body of the closest soldier. They hadn't gone completely cold yet. He ripped a hole in the dead man's throat and began to suck the blood from his corpse like a starving animal. If nothing else it began to ease the pain.

"What happened?" White asked.

"Hunters," Hans gasped, diving straight back in.

He could feel his body knitting back together as he drank. The blood wasn't as fresh as it could be, but he'd had worse. His bones were clicking back into place and fusing together. Soon he might even be able to walk. His mind was clearing too, although that wasn't entirely a good thing. The memory of confusing White for Stuart was a sickening one.

The demon was strolling through the carnage. His expression was unreadable as he surveyed the damage. Hans barely paid him any attention. He knew he should, he knew fooling them was the point, but he felt like he was dying. White returned to him quickly and dumped a fresh body on the old one.

"It looked like it was starting to run a bit dry," he offered.

"*Danke,*" Hans thanked him, moving on to the next one. It tasted better. The first man had been a smoker. It was funny the things that he stopped being fussy about when the alternative felt like death. After two bodies the injury was nearly healed. He still had some scarring and pain, but he could easily stand and walk again. He'd never drunk so much before in one sitting. Not even close. He sat back in the mud with a sigh and wiped his mouth with the back of his hand.

He wasn't the only one feeding. The sounds had been coming from behind him while he wasn't paying attention; slurping, tearing, bones cracking. He turned. White had started feeding off the wings. He was hunched over the broken feathery remains, devouring at speed. His silver eyes burned so bright they glowed. Luminous blood dripped from his chin. The wings shriveled in his hands as he sucked the light from them, quickly absorbing the essence like a vacuum, and discarding the husks as he finished. He scooped the glowing ooze from the remains of the eyeball, feeding it into his mouth with his fingers.

Hans thought he was going to vomit. He didn't know why the sight revolted him so, but it did. He had no right to protest. He'd just been feeding of the dead too, but something about the demon devouring the creature's remains made Hans want to scream. He turned his eyes away quickly, trying to collect himself. He couldn't watch. He heard White stand, heard the demon shiver. There was something ecstatic in the shiver. Something blissful. Hans cleared his throat, unable to look back and desperate to avoid the moment.

"Doctor Schmitt vas eviscerated," he admitted.

"Mm," White nodded. "I think I can smell which bits were him." The demon poked one of the husked wings with the toe of his shoe, letting it crumble to dust. "Your portal worked though, before the Hunters got here. You went where Schmitt said you could. You got one. Just a little one. One of the corrupted. Just a baby. Imagine if you'd got one of the big ones…"

Hans shuddered. He didn't understand what White was saying and he didn't want to. The demon was clean again, as though nothing had happened, but his eyes were so bright. He stepped closer again. Hans could feel a heat coming off him now. Unnatural. Radiant. The demon drew closer still.

"It all happened so fast…" Hans sighed, rubbing his face.

"Even so, I'm sure you can give a decent account," White smiled. "Good thing we hired you, Wagner. When I first arrived I thought there were no survivors."

"Vhat are you doing here anyvay?" Hans asked. "I zought you and Dame Rogue vere busy."

"We were," White grinned. "But we saw the explosion from the castle. You put on quite a show."

"Not the kind I vas intending…" Hans mumbled.

"No. Come on." White bent down and helped pull Hans to his feet. "Let's get you back up the hill. We can clean you up, get you a snack, and work out how to fix this mess. I'm not delivering the bad news myself."

* * *

It was snowing again. The flakes settled soft and quiet on the world, dulling all sound and generating a deceptively peaceful ambiance. Everyone was resting. Vincent was finally sleeping. At first, every time he closed his eyes, he saw Hans impaled on the machine. The dark wound, glinting bone, disturbing lack of blood… the agony on his face. It looked worse than Vincent had felt minutes before, when his blood had boiled. The pain so real and sharp he couldn't move. The sound of the creature's wings seemingly rupturing his veins. Hans had still looked worse. It had been such an alien thing to see someone that badly wounded and yet still alive. But he had sworn he would be alright, and

Vincent had believed him.

Now he was resting, finally asleep, without nightmares. He might not have stopped Rogue yet, but half the job was done and that was worth a nap. He was so deeply asleep he didn't hear the knocking at first. His mind shrugged it away until he heard others start to move. The sound had persisted. He struggled from his bed and staggered from the room. Owens was opening the front door. Vincent recognized the bobbly wool hat as soon as it burst in.

"Oskar?" he mumbled, rubbing his tired face.

"Chancellor, vhat did you do?!" Oskar cried, shoving his way into the house and shutting the door.

Owens stood back out of the way, clearly not prepared to make this his fight. The others were struggling up too. Vincent could hear the doors behind him as people spilled into the corridor to see what was happening.

"I don't know what you mean, Oskar," Vincent sighed. "If it's about the barn, I already—"

"I can fix that," Tony interjected behind him.

"*Wen interessiert die Scheune?!*" Oskar exclaimed. "Who cares about ze barn?! It has some little symbols! Ze massacre, Chancellor! You killed all zose soldiers!"

"It had to be done, Oskar," Vincent replied. "I'm sorry, but you know how it can be—"

"You kill zem ve have big problem now!" Oskar interrupted. "I listen for updates, like you ask. I listen for news at ze castle. Zey sending reinforcements now! Zey send... uh, eh..." Oskar waved his hands in frustration, trying to find the word. "Zey send *ein*

Luftschif!" he looked to Owens desperately.

"Airship," Owens translated, his eyes narrowing. "They're sending an airship of reinforcements? Here?"

"Ja! Ja!" Oskar nodded. "You see problem?!"

"The last thing we need is more troops swarming the region looking for us," Vincent growled.

"Especially if we still need to get to that castle to take out Rogue and White," Fred added.

"And given that we've killed German soldiers this is officially a national incident," Owens sighed, pinching the bridge of his nose. "We've interfered with a military operation. This could get messy."

"The Order works outside the borders of nations," Lucy insisted. "We're an international organization, and no one is immune to our intervention, not even governments. Our duty is to the world as a whole."

"That's great," Owens drawled. "Why don't you go tell the Nazi fascists and their great and powerful leader that? You're blonde, they'll like you."

"Don't be rude, Stuart," she sniped.

"He's right though," Vincent sighed. "Germany is looking for a fight. Their Chancellor is a madman driving people from their homes and their country. We cannot give them a reason to start a war. Not another one."

"Like that's not where the world's heading anyway…" Owens muttered.

"Don't even joke," Vincent warned. "We need to deescalate the situation. We need to make it about Rogue and White and their witchcraft, and not about the German military operation."

"They're the same thing," Tony protested.

"Not when you start getting into the politics of it," Lucy sighed. "So how do we do that?"

"Focus on ze foreigners," Oskar suggested. "Zey have brought in more outside help. Ze military can't make ze project vork alone."

"More outside help?" Vincent queried, wishing he'd stayed in bed.

"*Ja*," Oskar nodded. "Ze Professor zat had been communicating about ze project. He arrived last night. I vas going to come and tell you about it, but zen I heard about ze *Luftschiff* and zought zat vas more important."

Vincent gave him a nod.

"Professor from where, exactly?" Owens asked. "I never got a name from Hans."

"Not *Deutschland*," Oskar shrugged. "I don't know exactly. I zink in *Afrika* somevhere maybe? I never seen the name before. Goes by Professor Isfet."

* * *

Hans made it back to the castle before dawn, but it felt like they cut it quite fine. He still felt strangely dizzy. Possibly the winged creature had affected him more than he realized, or possibly his body was still in shock from its near-death experience. Some of the legends were true. Vampires could survive most things, short of a punctured heart or severed head. Sunlight burns could be hideous but death would take hours. That didn't mean Hans wanted to test them. All of them took fresh blood to recover from.

White half carried him back into the basement. He was able to walk on his own, but he knew it didn't feel right. Apparently it didn't look right either. The demon had insisted on aiding him. Hans wondered if the creature knew it made him uncomfortable and if that was why it hung about. They burst into the room without knocking and Greta startled in the bed. The young woman leapt up and backed away from them.

"Where do you think you're going?" White demanded.

"*Bleib zurück,*" Hans warned her, confident that Greta didn't speak English and White didn't speak German. He turned to the demon. "Leave me here. I vill feed and change. Ve must find out if anyzing is salvageable."

"I wouldn't hold my breath," White commented.

"I never do," Hans winced.

White flashed him a grin.

"I'll see what I can do," the demon promised. "Come downstairs when you're ready. We have a surprise for you."

He set Hans down in the chair by the desk and catered to his request, leaving the room and shutting the door with a snap. Hans and Greta waited, watching the door, ears strained. Hans heard him leave. He wasn't sure he trusted it, but he didn't have much choice. Greta broke first. As soon as it was quiet she dashed over.

"*Hans! What happened?!*" she exclaimed in German, taking in the damage.

"*I ruined a perfectly good suit,*" he replied. His body was mostly healed, but he still felt weak. He knew he wasn't at his best, and his mind was hazy. It left him feeling anxious and vulnerable.

Greta pulled up her sleeve and held out her wrist. Hans took it gratefully and drank to clear his head. He let his breath heal her arm after and was pleased to note that ability worked as well as ever. She waited patiently but her resolve didn't waver.

"What happened?" she repeated.

"The machine was destroyed and Doctor Schmitt was killed," Hans answered carefully.

Greta stayed silent. Her eyes were accusing him of sabotaging the project and hurting himself. He didn't deny it. His look was pointed. They had to do something if they ever wanted to escape this place with their lives. She sighed and patted his head.

"Do you want me to scream and break the drawers?" she asked.

"No," he smiled. *"Neither of us have the energy for that."* He was injured and she had just given blood. *"I will go and wash and change, then I'll see what the situation is with White downstairs."* He carefully collected some clean clothes to take through to the washroom. His hands were steady now but they didn't have their usual sharpness or surety of movement. He wasn't sure if he could flicker. How long did it take to recover from such an injury? Small injuries were nearly instantaneous. This felt more like when Stuart had found him staving. That had taken some time to recover from.

"Hans..." Greta called softly.

He turned back to her, nearly at the door. She was perched demurely on the end of the bed. His eyes narrowed. She was nervous about something.

"*Is it nearly over…?*" she asked.

"*I hope so,*" he sighed. "*But I can't be certain.*"

"*Is there any way we could—if someone could help—maybe I could—*"

Hans tried to catch up with her train of thought, but his mind still felt slow. He quickly assembled everything he knew about her here. Someone else? Ah. She had been growing rather fond of the soldier assigned to care for her and bring her meals. Hans had already warned her about not disclosing their plan to anyone else.

"*Is this about Gefreiter Voss?*" he asked.

"*We could elope,*" she offered hopefully. "*We could run away and you could give chase. We could fake it. You could come back and say you'd killed us. No one would ever look for us again. We could get away. I could…*"

"*It is not wise, Greta,*" Hans sighed. "*I don't want to say no, but… if you did that now I couldn't guarantee that White would not pursue. If you do anything to provoke their wrath while they are alive I cannot promise your safety. I just… I know I ask a lot, but I need you to trust me. I'm trying to get us out alive. Plans are in motion, I swear. Once they are gone you can run off with whomever you want. If you want to trust the solider then, I will not stop you.*"

"*He's trustworthy,*" she assured.

"*I believe you believe that,*" Hans sighed. "*But I have been hunted most of my existence. In more than a hundred years, I have only truly trusted three people. Two of them are long dead. Please, Greta, play this one safe. I don't want you to get hurt.*"

She sighed in reluctant agreement. He gave her a grateful nod.

"*Don't get yourself killed,*" Greta ordered.

"*As long as you don't either,*" he smiled. He left the room to bathe and change. The hot water was pleasant after a night spent dying in the snow. He sat in it long enough to stop feeling cold. White was expecting him, but Hans felt the demon could wait. He was prepared to be snarky about it, and White always seemed to appreciate that. He was the strangest creature Hans had ever met, and the memory of White feeding on the luminous wings caused a flood of revulsion. Hans stilled himself. It didn't do to dwell.

As he changed he worried about the situation with Greta. He realized she didn't know about Stuart. Hans had never told her. He'd never actually told anyone. She probably thought she was the last living person he trusted. He wished he could include her in the list, but the truth was that as much as he tried to trust her, as much as he wanted to, she was young and impulsive and he worried. If she tried to run with the soldier they could all end up in trouble. He didn't need that drama now, not on top of everything else.

Once he was clean and dressed appropriately, he set off down to the deepest levels of the basement. The caves beneath the castle. He half expected White to be loitering in the tunnels again and was surprised when the demon didn't try and sneak up on him. That was nothing compared to the surprise waiting in the cave. He heard the noise before he saw it. Soldiers.

He entered the massive cave to see a group of

soldiers assembling a new machine. It was similar to his, but with slight differences. Better. If you could call an effective means of ending the world better. White appeared at his shoulder with a grin. Hans didn't have to look to see it, he could feel the bared fangs by his neck even if they didn't exist in this form. The demon was still unusually hot and his eyes bright.

"Isn't it great?" White smirked.

"How…?" Hans muttered, trying to keep the horror from his voice.

"The new and improved version!" Rogue announced dramatically, sweeping into view around the machine. "Courtesy of the great Professor Isfet, our Lord and benefactor!"

The Professor strode from the center of the machine where he had been overseeing the assembly, a wide grin splitting his face.

"I couldn't for the life of me figure why your machine didn't work, Vampire. Its design was nearly perfect," he complimented in a voice as smooth and rich as black coffee.

Hans felt terror freeze every fiber of his body. Professor Isfet was a tall handsome man with dark skin in a long black coat. At least, that was how he presented. It was, in fact, not what he was at all. Hans recognized the lack of blood and heartbeat. Just like him. Except worse. So much worse. The Darkness given form. Human skin stretched over the end of existence and paraded as attractive. Something that didn't belong here. A figure of a different world, a different time, a different legend. A myth that had stepped through to stalk an elusive prey and bring destruction to any life that crossed its path. Hans felt very much like that life now.

"I heard you were badly injured in a Hunter attack," Isfet commented, looking Hans up and down.

"*Ja*," Hans admitted. "I only escaped alive because I can vizstand damage zat vould kill a human..." he trailed off.

Isfet *knew*. Hans didn't know how to explain it, but that thing knew everything about him. All his secrets. Everything he'd done. He'd made the comment about the machine Hans had built because he knew that it should have worked. He knew Hans had been sabotaging it. He knew about the Hunters and their Chancellor and the alliance. He knew about Stuart. That's why he was smiling like that.

"Thank the melody of the universe you're still with us," Isfet purred.

White grabbed Hans enthusiastically by the shoulders. "It would take stronger stuff than that to kill you, Wagner," the demon grinned.

Hans conceded very silently that it would, and he had a horrible feeling he was about to find out what. He was trying to meet the eyes of the Darkness, but staring into the void was terrifying. Rogue sidled up beside the Professor. Hans was painfully aware that he was pinned between the three of them. They were all smiling.

"Remind me again how you survived..." Isfet coaxed.

"I vas impaled by a broken piece of machine," Hans

replied stiffly. "Viz no heartbeat or breaz ze Hunters vould have assumed I vas dead." He let that hang there a moment before trying to buy himself more favor. "It is possible zat vizout Herr Vhite I vould not have made it. If ze sun had risen before I could get free I might have perished."

"A tragedy…" White murmured.

Hans took stock. The demon didn't know. Isfet might have been privy to the entire events of the world, but he hadn't shared. Hans wasn't the only one getting played with. Of course. The Darkness played with everyone equally, even its supporters.

"And what did you find in the pocket of his coat, Cazial?" Isfet pressed.

It took Hans a moment to realize who Isfet was talking to, but he felt the movement. Obviously the demon's real name wasn't Ezra White. It fished in the pocket of its suit and pulled out the pin. Hans couldn't believe he wasn't dead already. He had never felt White palm it.

"A pin he ripped off one of the Hunters," White stated proudly.

Isfet and Rogue both directed dubious looks their way. The witch was catching up. She knew it didn't make sense.

"So if we were to ask our Queen's magic what our vampire here wanted most…" Isfet kept leading, opening the invitation up.

Hans tried to move back, but White stayed behind him, holding him in place. Rogue reached out and touched one hot finger to the center of Hans' forehead.

Her blood red nail scratched against his skin. When she pulled her finger back it traced a thin ghostly line in the air, as though drawing a soul from his body. It stretched and dripped as it pulled from Hans' skin. He didn't want to look, but he couldn't help himself. He would have given anything to fool the spell, but he couldn't. He knew what shape it was taking. He could see it grow. A soft ghost of Stuart ignored them all, going about its business like they weren't there.

"Revenge on the Hunters," White nodded approvingly. "I remember that one. We will take him apart piece by piece."

"The notion doesn't appeal, Herr Wagner?" Isfet taunted, grinning.

Hans didn't rise to the bait. He knew Isfet was messing with him. He stared the creature down. The ghost was starting to fade and Rogue was still admiring it.

"I never saw this one before the train. He's very handsome..." she commented, her fingers tracing against it and messing the illusion. "Why the bite marks on his neck...?"

It was a rhetorical question. Hans knew he was caught. Isfet and Rogue were playing with them while they waited for White to catch up. He'd just got there. Hans felt the demon's hands tighten on him like a vice. He was done lying. Unfortunately, that probably meant he was done with everything else too.

* * *

Lucy had been watching Vincent when Oskar had told them about the visitor to the castle. She had seen him freeze. She'd felt her own blood ice over. This was it. This was what she'd been searching for. A dark chill had settled over the room. They all knew what this meant. They had unanimously agreed they needed to get into the castle, preferably before the reinforcements arrived, but they were still no closer to breaching the castle's defenses. Asking Hans to smuggle them in was a huge risk, if it was even an option at all. Vincent had made a comment about their ally's wellbeing in the face of this new threat that had drained the color from Stuart's face. The poor man had looked like he might faint.

Tony had ducked back into the bedroom almost as soon as the name had been spoken. Lucy had caved quickly to follow him. She'd let him back into their bed after the stunt at the railyard, although they were still not over the barn incident. He was digging through the pockets of his coat.

"Tony...?" she queried, watching him rummage.

He turned back to her, eyes imploring, and held something out. A bullet. Lucy took it from his fingers. It was a holy bullet, heavier than the ones she usually made. At first she thought the metal was strangely textured when she touched it, then she realized that it was engraved with etchings so small she would need a microscope read them.

He'd done it. He'd made the new bullet.

"How?" she gasped, inspecting it closely.

"The book," he answered. "That's what I was doing

in the barn. I was learning how. The monster was a mistake. It won't happen again. I could make more though, if we got the right ingredients."

"Why didn't you tell me?!" she protested. "We were supposed to be doing this together!"

"I know," Tony nodded. "That was wrong. I... I shoulda said, Luce. I'm sorry. I just... I didn't... I didn't really know what I was doing, I just knew what had to be done. I didn't want you to get hurt. I had to go somewhere else to find out how to finish what I started, somewhere I knew I could come back from, but you mighta gotten stuck. Somewhere no one should ever go."

"You went back to the tree..." Lucy breathed. "You used the book to go back to where it took you... oh Tony!" She threw her arms around him.

"I had to," he muttered, holding her close. "I had to go back. If I didn't go back, if I didn't see how it worked, how I worked, I'd be a slave to it forever. He wants us dead. Ever since Egypt. Now it's worse. He's recruiting to kill us. My magic is their magic, and he wants it back. The guardians stand neutral, waiting to see how everything plays out, but his game with Vincent is coming to an end. There is a curse on the Temple name, and Vincent is walking straight into his hands."

"A curse?" Lucy echoed. "What... what kind of curse?"

"I'm not sure," Tony admitted. "Most of this is vibes, it didn't come with an instruction book."

"Is it... my curse?" she whispered.

He looked at her in confusion. She pulled away,

sitting on the end of the bed and placing a hand to her mouth.

"I... I have a curse..." she muttered. "It's a little one. Easy to lift. I... I just... I didn't... Fred helped me! She..."

"I know," Tony gave her a nod. "That's not the one."

Lucy looked up at him hesitantly. He looked completely calm and the nod he gave her was reassuring.

"You knew...?" she asked. "How?"

"I recognized the magic," Tony shrugged.

"You never said anything..."

"Neither did you," he pointed out. He hunched his shoulders awkwardly, as though he had no idea what to say, but it wasn't going to stop him from trying. "I figured if you wanted to tell me about it, you would. It's your body, Lucy, you have to do what's right for you. I figured once you were ready, hopefully, we'd talk about it or something... I dunno. I guess... I thought it was your business."

"I should have told you..." she sighed. "I know I should have... I just didn't know how..."

"And I should have told you what I was doing," he shrugged. "I should have told you what it was and how I was planning it, but I can't always communicate these things I know, and I thought it'd be easier to just do it and show you than try and explain. I won't make that mistake again. I promise. I'll always try to tell you, even if the words aren't so good."

Lucy stood again and slipped her arms around him once more.

"We'll both try and do better," she promised, kissing him firmly. He kissed her back, tangling his fingers in the stray curls he brushed from her cheeks. When she let him go and stepped back she held up the bullet again. It gleamed in her fingers as she held it between them.

"I can make more," Tony repeated. "I just need some more stuff."

"It will do for now," Lucy assured. "We can finish this."

She pocketed the bullet and took Tony's hand, dragging him back into the main room where the others were still debating what to do. A weary Vincent stood with Oskar, while Fred comforted a concerned Stuart on the couch. Gio stood by the fireplace looking, as usual, like he was searching for answers at the bottom of a cigarette.

"Vincent," Lucy announced their return by addressing her mentor. "Tony says there's a curse on the Temple name."

"It's not a curse, it's a prophecy," Vincent replied instantly, like he had heard this argument made to the Hunters' Council. "The House of Faith will vanquish the Darkness."

"That's not a prophecy, that's a motto," Tony declared.

"That's all I know," Vincent shrugged. "No one much talks about it anymore. It was from my grandfather's time. I believe it was spoken by one of his enemies, and translated. Originally it sounded more like a curse, but I don't see how it could be read as such.

Why is this important?"

"Because if it is a curse maybe that's what keeps drawing the Prince to you?" Lucy shrugged. "Why else would something like that take such a vested interest in a single mortal?"

"So many reasons," Tony sighed. "Honestly, a family motto don't seem the likely one."

"Our family motto is *Ut Sol Oriatur*," Vincent offered. "You kids should learn it, being that it's yours now. As for the Prince... he is what all Hunters seek. His complete and utter annihilation is our ultimate goal, and I have sworn my life to it. How many ways I have failed, we will never know, but I won't fail this time."

"We won't fail," Lucy insisted. "I have a plan."

"Oh you do, do you?" Vincent smiled at her as though humoring her.

"Yes," she told him firmly. "Oskar, can you please tell me everything you know about the airship of reinforcements? This is going to take some doing."

FORTRESS OF THE SHADOW REICH

16

They had waited as late as they could. Oskar had given them the location of the airfield on the nearby hill and an estimated landing time for the reinforcements. Lucy's plan was, as Vincent politely put it, insane. However, no one had come up with a better one. They had all agreed to wait until nightfall in the hope that Hans would return with more intel and better ideas. Vincent had made the final call on that and hated every second of it.

The worst part was knowing. Deep in his soul he knew the vampire wasn't coming, and he couldn't meet Stuart's eye. He'd been the one to help injure the creature, and now there was no sign of what might have happened to him. Only the absence. Still, if they had needed anything to drag Owens on board with the insanity, that had done it. Watching darkness fall across the land with no sign of Hans seemed to have flipped a switch in his brain. He was prepared to try Lucy's plan, and damn however many people got killed in the process. Vincent was the one worried about the casualties, but he thought about how he would feel if it were Fred or Lucy missing, and he couldn't judge Owens. He just didn't want to start another war.

The airfield was a large, fenced area on a neighboring hill to the castle. It wasn't guarded nearly as well as the fortress. Sneaking in had been as easy as clipping the wire fence and getting Fred and Tony to conjure a little concealment. Staying hidden was proving more difficult. They were crammed in tightly behind a stack of heavy crates near the opening in the fence. The entire area was lit up with floodlights. The airship had landed. Harsh glows bounced off the underside of the grey zeppelin and reflected off the wet concrete ground. All the snow inside the station had been cleared. At least they wouldn't have to worry about leaving tracks.

They did have to worry about witnesses. More than a hundred of them. The airship had unloaded its reinforcements. Vincent could see ranks of troops lined up and ready to head out. Rows of men in uniform stood facing away from them, but their commanders were staring straight at the path the Hunters needed to take. They stuck to the shadows as best they could, clinging to the darkness like bats. Vincent wasn't sure how much magic Fred and Tony were spending to try and conceal them. Fred always said it was easy enough to conceal movement from imps... human minds were harder to fool.

He stared out at the ranks of humans who could turn on them, guns drawn, at any second. They really needed this to work. He sent Owens up first. Lucy might have been his rival for agility, but he trumped her in experience. He also seemed the most motivated right now, and Vincent would take the enthusiasm where he could get it. He let the girl follow after, with her husband and his cousin next. He and Fred brought up the rear. How Lucy had talked them into scaling the mooring lines of a zeppelin he would never know.

The ship blocked most of the view, drifting in the breeze as they climbed towards it. Vincent clutched the coarse rope tightly in his gloved hands. He inched along. It just kept getting higher. That was the point. He was holding his breath. Stop it. Goddamn. Usually when he did something this stupid it was at speed during the heat of battle. He didn't have time to think about it. He didn't have time to dwell on the height or the bounce of the rope or the way he kept holding his breath. Stop that! Breathe! The way his hands were slipping…

Even in gloves his fingers were going numb in the cold. He clutched tighter, but the grip wasn't there. He clambered, hand over hand, breath steaming as he panted. There was no way someone hadn't seen him. Surely. Any second. The ground felt so far away now. If he fell he wasn't getting back up in a hurry. He couldn't stop looking down. The soldiers were out of sight now, but he was waiting for them. Someone would come and investigate. Any second…

He reached forward. A hand grabbed his own. He looked up. Fred pulled him up into the central gondola. There were only three guards. Two of them were lying unconscious on the floor. The other one had Gio's elbow around his throat. His feet were starting to twitch.

"You alright, Sir?" Fred asked.

"Peachy," Vincent gave her a nod. He knew she'd

seen him struggling, felt the failing strength in his hand, but as far as he was concerned the hard part was over.

Gio dropped the guard. He'd stopped struggling, and he hit the floor with a thud. The young gangster pulled out a cigarette.

"Don't even think about it," Owens ordered.

"He's right," Lucy gave Gio a warning look. "We're going upstairs. If anyone blows this thing up with us inside it, I will haunt you for eternity."

Gio sighed and stuck the cigarette behind his ear. Lucy took point and headed for the door first. Vincent followed after her. They had a strict no-guns policy while they were up here. No noise. No sparks. He drew his sword carefully before they took the stairs.

The passageway inside the airship was a thin paneled path, sturdier than it looked. Crisscrossing steel beams reinforcing the blimp nested like a tunnel around it. They sprung up either side and crossed over the top like an infinite mirror of triangles. The balloon rose massive around them, yet the single file walkway, straight and long and exposed, felt desperately claustrophobic. It was like sneaking through the bowels of a giant steel beast.

Vincent was holding his breath again. If so much as a spark caught up here... He couldn't think about it. He had spent a lot of his life staring down death. Of all the ways he didn't want to go, exploding in a giant case of hydrogen was right up there. The metal creaked around him. He was starting to worry his body was pumping more adrenaline than blood.

They reached the door to the bridge. Lucy burst out

first. Startled guards stayed surprised that much longer when it was a young woman surprising them. As it was, they took the captain and his soldiers completely by surprise. Lucy leapt into the room, dagger drawn, and caught the first man by the throat. Vincent was right behind her, decapitating the captain as the man turned around. The third whirled and dropped, with one of Stuart's daggers sticking abruptly out of his eye.

"Good shot, *Capo*," Gio complimented his boss, strolling down the stairs behind them. He'd taken the cigarette out from behind his ear and was now chewing on the end of it. Fred hadn't let him smoke in the car on the way up either.

"Let's get this thing moving before anyone notices we're here," Fred suggested, making sure everything was firmly closed up behind them.

Everyone nodded their agreement. The Italians took the helm while the other three cleaned their blades.

"You know how to drive one of these things?" Tony asked.

"Can't be that hard," Gio shrugged.

"Boost it," Owens ordered, stepping in and taking over. "Every mooring line we didn't undo is one we're going to have to rip."

The boys stepped back as the ex-Hunter took the controls and fired the engines full bore.

"Is there anything he doesn't know how to do?" Tony muttered.

"Not really," Gio whispered. "It gets kinda annoying." Neither acknowledged that Owens was the only one who could read the controls.

The ship lurched as it set off. Vincent risked a peek out the window. The troops were startled now, though no one was taking up weapons yet. They didn't know they'd been compromised. They just didn't know why their ship was taking off again. There was yelling and chaos below them. Vincent could see it, but he couldn't make anything out over the roar of the engines. Owens set their course and hit the thrusters, tearing away from the mooring and firing away. Vincent felt a small smile tug his lips. He couldn't believe her crazy plan was working.

"Where are you going?" Lucy demanded.

"Our best option is to crash into the castle at this angle," Owens motioned. "Coming in from the side here. If I'm right, there should be a doorway down into the caverns beneath from that side of the courtyard. It will lead through the dungeons. Shortest and safest path for us to get straight from here down under the castle."

"We're not crashing," Lucy sighed. "We're landing at the castle, because they didn't have the sense to do that themselves."

Owens turned to her but she met his raised eyebrow with a completely straight face.

"Lucy, landing somewhere there's no space to land that will therefore cause damage to the area and/or vehicle is the definition of crashing," he stated in his best teaching voice.

She grinned at him and bopped the tip of his nose with her finger. He allowed it, with a longsuffering expression of tested patience. Vincent smirked. He wondered if that was what he looked like most of the time. It was the spitting image of the expression Fred used to wear during lessons with Tony. For different reasons, he was sure.

Still, the girl was allowed to be a little bit cheeky. This was her plan to save Stuart's boyfriend and take out Isfet. Vincent couldn't believe it was working. When she had suggested they steal the airship and fly it to the castle they all thought she'd gone mad. But she wasn't wrong. It was their best chance. The enemy weren't going to fire on their own ship. The reinforcements at the airbase didn't know what had gone wrong, and the soldiers at the castle wouldn't know anything had gone wrong. They could fly right over the defenses that barred them from infiltrating the fortress.

It was working. They shot through the sky, the castle rushing towards them at speed. Vincent and Fred fixed the getaway ropes and tested their strength. Somehow, the plan was less intimidating when it reached full madness. There was tension to sneaking. Jumping out of a crashing airship? That was just another Thursday.

"You might want to slow us up a bit, Stuart," Fred warned. "I ain't jumping at this speed."

"Seconding that," Tony raised a hand.

Owens threw the engines in reverse. Vincent looked out as the lights from the zeppelin illuminated the defenses they sailed over. Switchbacks, gatehouses, bunkers, barbed wire disappeared beneath them. The girl had been right.

Sirens began to blare.

"Sounds like they noticed us…" Gio commented.

Owens gave him the 'no shit, we're about to crash into them' look.

"Time to get a wriggle on then," Fred encouraged.

"Is the bridge going to make it over the wall before the front of the ship hits the towers?" Tony asked nervously.

"Maybe," Lucy answered. "Close run thing, so, ugh–!" She smashed through the windshield with a fire extinguisher and raked the glass across the bottom. "Recommend we go out the front window."

Owens kept the engines in full reverse, slowing the ship as it drifted lazily towards the towers.

"Now or never, people," Vincent ordered.

They began to grab the ropes and throw the ends out the broken window.

"How do we know they won't shoot us?" Tony asked, readying himself to propel down.

"We don't," Lucy admitted. "But I honestly think they have bigger problems."

The nose of the ship was drifting closer to the nearest tower. Owens had aimed it to scrape by. They were pushing it close. Everyone clambered over the broken window and jumped. Vincent made sure they all got out and followed last.

This was the kind of hunting that came naturally to him. His tattered coat billowed around him and the cold wind whipped through his steel-grey hair. The rope held tight as he swung down, cobbled courtyard rushing to meet him. His knees were already screaming in protest at the idea of the landing. He ignored them. As the ground came closer he could hear orders being screamed in German over the sound of the sirens. They didn't have enough people left here to manage what was about to happen. The ship was still trying to go in reverse though. It was possible it might–

The nose of the airship smashed into the tower. It crumpled. The metal tore. It sparked. Vincent hit the ground and rolled. He could feel the vibrations from the exploding airship above him in his bones. The sky became an ocean of fire. Hot air beat down on him. The ringing in his ears was compounded by the cracking of stone as the tower fell. A hand grabbed his coat and hauled him away. Vincent crashed away from the heat and light. He staggered and hit a wall. Dark. Cool. A door was slammed shut. He blinked, trying to get his hearing and vision back.

"You doing okay, Doc?" Gio asked.

Vincent nodded, letting reality slowly come back into focus. Outside the door, the rumble of destruction continued.

"That was the craziest thing we've ever done," Tony commented to Lucy.

She grinned at him.

"I think it's pretty safe to say them Nazis are well distracted," Gio grinned. "Where to now, boss?"

"Down these stairs," Owens lifted a torch and illuminated a spiral staircase. "Hans said he was staying in the basement beneath the castle, and the cavern they set up as the lab is beneath the dungeons."

"Why the basement?" Tony pondered as they began down. "Seems a strange place to put a guest."

"No windows," Owens replied curtly. "Windows

can be extremely dangerous for someone who has to avoid sunlight."

"I can't imagine having to live without sunlight," Lucy sighed. "It would be awful."

"It's not his favorite part of existence," Owens replied. There was a sharpness to his tone that shut everyone up. They knew it wasn't personal. They knew he was just stressed. It was better to stay silent for now. They kept their mouths shut and descended deep into the lion's den. Owens led them down, pausing at every landing. Each time he reached a doorway he hesitated, as though compelled to check it. Down here the silence just grew. Occasional echoes from the carnage above rumbled deep after them, but all the passages down here were quiet. Logic dictated they go as far down as they could, so Owens did his best to ignore other paths.

It was the sensible choice. At the bottom of the staircase they hit rock. The corridor became an unpaved tunnel of dusty stone, deep under the earth. It was cold and dark and ominous. Strange sounds echoed back through the tunnel, like whispers from another world bouncing through the fissure. Owens looked back at them. Vincent gave him a nod. Lucy patted his shoulder. He led on.

The sounds grew louder as they went. The sinister shadows from the torch stretched and danced like nightmare figures looping over the naked rock walls. The weight of the earth above them pressed down forebodingly. Every now and again the tunnel would shiver. Dust rained down. It was hard not to think about the castle collapsing over them, but this was their best shot. It was their only chance to take out Rogue and White before Isfet helped them do something irreversible.

The tunnel split. They came around the corner slowly and found the path branching in two. Both tunnels looked nearly identical. Owens was crouched instantly, looking for footprints and signs of wear. Vincent joined him. Fred placed her hands out and a faint red glow grew from her palms. She grimaced and let the glow die.

"I'm not getting a reading on either of them," she admitted.

"They both look used," Owens agreed reluctantly. "Do we split up? Check both?"

Vincent shared a look with Fred. He didn't trust Owens to lead a team right now. That left him and Fred.

"Take Lucy and Giovanni," he instructed her. "Go right."

"And you?" she raised a sharp eyebrow.

"I'll take Owens and Tony left," he replied. "Two Hunters and a mage each side. Play it careful. Watch for traps."

"If anyone finds Hans let him know what we're doing and where we've gone," Owens insisted.

An awkward pause filled the air. Banging noises filtered up from both tunnels and did nothing to clarify which path with the best one to take.

"Of course," Lucy reassured, touching his shoulder. No one would meet his eye. They didn't want their gaze to betray the thought that if he were still here his super-human senses would have found them by now.

"Good luck, *Capo*," Gio took Stuart's hand.

"*Grazie e tu*," Owens replied.

Lucy and Tony shared a kiss and some quiet words. Vincent looked to Fred. He put an arm around her shoulders and kissed her forehead.

"Stay safe," he ordered.

"You too," she replied.

He could see the concern in her eyes. One hand had slipped into the pocket of her coat. He could see her grip tightening. Whatever vibes she had been able to read off the tunnels, they weren't good. Another loud boom echoed from above, rattling the caves. Dust sifted down. A metallic clang banged down the tunnels. They finished their goodbyes and parted ways. Vincent dragged Tony and Owens in his wake, stalking off down the left-hand tunnel.

It stayed dark and cold, and the instant they were out of sight he began to worry about Fred and Lucy. He should have kept them with him, but he hoped they would be safer down their path. The tunnel they followed began to snake back and forth. Vincent kept a slow pace. He could feel Owens itching to take off behind him. At least his impatience was tamed by his common sense, for now.

A faint glow tempered the darkness ahead. Vincent bade Owens stay his torch and snuck forward. The others followed. He wasn't sure what he'd been expecting, but it wasn't this. A faint ethereal light shone before them. Vincent looked to Tony. This was going to be his area of expertise. In an almost synchronized movement, the three of them drew their guns and started forward. Tony took the lead, barely half a step, and the Hunters flanked him. The kid raised a hand, but he'd barely signed when the illusion took shape.

The ghostly apparition of a familiar, beautiful woman hung in the air before them. Her hair and lips were robbed of their ruby color, but her smoky eyes called alluringly to them.

"Come to me..." the ghost whispered seductively. "I can grant you all that you seek... Follow my voice and I will fulfill your innermost desires..."

No one moved. The ghost curled her fingers at them, tempting them forward. Tony broke first. He gave a snort of laughter and that set the other two off. Vincent knew he shouldn't laugh, but the kid started it. A flicker of annoyance crossed the illusion's face.

"Sorry," Tony apologized to it. "You're probably not used to that response. I... geez lady, I almost feel bad for you. This is a fairly solid triple strike. You'll have better luck with the others, if you want to try them."

"You're not sending it after the others!" Vincent protested.

"Pfft," Tony scoffed. "It's pansy magic. Besides, it's not tempting you, Doc. It's certainly not tempting the Professor here. And me? *No buono.* Sorry, *signora*, if you met my wife, you'd understand."

Rogue's expression changed, settling into a smug glare. Highlights of color returned. Her voice became more certain.

"Then I guess we'll have to coax you another way..." she purred.

Tony flicked his finger at her. There was spark and

the apparition vanished before it could solidify further. Vincent opened his mouth to ask Tony exactly what that had been, but his words were cut off. A sharp scream pierced the air. The agony was so thick you could taste it. Owens went white.

* * *

The tunnel stayed dark and it wound in a long arc. Fred could feel it veering further and further right. It pulled tighter, shrinking in size and curving sharply. She was far from banging her head, but she still felt a strong urge to duck and hunch. Lucy and Gio stalked either side of her, guns drawn. Every now and again she let her fingers touch the photo in her pocket. Just a gentle reminder. Something warm. A piece of home.

Light flickered ahead. Arcane light. Magic. She motioned Lucy and Gio behind her, for all the good it did. They weren't keen to let her go ahead. The light grew brighter as they came around the corner. It began to take shape as they reached it. A form. A woman. Rogue. The apparition opened its mouth. Fred fried it.

Red lightning sparked from her hands. The ghost yelped, recoiling as the magic tried to rip it apart. Color began flare across it, adding an opaque quality to the illusion. It grabbed the lightning and tried to fire it back. Fred raised a shield of light. The magic hit hers and vanished. She stood, braced, light hanging off her arm like a weightless buckler. The set of her smirk was confident, and she tossed her dark hair from her eyes as though daring Rogue to try again.

The apparition glowered.

"It is no matter," Rogue scorned. "We don't need you. We need only the sacrifice. The pure life that will usher in the new world. You'll be dead before you can stop us."

"You first," Fred snarled. She blasted out from the shield, destroying the illusion. The magic went out and they were left in a deep semi-darkness again.

Gio flicked a match and held it up. They could see him desperately fighting the urge to light his cigarette still.

"What is it with the sacrifice?" he asked. "Always a pure life?"

"It means virgin," Lucy rolled her eyes. "It's a myth, but they buy into it."

Gio gave a snort of laughter. "Alright, good luck to 'em. Where they think they'll find that in the bottom of a cave?"

Fred paused. A sudden sharp alarm prickled the back of her neck. Lucy met her eye. The revelation was contagious.

"Vincent..." Fred whispered.

"Wait, what?" Gio startled.

"You sure?" Lucy checked.

"No, I'm not sure," Fred countered. "But my guess is as good as yours."

"The old Doc?" Gio pressed. "Seriously?"

Fred and Lucy ignored him, staring at each other. Fred could see Lucy's brain ticking over the same thoughts as hers. Would Isfet take great pleasure in using the Chancellor of the Hunters as his ultimate sacrifice? There was probably no greater infinite delight.

Fred cracked, taking off down the tunnel. Lucy sprinted after her and Gio bolted behind them.

* * *

Vincent chased Owens down the tunnel. The younger man had broken at the sound of the scream and raced toward danger. The noise had turned into a banging din and the light was growing as they neared the end of the tunnel. Tony ran faster. He caught Stuart's coat, yanking him back. Vincent grabbed him and slammed him into the wall. Just in time. It sounded like an assembly factory around the corner. A laugh echoed from the cavern beyond.

"I smell humans..." White's voice taunted. "Which one of you is Stuart? I have something of yours." His pronouncement was punctuated by a piercing scream. They all recognized Hans' voice.

It took Vincent and Tony's combined strength to hold Owens back. He looked like the one being tortured. Vincent could barely bring himself to look at his friend's pained face. He forced himself to, if only to mouth 'he's still alive', trying to put things in perspective. If Hans was screaming, he wasn't dead yet. The scream tapered into whimpering grunts.

"Stay back! It's a trap!" Hans cried weakly.

Owens rolled his eyes, unable to do much more being pinned to the wall.

"No doy," Tony muttered.

"The man's being tortured," Vincent countered in a whisper. "He can be excused for stating the obvious."

"*D'accord,*" Owens sighed, calming enough to shrug Vincent and Tony away. "Nice of them to set a trap for us. Let's spring it." He pulled open his coat to access the small satchel bag slung on safely beneath it. Inside were vials of holy water, at least two types of grenades, and several boxes of holy bullets. Owens drew out a smoke grenade and handed it to Vincent. "Cover me."

"Cover all of us," Tony countered, grabbing another one. "Before anyone does anything stupid, let's toss these around the corner. I'll create a few illusions in the smoke, that should trigger their response and then we'll have a better idea what we're up against. If there's enough smoke it might help extend a concealment spell too – I could sneak us through."

"When did you get so smart?" Vincent demanded.

"Been around Lucy for years, Doc," Tony grinned. "Something was bound to rub off."

They both ripped the tabs on their grenades and hurled them around the corner. Smoke gushed into the air. Tony flicked his fingers and shadows dashed through the smoke. Gunfire erupted. Vincent, Owens, and Tony hunched close to the wall as a wave of bullets screamed into the mouth of the tunnel. The wall across from them exploded in shards of rock. That was a lot of guns. The gunfire paused. Vincent took his fingers out of his ears to look at the other two in alarm.

Smoke was still pouring thick and heavy, obscuring the entrance. Tony motioned to them, signaling that he would send a distraction one way and try to conceal them the other. Owens nodded. He pulled out a couple of shrapnel grenades and handed one to Vincent. They moved on Tony's signal. Vincent wasn't sure how the concealment worked given that he was standing in it, but they burst out into the cavern while the bullets went safely wide.

The massive room was well lit. Vincent could see everything at once. The machine was back. The one they'd just destroyed at the railyard. It took up most of the center of the cave, a shining and ominous doorway to hell. A ring of soldiers stood guard around it as the last pieces were fixed together. Most of the uniformed men were grouped to face the entrances of the many tunnels that lined the walls.

On the far side, in a corner with no exits, White had Hans chained to a rack. Even from this distance Vincent could see where the silver shackles against his bare wrists and ankles were burning him. Silver could do terrible things to the undead. Three swords protruded from the vampire's bare torso. Vincent could see the entry wounds scorched around the edges. Holy blades. Some of them even had old Hunter insignia on them. White was in the process of turning their friend into an artistic pincushion. He had an entire ring of swords beside him, set in a convenient stand, as a painter would set their colors. The demon was clearly enjoying himself, but Vincent knew how that was going to end. He could feel his own blood chill in outrage.

They lobbed their grenades behind the line of soldiers. Vincent and Tony leapt for the cover of a nearby stack of crates. Owens went forward. The grenades went off, blowing a large hole in the soldiers' defense. Owens went for the gap. Half the men had died from the impact. The blasts had hit them from behind. The injured staggered to fill the hole. They saw the man in the suit streaking towards them. They took aim. Owens hit them like a freight train. He grabbed a soldier by the throat, swinging him forward like a human shield. The man sank the bullets intended for Stuart, dying quickly in his hands. Owens aimed the dead man's machine gun and mowed through the Nazis firing at him. He dropped the corpse and ran.

Other soldiers turned to face him but he was already throwing another grenade. Screams echoed through the cavern as it blew through more men. He didn't slow. White had turned from Hans and was watching the approach with a vicious grin. Owens shot through the last Nazis between him and the demon, tossed the empty gun, drew his pistol, aimed, and fired. White flickered. The bullet sent up chips of stone as it pierced the wall. White flickered into position at Stuart's shoulder.

"You think I didn't see that coming?" he taunted.

Owens kicked him in the face. The action was instant, unflinching. The sole of his shoe smashed into White's chin like he'd been waiting for it.

"You see that coming?" he retorted.

Across to the right, the last of the soldiers were converging on another tunnel. A dark red glow was burning deep inside it, becoming brighter, closer. They opened fire. The roar of machine guns filled the air, bouncing around the cavern. As quickly as the soldiers

fired, they fell. The bullets ricocheted straight back at
them. Blood spurted from the black uniforms, bodies
dancing grotesquely before they hit the ground. Fred
charged out, a snarl of righteous fury on her face and a
giant glowing red shield held before her. Lucy and Gio
appeared at either side; guns drawn, they rushed in
firing. The last of the soldiers didn't stand a chance as
the Hunters' bullets felled them.

"Sir, we married some badass ladies..." Tony
commented from behind the crates.

"That we did, son," Vincent conceded. He leapt out
of cover, running in to take out the machine. Someone
stepped in his way. A very familiar someone. "You!"
Vincent hissed.

"Hello darling," Isfet grinned.

Vincent lunged. He was too angry to think clearly.
He pounced, arms outstretched, to throttle the dark
entity. Isfet caught his wrists. Vincent kicked. Isfet
dodged. Vincent shoved him back, yanking his wrists
free. He drew his pistol, aimed, fired. Isfet closed his
hand over the end of the barrel. His limb rippled as
Vincent's bullets vanished into his otherworldly flesh.

"Oops," Isfet smiled.

Vincent ripped his gun free and attacked. He
punched and kicked and spun. Isfet blocked him
effortlessly.

To the side, Fred was still charging through, shield
raised. She stumbled and cried out. The shield was
ripped in half. Her magic vanished. The assault came
from the center of the machine. Rogue floated up, red
light burning from her hands and sparking around her

body. Gio aimed and fired. The sorceress vanished. His bullet pinged off one of the giant metal rings.

"Sir, get back!" Fred yelled, catching sight of Vincent and unleashing a storm of red light.

Rogue caught the lightning before it came close to Isfet. The two mages pushed the crackling magic between them, trying to force each other back.

Lucy sprinted and leapt. She kicked off one of the generators rigged to the machine. Pouncing like a cat, she cartwheeled over the machine, tossing a grenade into the center, and leaping to the other side of the room.

In the corner, White had Owens by the throat. His hand tightened and his snarl twitched. Owens struggled, raising a shaking hand, and shot him in the side. White dropped him to dodge. The bullet grazed the demon's ribs. Lucy's foot collided with his back. He staggered. Owens struggled up, coughing and gasping. Lucy pulled him up by the elbow. She drew her gun on White and fired. He flickered away.

Near the tunnel, Isfet shoved Vincent back. The blow knocked him down. Vincent hit the ground on one knee with a grunt.

"You're getting a bit old, friend," Isfet commented. "Here, catch."

With a small flick of his hand, Lucy's grenade shot out of the machine towards Vincent. There was no time to throw it back. It was about to blow. Vincent threw his arms over his face. The pain never came. He heard the blast erupt near the ceiling. The whole cavern shook. Above them, the castle was still falling. Vincent opened his eyes. Tony stood over him. A golden glow surrounded his hands and a giant arcane circle of light shielded them from harm.

"Ah," Isfet sneered. His smirk was long gone and distaste curled his lip.

"Wanna try again?" Tony invited. "You lost this fight last time you lunged me."

"There's always the next round, babyface," Isfet hissed, but he didn't attack. He stepped back, eyeing the situation and dashing away to the machine.

Vincent had never seen the Prince run from anything. Not like that. Not like he was afraid. Tony turned and offered Vincent a hand up. Vincent saw what Isfet saw. The light wasn't just about the kid, it was in him. His eyes glowed with it. The days of the Darkness trying to creep out of his body were gone. He looked holy.

"Tony..." Vincent muttered, unsure what to ask next but prepared to take his hand.

"I got you, Doc," Tony promised, pulling him to his feet like nothing was different.

Across the room, Hans cried out. He still struggled feebly against his bonds, weak and wounded by his restraints.

"*Aufhören!*" he bellowed, dark eyes fixed on the machine. "Stop! Greta!"

They all looked. Isfet stood at the base of his machine. He was holding a terrified young woman by her hair, pressing a knife to her throat. His expression clearly stated he was done playing games.

"Aw, what's wrong, Wagner?" White taunted. "You

weren't using her. Means we can."

Hans looked like he was about rip free, but the silver scorched him when he moved and the blades impaling him cut deeper. Lucy rushed forward, but even she couldn't get there in time. Isfet slit the girl's throat, ear to ear, deep enough to hit bone. Her blood sprayed across the bottom of the rings and Isfet dropped her body into the basin beneath them. The metal began to light up where the blood touched it. The glow spread, traveling across the engraved runes. The rings started to spin. In the center, a portal began to emerge.

FORTRESS OF THE SHADOW REICH

17

The portal ripped open. Energy rippled out from it, blasting across the room. Lucy threw her arms up, shielding her eyes from the light. It hit her first. She skidded back, but stayed on her feet. Behind her, Owens staggered to Hans and ripped the swords from his body.

"Stu–!" Hans gasped. He didn't get further, but Owens took the warning. He jerked away as White tried to stab him in the back. The blade caught the edge of his sleeve, but he turned firing. White flickered away from the shot. It grazed his leg.

The magic between Fred and Rogue flickered out as the portal energy hit it. Both women paused to look. Gio emptied his gun into the machine, trying to jam it. He grabbed one of the machine guns from the floor and kept going. Half the bullets ricocheted off the spinning rings. The others vanished into the growing portal. The same eerie blue light as last time began to fill the cavern. Lightbulbs began to burst. A cold wind exploded through the cave. It stank of death and emptiness. The gravity began to change. Everything felt heavier, tighter. Pressure from the portal was building.

"This one's on us, Doc," Tony insisted. He and

Vincent were crouched by the crates, arms raised as the portal winds buffeted them.

Vincent gave him a nod. They forced themselves up. Vincent drew his sword in one hand and his pistol in the other. He ran forward, pushing through the wind. Tony started to glow brighter. The golden ropes of light uncoiled from his hands. He threw them hard, lashing out and catching the rings. He pinned them in place, locking them down and halting the spinning. The force of the machine pulled. Tony gritted his teeth, bracing himself and holding the ropes tightly.

Isfet strode towards him. Vincent met him coming. The old Hunter narrowed his eyes, his glare meeting the Prince's look. Isfet broke first, trying to get to Tony. Vincent lunged. He fired straight at him, slowing him with bullets even if he couldn't stop him. Isfet raised his arms to meet Vincent's sword. He swung it true. Isfet smashed his forearms down on the blade. Anyone else it would have severed the limbs. His flesh oozed around the sword, but black blood dripped from the wounds.

"What are you really doing here, Vincent?" Isfet pushed, his flesh crawling up Vincent's sword. "You think you came halfway around the world chasing a witch and a demon? No. You know better than that. You're always looking for something… you just can't seem to remember what it is."

"You don't have my memories anymore," Vincent grunted, trying to cut through him.

"I don't need memories, my love, I have you," the Prince oozed along the blade, his grin growing more insane. "I am what you've been searching for, Hunter.

I'm what you've always been searching for, what you taught your little girl to search for with the same single-minded drive that doomed you. You believe it's your family's destiny to defeat me? You're nothing without me! I need you to look, Vincent. I need you to look for me, and I need to see you realize that I will always be just out of reach. I need to see that beautiful madness consume you as you comprehend that the one thing you have always sought is the one thing you will never quite have. You need me, Vincent. You need me and I will always, *always* be here for you... just out of reach."

The portal was still growing. Even though the rings weren't spinning, the momentum was there. The light hit the metal with a stabilizing thunk. Deep inside the shimmering force, something stirred. A distant groan. A crack. A cry.

Tony pulled harder, his golden light trying to rip the rings and destabilize the portal. His ropes heaved. The rings creaked.

Rogue went for him. She flashed across the room in a sea of crimson light. Then Fred was there. She threw herself in front of her apprentice, shield raised in a half dome. Rogue's magic smashed into them like a wave against a cliff. Red light sprayed into the air. Fred roared with effort, but her shield held. The light around her hands flared painfully.

Bullets sprayed across the shield. Three caught Rogue down the leg. The sorceress spun in the air, red lightning erupting from her like a storm. Gio kept the gun on her. His finger didn't ease on the trigger. Rogue screamed, unleashing her rage. Gio ran and dove behind the portal, rolling away. The wall behind him ripped apart. Shards of rock exploded into the air.

On the other side of the cave, Owens was trying to break the chains binding Hans.

"Vhite has ze key!" Hans gasped over the noise. "Stop him!"

A hand grabbed Stuart's shoulder.

"Uh-oh, did I steal your plaything?" White smirked.

Owens was already driving his dagger towards White's gut. The demon caught his wrist. He swung his other hand through, firing his pistol. White caught that wrist too. The bullet went wide. White grinned, looming over Owens and squeezing. Stuart's eyes creased with pain.

"Missed me..." the demon hissed.

"Dodge this," Lucy taunted. She was already pulling the trigger, her gun pressed to White's lower back. The holy bullet ruptured his flesh, spraying black blood.

White snarled, dropping Owens. He whirled, striking Lucy so hard she smashed into the ground. Owens lifted his gun and fired. This time he got White through the shoulder. Another dark stain spread across the demon's suit jacket. White didn't even flinch. He snatched Lucy up in both hands, wheeling around, and threw her into Stuart. They both went flying. Owens hit the ground hard. He wasn't sure if the crack came from him or the cave. The girl wasn't heavy, until she landed on his ribs. This fall was even harder than her last. Grazes marked her knees and forearms.

A deep groan shook the cave. Something was coming through the portal. Something dark and sharp began to extend through the ether. Something easily six feet long. A claw. Five. Fingers the size of ancient trees began to slide through the hole. Vincent stared it horror, locked in battle with Isfet. Behind the Prince, something too big for this cave was trying to break through.

Tony pulled harder. His knuckles were white and the veins in his neck stood out as he fought desperately against the machine. He cried out from the exertion, struggling to counter the magic of the runes. One began to flicker where Tony's magic bound it. The rings buckled. A hand the size of a ship reached through the portal, groping for the heart of a new world. Tony screamed and unleashed. The light burnt up his arms, bursting through the ropes. The metal began to tear. A sharp screech sounded as the bolts gave. The rings ripped apart. Tony flung the pieces away. One embedded in the ceiling. Two smashed into the walls. The portal choked. It shrank. Vanished. The light went out with sharp sound. The giant hand abruptly fell, sheared at the wrist.

Everyone froze.

Tony whimpered as his light went out, staggering weakly and leaning on his knees. Sweat dripped down his cheeks. He looked up. His dark eyes met Isfet's, fatigued but full of challenge.

The Prince was not happy. There was a loathing in his gaze colder than the deepest part of Hell. He sighed. A deep sound that carried. His weary breath suffocated the sounds of the battle. Nothing was more powerful than his impatience.

"If you want something done right…" he muttered.

Isfet shoved Vincent back. The Hunter hadn't been expecting the force. He crashed to the ground, confused as to where the Prince had found such strength. Isfet stared Vincent in the eye, his smirk returning as he raised his hands to his face. He sunk his fingers into his flesh, ripping the skin away. Black ooze dripped like blood. Something else erupted from within him. The faceless figure. The Darkness.

It grew, shifting, heaving, pulsing. Vincent staggered, desperately trying to get back to his feet. The ooze bubbled up, overflowing. Gushing closer. Vincent scrambled away. The Prince's laughter echoed through the cavern. The Darkness kept expanding. It was massive. Endless. Vincent could feel it reaching for him. He ran. The monster began to take form.

It was huge. Vincent leapt as it reached for him. A six-fingered hand the size of the severed one crashed into the cavern floor. Rock fractured beneath its weight. Shoulders twisted and heaved up to the ceiling. A face began to tear through the dark ooze. Beady glowing eyes peered down through a mask of fangs and horns. The Prince bellowed. The sound shook the cave. Cracks snapped through the walls. Dust rained from the ceiling. All the Hunters flinched, terror plain on their faces. Rogue turned her face to the monster, devotion softening her features.

"My King..." she breathed lovingly.

Fred went for her. She threw magic and her shield dove around Rogue, trapping her in a cylinder of light. Lightning burst from the sides, zapping the sorceress mercilessly. Rogue screamed, throwing her arms either side. The cage ruptured, tearing apart in flecks of broken magic. She leapt. Magic still lit her hands, but she didn't turn to it. She lunged at Fred, tackling her to the ground. Fred struggled in her arms. Rogue clawed at her, hissing in outrage, trying to throttle her. Fred punched her across the face. Her right hook drew blood, but Rogue didn't stop. Her hands caught Fred's neck and tightened.

Gio ran in. He paused, aimed, then lowered the gun. The women were too tangled. He couldn't risk it. Instead he went old school. His running kick caught Rogue full in the ribs, ripped her off Fred and knocked her down. He grabbed Fred's arm, pulling her up. She was coughing and choking, but her grip was strong. Rogue snatched at them. She caught Fred's coat, tearing the pocket away. A small square photo fell to the floor. Fred paused.

"Fred!" Gio warned, shoving her out of the way.

Rogue threw a hand out, blasting him. Gio took the hit. Red lightning smacked him full in the chest. The blast lifted him off his feet, ripping his grip on Fred and firing him across the room. He hit his head against the cave wall. A trickle of blood smeared down the side as he slid, unmoving, to the ground.

Owens saw his apprentice go down, but White didn't appreciate the distraction. Isfet and Rogue were responsible for the dawning horror in Stuart's eyes. White didn't like being shown up. He stabbed at the Hunter. Owens barely dodged. The blade grazed his ribs. He gave as good as he got, swinging back with a short blade in his fist. White flickered back from the attack. Owens paused as the great beast in the center of the room shifted. He shot at it, his holy bullet sparking gold in the creature's back.

"Forgetting your priorities?!" White called to him.

Owens whirled back. White grabbed the wheel of swords by its stand. Hans writhed against his bonds, but he couldn't get free. White flashed his proudest grin at the look on Stuart's face.

"NO!" Stuart screamed.

White drove the stand down. Hans howled once as he was impaled by more than a dozen swords. Owens moved like lightning. He lunged for the demon like the cure to death itself was in its pocket. White danced back from him, laughing manically. Owens didn't pause. He didn't think. He stabbed and fired as if God himself had ordered him to kill that thing. White was grinning with joy. Until a bullet struck him. It caught his leg. He stumbled. Owens was reloading as he went. His homicidal gaze never dropped from White's face. The demon's smile wavered.

The monster in the center of the room was moving. It took up nearly half the cave on its own. One hand slapped forward over the ground. Vincent and Tony leapt out of the way. Vincent yelped, stumbling. His knee buckled as he tried to avoid being crushed. Shots sounded. The beast roared. Golden sparks erupted from its wrist. Lucy came rushing in. She appeared around the side, pistol in each hand. Black ooze sprayed where she shot it, but the wounds began to seal as soon as the light died.

Tony was panting, gulping air like he needed a rest.

There was no time. He tried to focus. Golden light sparked in his eyes and around his hands. It flickered, sparking on and off like a dodgy bulb. Vincent shoved him out of the way as the monster slashed at them. Vincent slashed back. His sword caught it across the knuckles, and his gun fired into its palm. The attacks barely slowed it. It snatched for him. He dodged. A claw caught his coat. It knocked him down. The sword clattered from his hand. Tony finally got the light to hold. He blasted it at the creature's chest. It flinched. The light wounded it. That made it angry.

The anger was nothing in the face of Stuart's wrath. White's smile was gone. He had the confused look of an immortal who just realized they might be able to die. Owens saw him stumble. He shot out White's knees before he could flicker. The demon blinked, barely comprehending what was happening to him. Owens didn't let him fall. He caught White, jamming him against the wall, and burying his dagger in the demon's stomach. White blinked, struggling. It hurt. He was bleeding. Owens thrust the blade deeper, unloading two bullets straight where White's heart should be.

White fell, sliding down the wall, tasting his own blood. Black stained his lips. It smeared the rock behind him.

"Let me help you with that," Owens offered. It sounded like a death threat. It was.

He grabbed a bottle from his bag, ripping out the stopper and shoving it in White's mouth. The demon's scream became a gurgle as the holy water gushed down his throat. Owens lined his pistol up with the bottom of the bottle. He fired. Holy water and demon brain plastered the wall.

No one else saw White die. Fred had problems of her own. She couldn't make it to Gio. Rogue was on her feet again. The sorceress was furious. Red light coursed about her like an aura. Flames erupted at her every step. Fred panted weakly as she watched one flaming heel come down on her photo. Her family. Wee Toby and his beautiful mother. Helen.

"You can't win this," Rogue warned venomously. "I was ancient before you were born, witch! I know magic you could never hope to learn! My King has risen! This world will be cleansed! Your magic is little more than a thorn in my side."

Fred raised a hand to blast her. Rogue brushed the attack aside. Fred struggled back. Rogue reached down, snatching her by the throat and hauling her up, into the glow of the sorceress's magic. Fred struggled, flailing. She wasn't a witch. She was a mage. A damn good mage, but Rogue was right. Her magic couldn't match this. The photo smoldered on the ground as Fred dipped a hand inside her torn coat. She was so much more than a mage.

"Say goodbye," Rogue ordered, lifting Fred with one hand, and summoning a giant fiery blade of red light in the other. She drove it through Fred's chest. Fred felt her body stiffen. Pain exploded through her. Her lungs tightened, trying not to breathe to stave off the pain. She positioned her hand as Rogue removed the blade.

"Goodbye," Fred wheezed. She pulled the trigger. Three shots, pressed against Rogue's stomach, pointing up.

The sorceress stared at her, bewildered. The strength vanished from her arm. Fred's feet hit the ground. She smiled. Not just a mage. Rogue touched a hand to the wounds in her torso as death began to cloud her eyes. She let go. Neither had the strength to stand alone. They collapsed to the floor. Fred felt the gun slip from her fingers. She didn't need it. She closed her eyes, smiling at the sky. They fought the fight for others. That was why they acted, why they were Hunters, she remembered as blood pooled beneath her.

The ground shook. The whole cavern rattled like it wanted to come down. The Prince attacked viciously as the remaining Hunters fired at him. One blow from that creature could be fatal. Vincent was painfully aware that the thing could crush him with a finger. Tony couldn't hold his magic. He had brought one rope back, catching the monster around the arm, but he couldn't bind it. Not yet. He needed more time. Lucy was dodging and weaving dangerously. Vincent saw the strike before it happened.

"Lucy!" he bellowed, charging in.

She faltered at his call. It slowed her. Not enough. He rammed her with his shoulder, knocking her back. The Prince's hand snatched him instead. Giant dark fingers caught him under the arms. He fired into the wrist. Light sparked from the wound. It bubbled and settled. The hand squeezed. Pain blossomed through Vincent's body like a sudden spring bloom. His life flashed before his eyes. All his ribs cracked. He felt them shatter, piercing his lungs. A choked sound escaped his lips, along with a spray of blood. He felt suddenly dizzy. Everything was happening slowly. His head was near the ceiling, but he didn't remember moving. He was being lifted. Lowered. His body was descending towards the biggest teeth he'd ever seen.

The Prince's eyes glowed with unholy fire. Familiar eyes. He'd spent all those years thinking of the Prince as faceless, but no. Those eyes had been watching him his whole life. Now they watched his death. He couldn't even kick as the Prince finally got to eat him. This was how he'd known it would end for some time. The pain was too much to fight. He tried, flailing weakly. The teeth closed on his left leg. They bit down. He screamed as his leg was severed, right through the thigh. The creature's teeth crushed through his femur. He wasn't sure if the amputation or the scream hurt more.

Everything went bright. He felt nothing.

"Vincent!" Lucy shrieked.

Tony's ropes were back. Not just one. Hundreds. Every rope that caught the monster made the boy's eyes burn brighter. The arcane circle that lit beneath his feet grew. Soon it encompassed the entire floor of the cave. The Prince was growing smaller. He thrashed and growled and struggled, but Tony had his hooks in him. The smile on his face was strangely cruel as he tightened his magic, draining the Prince's power and inverting it. The monster slipped. Tony pinned it to the ground. Vincent's still body rolled limply away. Tony and Lucy approached, slowly.

The Prince hissed and snarled, thrashing against the ropes binding it, the light burning it. He was small again. Humanoid. The faceless shadow man. He seemed so little, bound in that much light.

"You think you've won," he spat in his deep voice. "But this is nothing! A minor setback!"

"That is a victory for us," Lucy told him coolly, slipping a bullet from her pocket.

"You are small and weak," the Prince taunted. "The best you can hope for is a mere scratch to the surface. I will always be here. I will always come back. Your Master feared his past, I'll give you a future his nightmares couldn't dream of! A war bigger than the last! A war to end all wars! I cannot be stopped! Humanity will fall!"

"Sure," Tony nodded to him. "How's that going for you right now?"

"Thief!" he accused.

"Maybe," Tony shrugged. "But I worked out how you did it, and I'm putting it to better use than you ever did. I don't think you're as invincible as you want to believe." He nudged the bound entity with his foot. "Even death may die."

"I cannot die!" the Prince spat.

"Well, me and my little friend are going to test that theory," Lucy stated, slipping the bullet into her revolver and jamming it under the Prince's chin.

"I will always come back," the Prince threatened.

"So will we," Lucy smiled grimly. "And we are not afraid of you. See you next time." She pulled the trigger.

A blinding light exploded through the Prince's head, shattering his cranium like a melon. The silhouette of the Darkness began to dissolve in its bonds.

"Stand back, Luce," Tony cautioned. He stepped forward, hands outstretched, and focused his magic. The ropes seemed to absorb the body dissolving in them. They glowed brighter and brighter, until they were too bright to look at. The light began to drift away, dispersing but not fading. It settled on the wounded. Tony stood patiently, eyes closed, fingers twitching. Lucy shaded her face with an arm, but she didn't take her eyes from her husband. She could feel his magic settling on the scrapes on her skin.

Vincent lay in a strange bath of light, beyond pain and comprehension. He saw the figure coming for him across space and time. Across all universes. His old friend. The Prince. The one who had caught him and carried him through so much. The one who had shared his secrets. He came closer, his hands resting warm and gentle on Vincent's body. The smooth dark featureless face. But there were features now. Just two. Those glowing eyes.

He blinked weakly. The pain was coming back. So was reality. The cave swam back in hazy focus behind the Prince's curious face. Vincent blinked again.

"You okay, Doc?" Tony asked, peering at him.

Vincent choked, coughing and spluttering. His body was aware that it hadn't been breathing, but his lungs worked again. There was no more blood. It was a miracle. Still hurt though. Some parts worse than others. Vincent reached down. His leg was missing. He lurched into a sitting position. The kids were helping him. Tony and Lucy were at his sides. He could feel Lucy's arm around him, scooping him up and he clutched at his stump. She kissed his grizzled cheek.

"You're okay," she soothed.

There was one person the light had not touched. Hans lay cold and still on the slab. Owens had ripped the wheel of blades from his body. He had felt the touch of Tony's magic on his own skin, but watched helplessly as it didn't transfer. Hans looked like he'd been stabbed all over with red hot pokers. His flesh was punctured and burned. Owens watched as his own tears splashed against his lover's pale skin, dry and cold and lifeless.

He could feel a scream building. He didn't know when it would get to his lips. If it ever would. Maybe it would sit in his chest for the rest of his life. He buried his face against Hans' cheek, clinging to him, weeping. His fingers tightened desperately. The gentlest breath tickled his cheek.

"Stuart...?" his voice came like a death rattle.

"Hans?" Stuart gasped, turning to him.

"Are you alright?" Hans wheezed.

"How?" Stuart looked him over. "How?! How are you–?"

"Are you alright?" Hans repeated.

"I'm fine! You're okay? You're alive?!"

Hans was clearly in profound pain, but he smiled. He turned his head to kiss Stuart's tears. Stuart was still crying.

"I... I thought–" he stammered.

"It's okay," Hans whispered. "Zey missed my heart..."

Stuart looked down, running his fingers over Hans' bare chest, seeing the placement of the injuries. They were many, but if they didn't pierce the heart or decapitate the body...

"I can recover," Hans promised.

On the other side of the cave, Fred rolled over with a groan. She had a vague feeling that she'd been lying in her own blood, but she felt alright. A sharp pain flared in her chest and she clutched her ribs.

"Here, Miss Winifred," Gio crouched by her and helped her to her knees. "You feelin' okay?"

"You still alive, Gio?" she gasped.

"Seem to be," he nodded.

"Am I still alive?" she asked.

"It certainly looks that way," he confirmed. He patted something against the side of his trousers, brushing away dirt, and held out the singed photo. It was scorched around the edges, but two smiling faces looked up at her from the black and white image. Fred was vaguely aware that her face was wet.

"Thank you," she said thickly, taking it from him.

"Of course," he replied. "Let me help you up. I don't got a lot of interest staying here longer than we have to."

She wasn't going to argue. He slipped an arm around her and helped pull her to her feet. Nearby, the kids were helping get Vincent up. He was standing with a stunned expression on his face, and a sizable portion of him appeared to be missing. It didn't seem the right time to comment.

From around the corner Stuart guided Hans gently towards them. The Vampire had been unshackled and he was wearing Stuart's coat over his torn trousers. He appeared to be in a great deal of pain, hobbling along carefully, but Stuart had a tight hold on him and wouldn't let him fall.

"*Erstaunlich...* I can't believe you actually did it..." Hans smiled wanly.

"I think we're a little surprised ourselves," Lucy admitted.

"I'm sorry about your injuries," Tony apologized. "I tried, but–"

"I felt you trying," Hans nodded. "It's best you didn't. Might have made it vorse. Ve do not heal as you do."

"Do what humans do," Vincent suggested dazedly. "Drink the pain away."

"Okay, Vincent," Lucy patted him gently on the chest as she helped balance him upright. "Let's get you somewhere with actual medical care."

18

The ship pitched and swayed gently in the dark ocean. The sun had just set, and the last faint touch of light was visible on the horizon. Hans woke sleepily in his soft bunk. His injuries still hurt. They were taking some time to heal. It took a lot of blood to heal holy scars. At least his body could withstand the damage. It wasn't like humans where the wounds would continue to weep. He blinked at the dim ceiling and became aware that he was not alone in the cabin. He turned his head.

"Oh, are you awake?" Lucy asked. She was sitting on the bunk across from him, reading a book. "Stuart's getting some fresh air. He asked me to wait with you, so that you weren't alone if you woke."

"Zat's very kind of you boz," Hans smiled gently. "I am fine, I assure you."

He moved to sit up. The pain caused him to grimace and hiss, he clutched his body where everything stung. Then Lucy was beside him. Her warm little hands helped lift him up and perch him on the edge of the bed.

"*Danke,*" he thanked her. "I am alright..."

She unbuttoned her cuff and rolled up her sleeve, exposing her wrist.

"Here," she offered.

"*Nein,*" Hans shook his head. "I cannot."

"You need it," she countered. "I don't mind, truly. I wouldn't offer if I did."

"Your husband vould be furious," Hans sighed.

"My husband is not as small minded as people think," Lucy replied. "Besides, it's my body, not his. There are so few people you can drink from on this ship, and I don't want Stuart hurting himself to help you recover, or you starving yourself to keep him safe." She gave him a very direct look. "If you were an injured human, and you needed blood, Tony would help me set up the needles. No one would care if I was giving you blood intravenously to help you. Don't let human prejudices put you off. You need to get better."

Hans was too weary to fight her, and she did smell good. All her men stank of various kinds of poison, but the girl had clean blood. Young and healthy. She didn't even flinch when he bit her. His pain began to ease instantly as he drank. Little by little, his wounds shrank with each daily feed. He didn't take much. Enough to ease his pain and settle her indignation. His breath still rattled in his injured lungs as he healed the new mark on her wrist.

"*Danke sehr,*" he murmured with a grateful nod.

"You feeling better?" she checked, rolling her sleeve back.

He nodded again. She seemed satisfied with his answer. He watched her curiously. She was not like most other humans he had known. Even from the first moment they had met, she had been unusual.

"Vhat did you expect of me?" he asked.

"What do you mean?" she asked, confused.

"Vhen ve met," Hans mused, "you had a strange look about you. I vasn't sure vhat it vas at first. Now I zink you vere disappointed in me. Vhy?"

"I– no! No, not at all!" Lucy shook her head.

"Zen vhat?" Hans pressed curiously. "Vhat did you zink vhen ve met?"

"I… I don't know," she shrugged. "You… hm…" she thought for a moment. "You were ordinary. That was what struck me first. Everyone was harping on about vampires, I think I expected some kind of monster, but when Stuart brought you inside you were just… this normal guy." Lucy pulled a face, grinning to herself. "I think the romantic in me was expecting some kind of beauty and the beast fairytale, and then, I suppose, yes… it was a bit disappointing. A bit anti-climactic, after all the fuss."

Hans laughed. It hurt, but he couldn't help himself. He clutched his chest. Lucy put a hand on his back.

"Sorry," she apologized.

"*Nein, nein.*" He waved it away. "Beauty and ze beast, huh," he smirked a little. "*Ja,* he is beautiful…"

Lucy snorted and they both laughed. Hans regretted it, but only for a second. It was still funny once the pain eased. Lucy pressed her lips together like she was trying to hold back her laughter. Hans shook his head at the ease with which he'd amused himself.

"You said he vas outside?" Hans asked.

"Out on deck," she nodded. "He said he needed some air."

"I might go check on him…"

She gave him a cheeky smile and they left the room together. Hans grabbed a coat from the back of the door, but didn't dress properly. He couldn't be bothered. The trousers and long-sleeved undershirt he wore were fine, and he didn't expect many people up and about outside after dark. Lucy turned down the hall towards their other cabins. He took the passage to the main stairs.

Out on deck the air was cold. The sky was lit by a large glowing moon, and Hans smiled at its brilliance when he saw it. Stuart wasn't hard to find. He was the only one up here. The moonlight bathed him in a divine glow as he stood at the railing, watching the waves. Hans approached him softly. He could be completely silent when he wanted to be, and somehow Stuart always still knew he was there.

"Hans," he murmured, wiping his face and turning to greet him.

Hans stopped before him, barely leaving a gap between them, and raised his hands to Stuart's cheeks. He could feel the damp tracks of his tears.

"Vhat's 'rong?" he whispered over the sloshing waves.

"Nothing," Stuart shook his head. He moved Hans' hands from his face and whispered. "It's a public ship..."

"Zere is no one else up here," Hans assured him.

"I remember last time you said that," Stuart reminded.

"I von't take zings so far this time," Hans smiled, kissing the salt from Stuart's tears. He turned his lips to Stuart's, seeking the wet heat of his mouth, tasting it, holding him. His hands slid again under Stuart's coat, around his body. He could taste the reluctance in Stuart's kiss. His fear was bitter.

"Vhat's 'rong?" he asked again, insistently this time, letting his lips trace across Stuart's cheek. "You are upset – *verärgert*. You vorry America vill not be safe for us again?"

"I don't know," Stuart breathed. "I don't know what's wrong. Maybe I'm still just processing everything that's happened."

"It has been much," Hans agreed. He brought his hands back up to touch Stuart's face, brushing his fingers affectionately against Stuart cheeks. "Do you love me?"

"*Selbstverständlich,*" Stuart answered instantly. "More than anything."

"Zen it doesn't matter," Hans smiled. "You are allowed to be unsure about ze rest. You are allowed to not know vhich of ze many horrors concerns you presently. As long as you are sure of zat. You are my everyzing, Stuart. As long as you love me, I don't care about ze rest. Ve vill make it vork. Ve vill veazer zat storm. Germany, America, vherever, as long as I have you."

He kissed him again and this time Stuart kissed him back without hesitation. Hans pulled him in tighter, pressing himself to Stuart's warm body. Stuart slipped his arms around Han's neck and held on like he'd never let go. Hans opened his mouth to Stuart's, kissing him hungrily. A bang sounded in the ship. They froze. The echoes of the metal clang died. They were still alone.

Stuart's heart was racing. Hans could feel it beat against his own chest like they shared the same pulse. He gave a soft chuckle.

"Perhaps ve take zis inside..." he suggested.

"*Ja*," Stuart agreed. He kissed him again, fleetingly, daringly.

Hans grinned, his lips still brushing Stuart's. He wanted to bend Stuart over the railing and devour him in the moonlight, but there were smarter options. Their cabin had a window. He breathed in the scent of his lover's kiss, teasing himself with the taste. Then he pulled away, taking Stuart's hand and leading him from the deck.

* * *

Lucy had left Hans and gone straight to her cabin. She steeled herself and entered. Tony and Gio were sitting at the table. The cigarettes were still out but at least the cards had been put away. Tony smiled and beckoned her over as soon as she came through the door.

"*Come stai amore mio?*" he asked, catching her around the waist and pulling her in with one arm.

"I'm good," she smiled back, kissing the top of his slick hair. "I gave Hans blood."

She stated it like a challenge. Her words hung in the air. Gio paused mid puff, actively holding his breath.

"Okay," Tony answered carefully, holding Lucy with one arm and tapping his cigarette into the ashtray with the other.

She gave him an expectant, imperious look, waiting

for the other shoe to drop. Tony shrugged like he didn't know what else to say.

"I think that's all the answer you're gettin'," Gio offered, cautiously resuming his cigarette.

"Good," Lucy settled. "As you said, it's my body, and he needs the help."

"Luce…" Tony sighed, stubbing out the smoke. "I trust you. You've never made a bad decision, *mi amore*."

"I dunno," Gio smirked across the table. "She married you, *amico*."

"*He*," Lucy leant on the word and Tony's shoulder for reinforcement. "…is the best thing that ever happened to me, and the only reason we're all alive right now. So you watch your mouth, Amarti."

Gio grinned and flashed her a cheeky wink. He blew a stream of smoke at the ceiling.

"How'd you do it, Tony?" he asked. "Professor Owens always said magic ain't gonna save you from death, so avoid it."

"I couldn't do it again," Tony sighed, rubbing his face with his spare hand. "Not like these." He reached into his pocket and pulled out a handful of delicately engraved bullets. He held them out. Lucy put her hand out and Tony tipped them over. They clinked gently as they were exchanged. "Healing people with magic… I always wanted to. No one knows how. Spells aren't designed that way, so I couldn't do it. I worked out how it might work… but I never had the power. No one does. It comes from a different place. But I stole it. The only reason we all made it was because I stole the Prince's energy and spent that to weave magic. I couldn't do it again. Not from scratch. Not without something to draw from."

"You did good, baby," Lucy told him, leaning over to kiss his cheek. "You have done more than enough miracles for one lifetime."

"Hallelujah! Lit it up like Christ himself!" Gio praised, making the sign of the cross.

"Hope Vincent's going to be okay…" Tony muttered, nervously tapping the butt of his extinguished cigarette again. "Couldn't mend what ain't there…"

"He'll be fine," Lucy assured.

"You best believe it'll take more than the apocalypse to kill that old bandit," Gio muttered.

"I might go check on him anyway," Lucy mused, rubbing Tony's shoulder. "Don't want to leave Fred to put him to bed alone. She's still a bit sore herself."

"Yeah, we'll come help you," Tony agreed. "Gotta watch out for the old folks."

"Don't let Miss Winifred catch you saying that, *amico*," Gio warned, climbing from his seat. "Wouldn't wanna give her something to really get sore about."

They all shared a grin as they untangled and clambered up to head for the door.

* * *

The moonlight filtered through the window and Vincent grimaced sharply, sitting on the edge of the bed and rubbing the stump of his leg. He could still feel it sometimes. The pain, like it was still there, like it was still being torn from his body. Tony had healed everything on the inside and stopped him bleeding out. Doctors had helped with the rest, but Owens had done all the translating, so who knew what he'd ordered done. Vincent was still keeping the stump bandaged. He shoved the case of files and trinkets further down the mattress so that he could turn and keep the partial limb elevated.

"You sure about this, Sir?" Fred asked. She sat on the bed across from him, leaning on her knees with her fingers linked. She'd stopped asking him if he needed anything two hours ago because he kept snapping. He'd already apologized for that. Well, he'd done his best.

"I'm sure," he grunted, trying to push the pain from his leg.

"Stuart?" Fred called through the open doorway.

There was a quick shuffle of footsteps, as though they had been going by and had to retrace a few steps. Owens poked his head through the door curiously. Hans was right behind him. The two of them still had their fingers entwined. Vincent shook his head wearily. They were going to get themselves killed. Not that he could make that critique about other people anymore.

"You two need anything?" Owens inquired hesitantly.

Vincent raised a hand and motioned them in impatiently. Owens led Hans into the room. Their hands teased letting go momentarily, but never committed to it. Owens still had his eyebrows raised in inquisition, waiting for an answer to his question.

"Here," Vincent held his hand out gruffly.

Owens took it. Vincent shoved the small metal pin into his fingers.

"Yours," he insisted. "I should have done this years ago."

Owens considered the pin in his hand. His curiosity had settled to resignation.

"You don't have to do this," he sighed.

"Like I said to your man there: you don't have to keep it," Vincent gritted his teeth, rubbing his thigh. "I'd never judge you for snubbing the Order after how we treated you, but we're trying to do better. It helps to shake things up if the people we're trying to do better by have a seat at the table and a voice to be heard. Truth be told, I can't rightly return Hans' pin and deny you yours. I think... I think it just slipped my mind. In my head you were still one of us. I'm sorry about that."

"There's nothing to be sorry for, Vincent," Owens smiled.

"We can agree to disagree on that," Vincent winced. "Owens, you're not going to convince me otherwise. I know I haven't always been the best to you. I don't know if you two have planned where you'll go yet, but I want you to know you will always have a home under my roof. Family look out for each other. What you two have done for me, for my kids... like it or not, you're part of this freakshow now. Whatever you decide, you have my support."

"That is more than kind of you, Vincent," Owens murmured. "You don't owe me anything. I owed you. You did right by me, more than, in a world that would have otherwise cast me out."

"Then take the pin," Vincent insisted. "Join us again, as a favor to me."

"Do you need me to have a look at your leg, Chancellor?" Hans inquired, reading Vincent's pain.

"I'm fine," Vincent grunted.

"I'll hold him down, Fred, you get his bandages," Owens joked.

"Sir," Fred warned him firmly. "Let the nice vampire have a look at your injury before you get manhandled by a bunch of gays."

Vincent did not laugh. The others did. Begrudgingly, he slid his empty trouser leg up over his bandages. Hans came forward, motioning politely. Vincent gave him a gruff nod of permission. Hans carefully unwrapped the wound. It was still unpleasantly sticky. The vampire's nose crinkled in distaste. Vincent assumed that meant his blood was still poisonous with tonic and probably always would be. Hans began to breathe gently on the wound. Vincent felt the pain start to ease instantly. He let out a long slow breath as the relief eased his temper.

"We should perhaps make a point of doing this once a day," Owens mused. "If you're up for it, *Schatz*?"

"*Ja, bestimmt*," Hans nodded. "I am happy to help."

"Thank you," Vincent sighed. "I appreciate it. I need all the help I can get." He cast a grimace to the window. "I'm going to need all the help I can get on every front."

"Then perhaps you shouldn't be fighting with your Council about reinstating me," Owens suggested.

"I won't be," Vincent growled. "I'm overruling them

on you two, and anyone who doesn't like it can come fight me!"

"You realize they might actually try now," Owens pointed out.

"Then they can fight my kids, 'cause I'm swearing them in too!" Vincent huffed. "Anyone who can fight for the cause. You got a good heart and a good weapon, you get a pin."

"Feeling less elitist now," Hans smiled, tagging out for Fred who came over with fresh bandages.

"That was always our biggest problem anyway," Vincent admitted. He paused a moment, a grateful expression tugging his eyes as Fred helped dress the wound again. "I heard what Isfet said, you know... when I was lying there dying... and he was threatening the kids. I heard him threaten a new war." He shook his head, fear creasing his face. "We can't survive another one. Not just the Order, although we were slaughtered down to half our former glory – humanity can't survive another one."

"You'd be surprised vhat humanity can survive, Chancellor," Hans replied.

"I just... I think about what we just left behind... and I worry," Vincent grated. "I remember the last one. We can't go through that again. We just can't. I... I don't know what's coming anymore. The fear of that... whatever the future holds..."

"We'll handle it," Lucy finished.

They all looked up. She stood in the doorway with her boys, who both dropped nods of agreement. The three of them entered the room and joined the party.

Lucy bounced down on the side of Fred's bunk. She outstared the room.

"I got a pocket full of magic bullets, married the best sorcerer in existence, got the most badass friends a girl could ask for, and trained under the greatest mentor that ever wore the badge," she declared. "I meant what I told that shadow: I'm not scared of him. Whatever the future brings, Vincent, we'll handle it. That's what we do. We're Hunters."

An air of agreement settled across the room at her words. Vincent felt a small smile of pride pull at his weary face. There was still an anxious weight on his heart, but perhaps that was inescapable. Perhaps the fear would always be there, and what made the difference was standing up and fighting it anyway. He'd always done it before. He would find a way to do it again, with their help. That's what it meant to be a Hunter.

Did you enjoy this book?

Please consider leaving a review for it on Amazon or Goodreads. Every positive review allows me to spend more time writing books for you to enjoy!

Other Books By Kate Haley

Welcome to the Inbetween

The Vincent Temple Trilogy

Gateway to Dark Stars

Tomb of Endless Night

Fortress of the Shadow Reich

The War of the North Saga

Footsteps into the Unfamiliar (short story collection)

1. Steel & Stone

2. Magic in the Marshes

3. Forest of Ghosts

4. Women of the Woods

5. Spirit & Sand

6. The Prince and the Witch

7. Gods & Dragons

ABOUT THE AUTHOR

Kate Haley is a speculative fiction author who works predominantly in fantasy and horror.

While currently content to fill their days with writing and table-top RPGs, their grander plans involve world domination. Something akin to the tyranny of the greatest city atop the Disc would be an acceptable standard. They believe a super-villainous overlord would be an upgrade, given that our current villains lack style and imagination.

After all, super-villainy requires Presentation.

If you like their references, consider visiting their website www.katehaleyauthor.com for short fictions and merchandise, and join the mailing list for early access and exclusive cool stuff.

You can also get in touch through the website regarding their work, your position in future slave armies, or a general interest in all things nerdy and wonderful.

FORTRESS OF THE SHADOW REICH

Printed in Great Britain
by Amazon

21169427R00226